WONDER WOMAN
WARBRINGER
THE GRAPHIC NOVEL

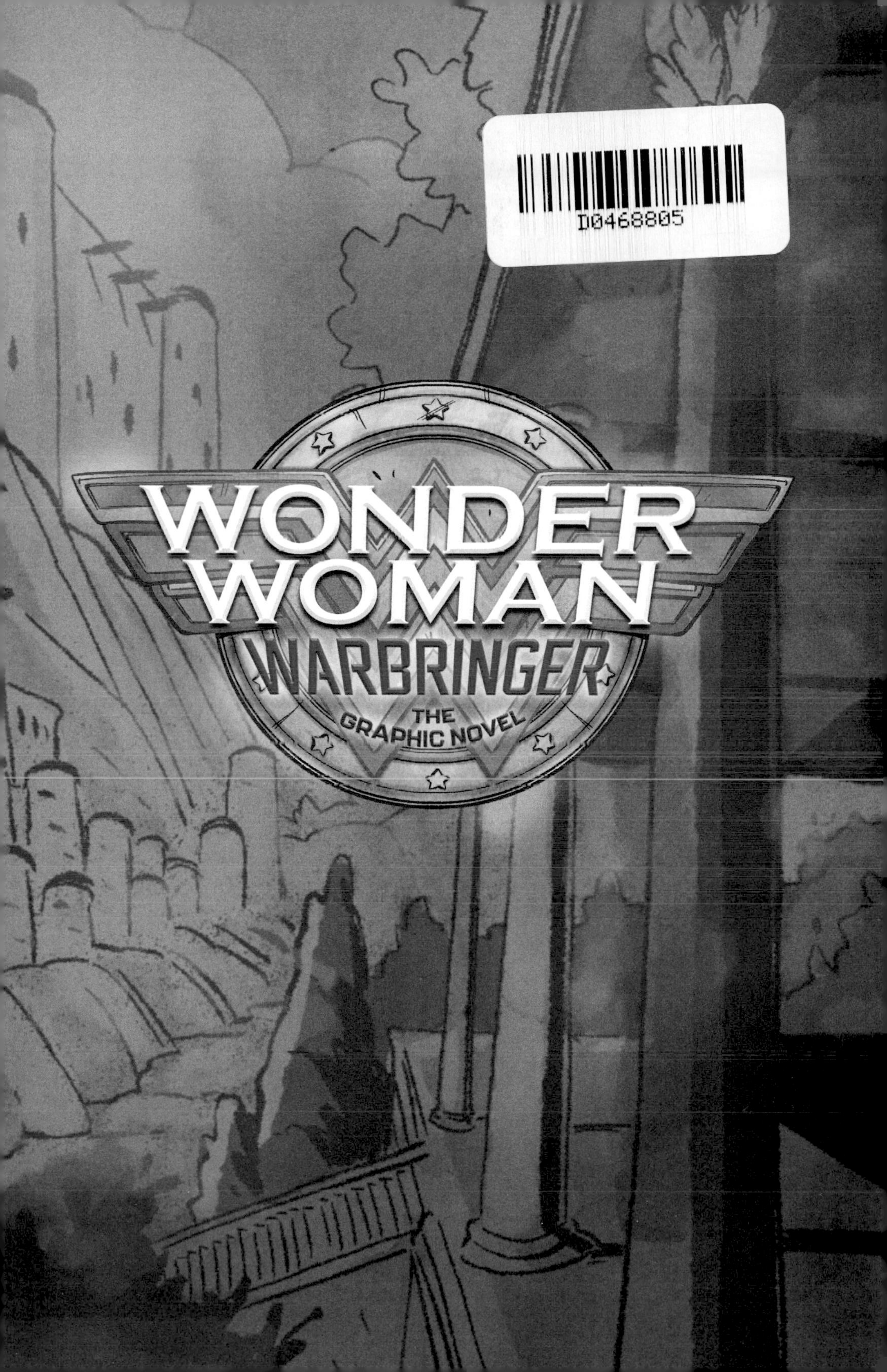

LAUREN BISOM Editor
STEVE COOK Design Director – Books
AMIE BROCKWAY-METCALF Publication Design

BOB HARRAS Senior VP – Editor-in-Chief, DC Comics
MICHELE R. WELLS VP & Executive Editor, Young Reader

DAN DiDIO Publisher
JIM LEE Publisher & Chief Creative Officer
BOBBIE CHASE VP – New Publishing Initiatives & Talent Development
DON FALLETTI VP – Manufacturing Operations & Workflow Management
LAWRENCE GANEM VP – Talent Services
ALISON GILL Senior VP – Manufacturing & Operations
HANK KANALZ Senior VP – Publishing Strategy & Support Services
DAN MIRON VP – Publishing Operations
NICK J. NAPOLITANO VP – Manufacturing Administration & Design
NANCY SPEARS VP – Sales

WONDER WOMAN: WARBRINGER

DC - a WarnerMedia Company.

DC Comics, 2900 West Alameda Ave., Burbank, CA 91505

Printed by LSC Communications, Crawfordsville, IN, USA.

11/29/19. First Printing.

ISBN: 978-1-4012-8255-4

School Market Edition ISBN: 978-1-77950-408-1

PEFC Certified
This product is from sustainably managed forests and controlled sources
PEFC
PEFC/29-31-337
www.pefc.org

Library of Congress Cataloging-in-Publication Data

Names: Simonson, Louise, adapter. | Seaton, Kristen, illustrator. | Woolley, Sara, colourist. | Bennett, Deron, letterer. | Bardugo, Leigh. Warbringer.
Title: Wonder Woman, Warbringer : the graphic novel / novel written by Leigh Bardugo ; adapted by Louise Simonson ; illustrated by Kit Seaton ; colors by Sara Woolley ; letters by Deron Bennett.
Other titles: Warbringer the graphic novel
Description: Burbank, CA : DC Comics, [2020] | "Wonder Woman created by William Moulton Marston." | Audience: Ages 13+ | Audience: Grades 7-9 | Summary: Diana risks exile from her land of warrior sisters to save Alia Keralis, a Warbringer - a direct descendant of the infamous Helen of Troy - as both face an army of enemies determined to either destroy or possess the Warbringer.
Identifiers: LCCN 2019040290 (print) | LCCN 2019040291 (ebook) | ISBN 9781401282554 (paperback) | ISBN 9781779501103 (ebook)
Subjects: LCSH: Graphic novels. | CYAC: Graphic novels. | Superheroes--Fiction. | Amazons--Fiction.
Classification: LCC PZ7.7.S546 Wo 2020 (print) | LCC PZ7.7.S546 (ebook) | DDC 741.5/973--dc23

PROLOGUE

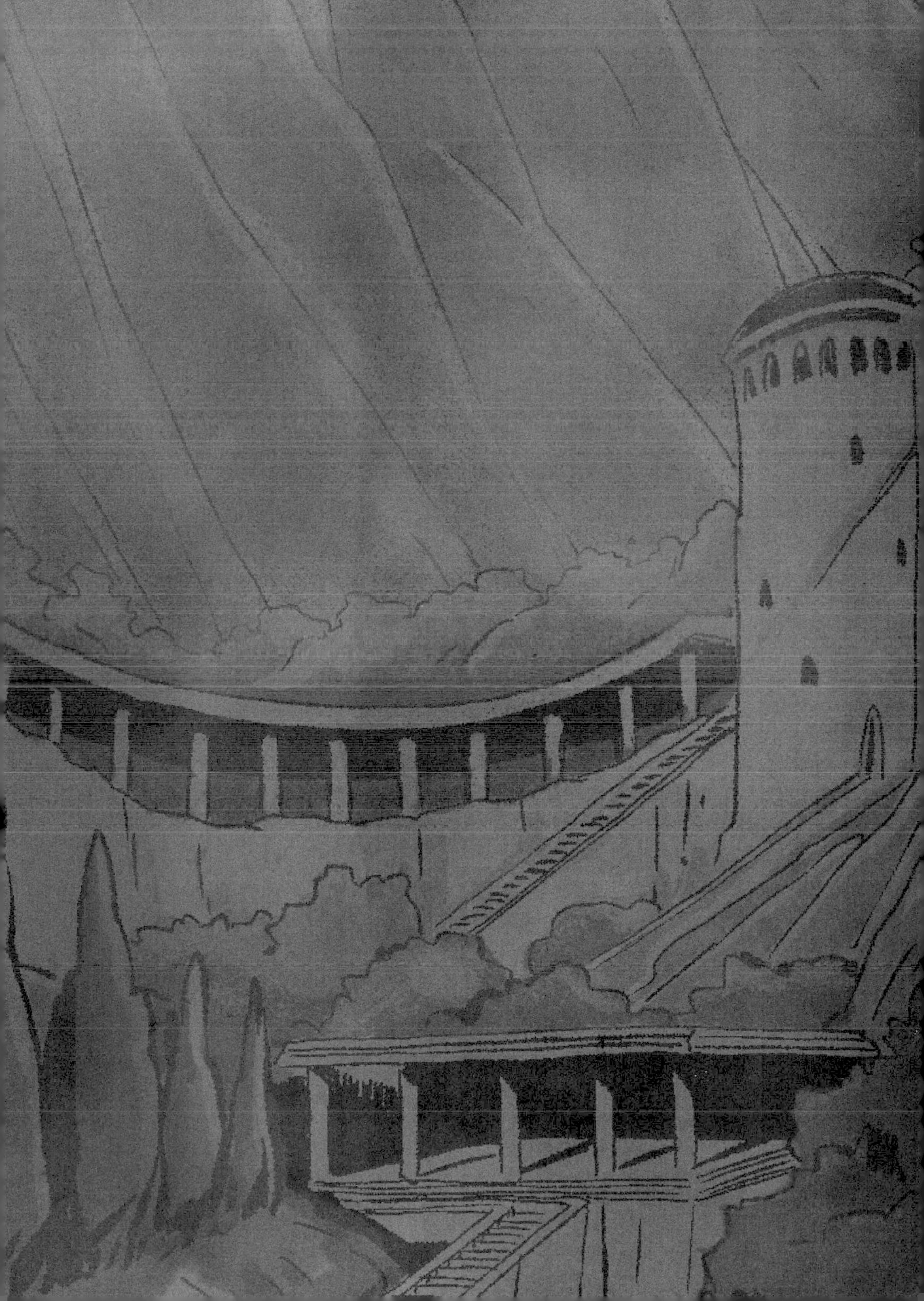

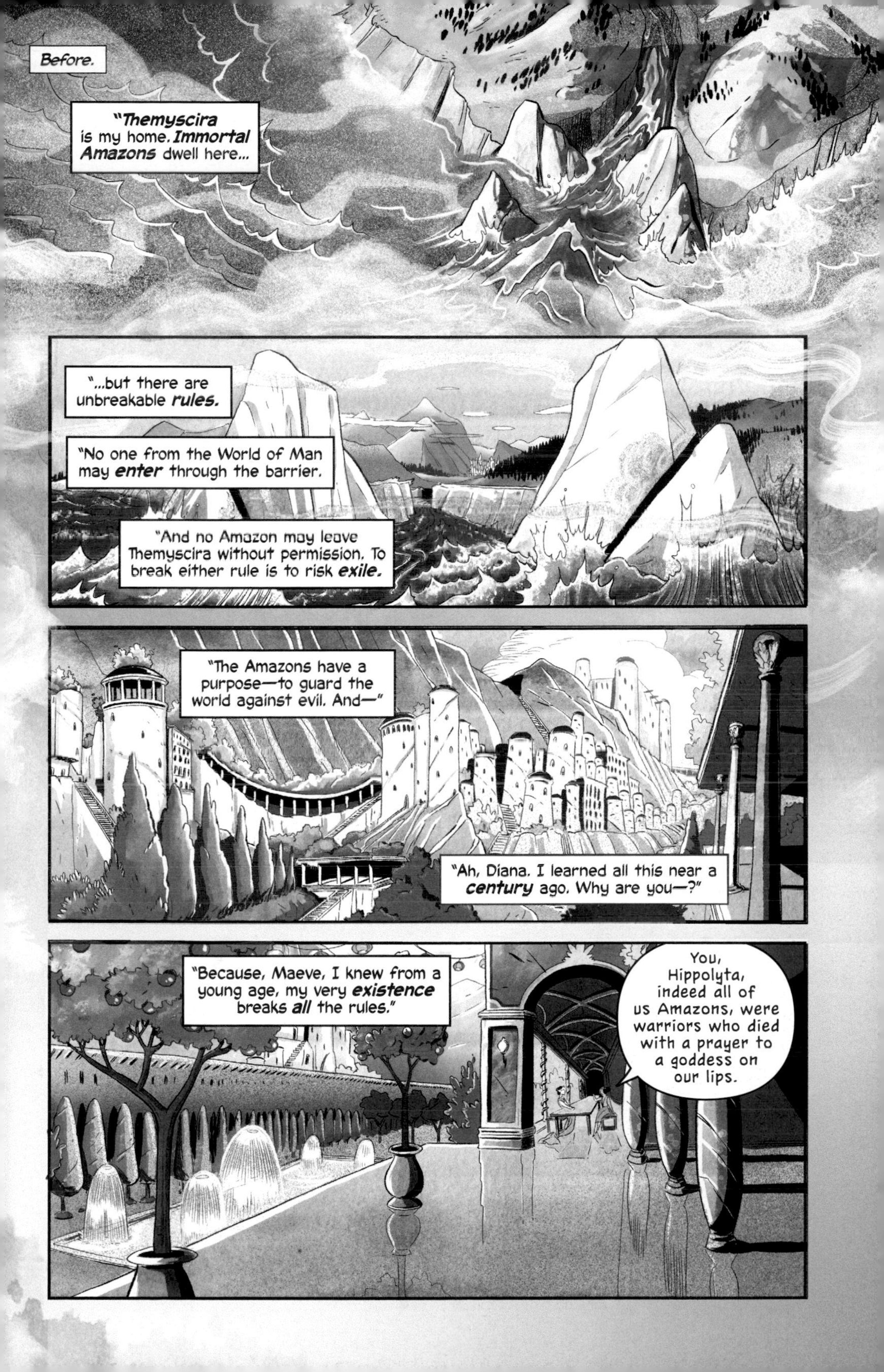
Before.
"Themyscira is my home. Immortal Amazons dwell here...
"...but there are unbreakable rules.
"No one from the World of Man may enter through the barrier.
"And no Amazon may leave Themyscira without permission. To break either rule is to risk exile.
"The Amazons have a purpose—to guard the world against evil. And—"
"Ah, Diana. I learned all this near a century ago. Why are you—?"
"Because, Maeve, I knew from a young age, my very existence breaks all the rules."
You, Hippolyta, indeed all of us Amazons, were warriors who died with a prayer to a goddess on our lips.

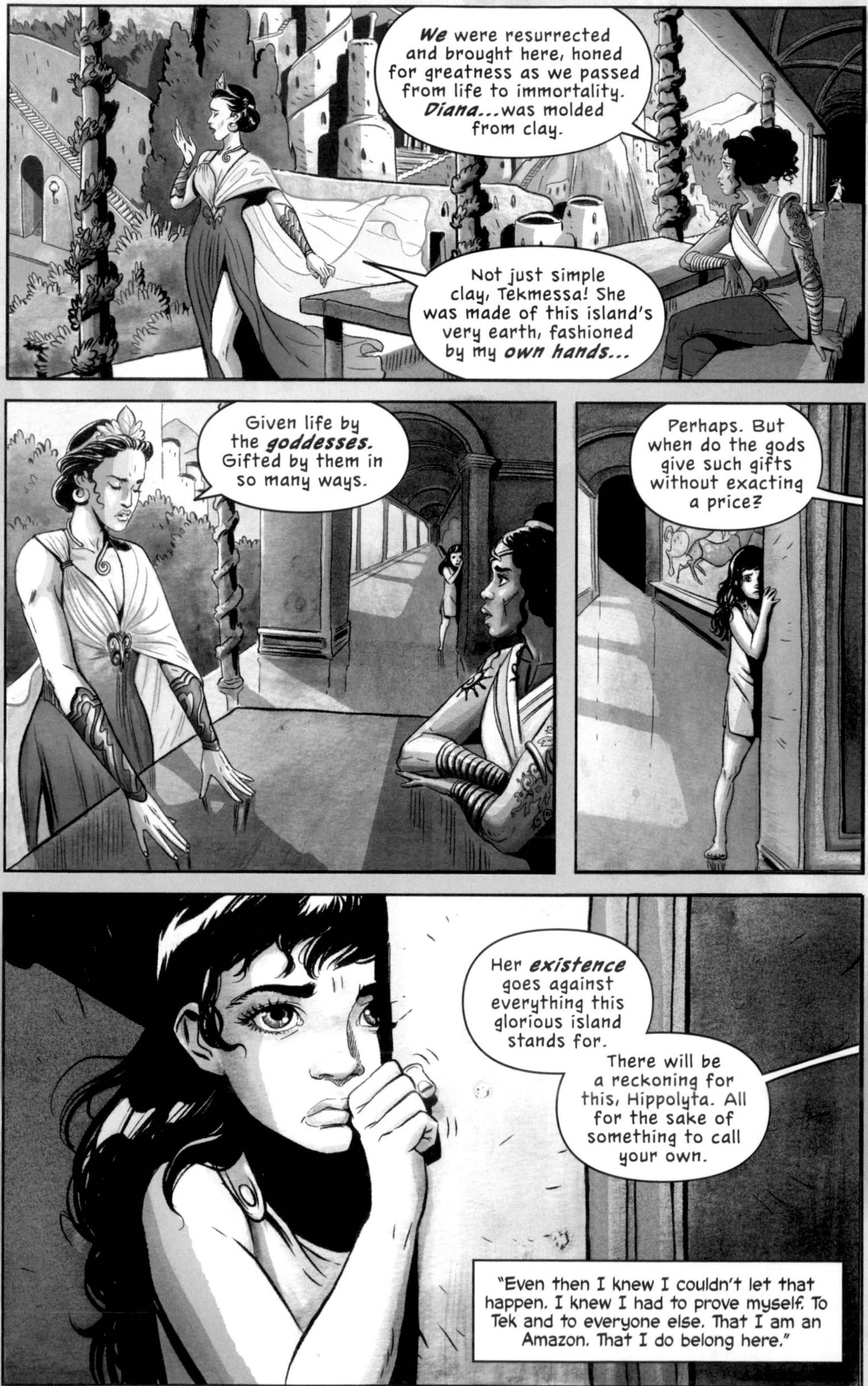

We were resurrected and brought here, honed for greatness as we passed from life to immortality. Diana...was molded from clay.
Not just simple clay, Tekmessa! She was made of this island's very earth, fashioned by my own hands...
Given life by the goddesses. Gifted by them in so many ways.
Perhaps. But when do the gods give such gifts without exacting a price?
Her existence goes against everything this glorious island stands for.
There will be a reckoning for this, Hippolyta. All for the sake of something to call your own.
"Even then I knew I couldn't let that happen. I knew I had to prove myself. To Tek and to everyone else. That I am an Amazon. That I do belong here."

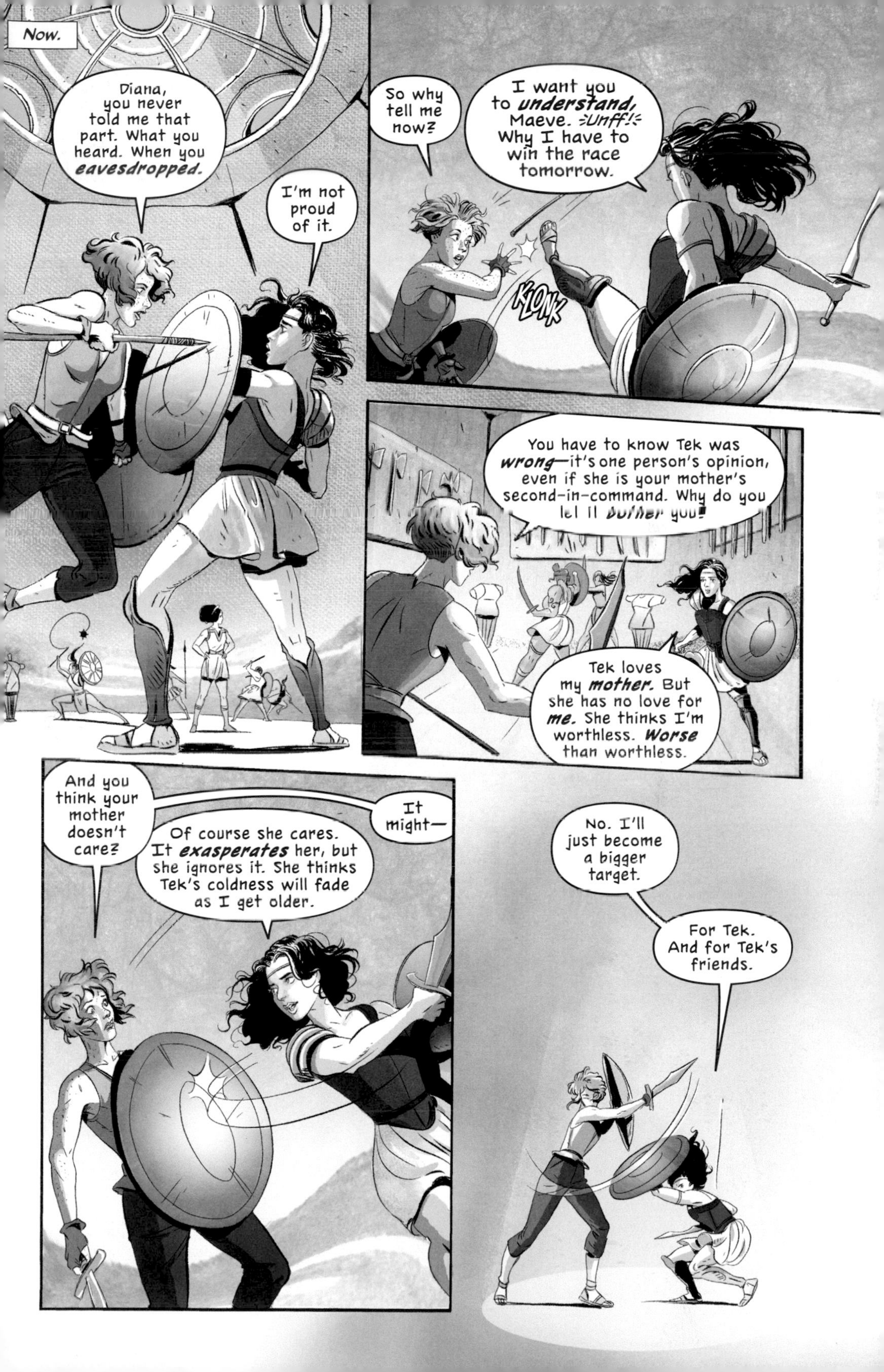
Now.
Diana, you never told me that part. What you heard. When you *eavesdropped.*
I'm not proud of it.
So why tell me now?
I want you to ***understand,*** Maeve. *Unff!* Why I have to win the race tomorrow.
KLONK
You have to know Tek was ***wrong***—it's one person's opinion, even if she is your mother's second-in-command. Why do you let it ***bother*** you?
Tek loves my ***mother.*** But she has no love for ***me.*** She thinks I'm worthless. ***Worse*** than worthless.
And you think your mother doesn't care?
It might—
Of course she cares. It ***exasperates*** her, but she ignores it. She thinks Tek's coldness will fade as I get older.
No. I'll just become a bigger target.
For Tek. And for Tek's friends.

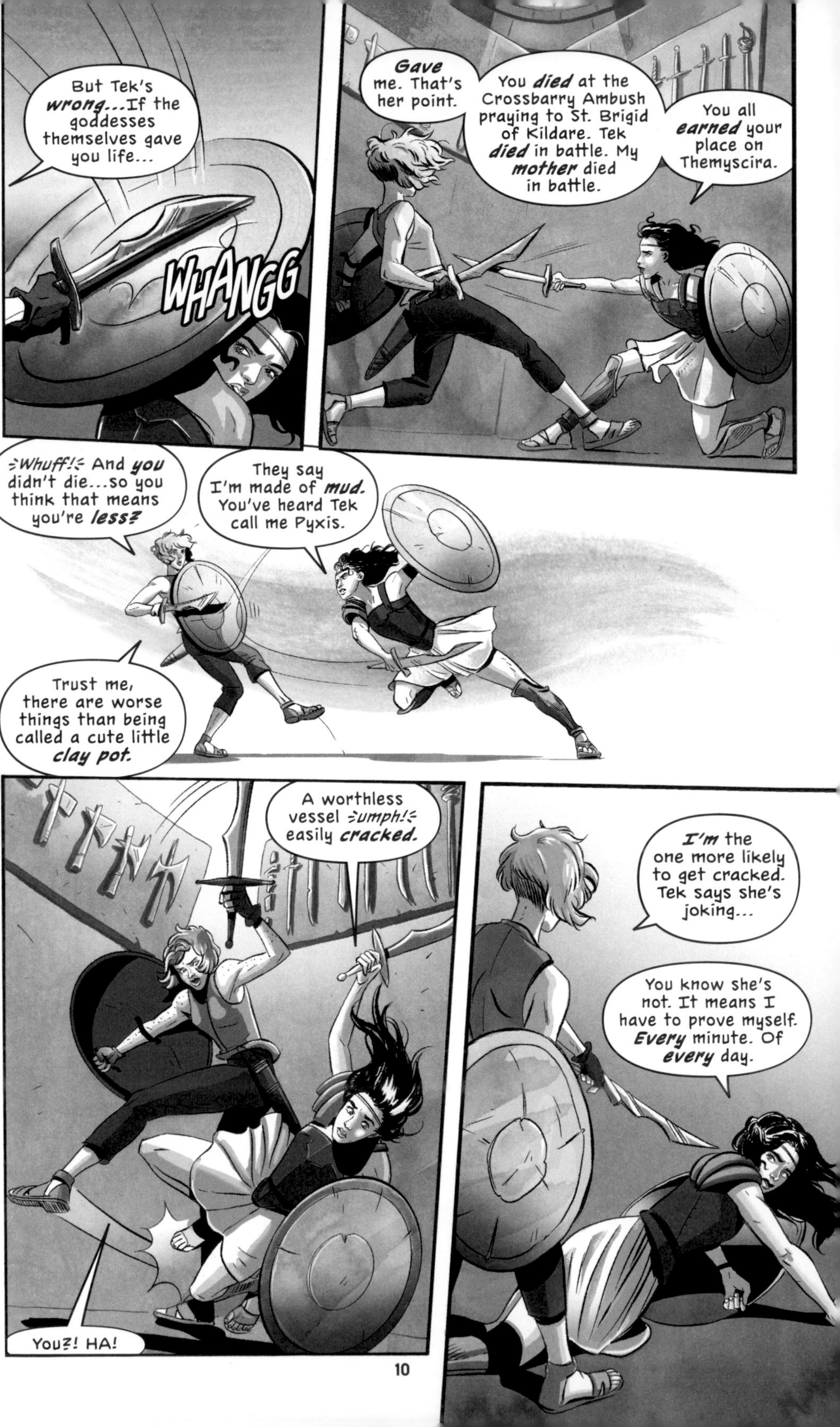

But Tek's *wrong...*If the goddesses themselves gave you life...
WHANGG
Gave me. That's her point.
You *died* at the Crossbarry Ambush praying to St. Brigid of Kildare. Tek *died* in battle. My *mother* died in battle.
You all *earned* your place on Themyscira.
Whuff! And *you* didn't die...so you think that means you're *less?*
They say I'm made of *mud.* You've heard Tek call me Pyxis.
Trust me, there are worse things than being called a cute little *clay pot.*
A worthless vessel *umph!* easily *cracked.*
You?! HA!
I'm the one more likely to get cracked. Tek says she's joking...
You know she's not. It means I have to prove myself. *Every* minute. Of *every* day.

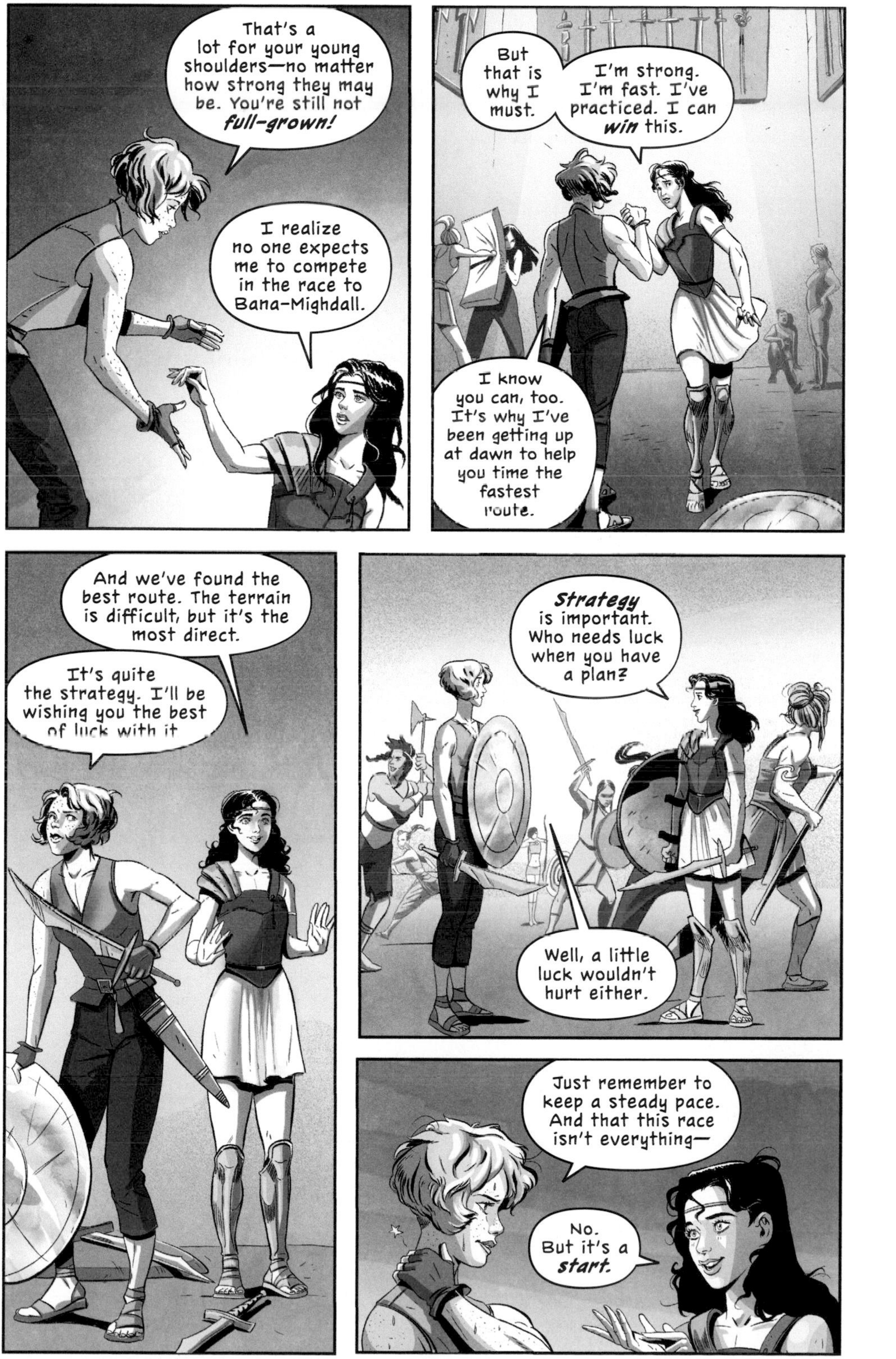
That's a lot for your young shoulders—no matter how strong they may be. You're still not *full-grown!*
I realize no one expects me to compete in the race to Bana-Mighdall.
But that is why I must.
I'm strong. I'm fast. I've practiced. I can *win* this.
I know you can, too. It's why I've been getting up at dawn to help you time the fastest route.
And we've found the best route. The terrain is difficult, but it's the most direct.
It's quite the strategy. I'll be wishing you the best of luck with it
Strategy is important. Who needs luck when you have a plan?
Well, a little luck wouldn't hurt either.
Just remember to keep a steady pace. And that this race isn't everything—
No. But it's a *start.*

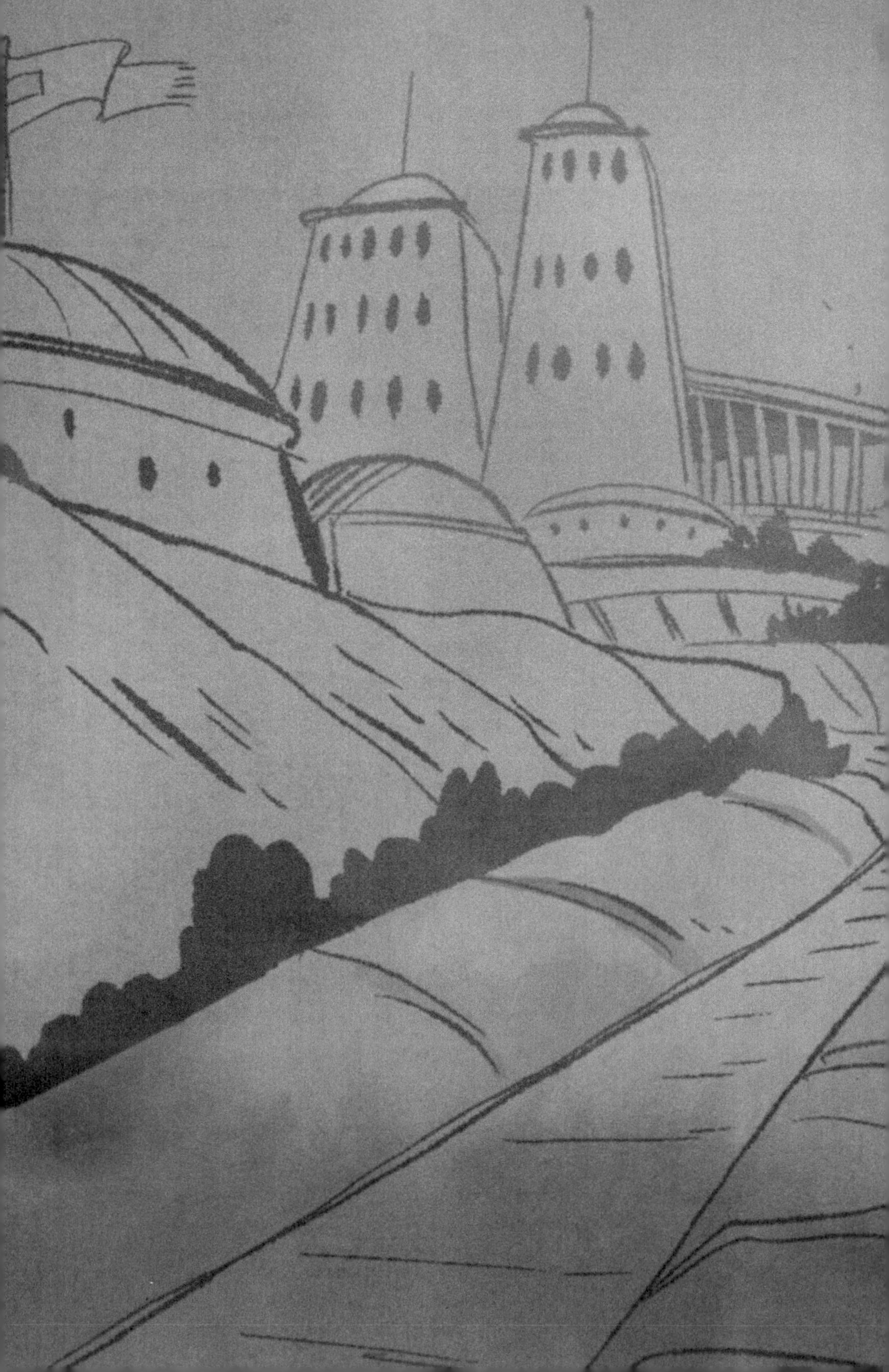

PART ONE

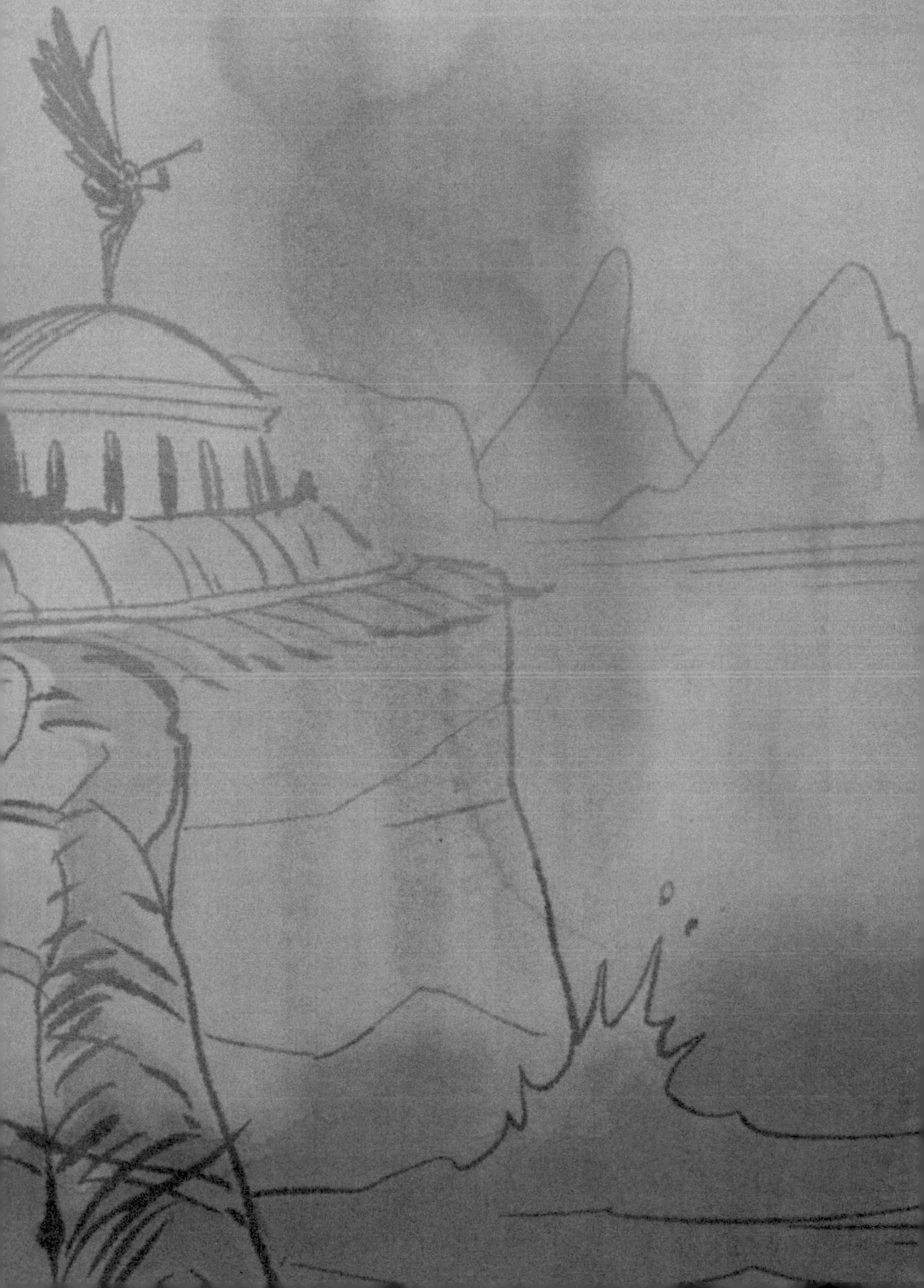

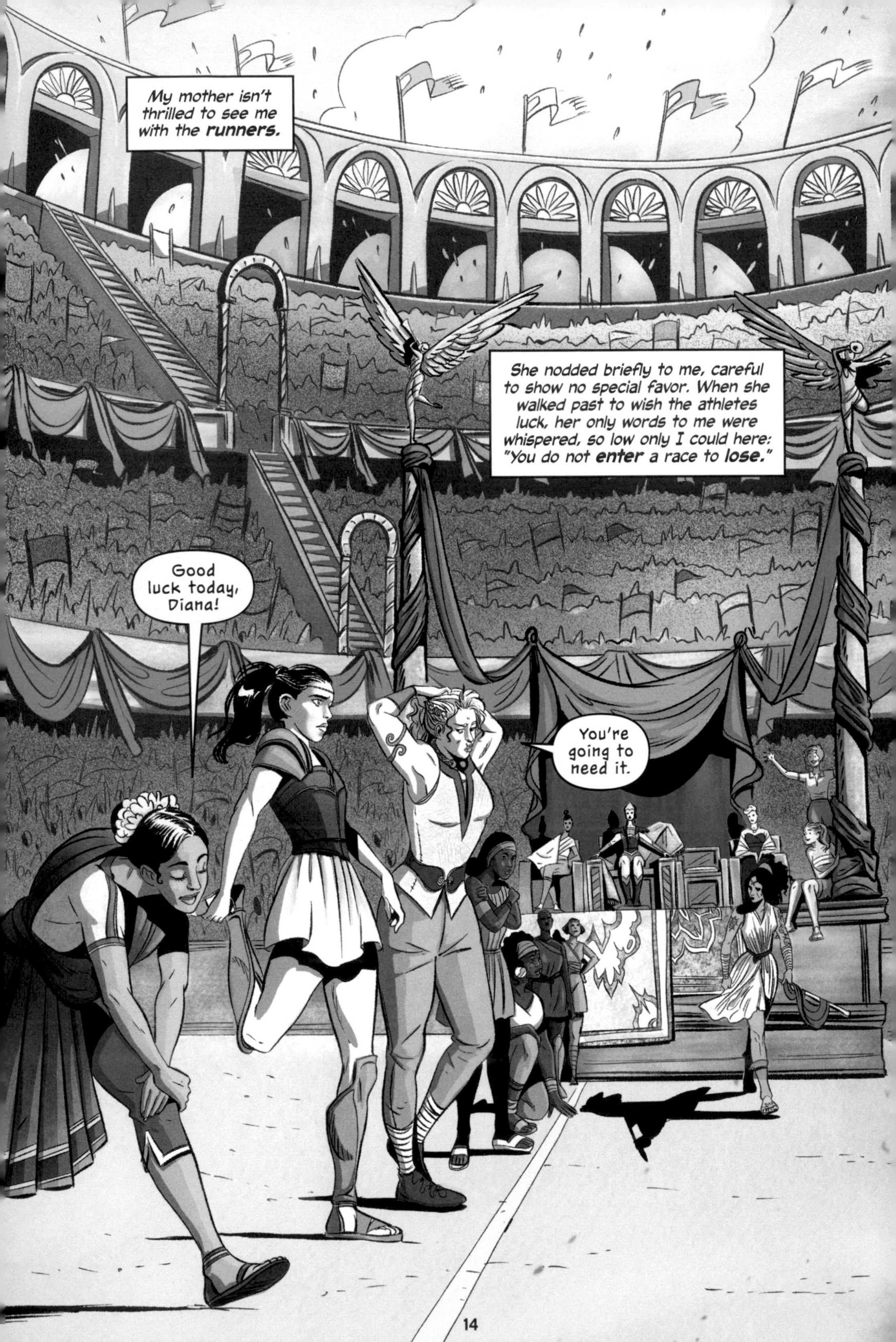
My mother isn't thrilled to see me with the runners.
She nodded briefly to me, careful to show no special favor. When she walked past to wish the athletes luck, her only words to me were whispered, so low only I could here: "You do not enter a race to lose."
Good luck today, Diana!
You're going to need it.

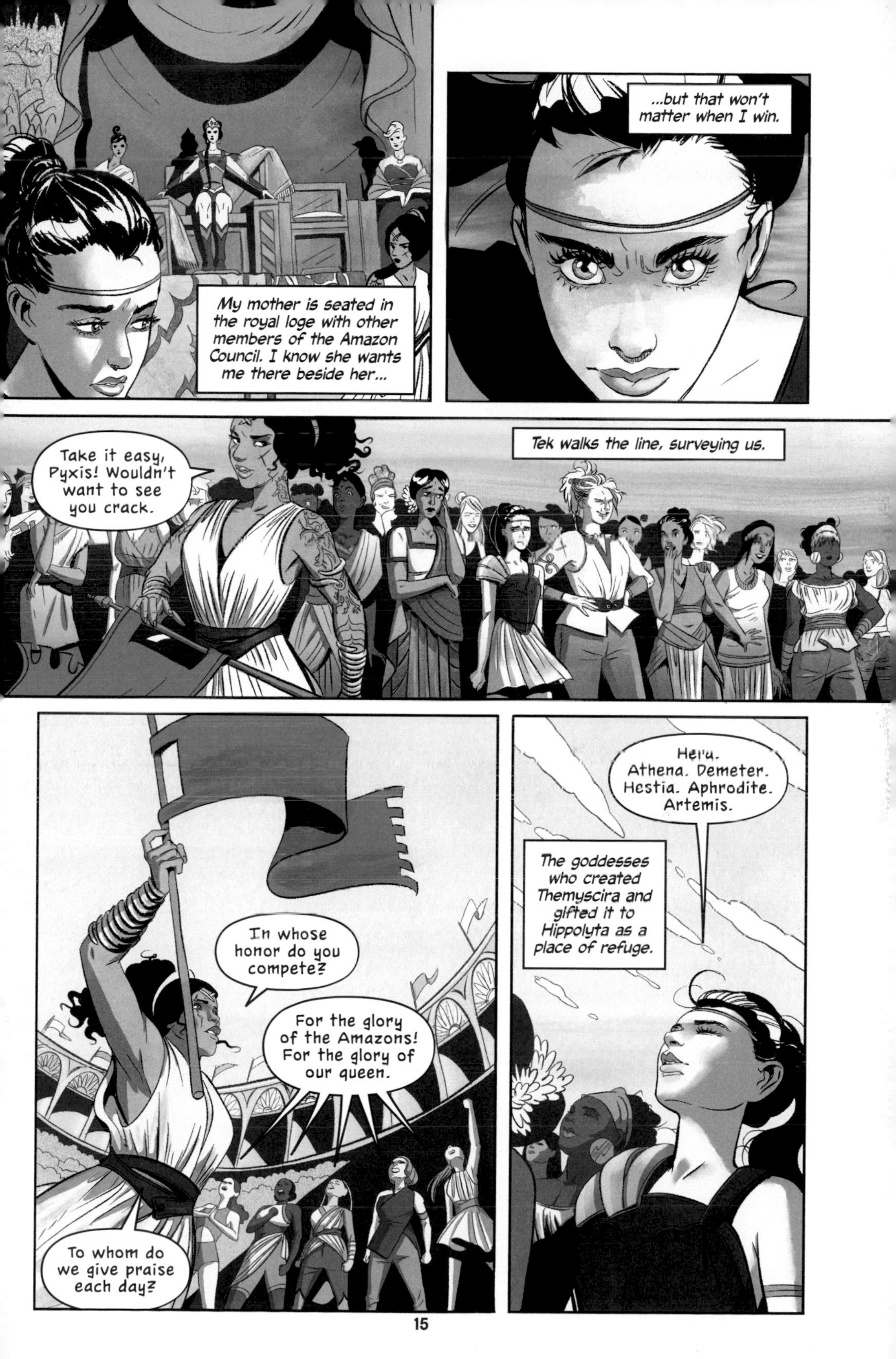
My mother is seated in the royal loge with other members of the Amazon Council. I know she wants me there beside her...
...but that won't matter when I win.
Tek walks the line, surveying us.
Take it easy, Pyxis! Wouldn't want to see you crack.
In whose honor do you compete?
For the glory of the Amazons! For the glory of our queen.
To whom do we give praise each day?
Hera. Athena. Demeter. Hestia. Aphrodite. Artemis.
The goddesses who created Themyscira and gifted it to Hippolyta as a place of refuge.

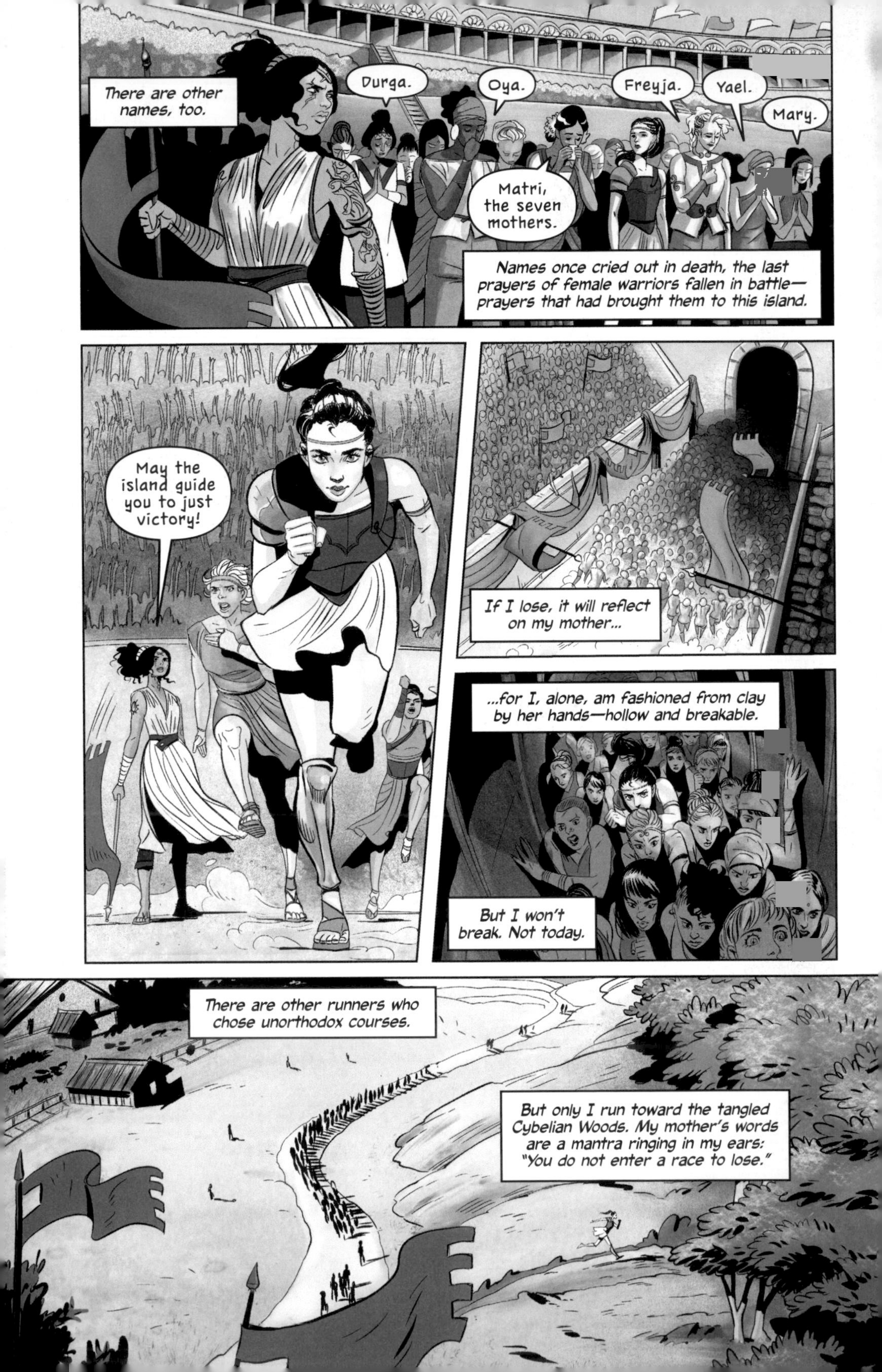
There are other names, too.
Durga.
Oya.
Freyja.
Yael.
Mary.
Matri, the seven mothers.
Names once cried out in death, the last prayers of female warriors fallen in battle—prayers that had brought them to this island.
May the island guide you to just victory!
If I lose, it will reflect on my mother...
...for I, alone, am fashioned from clay by her hands—hollow and breakable.
But I won't break. Not today.
There are other runners who chose unorthodox courses.
But only I run toward the tangled Cybelian Woods. My mother's words are a mantra ringing in my ears: "You do not enter a race to lose."

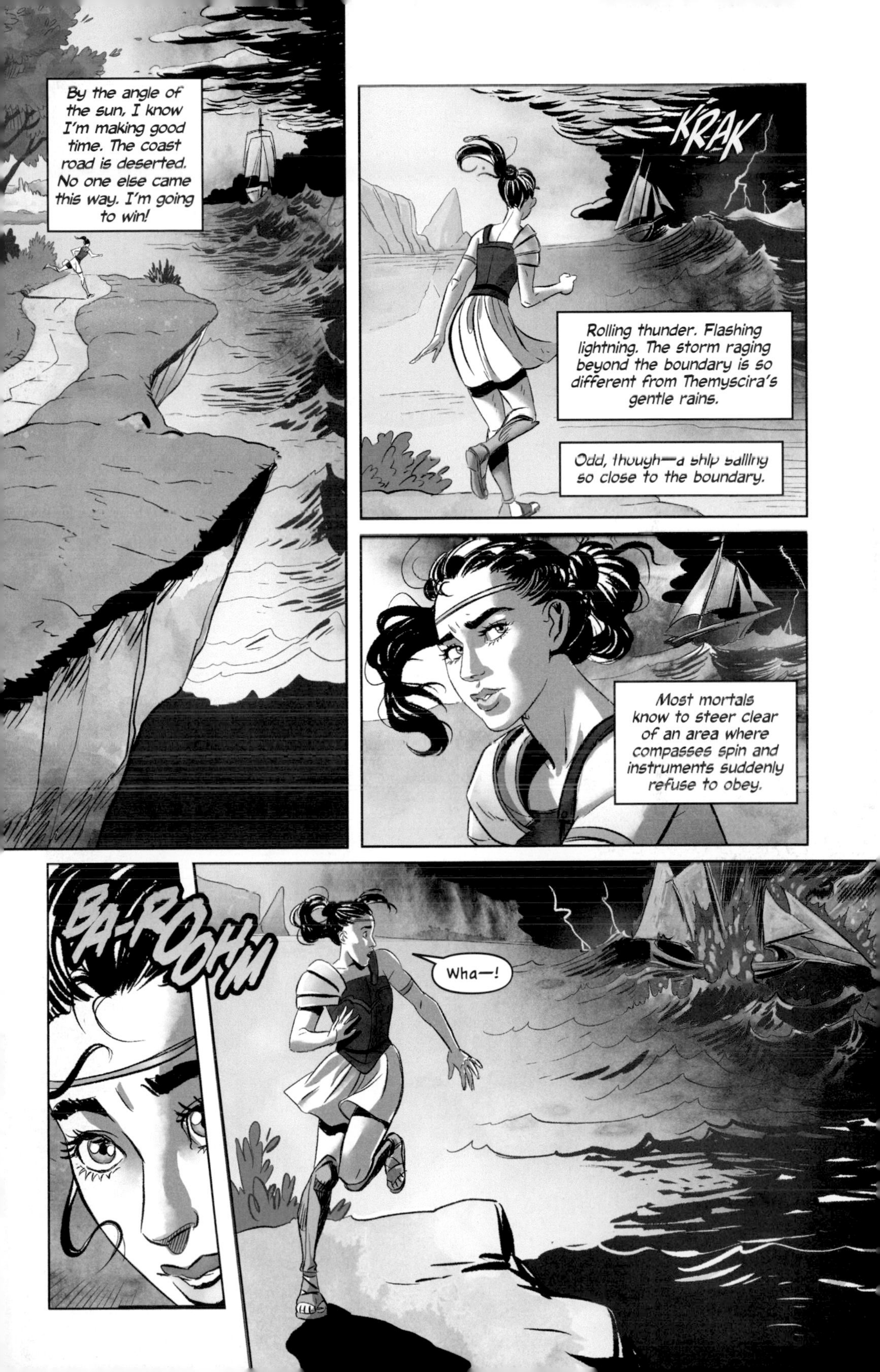

By the angle of the sun, I know I'm making good time. The coast road is deserted. No one else came this way. I'm going to win!
KRAK
Rolling thunder. Flashing lightning. The storm raging beyond the boundary is so different from Themyscira's gentle rains.
Odd, though—a ship sailing so close to the boundary.
Most mortals know to steer clear of an area where compasses spin and instruments suddenly refuse to obey.
BA-ROOHM
Wha—!

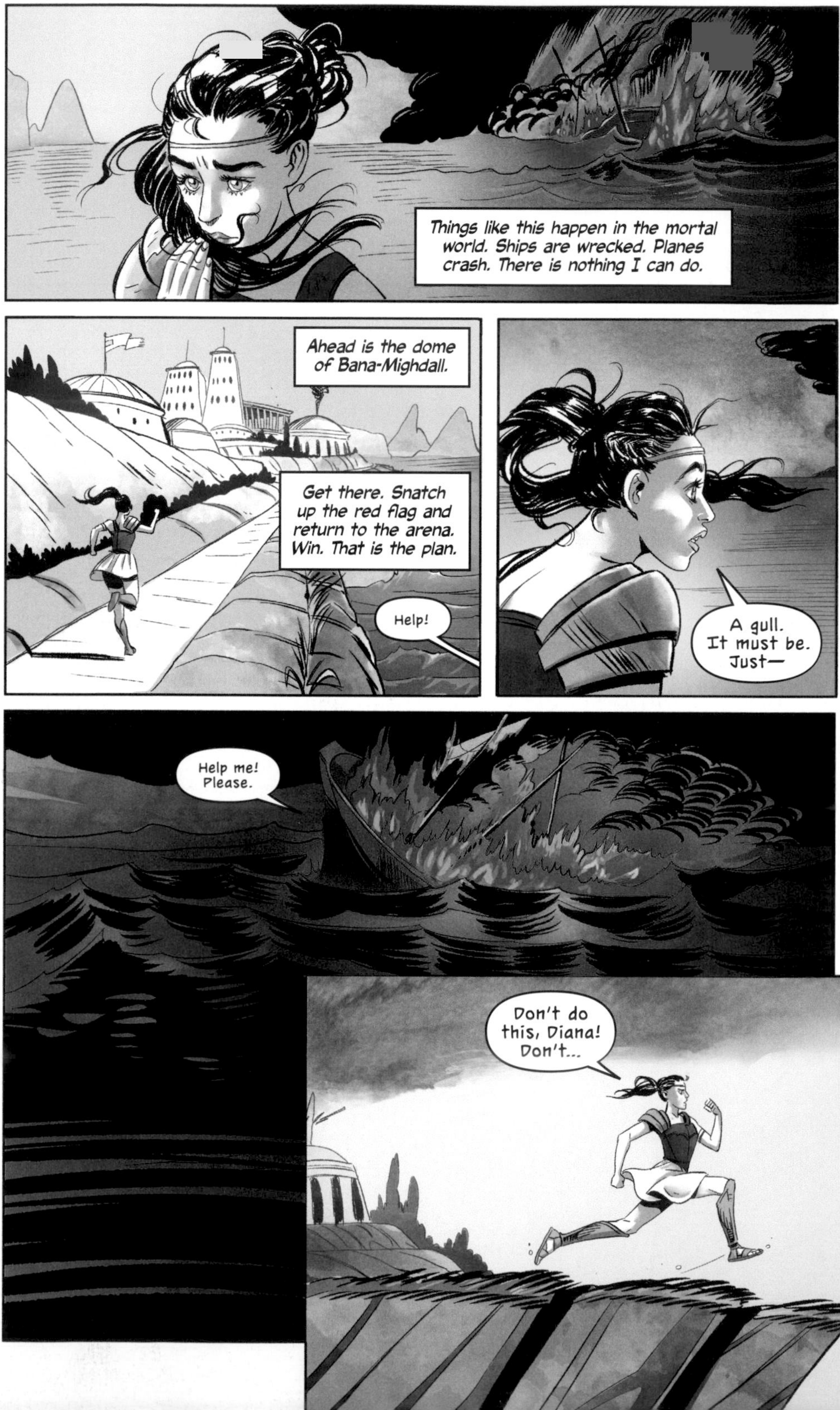
Things like this happen in the mortal world. Ships are wrecked. Planes crash. There is nothing I can do.
Ahead is the dome of Bana-Mighdall.
Get there. Snatch up the red flag and return to the arena. Win. That is the plan.
Help!
A gull. It must be. Just—
Help me! Please.
Don't do this, Diana! Don't...

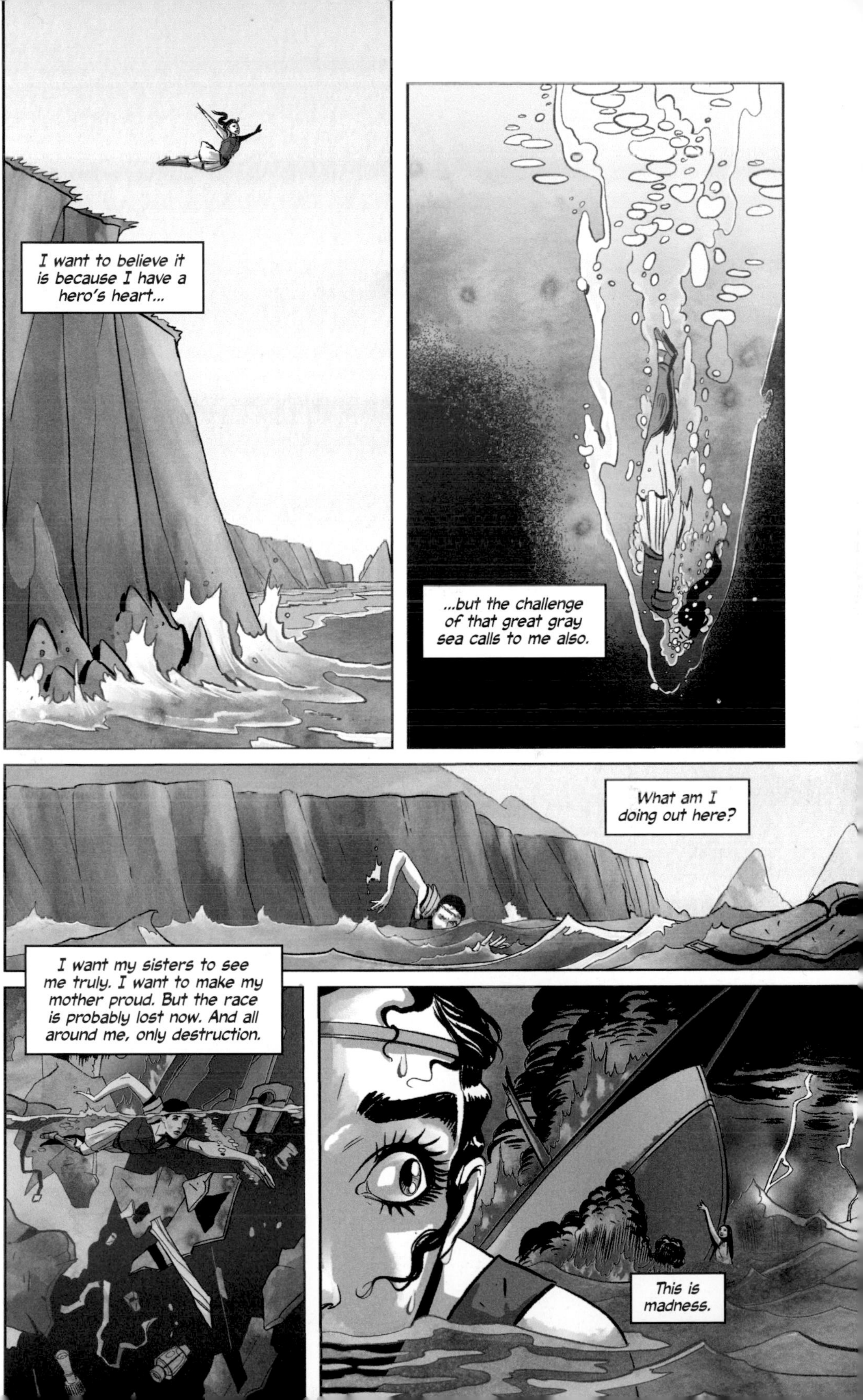
I want to believe it is because I have a hero's heart...
...but the challenge of that great gray sea calls to me also.
What am I doing out here?
I want my sisters to see me truly. I want to make my mother proud. But the race is probably lost now. And all around me, only destruction.
This is madness.

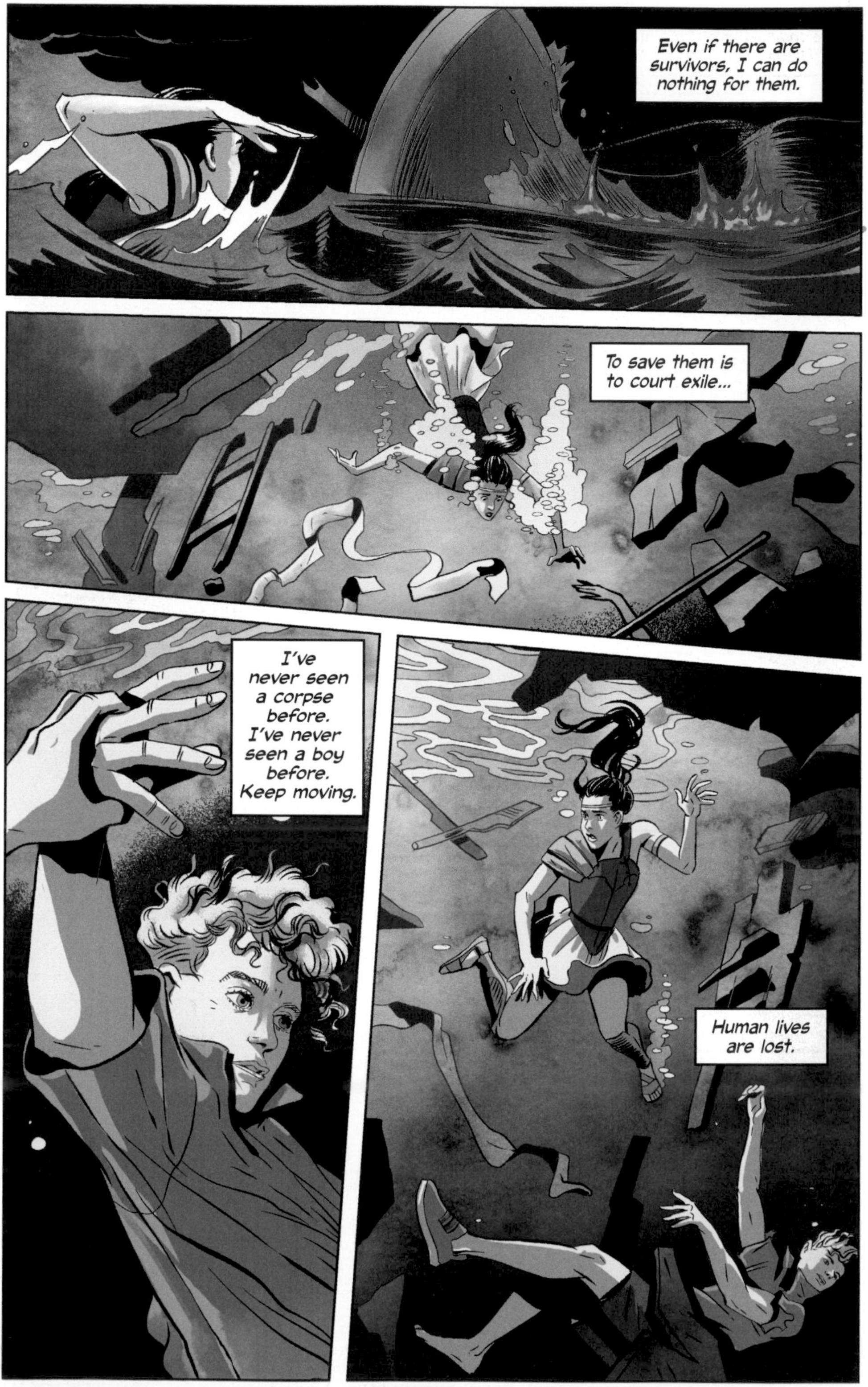
Even if there are survivors, I can do nothing for them.
To save them is to court exile...
I've never seen a corpse before. I've never seen a boy before. Keep moving.
Human lives are lost.

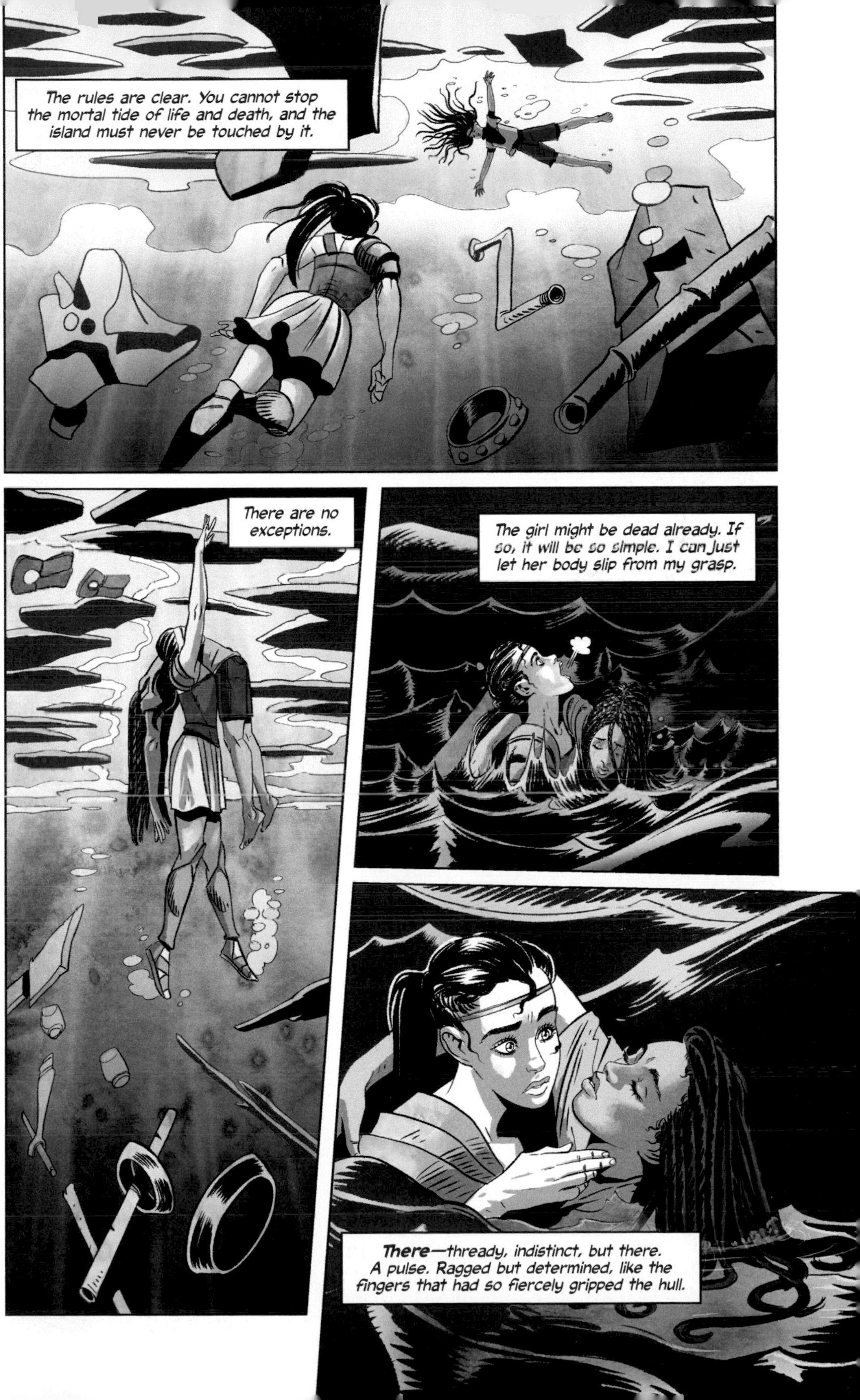
The rules are clear. You cannot stop the mortal tide of life and death, and the island must never be touched by it.
There are no exceptions.
The girl might be dead already. If so, it will be so simple. I can just let her body slip from my grasp.
There—thready, indistinct, but there. A pulse. Ragged but determined, like the fingers that had so fiercely gripped the hull.

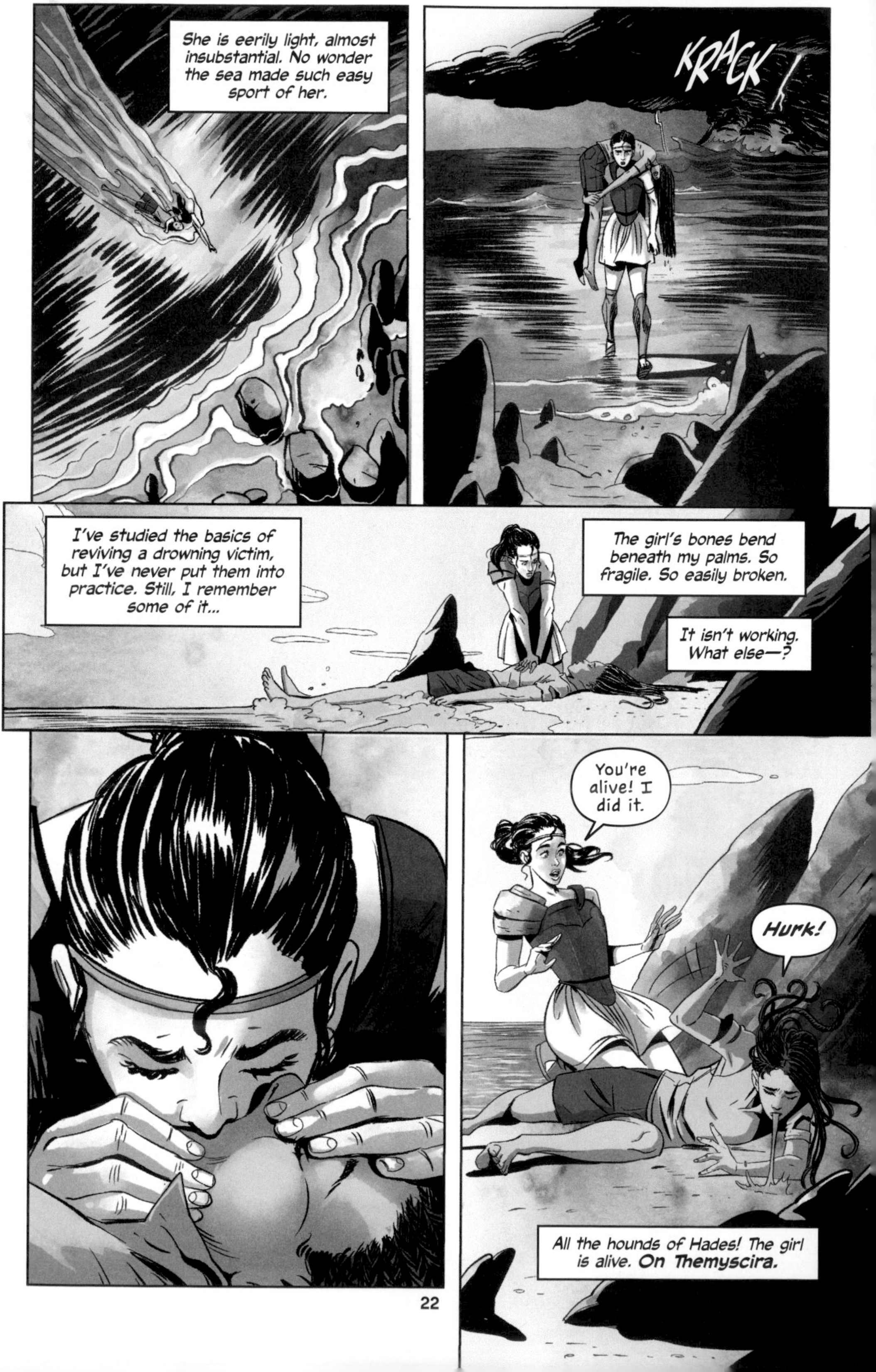
She is eerily light, almost insubstantial. No wonder the sea made such easy sport of her.
KRACK!
I've studied the basics of reviving a drowning victim, but I've never put them into practice. Still, I remember some of it...
The girl's bones bend beneath my palms. So fragile. So easily broken.
It isn't working. What else—?
You're alive! I did it.
Hurk!
All the hounds of Hades! The girl is alive. On Themyscira.

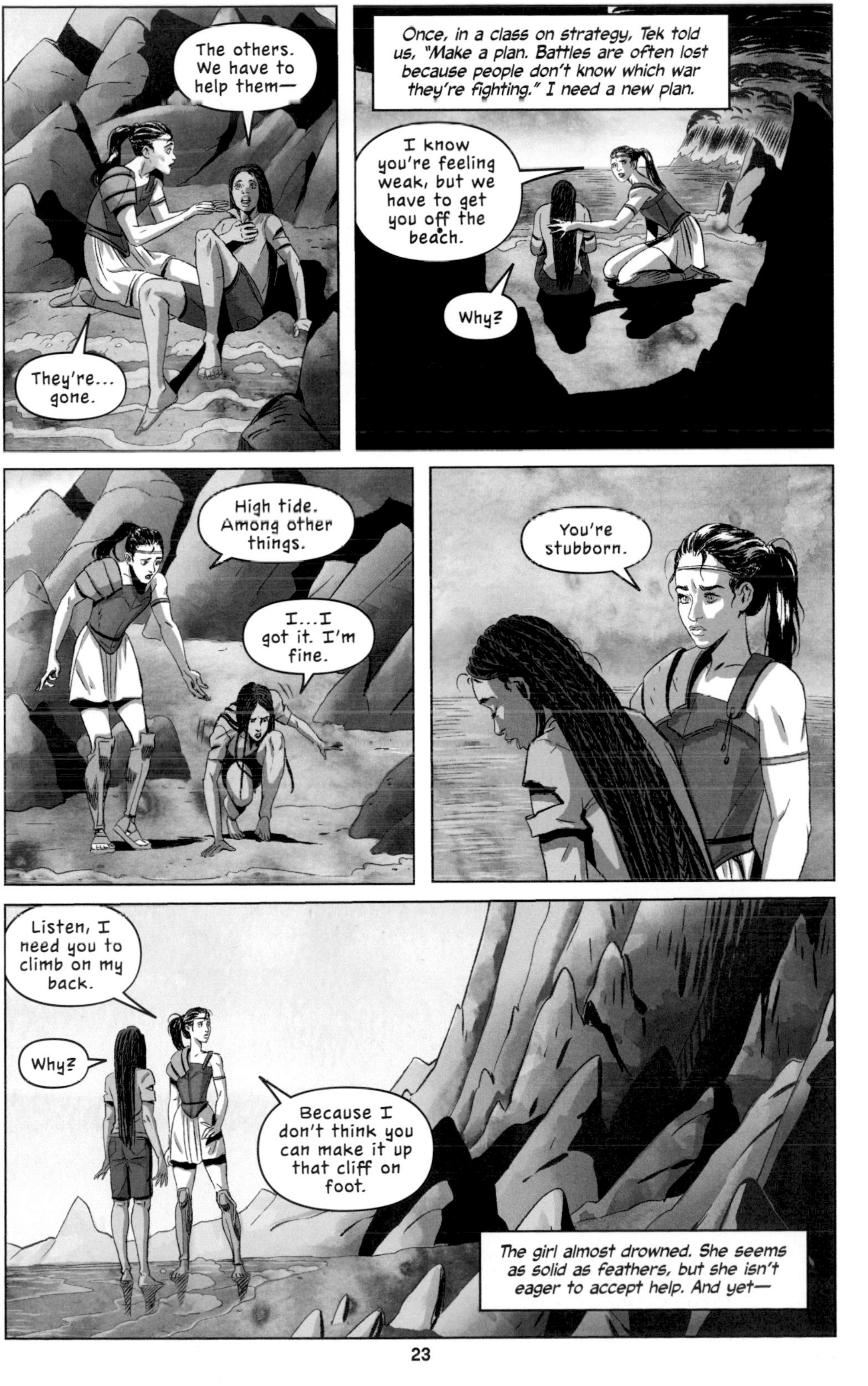

The others. We have to help them—
They're... gone.
Once, in a class on strategy, Tek told us, "Make a plan. Battles are often lost because people don't know which war they're fighting." I need a new plan.
I know you're feeling weak, but we have to get you off the beach.
Why?
High tide. Among other things.
I...I got it. I'm fine.
You're stubborn.
Listen, I need you to climb on my back.
Why?
Because I don't think you can make it up that cliff on foot.
The girl almost drowned. She seems as solid as feathers, but she isn't eager to accept help. And yet—

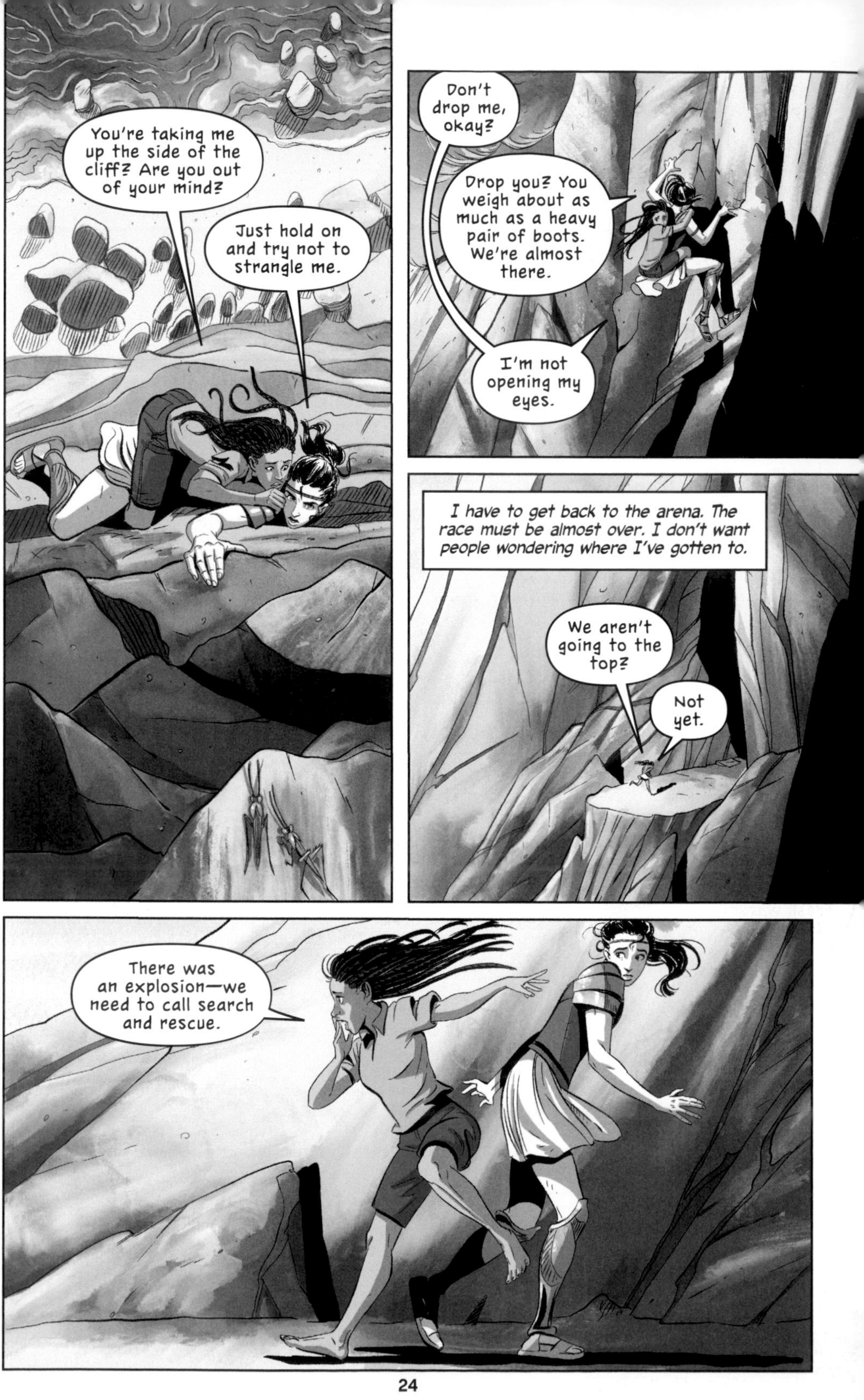
You're taking me up the side of the cliff? Are you out of your mind?
Just hold on and try not to strangle me.
Don't drop me, okay?
Drop you? You weigh about as much as a heavy pair of boots. We're almost there.
I'm not opening my eyes.
I have to get back to the arena. The race must be almost over. I don't want people wondering where I've gotten to.
We aren't going to the top?
Not yet.
There was an explosion—we need to call search and rescue.

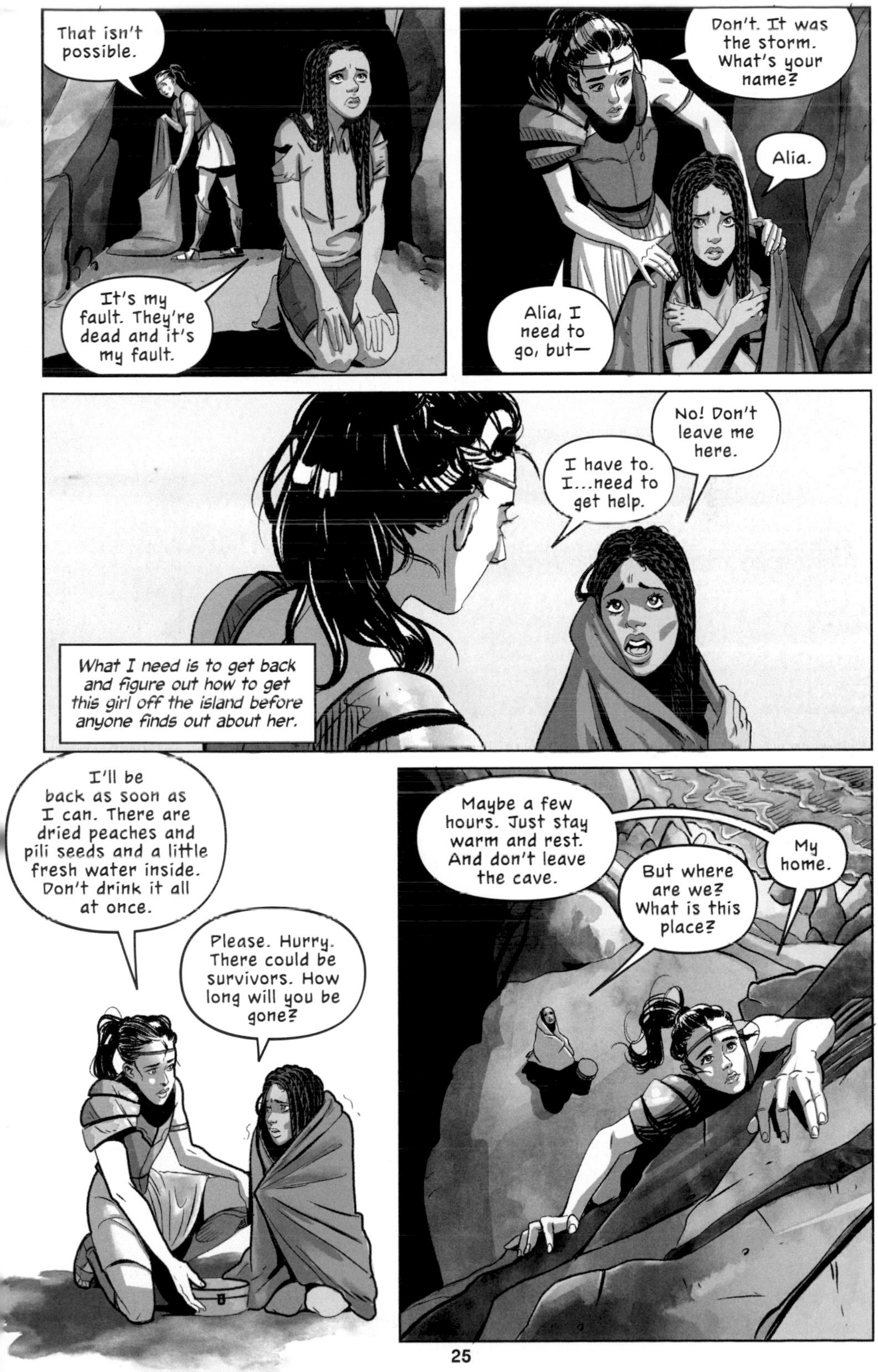
That isn't possible.
It's my fault. They're dead and it's my fault.
Don't. It was the storm. What's your name?
Alia.
Alia, I need to go, but—
No! Don't leave me here.
I have to. I...need to get help.
What I need is to get back and figure out how to get this girl off the island before anyone finds out about her.
I'll be back as soon as I can. There are dried peaches and pili seeds and a little fresh water inside. Don't drink it all at once.
Please. Hurry. There could be survivors. How long will you be gone?
Maybe a few hours. Just stay warm and rest. And don't leave the cave.
But where are we? What is this place?
My home.

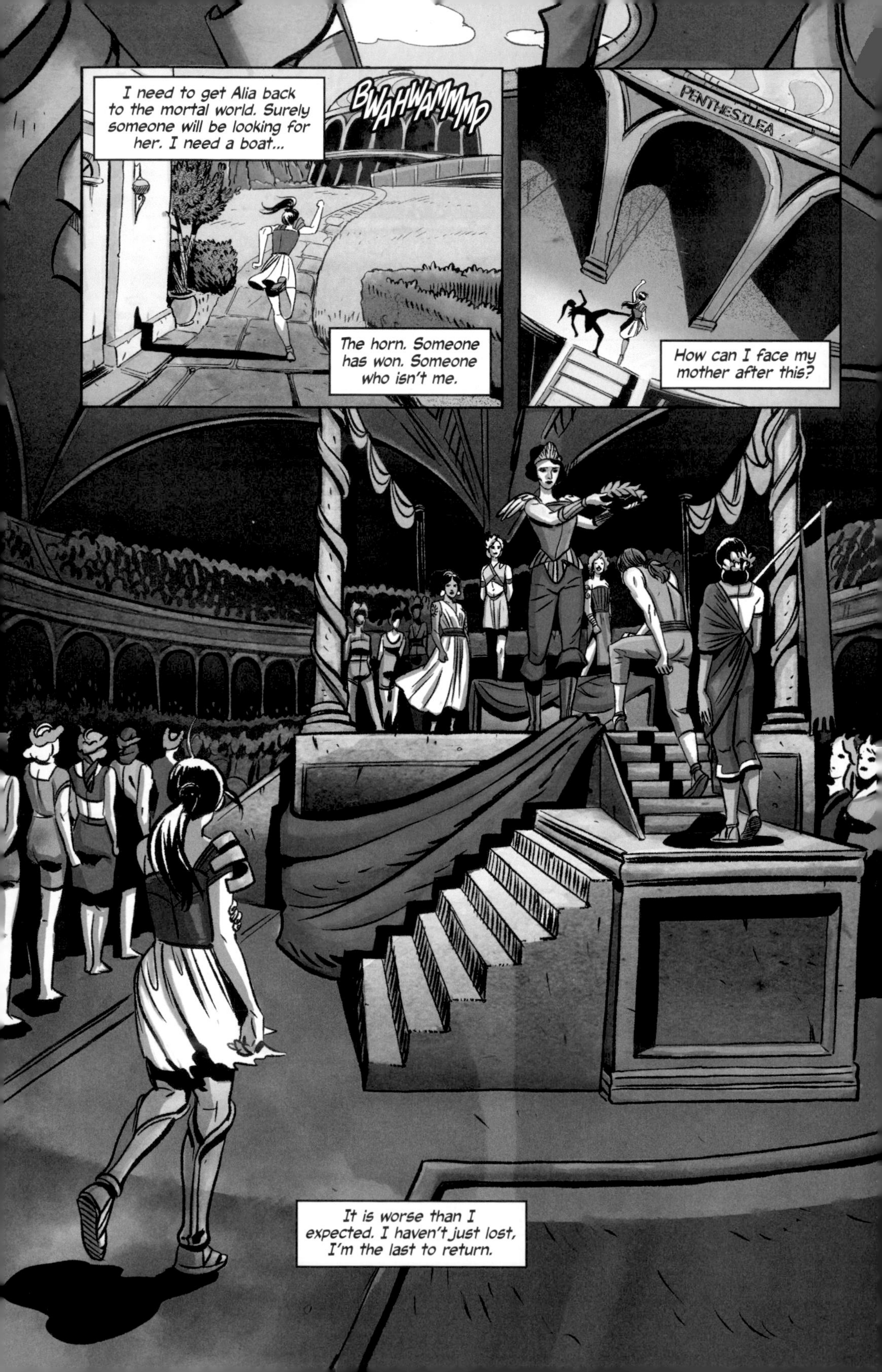
I need to get Alia back to the mortal world. Surely someone will be looking for her. I need a boat...
BWAHWAMMMP
The horn. Someone has won. Someone who isn't me.
PENTHESILEA
How can I face my mother after this?
It is worse than I expected. I haven't just lost, I'm the last to return.

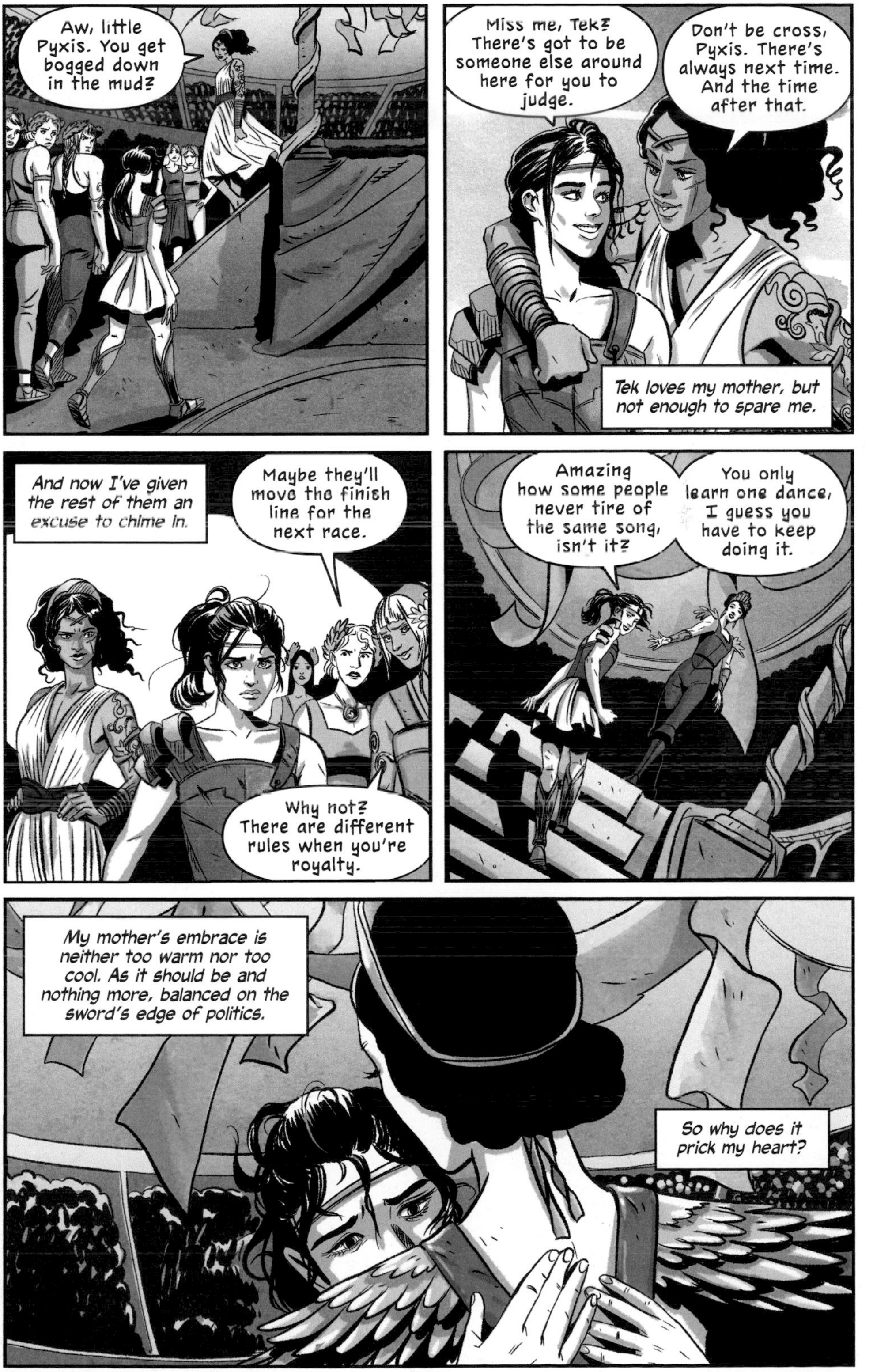

Aw, little Pyxis. You get bogged down in the mud?
Miss me, Tek? There's got to be someone else around here for you to judge.
Don't be cross, Pyxis. There's always next time. And the time after that.
Tek loves my mother, but not enough to spare me.
And now I've given the rest of them an excuse to chime in.
Maybe they'll move the finish line for the next race.
Why not? There are different rules when you're royalty.
Amazing how some people never tire of the same song, isn't it?
You only learn one dance, I guess you have to keep doing it.
My mother's embrace is neither too warm nor too cool. As it should be and nothing more, balanced on the sword's edge of politics.
So why does it prick my heart?

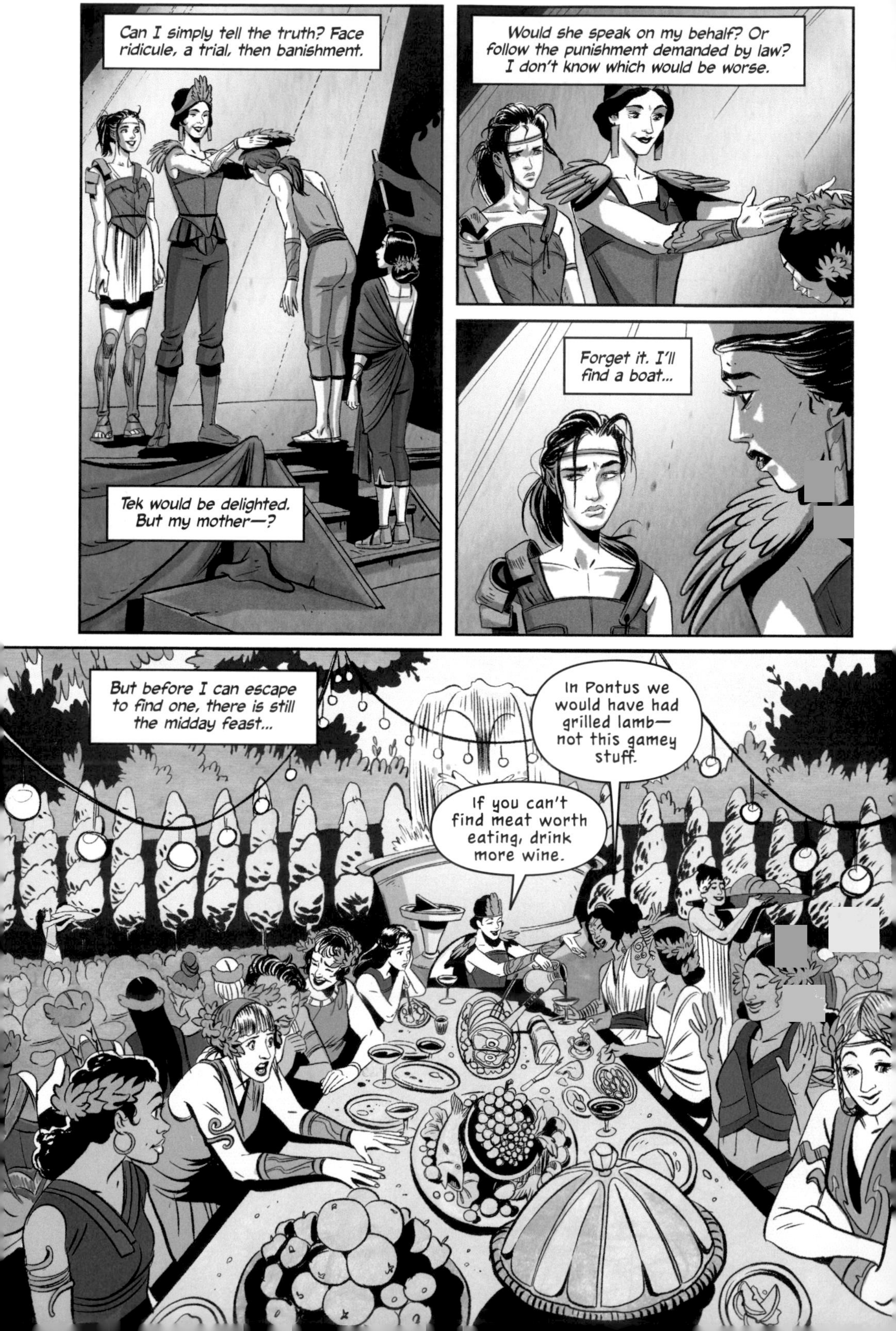
Can I simply tell the truth? Face ridicule, a trial, then banishment.
Tek would be delighted. But my mother—?
Would she speak on my behalf? Or follow the punishment demanded by law? I don't know which would be worse.
Forget it. I'll find a boat...
But before I can escape to find one, there is still the midday feast...
In Pontus we would have had grilled lamb—not this gamey stuff.
If you can't find meat worth eating, drink more wine.

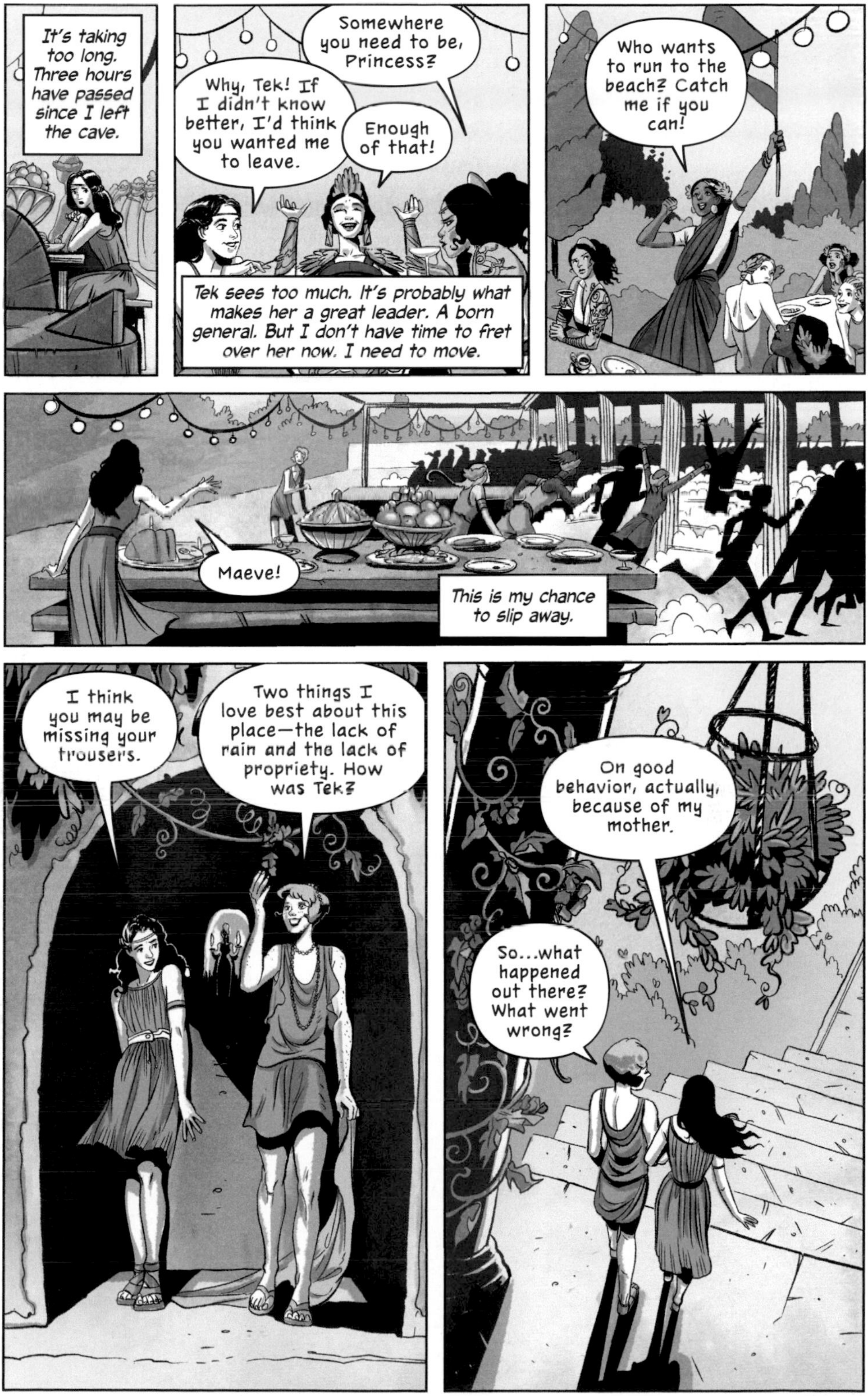
It's taking too long. Three hours have passed since I left the cave.
Why, Tek! If I didn't know better, I'd think you wanted me to leave.
Somewhere you need to be, Princess?
Enough of that!
Tek sees too much. It's probably what makes her a great leader. A born general. But I don't have time to fret over her now. I need to move.
Who wants to run to the beach? Catch me if you can!
Maeve!
This is my chance to slip away.
I think you may be missing your trousers.
Two things I love best about this place—the lack of rain and the lack of propriety. How was Tek?
On good behavior, actually, because of my mother.
So...what happened out there? What went wrong?

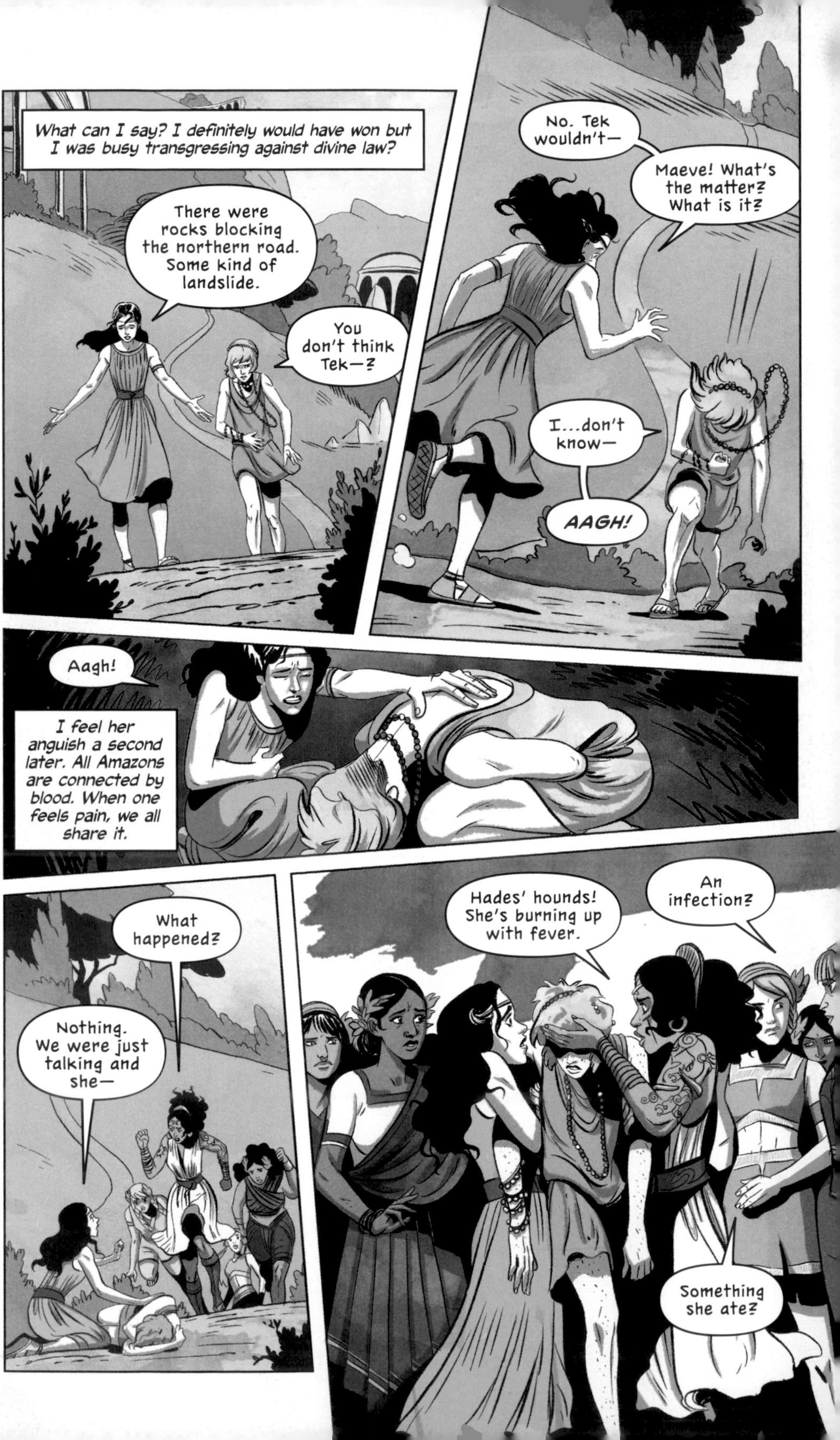
What can I say? I definitely would have won but I was busy transgressing against divine law?
There were rocks blocking the northern road. Some kind of landslide.
You don't think Tek—?
No. Tek wouldn't—
Maeve! What's the matter? What is it?
I...don't know—
AAGH!
Aagh!
I feel her anguish a second later. All Amazons are connected by blood. When one feels pain, we all share it.
What happened?
Nothing. We were just talking and she—
Hades' hounds! She's burning up with fever.
An infection?
Something she ate?

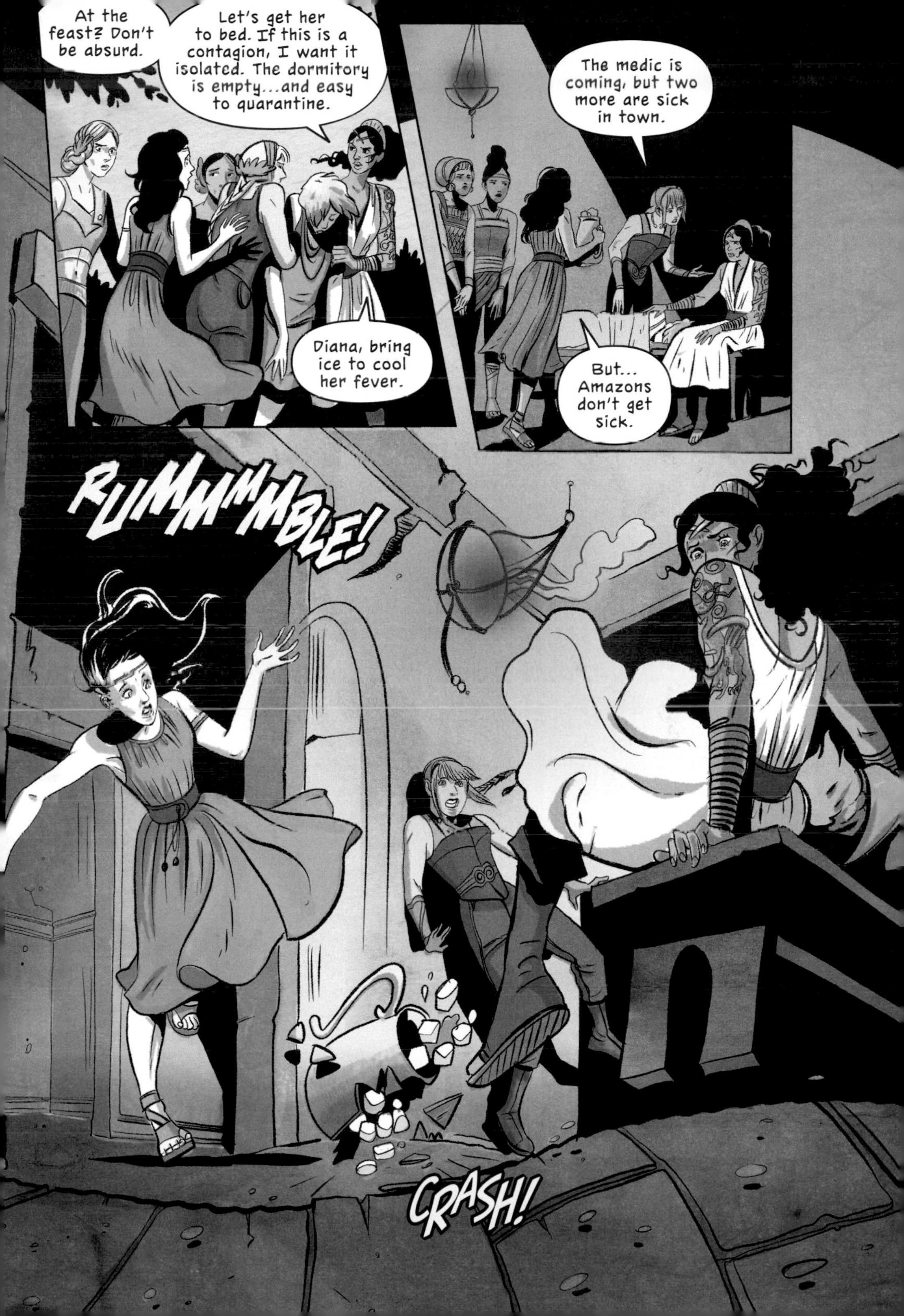
At the feast? Don't be absurd.
Let's get her to bed. If this is a contagion, I want it isolated. The dormitory is empty...and easy to quarantine.
Diana, bring ice to cool her fever.
The medic is coming, but two more are sick in town.
But... Amazons don't get sick.
RUMMMMMBLE!
CRASH!

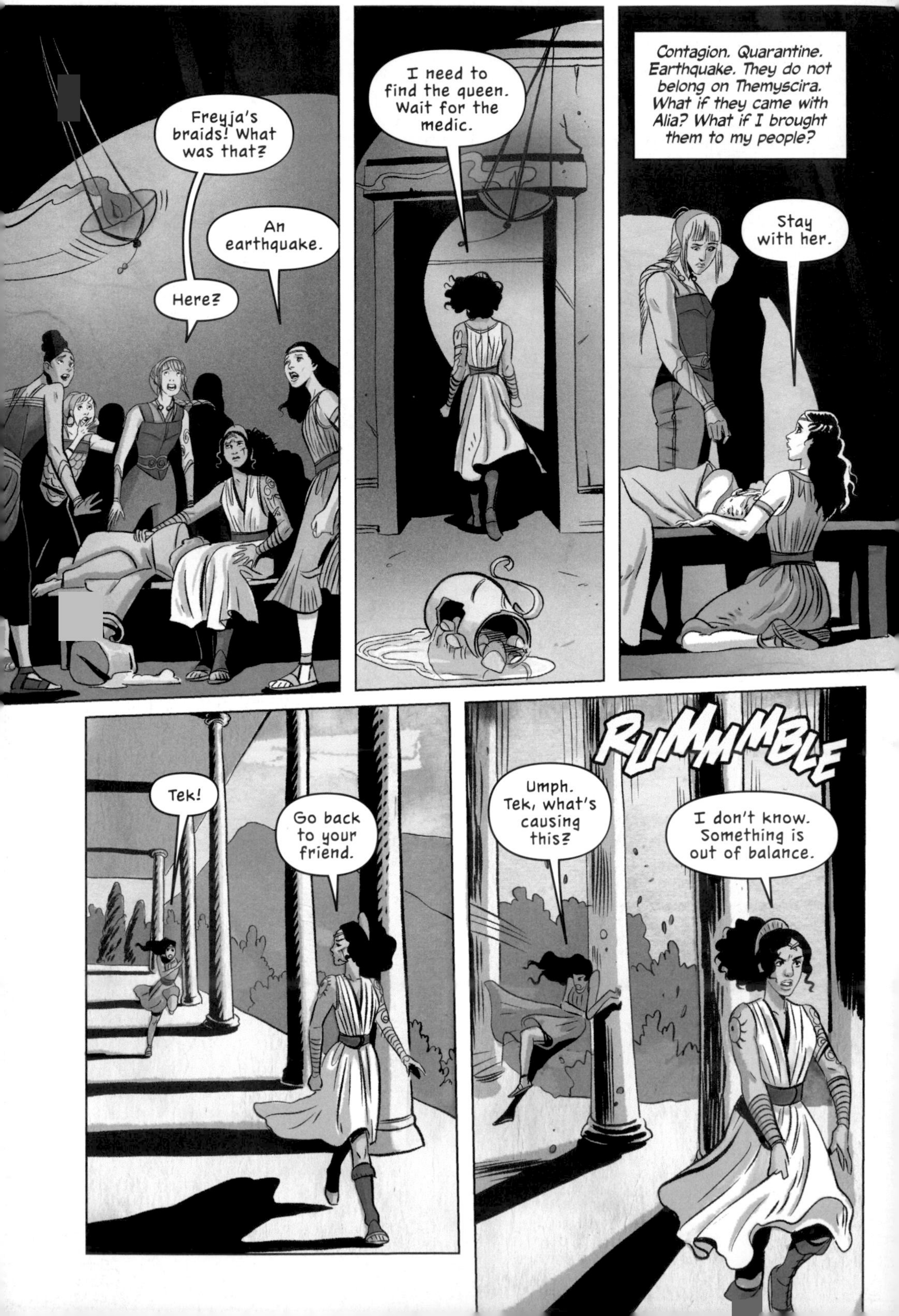
Freyja's braids! What was that?
Here?
An earthquake.
I need to find the queen. Wait for the medic.
Contagion. Quarantine. Earthquake. They do not belong on Themyscira. What if they came with Alia? What if I brought them to my people?
Stay with her.
Tek!
Go back to your friend.
RUMMMBLE
Umph. Tek, what's causing this?
I don't know. Something is out of balance.

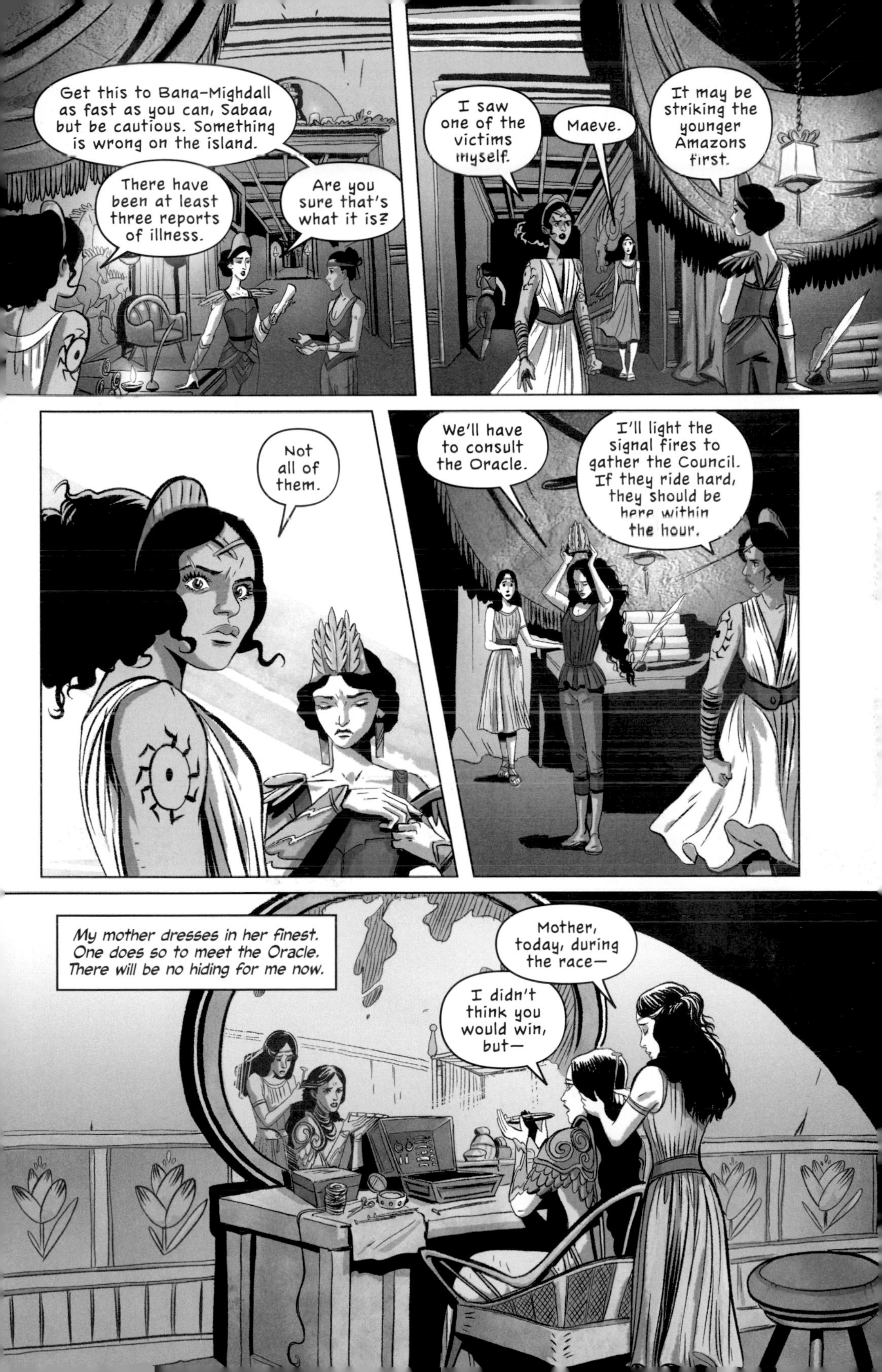
Get this to Bana-Mighdall as fast as you can, Sabaa, but be cautious. Something is wrong on the island.
There have been at least three reports of illness.
Are you sure that's what it is?
I saw one of the victims myself.
Maeve.
It may be striking the younger Amazons first.
Not all of them.
We'll have to consult the Oracle.
I'll light the signal fires to gather the Council. If they ride hard, they should be here within the hour.
My mother dresses in her finest. One does so to meet the Oracle. There will be no hiding for me now.
Mother, today, during the race—
I didn't think you would win, but—

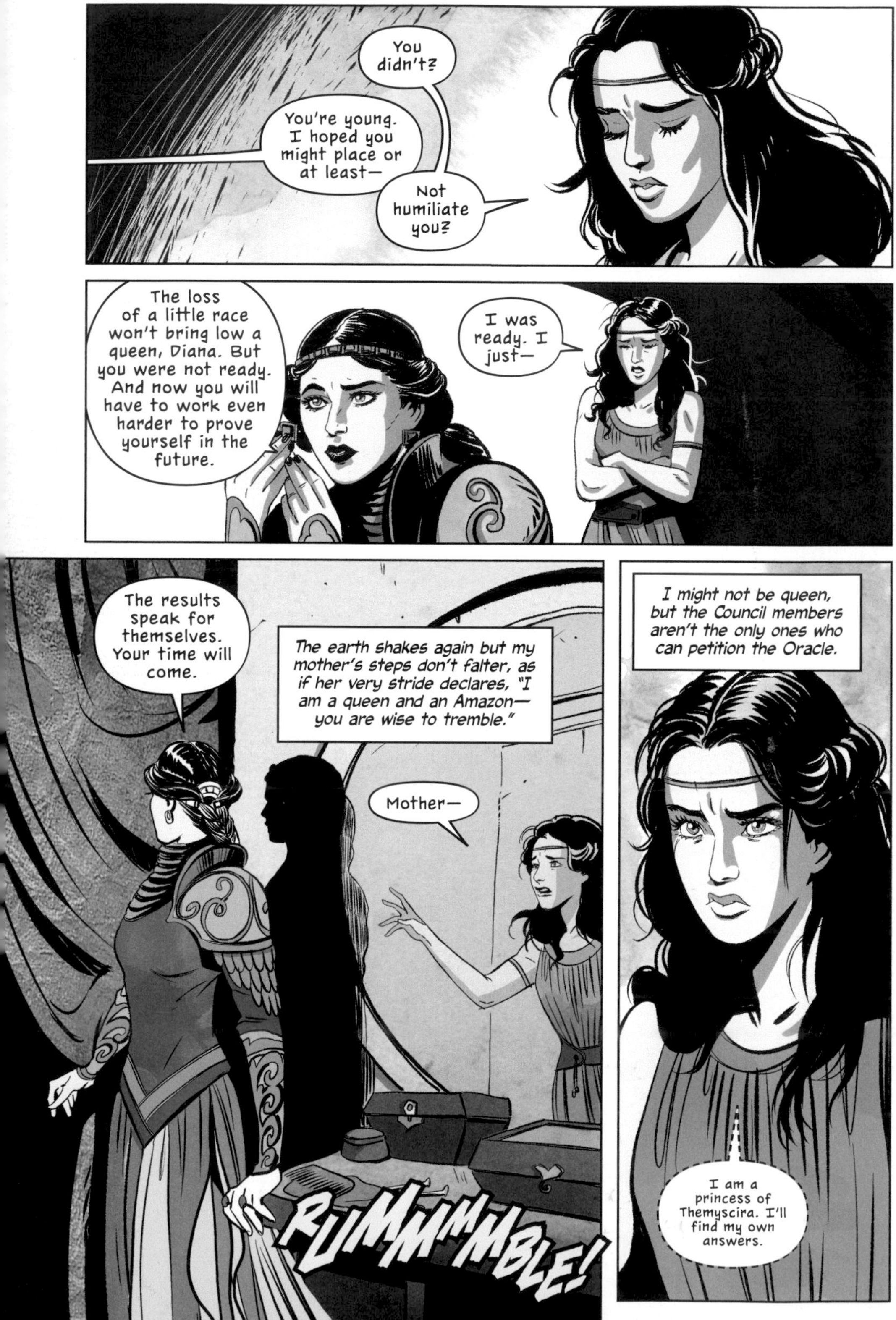
You didn't?
You're young. I hoped you might place or at least—
Not humiliate you?
The loss of a little race won't bring low a queen, Diana. But you were not ready. And now you will have to work even harder to prove yourself in the future.
I was ready. I just—
The results speak for themselves. Your time will come.
The earth shakes again but my mother's steps don't falter, as if her very stride declares, "I am a queen and an Amazon—you are wise to tremble."
Mother—
RUMMMMBLE!
I might not be queen, but the Council members aren't the only ones who can petition the Oracle.
I am a princess of Themyscira. I'll find my own answers.

PART TWO

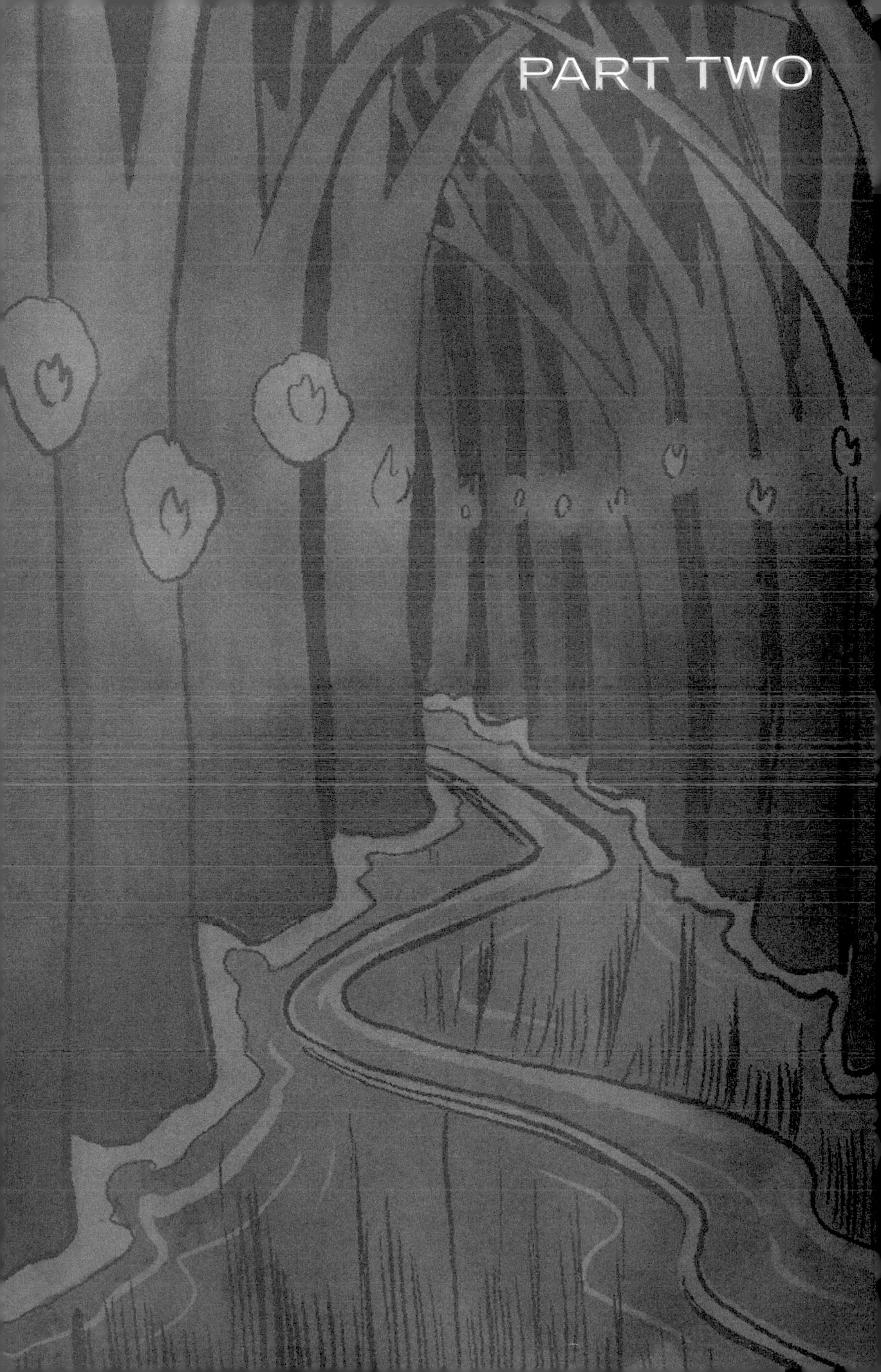

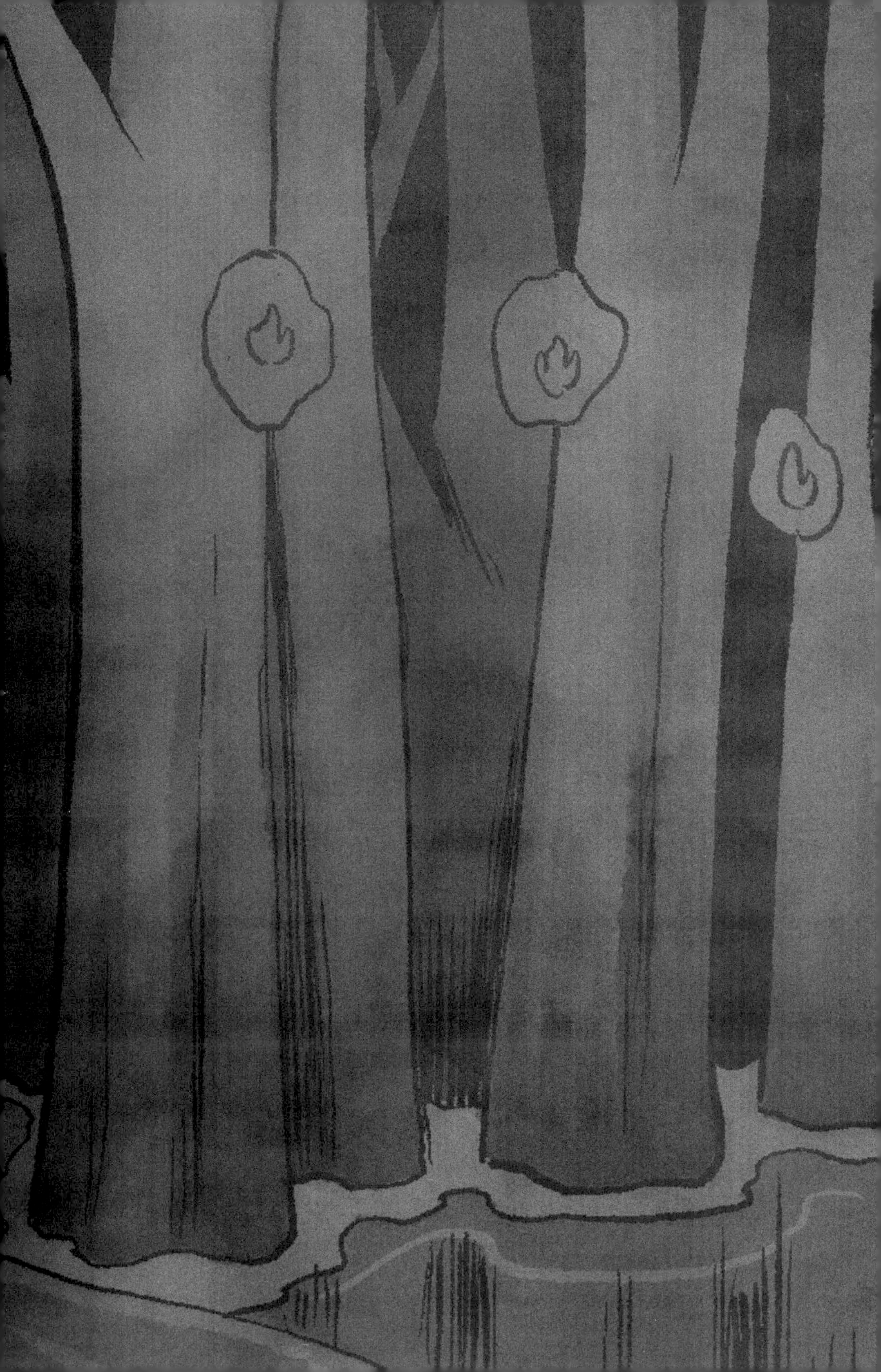

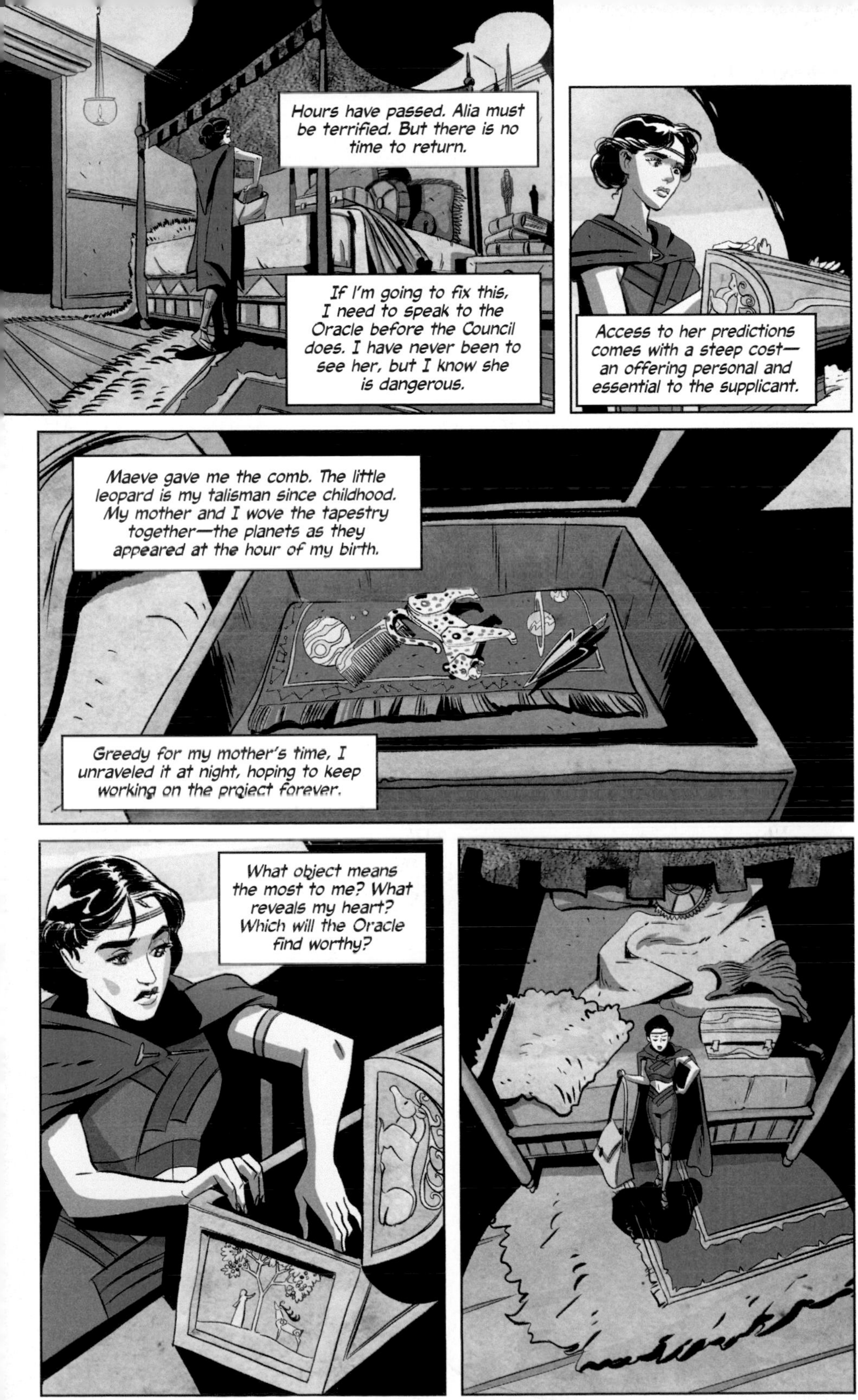
Hours have passed. Alia must be terrified. But there is no time to return.
If I'm going to fix this, I need to speak to the Oracle before the Council does. I have never been to see her, but I know she is dangerous.
Access to her predictions comes with a steep cost—an offering personal and essential to the supplicant.
Maeve gave me the comb. The little leopard is my talisman since childhood. My mother and I wove the tapestry together—the planets as they appeared at the hour of my birth.
Greedy for my mother's time, I unraveled it at night, hoping to keep working on the project forever.
What object means the most to me? What reveals my heart? Which will the Oracle find worthy?

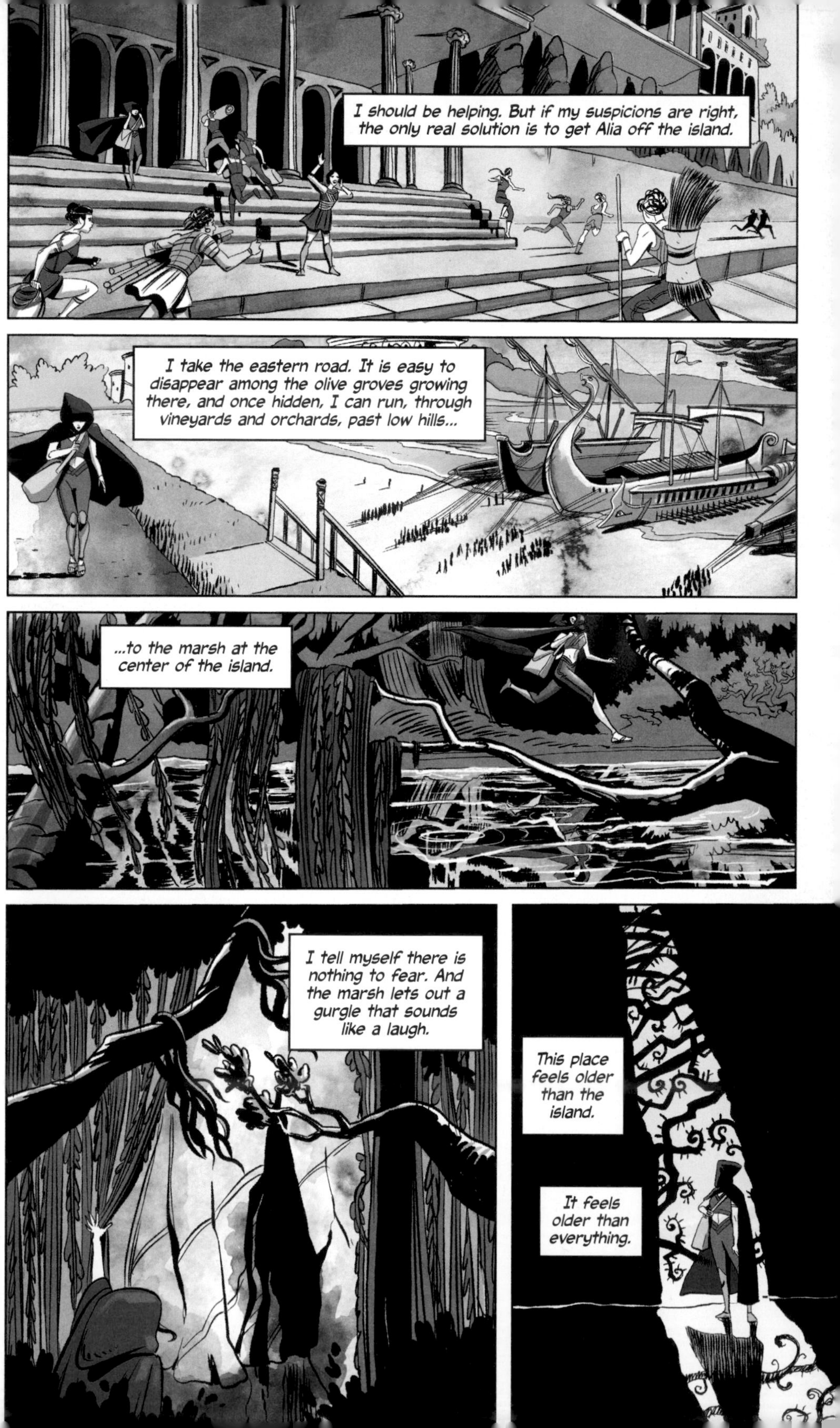
I should be helping. But if my suspicions are right, the only real solution is to get Alia off the island.
I take the eastern road. It is easy to disappear among the olive groves growing there, and once hidden, I can run, through vineyards and orchards, past low hills...
...to the marsh at the center of the island.
I tell myself there is nothing to fear. And the marsh lets out a gurgle that sounds like a laugh.
This place feels older than the island.
It feels older than everything.

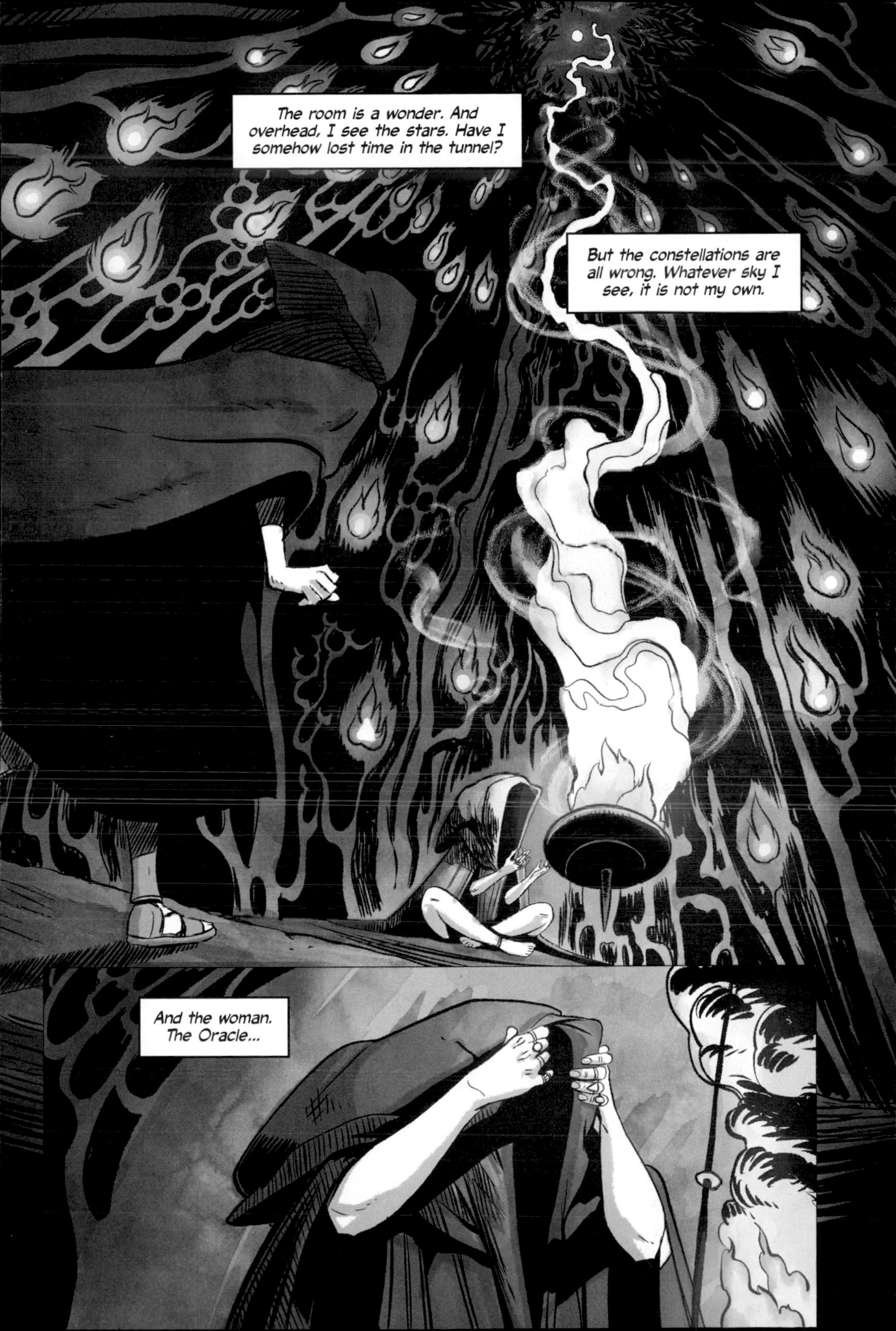
The room is a wonder. And overhead, I see the stars. Have I somehow lost time in the tunnel?
But the constellations are all wrong. Whatever sky I see, it is not my own.
And the woman. The Oracle...

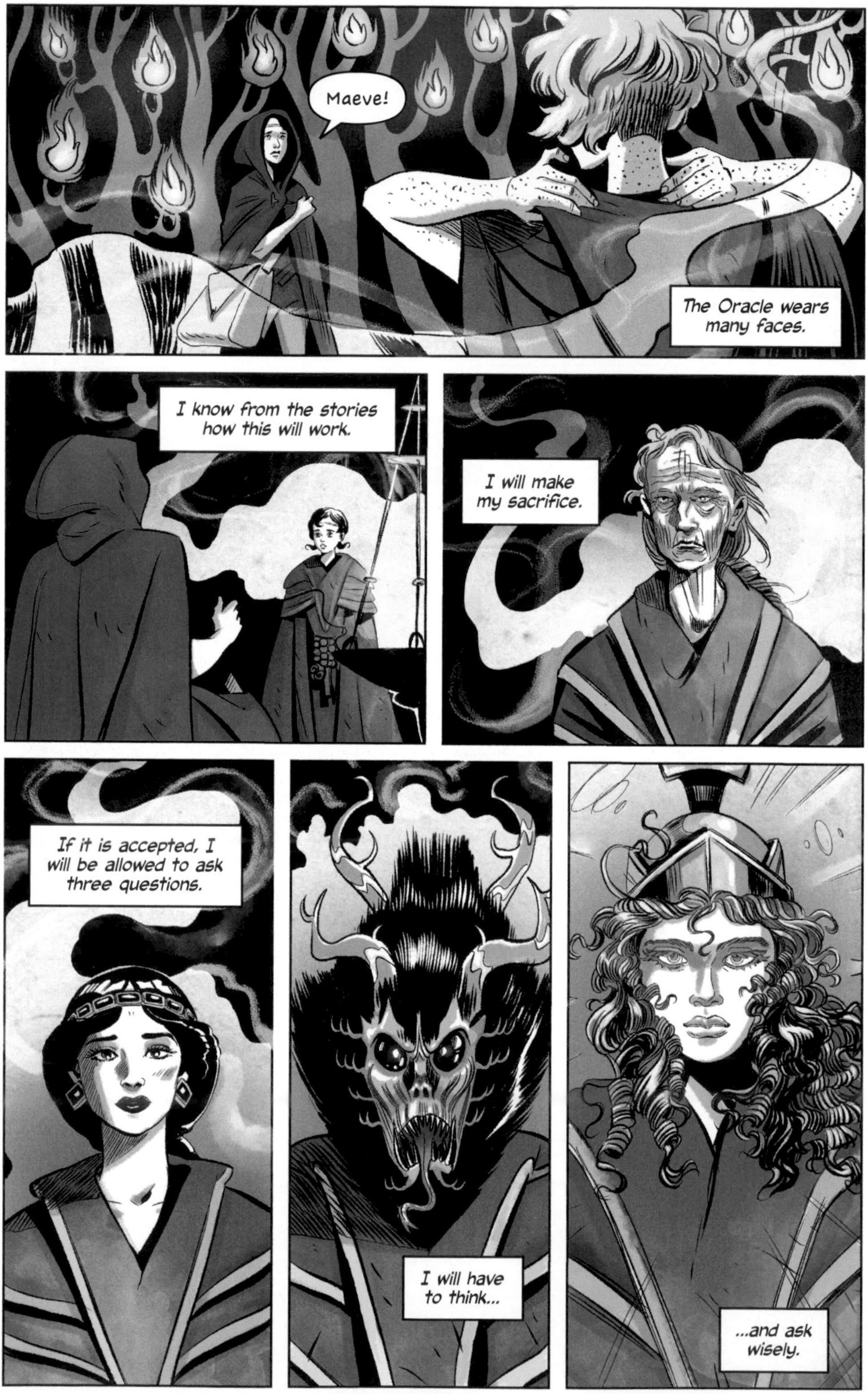
Maeve!
The Oracle wears many faces.
I know from the stories how this will work.
I will make my sacrifice.
If it is accepted, I will be allowed to ask three questions.
I will have to think...
...and ask wisely.

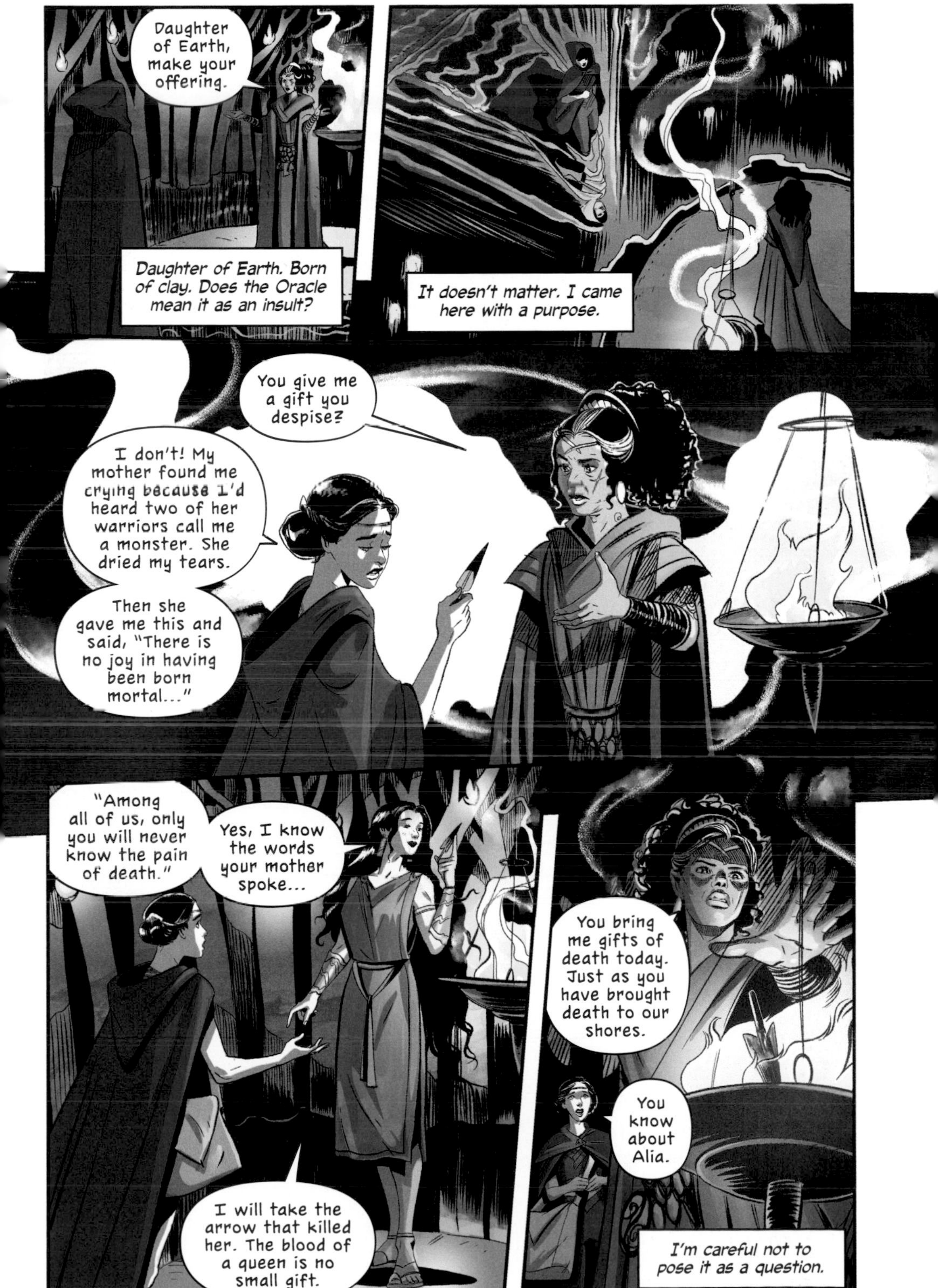

Daughter of Earth, make your offering.
Daughter of Earth. Born of clay. Does the Oracle mean it as an insult?
It doesn't matter. I came here with a purpose.
You give me a gift you despise?
I don't! My mother found me crying because I'd heard two of her warriors call me a monster. She dried my tears.
Then she gave me this and said, "There is no joy in having been born mortal..."
"Among all of us, only you will never know the pain of death."
Yes, I know the words your mother spoke...
I will take the arrow that killed her. The blood of a queen is no small gift.
You bring me gifts of death today. Just as you have brought death to our shores.
You know about Alia.
I'm careful not to pose it as a question.

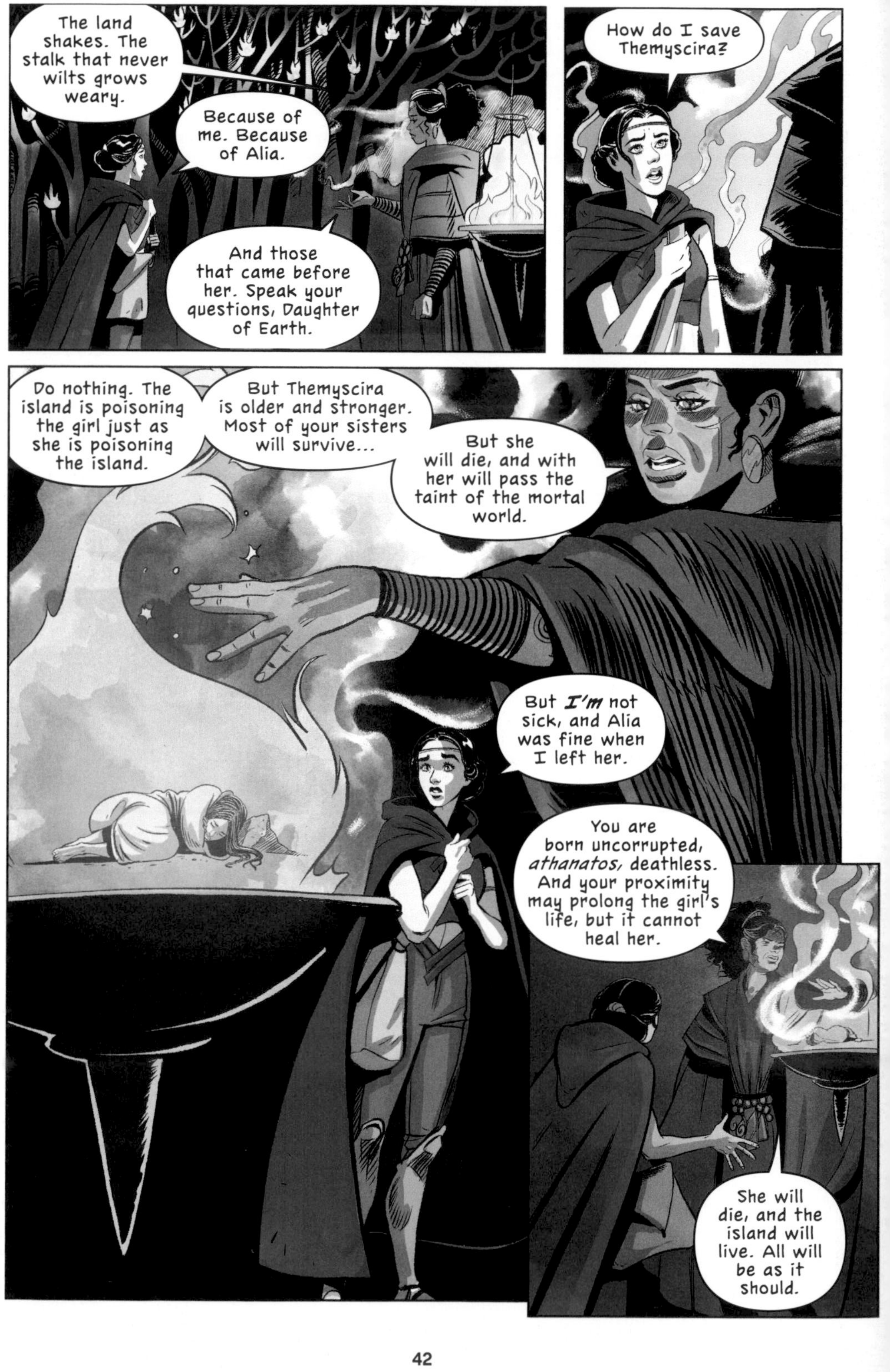
The land shakes. The stalk that never wilts grows weary.
Because of me. Because of Alia.
And those that came before her. Speak your questions, Daughter of Earth.
How do I save Themyscira?
Do nothing. The island is poisoning the girl just as she is poisoning the island.
But Themyscira is older and stronger. Most of your sisters will survive...
But she will die, and with her will pass the taint of the mortal world.
But *I'm* not sick, and Alia was fine when I left her.
You are born uncorrupted, *athanatos,* deathless. And your proximity may prolong the girl's life, but it cannot heal her.
She will die, and the island will live. All will be as it should.

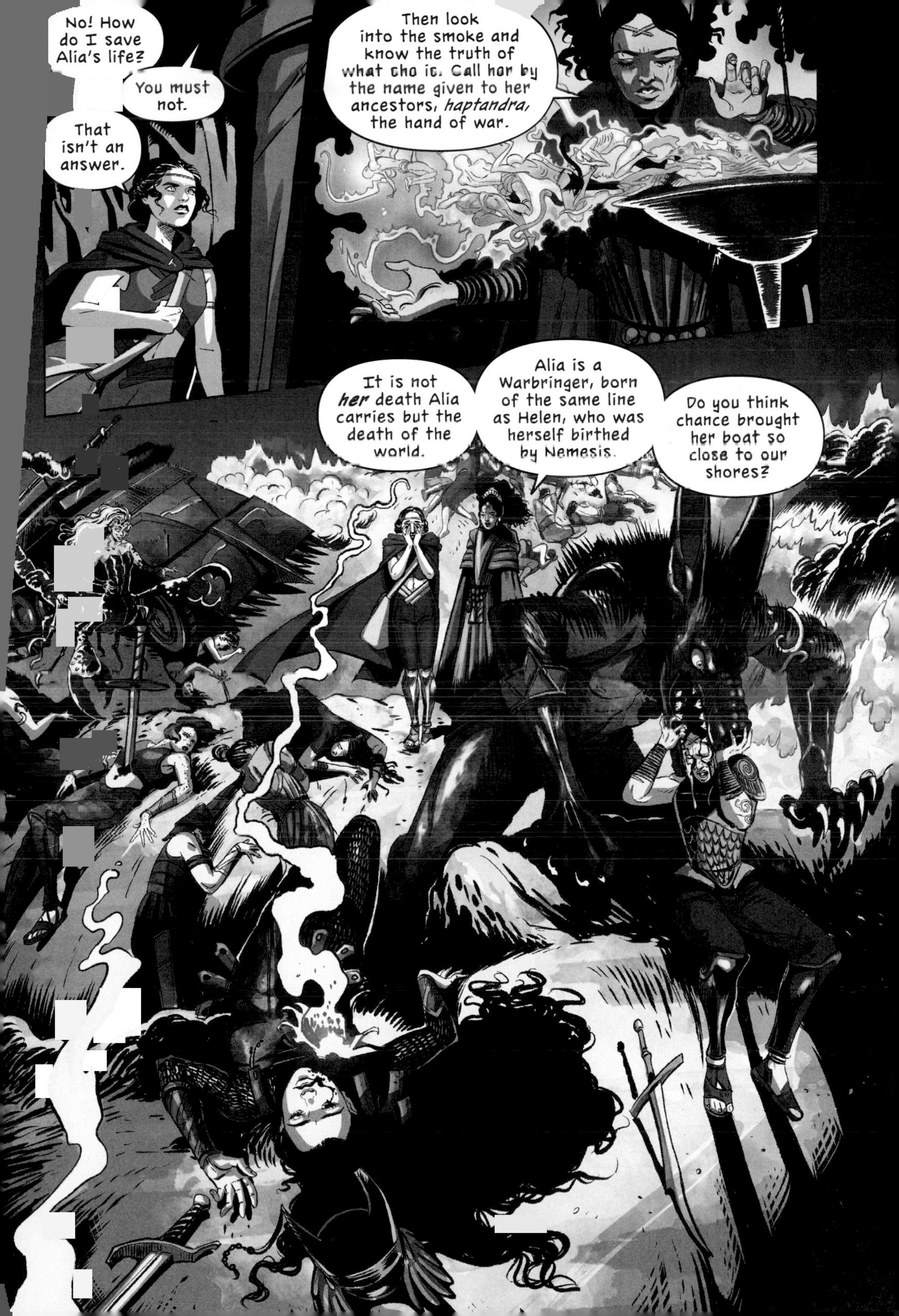
No! How do I save Alia's life?
You must not.
That isn't an answer.
Then look into the smoke and know the truth of what she is. Call her by the name given to her ancestors, *haptandra,* the hand of war.
It is not ***her*** death Alia carries but the death of the world.
Alia is a Warbringer, born of the same line as Helen, who was herself birthed by Nemesis.
Do you think chance brought her boat so close to our shores?

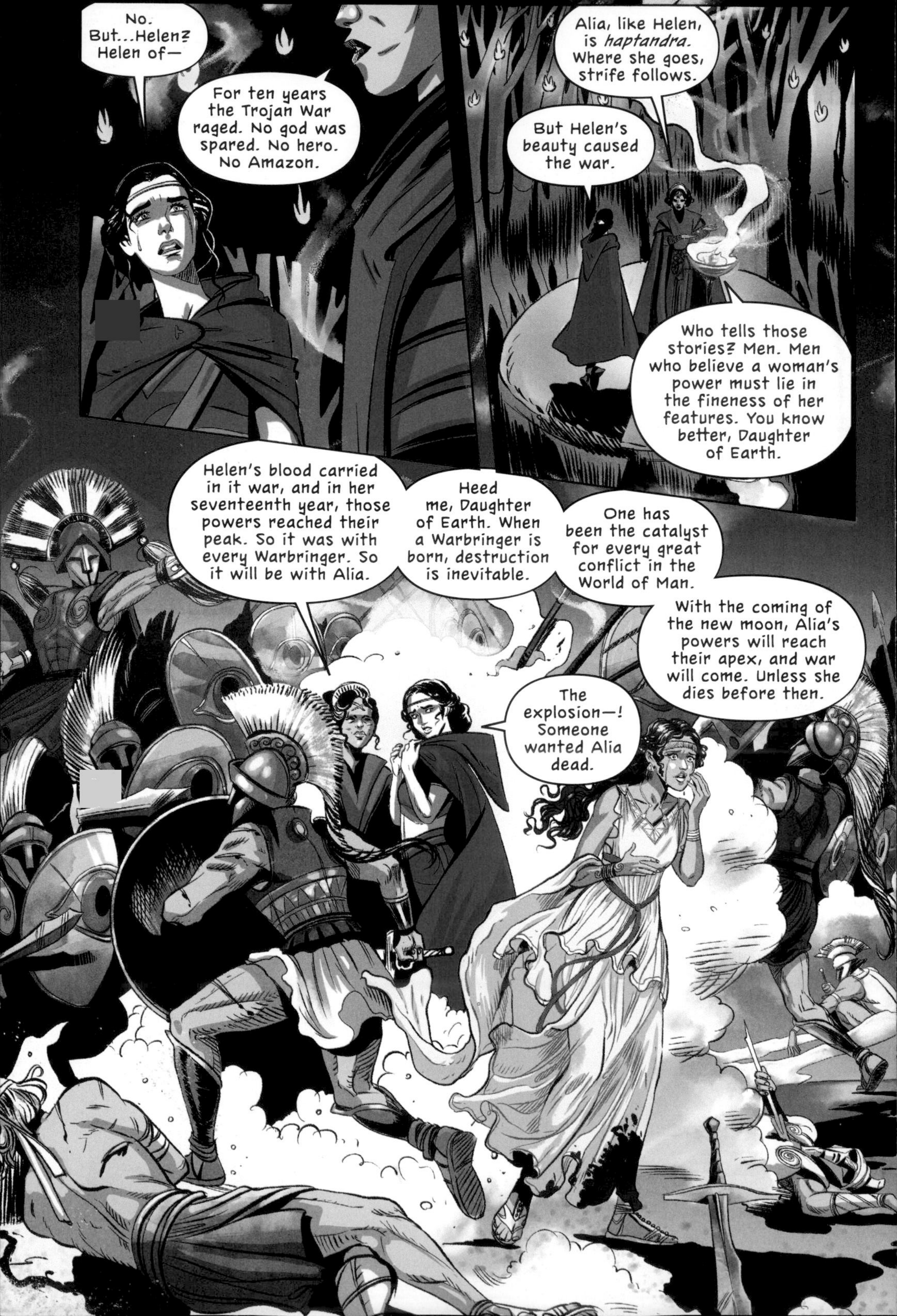
No.
But...Helen?
Helen of—
For ten years the Trojan War raged. No god was spared. No hero. No Amazon.
Alia, like Helen, is *haptandra.* Where she goes, strife follows.
But Helen's beauty caused the war.
Who tells those stories? Men. Men who believe a woman's power must lie in the fineness of her features. You know better, Daughter of Earth.
Helen's blood carried in it war, and in her seventeenth year, those powers reached their peak. So it was with every Warbringer. So it will be with Alia.
Heed me, Daughter of Earth. When a Warbringer is born, destruction is inevitable.
One has been the catalyst for every great conflict in the World of Man.
With the coming of the new moon, Alia's powers will reach their apex, and war will come. Unless she dies before then.
The explosion—! Someone wanted Alia dead.

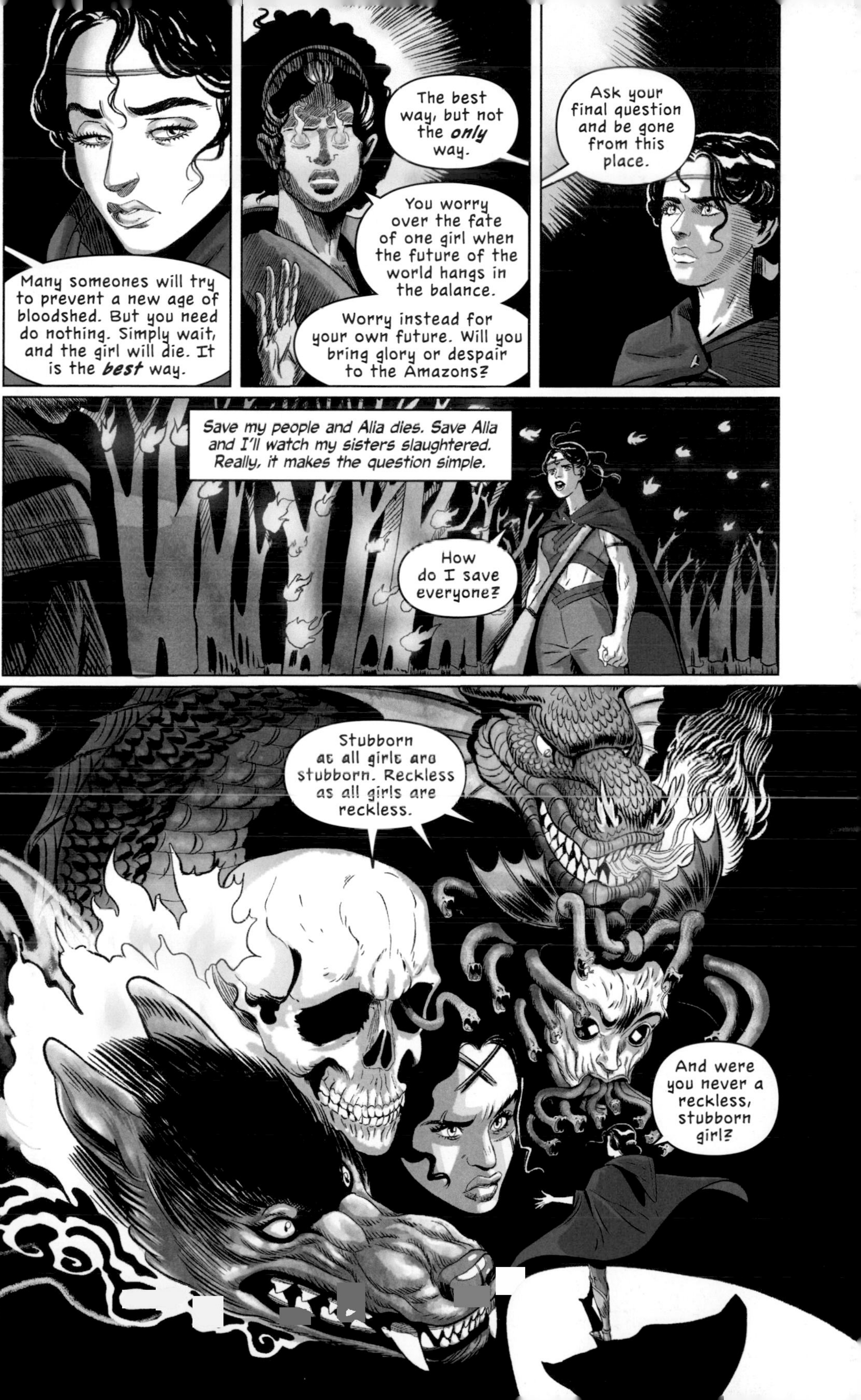
Many someones will try to prevent a new age of bloodshed. But you need do nothing. Simply wait, and the girl will die. It is the *best* way.
The best way, but not the *only* way.
You worry over the fate of one girl when the future of the world hangs in the balance.
Worry instead for your own future. Will you bring glory or despair to the Amazons?
Ask your final question and be gone from this place.
Save my people and Alia dies. Save Alia and I'll watch my sisters slaughtered. Really, it makes the question simple.
How do I save everyone?
Stubborn as all girls are stubborn. Reckless as all girls are reckless.
And were you never a reckless, stubborn girl?

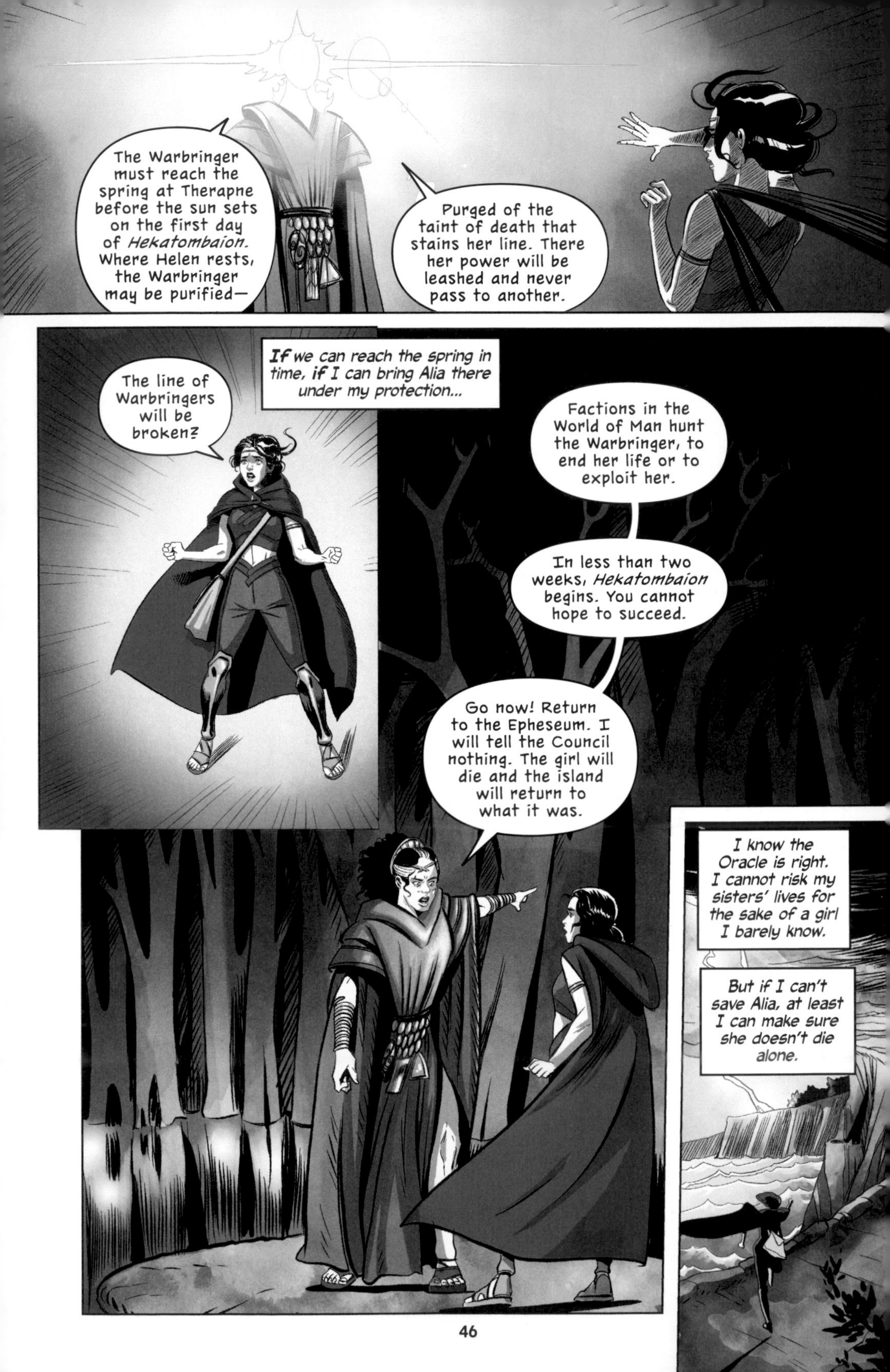
The Warbringer must reach the spring at Therapne before the sun sets on the first day of *Hekatombaion.* Where Helen rests, the Warbringer may be purified—
Purged of the taint of death that stains her line. There her power will be leashed and never pass to another.
The line of Warbringers will be broken?
If we can reach the spring in time, if I can bring Alia there under my protection...
Factions in the World of Man hunt the Warbringer, to end her life or to exploit her.
In less than two weeks, *Hekatombaion* begins. You cannot hope to succeed.
Go now! Return to the Epheseum. I will tell the Council nothing. The girl will die and the island will return to what it was.
I know the Oracle is right. I cannot risk my sisters' lives for the sake of a girl I barely know.
But if I can't save Alia, at least I can make sure she doesn't die alone.

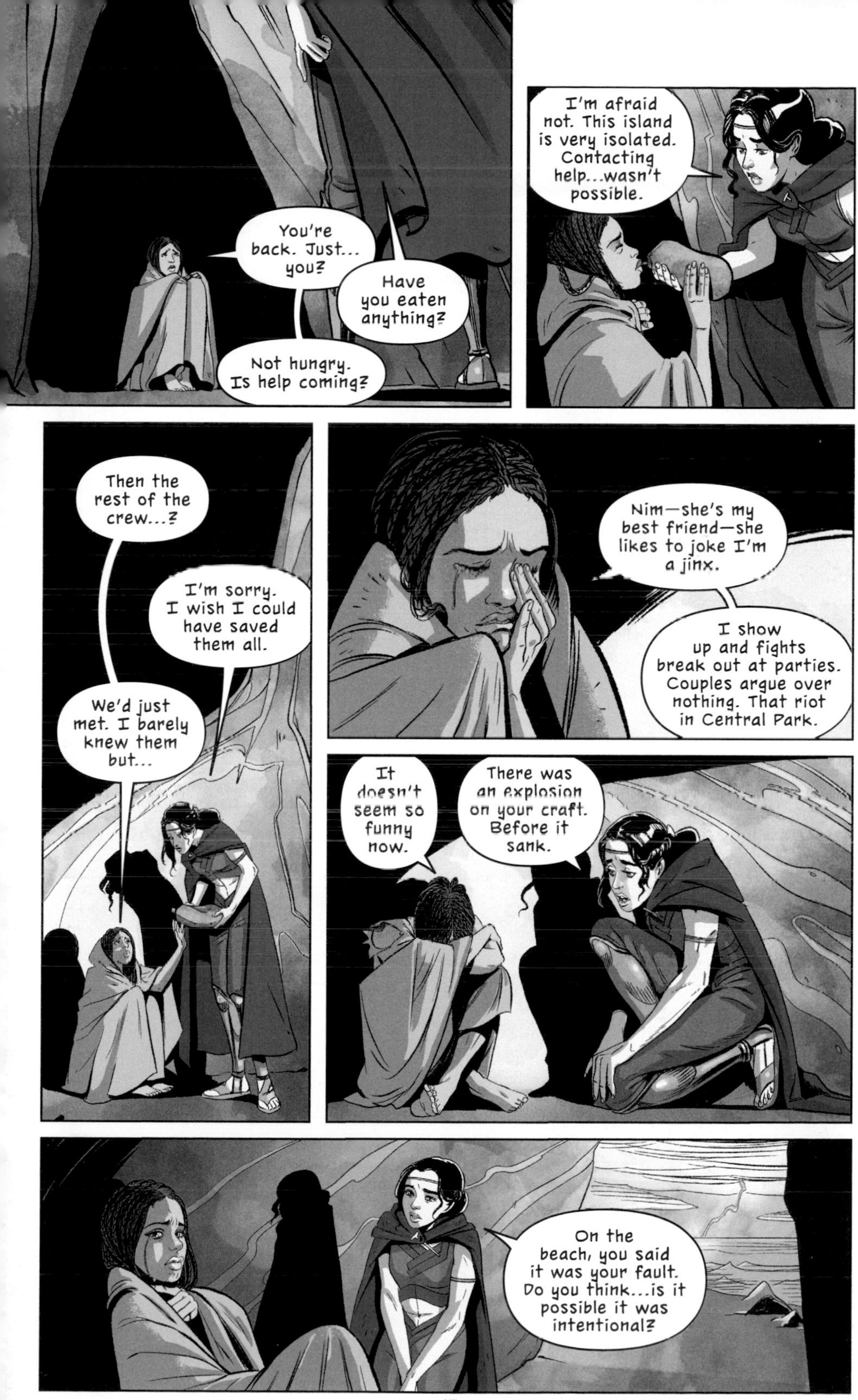
You're back. Just... you?
Have you eaten anything?
Not hungry. Is help coming?
I'm afraid not. This island is very isolated. Contacting help...wasn't possible.
Then the rest of the crew...?
I'm sorry. I wish I could have saved them all.
We'd just met. I barely knew them but...
Nim—she's my best friend—she likes to joke I'm a jinx.
I show up and fights break out at parties. Couples argue over nothing. That riot in Central Park.
It doesn't seem so funny now.
There was an explosion on your craft. Before it sank.
On the beach, you said it was your fault. Do you think...is it possible it was intentional?

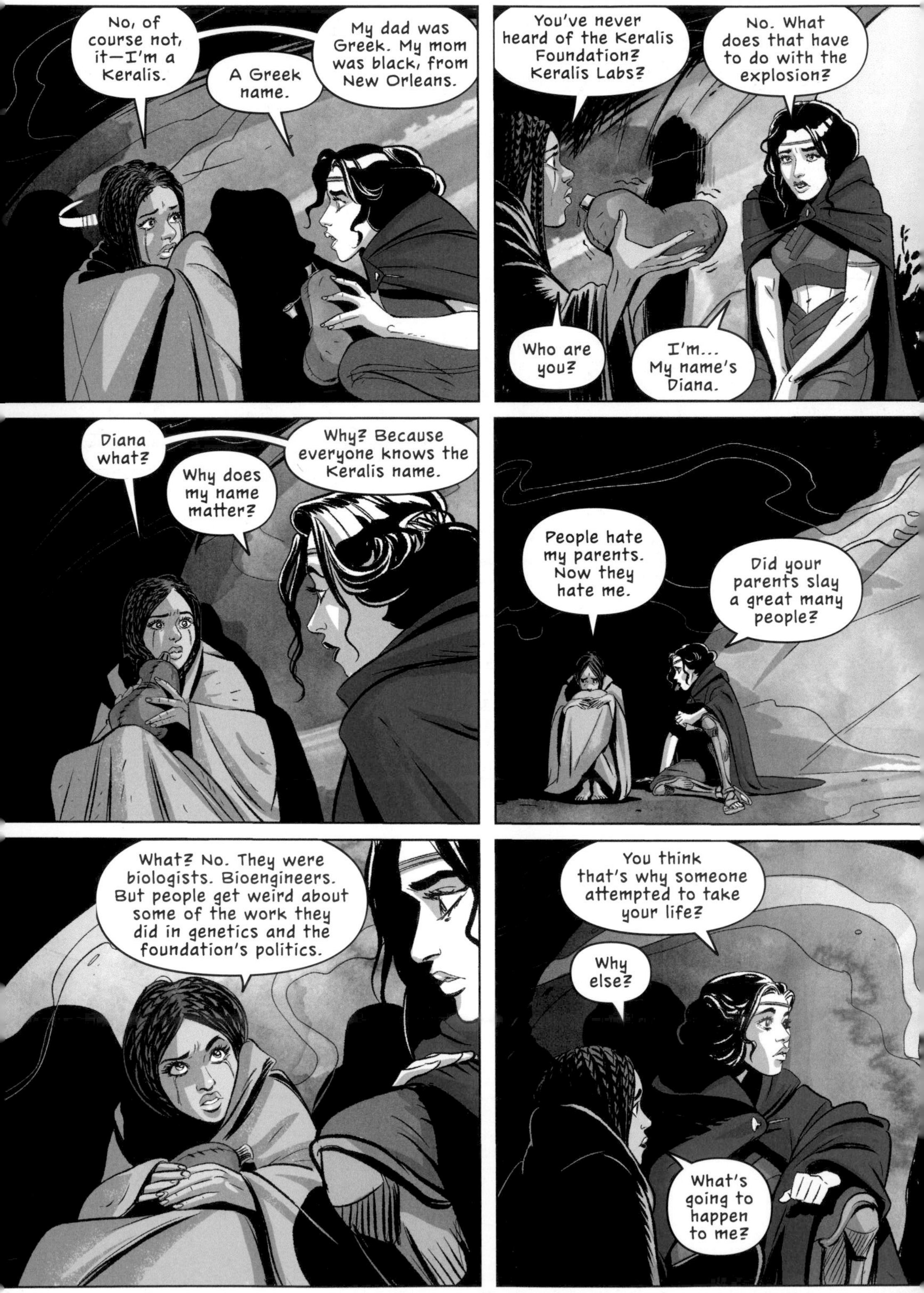
No, of course not, it—I'm a Keralis.
A Greek name.
My dad was Greek. My mom was black, from New Orleans.
You've never heard of the Keralis Foundation? Keralis Labs?
No. What does that have to do with the explosion?
Who are you?
I'm... My name's Diana.
Diana what?
Why does my name matter?
Why? Because everyone knows the Keralis name.
People hate my parents. Now they hate me.
Did your parents slay a great many people?
What? No. They were biologists. Bioengineers. But people get weird about some of the work they did in genetics and the foundation's politics.
You think that's why someone attempted to take your life?
Why else?
What's going to happen to me?

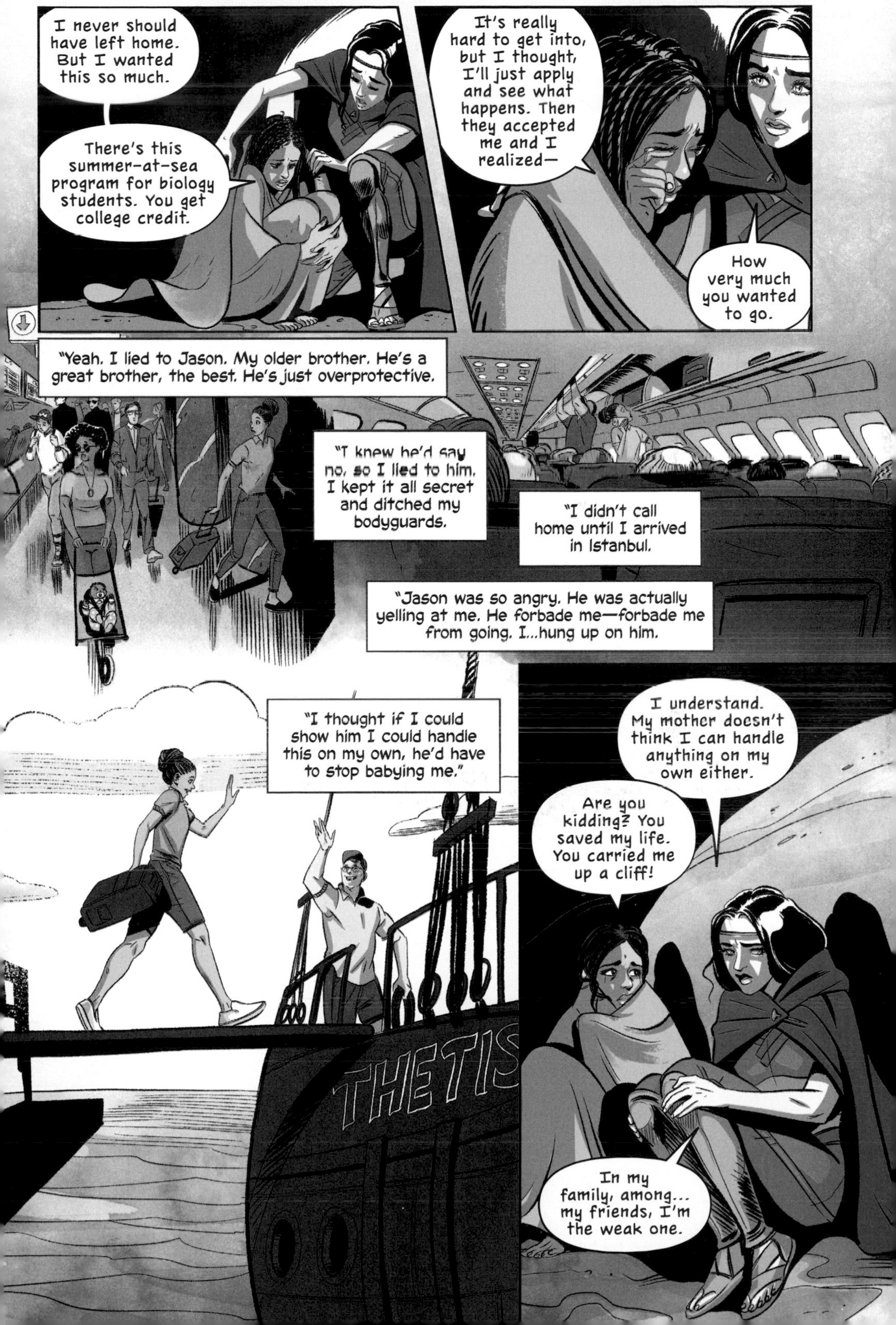
I never should have left home. But I wanted this so much.
There's this summer-at-sea program for biology students. You get college credit.
It's really hard to get into, but I thought, I'll just apply and see what happens. Then they accepted me and I realized—
How very much you wanted to go.
"Yeah. I lied to Jason. My older brother. He's a great brother, the best. He's just overprotective.
"I knew he'd say no, so I lied to him. I kept it all secret and ditched my bodyguards.
"I didn't call home until I arrived in Istanbul.
"Jason was so angry. He was actually yelling at me. He forbade me—forbade me from going. I...hung up on him.
"I thought if I could show him I could handle this on my own, he'd have to stop babying me."
THETIS
I understand. My mother doesn't think I can handle anything on my own either.
Are you kidding? You saved my life. You carried me up a cliff!
In my family, among... my friends, I'm the weak one.

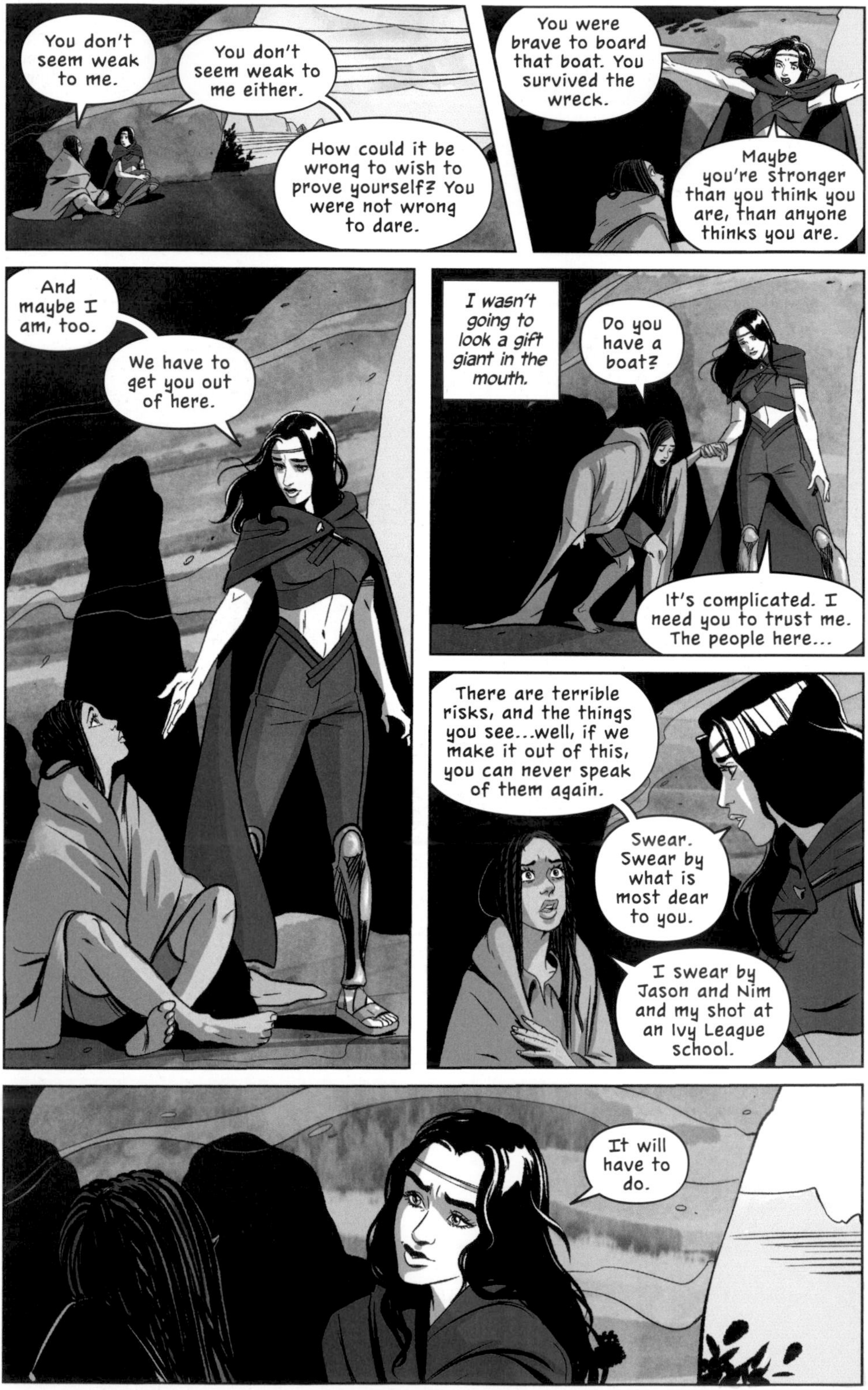
You don't seem weak to me.
You don't seem weak to me either.
How could it be wrong to wish to prove yourself? You were not wrong to dare.
You were brave to board that boat. You survived the wreck.
Maybe you're stronger than you think you are, than anyone thinks you are.
And maybe I am, too.
We have to get you out of here.
I wasn't going to look a gift giant in the mouth.
Do you have a boat?
It's complicated. I need you to trust me. The people here...
There are terrible risks, and the things you see...well, if we make it out of this, you can never speak of them again.
Swear. Swear by what is most dear to you.
I swear by Jason and Nim and my shot at an Ivy League school.
It will have to do.

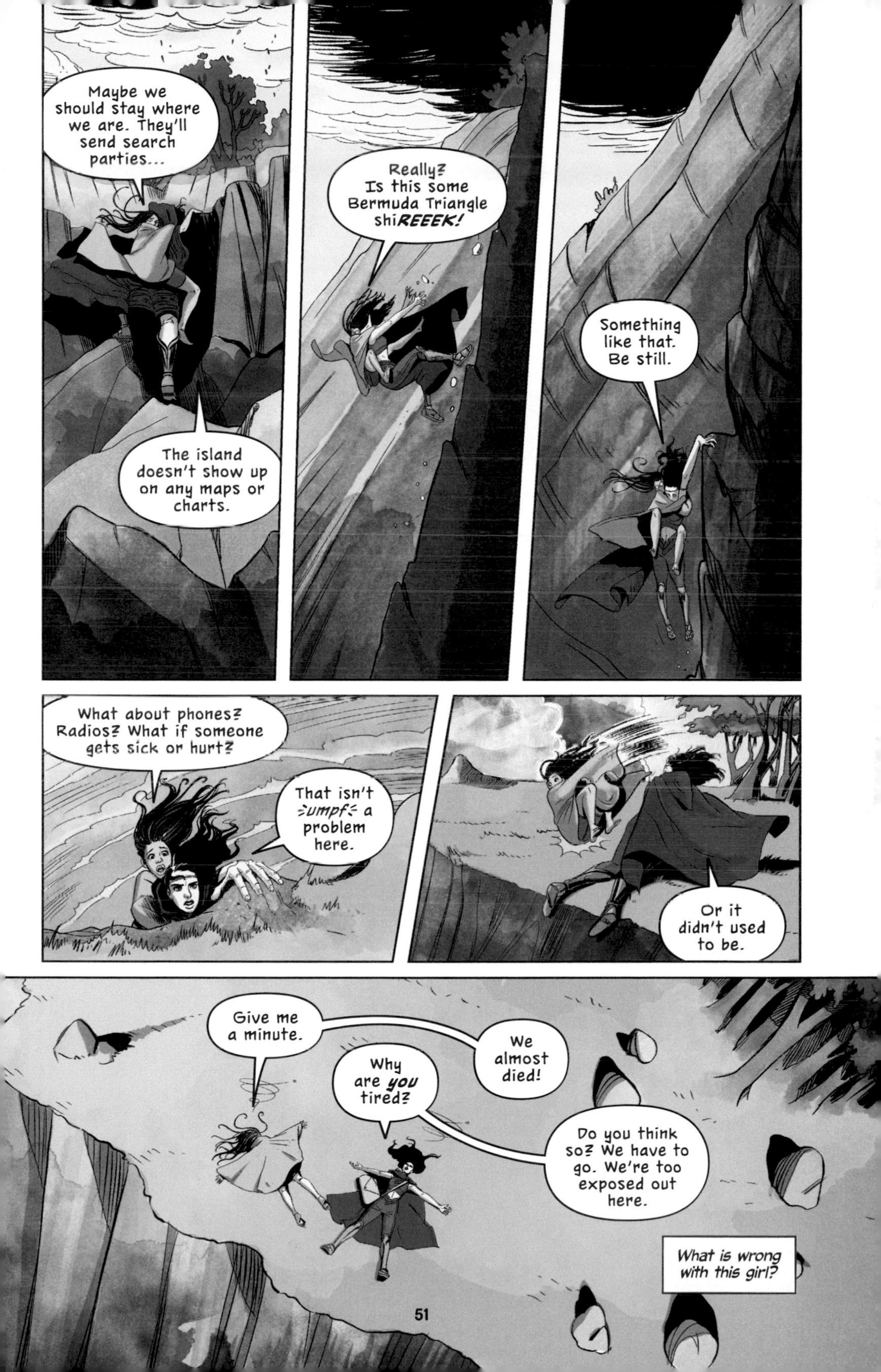
Maybe we should stay where we are. They'll send search parties...
The island doesn't show up on any maps or charts.
Really? Is this some Bermuda Triangle shiREEEK!
Something like that. Be still.
What about phones? Radios? What if someone gets sick or hurt?
That isn't =umpf= a problem here.
Or it didn't used to be.
Give me a minute.
We almost died!
Why are *you* tired?
Do you think so? We have to go. We're too exposed out here.
What is wrong with this girl?

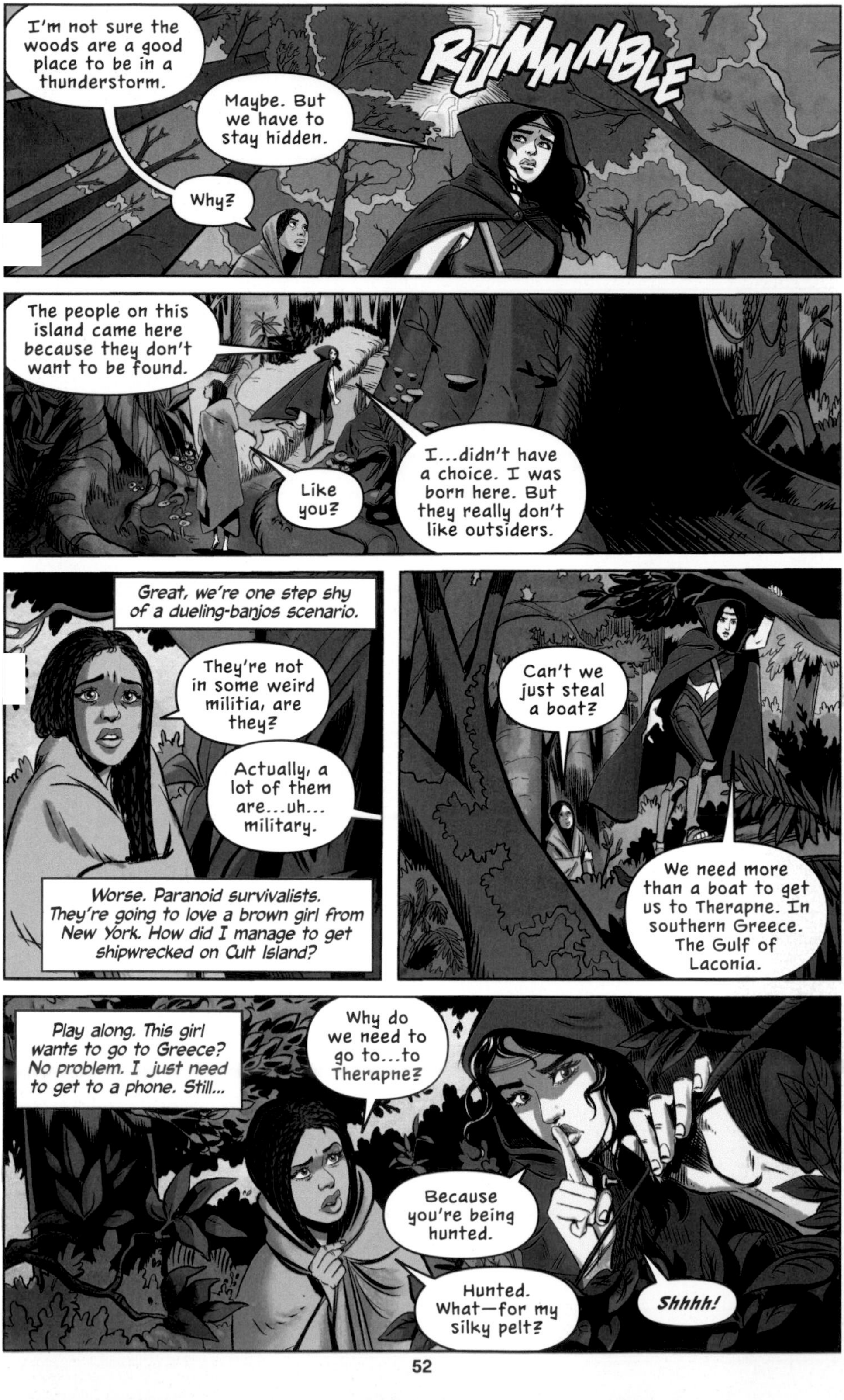
I'm not sure the woods are a good place to be in a thunderstorm.
RUMMMBLE
Maybe. But we have to stay hidden.
Why?
The people on this island came here because they don't want to be found.
Like you?
I...didn't have a choice. I was born here. But they really don't like outsiders.
Great, we're one step shy of a dueling-banjos scenario.
They're not in some weird militia, are they?
Actually, a lot of them are...uh... military.
Worse. Paranoid survivalists. They're going to love a brown girl from New York. How did I manage to get shipwrecked on Cult Island?
Can't we just steal a boat?
We need more than a boat to get us to Therapne. In southern Greece. The Gulf of Laconia.
Play along. This girl wants to go to Greece? No problem. I just need to get to a phone. Still...
Why do we need to go to...to Therapne?
Because you're being hunted.
Hunted. What—for my silky pelt?
Shhhh!

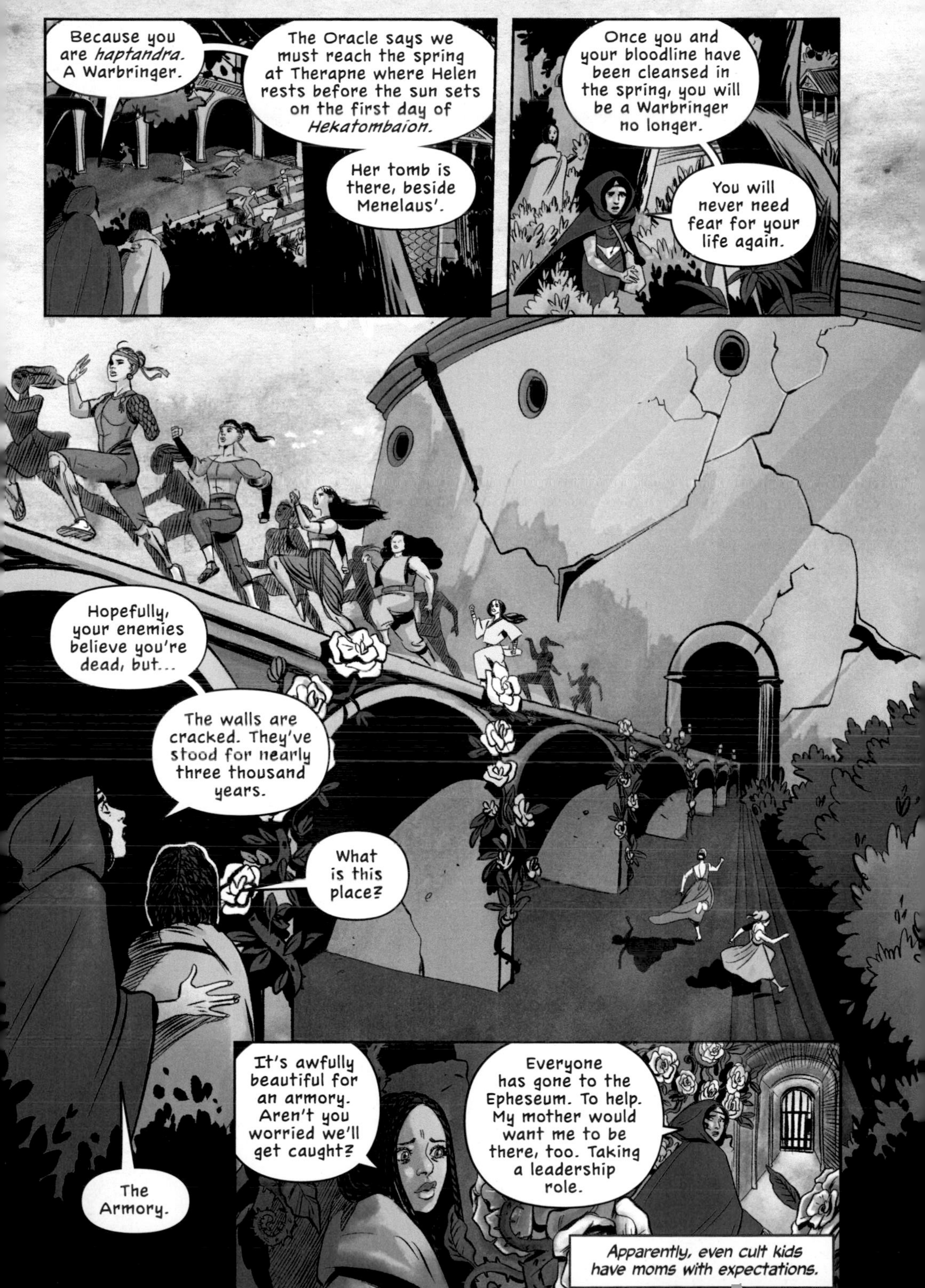
Because you are *haptandra.* A Warbringer.
The Oracle says we must reach the spring at Therapne where Helen rests before the sun sets on the first day of *Hekatombaion.*
Her tomb is there, beside Menelaus'.
Once you and your bloodline have been cleansed in the spring, you will be a Warbringer no longer.
You will never need fear for your life again.
Hopefully, your enemies believe you're dead, but...
The walls are cracked. They've stood for nearly three thousand years.
What is this place?
The Armory.
It's awfully beautiful for an armory. Aren't you worried we'll get caught?
Everyone has gone to the Epheseum. To help. My mother would want me to be there, too. Taking a leadership role.
Apparently, even cult kids have moms with expectations.

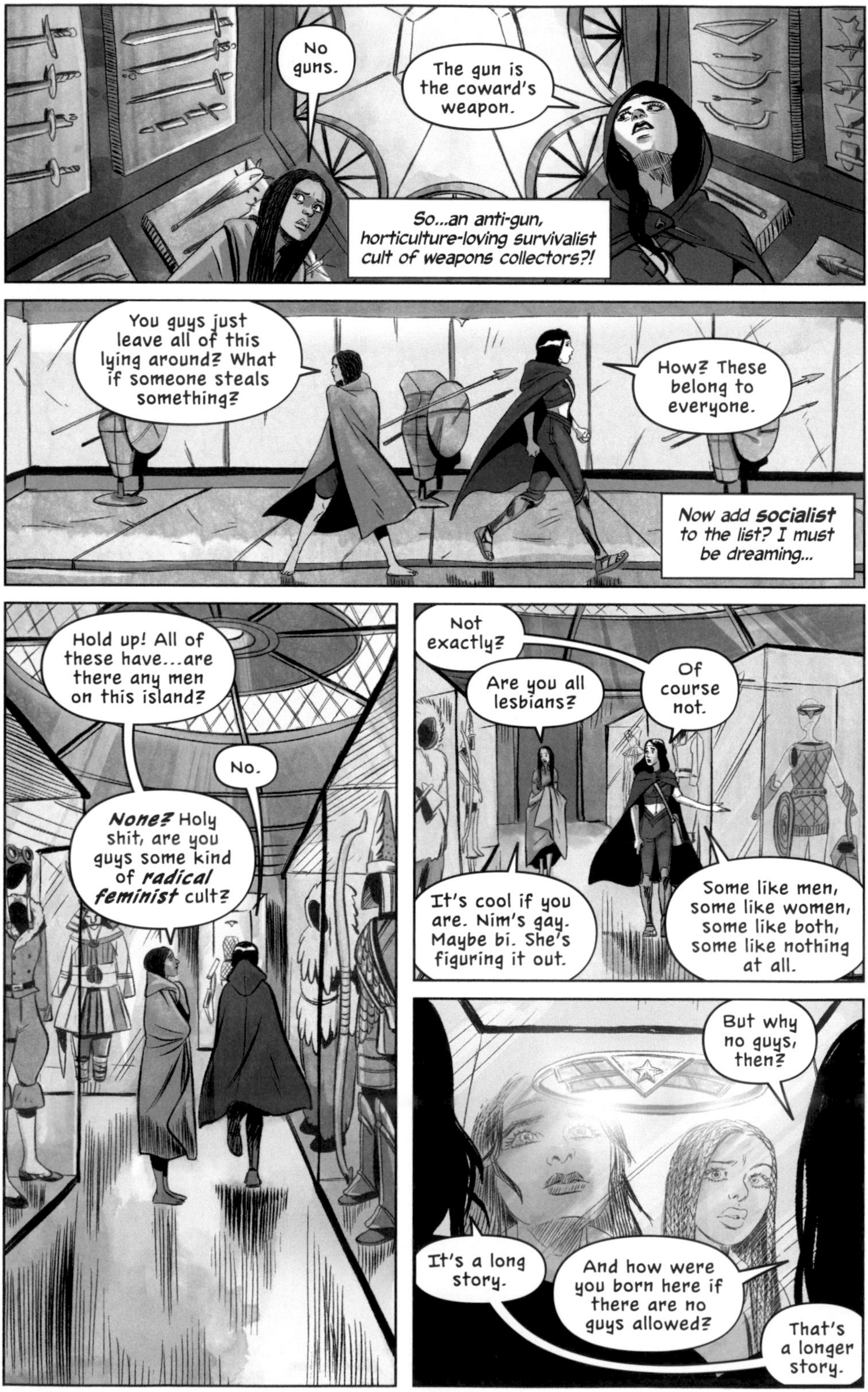
No guns.
The gun is the coward's weapon.
So...an anti-gun, horticulture-loving survivalist cult of weapons collectors?!
You guys just leave all of this lying around? What if someone steals something?
How? These belong to everyone.
Now add **socialist** to the list? I must be dreaming...
Hold up! All of these have...are there any men on this island?
No.
None? Holy shit, are you guys some kind of ***radical feminist*** cult?
Not exactly?
Are you all lesbians?
Of course not.
It's cool if you are. Nim's gay. Maybe bi. She's figuring it out.
Some like men, some like women, some like both, some like nothing at all.
But why no guys, then?
It's a long story.
And how were you born here if there are no guys allowed?
That's a longer story.

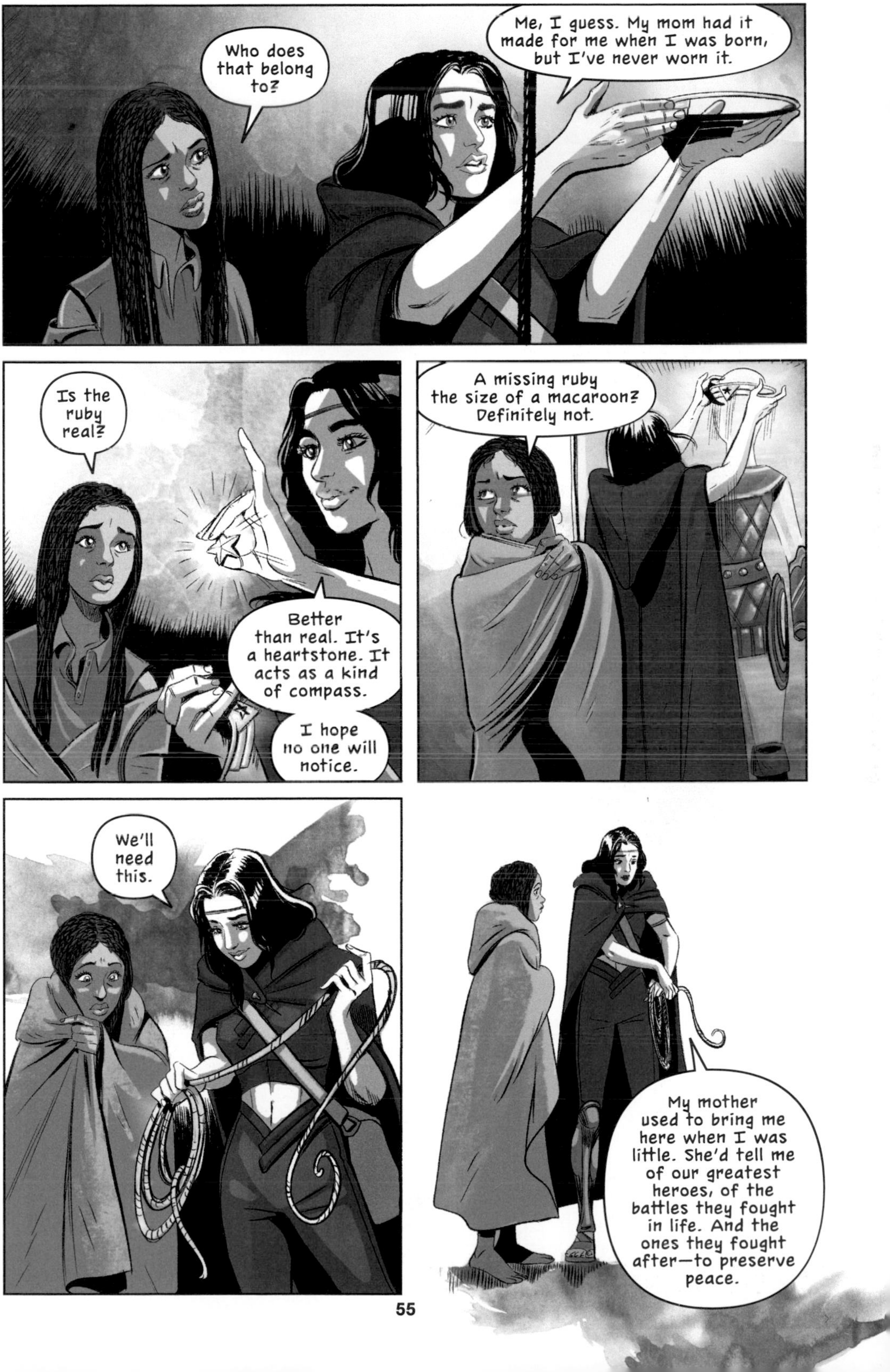
Who does that belong to?
Me, I guess. My mom had it made for me when I was born, but I've never worn it.
Is the ruby real?
Better than real. It's a heartstone. It acts as a kind of compass.
I hope no one will notice.
A missing ruby the size of a macaroon? Definitely not.
We'll need this.
My mother used to bring me here when I was little. She'd tell me of our greatest heroes, of the battles they fought in life. And the ones they fought after—to preserve peace.

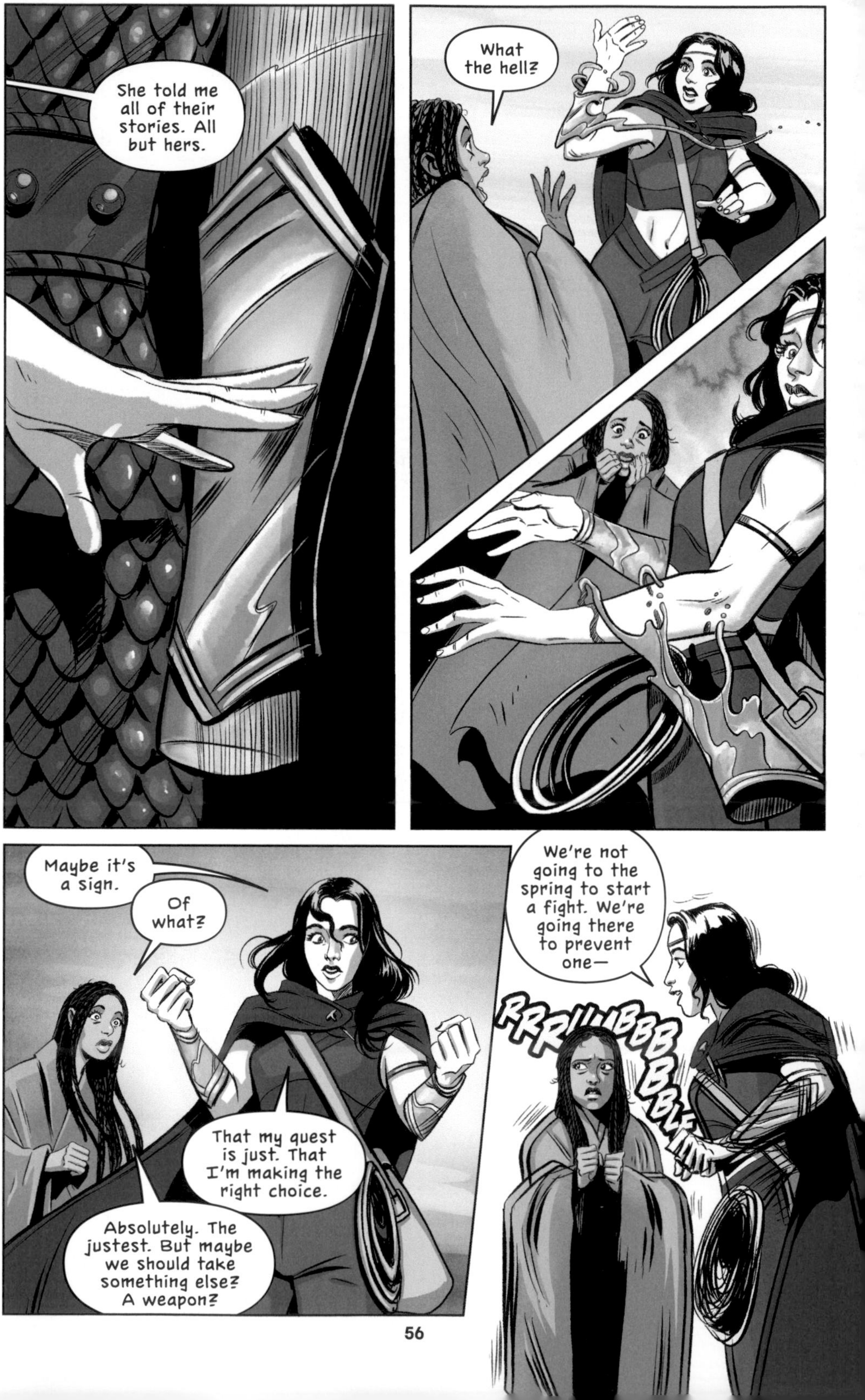
She told me all of their stories. All but hers.
What the hell?
Maybe it's a sign.
Of what?
That my quest is just. That I'm making the right choice.
Absolutely. The justest. But maybe we should take something else? A weapon?
We're not going to the spring to start a fight. We're going there to prevent one—
RRRUUBBBBBLE

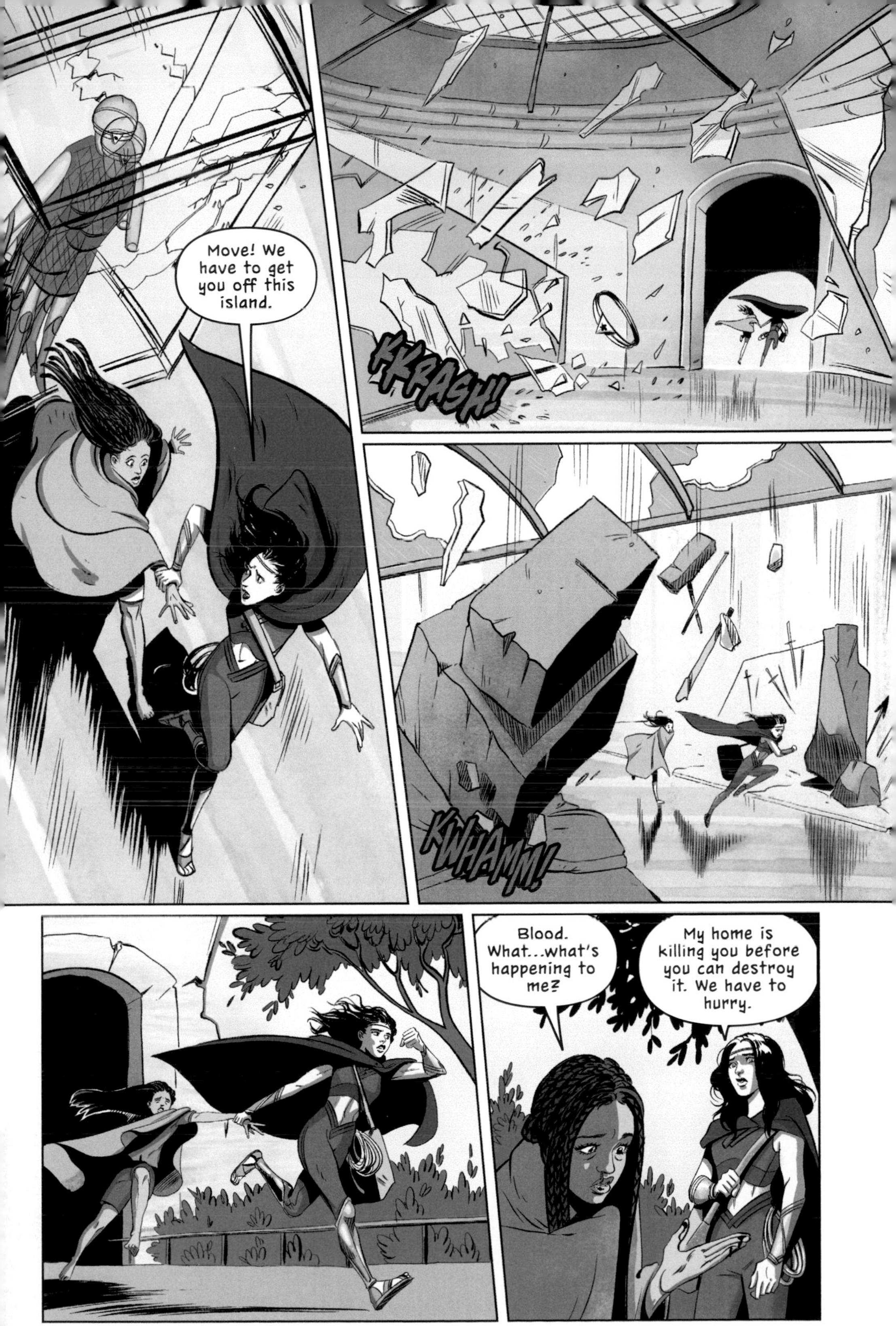
Move! We have to get you off this island.
KKRASH!
KWHAMM!
Blood. What...what's happening to me?
My home is killing you before you can destroy it. We have to hurry.

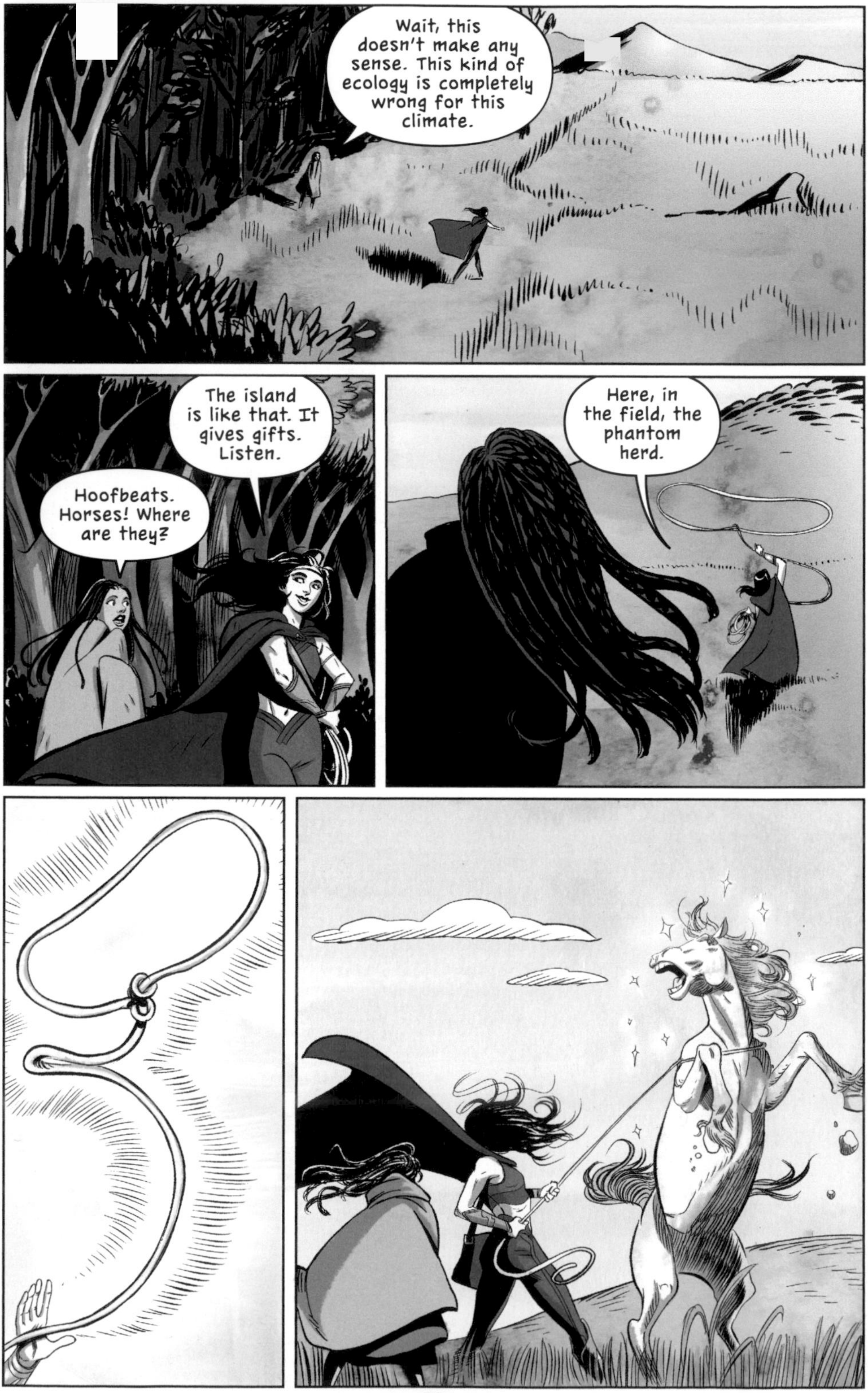
Wait, this doesn't make any sense. This kind of ecology is completely wrong for this climate.
The island is like that. It gives gifts. Listen.
Hoofbeats. Horses! Where are they?
Here, in the field, the phantom herd.

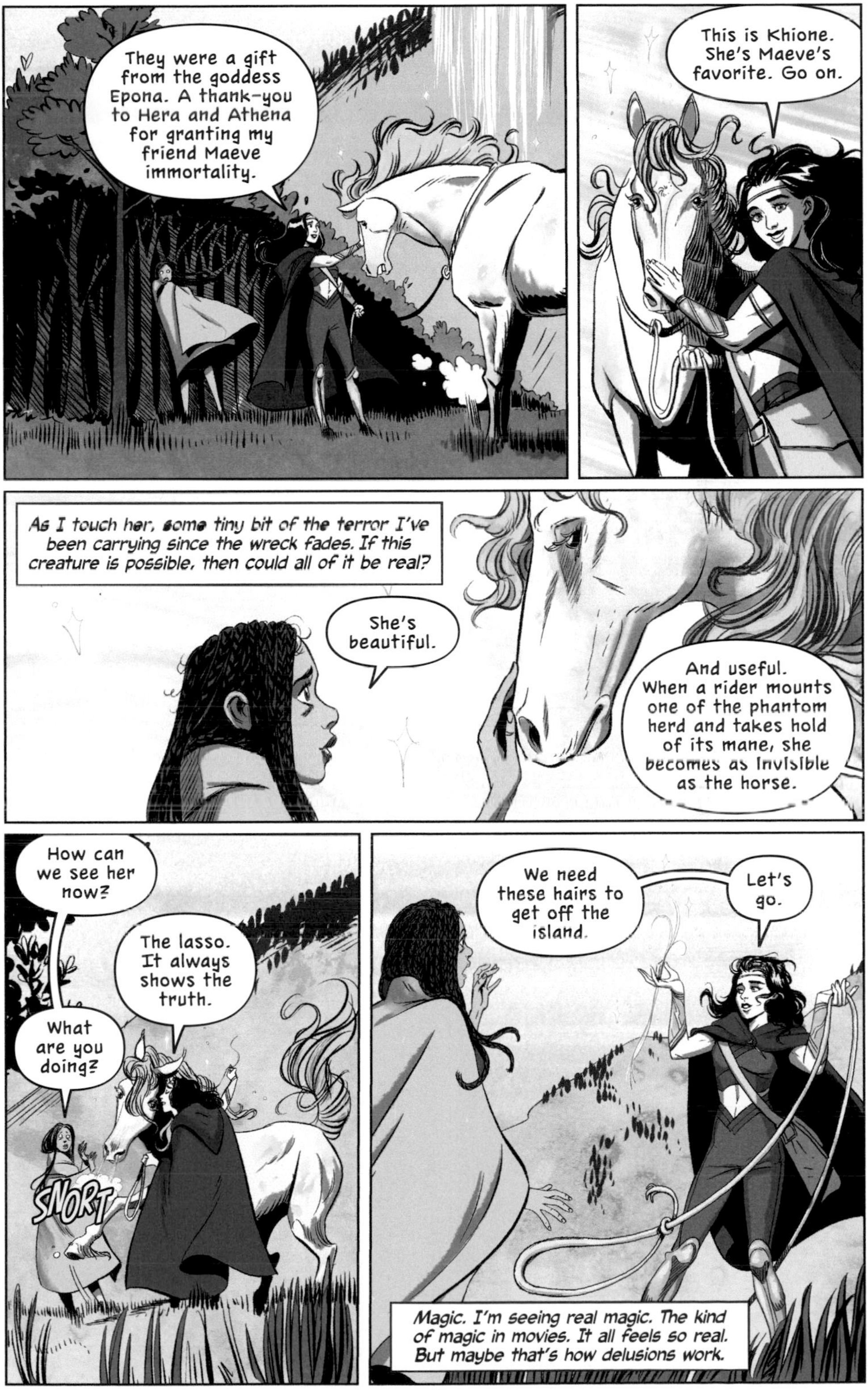
They were a gift from the goddess Epona. A thank-you to Hera and Athena for granting my friend Maeve immortality.
This is Khione. She's Maeve's favorite. Go on.
As I touch her, some tiny bit of the terror I've been carrying since the wreck fades. If this creature is possible, then could all of it be real?
She's beautiful.
And useful. When a rider mounts one of the phantom herd and takes hold of its mane, she becomes as invisible as the horse.
How can we see her now?
The lasso. It always shows the truth.
What are you doing?
SNORT
We need these hairs to get off the island.
Let's go.
Magic. I'm seeing real magic. The kind of magic in movies. It all feels so real. But maybe that's how delusions work.

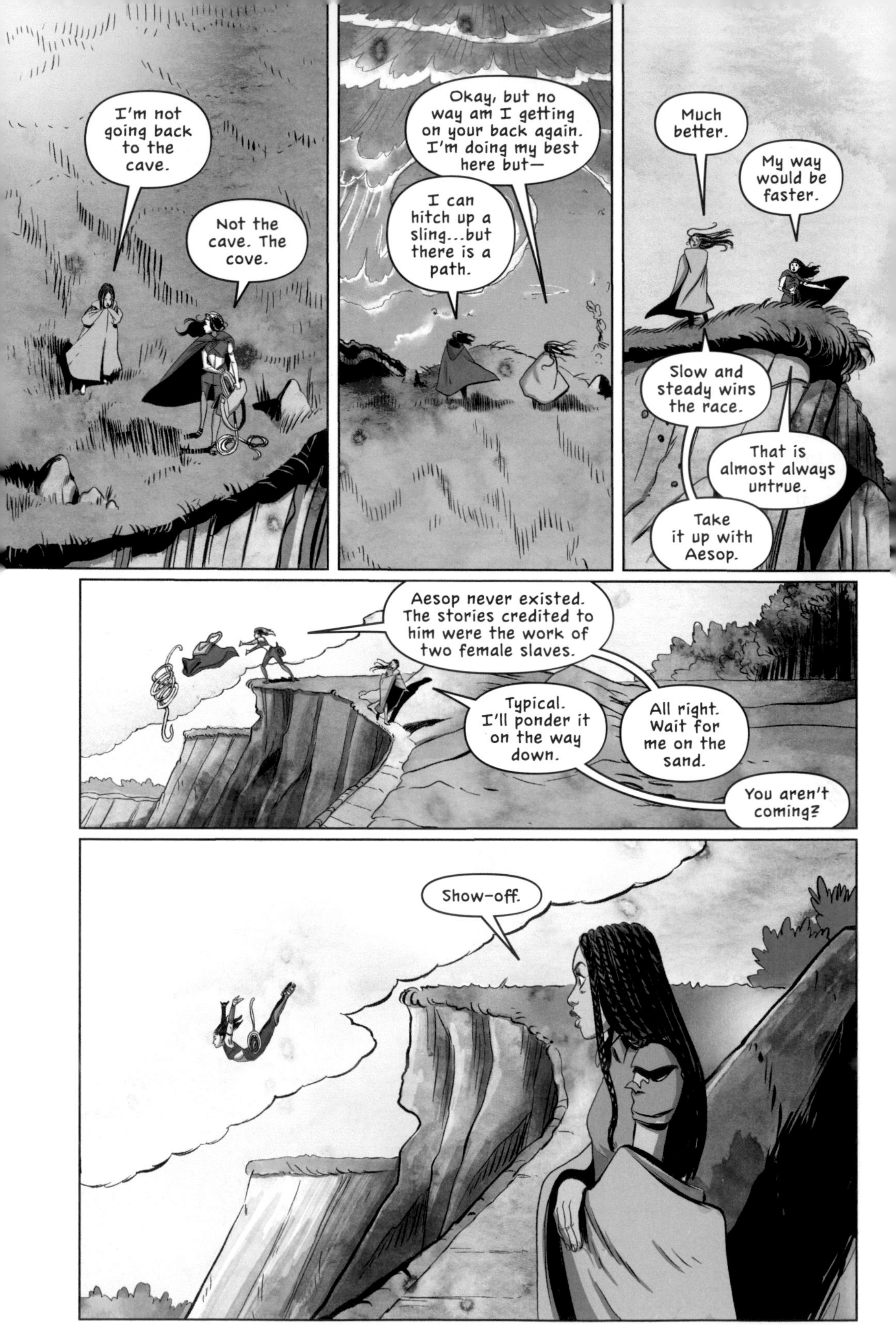
I'm not going back to the cave.
Not the cave. The cove.
Okay, but no way am I getting on your back again. I'm doing my best here but—
I can hitch up a sling...but there is a path.
Much better.
My way would be faster.
Slow and steady wins the race.
That is almost always untrue.
Take it up with Aesop.
Aesop never existed. The stories credited to him were the work of two female slaves.
Typical. I'll ponder it on the way down.
All right. Wait for me on the sand.
You aren't coming?
Show-off.

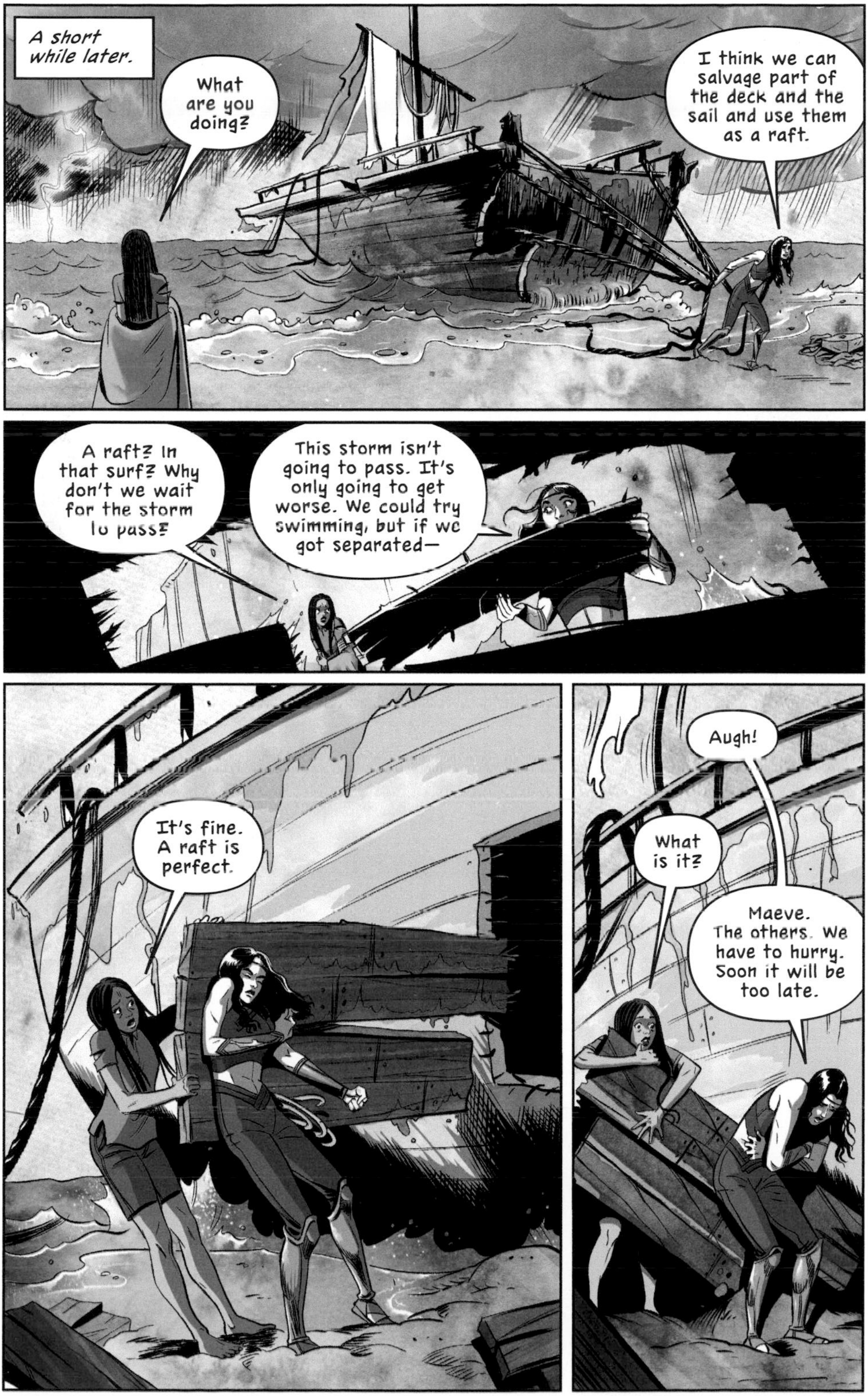
A short while later.
What are you doing?
I think we can salvage part of the deck and the sail and use them as a raft.
A raft? In that surf? Why don't we wait for the storm to pass?
This storm isn't going to pass. It's only going to get worse. We could try swimming, but if we got separated—
It's fine. A raft is perfect.
Augh!
What is it?
Maeve. The others. We have to hurry. Soon it will be too late.

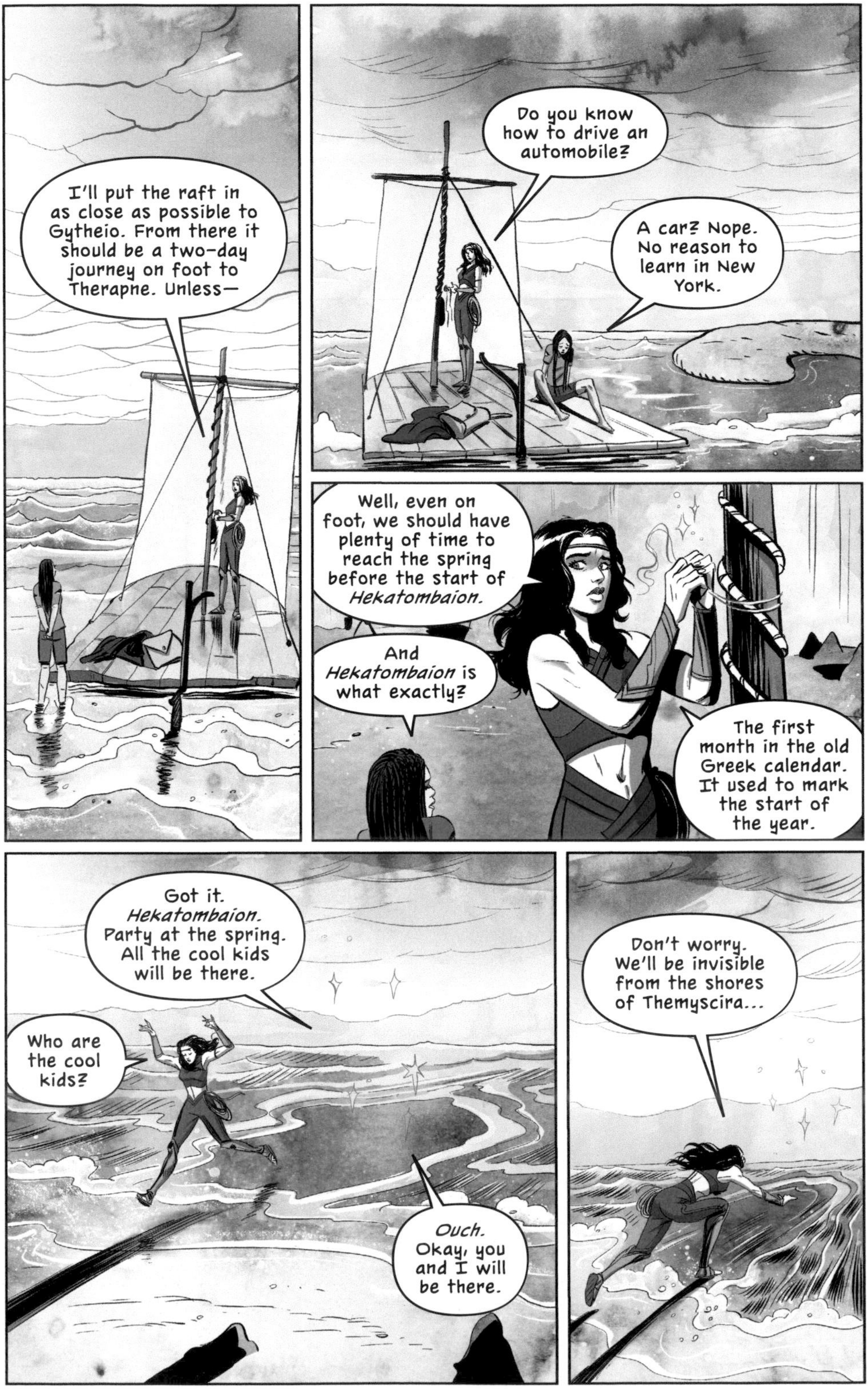
I'll put the raft in as close as possible to Gytheio. From there it should be a two-day journey on foot to Therapne. Unless—
Do you know how to drive an automobile?
A car? Nope. No reason to learn in New York.
Well, even on foot, we should have plenty of time to reach the spring before the start of *Hekatombaion.*
And *Hekatombaion* is what exactly?
The first month in the old Greek calendar. It used to mark the start of the year.
Got it. *Hekatombaion.* Party at the spring. All the cool kids will be there.
Who are the cool kids?
Ouch. Okay, you and I will be there.
Don't worry. We'll be invisible from the shores of Themyscira...

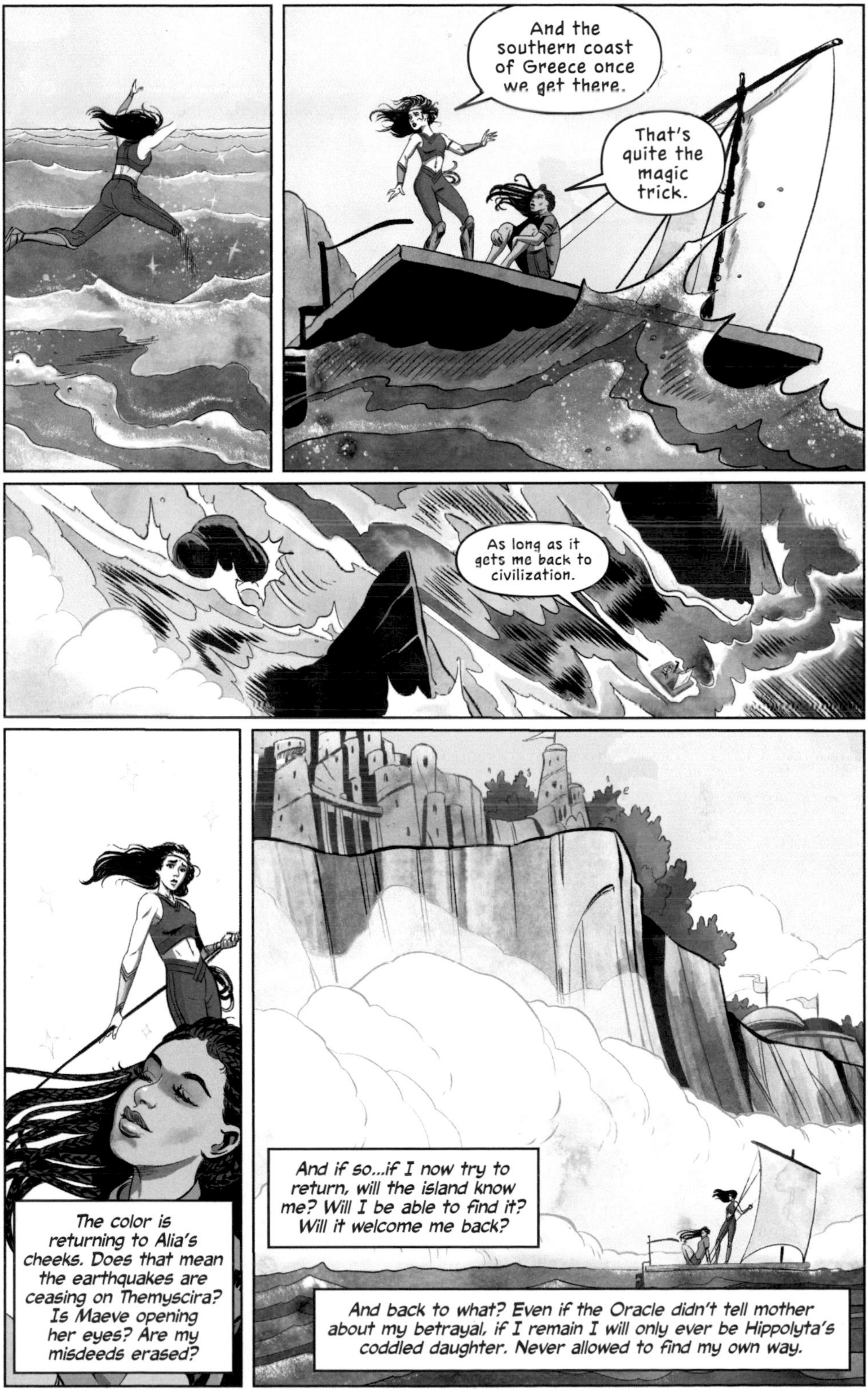
And the southern coast of Greece once we get there.
That's quite the magic trick.
As long as it gets me back to civilization.
The color is returning to Alia's cheeks. Does that mean the earthquakes are ceasing on Themyscira? Is Maeve opening her eyes? Are my misdeeds erased?
And if so...if I now try to return, will the island know me? Will I be able to find it? Will it welcome me back?
And back to what? Even if the Oracle didn't tell mother about my betrayal, if I remain I will only ever be Hippolyta's coddled daughter. Never allowed to find my own way.

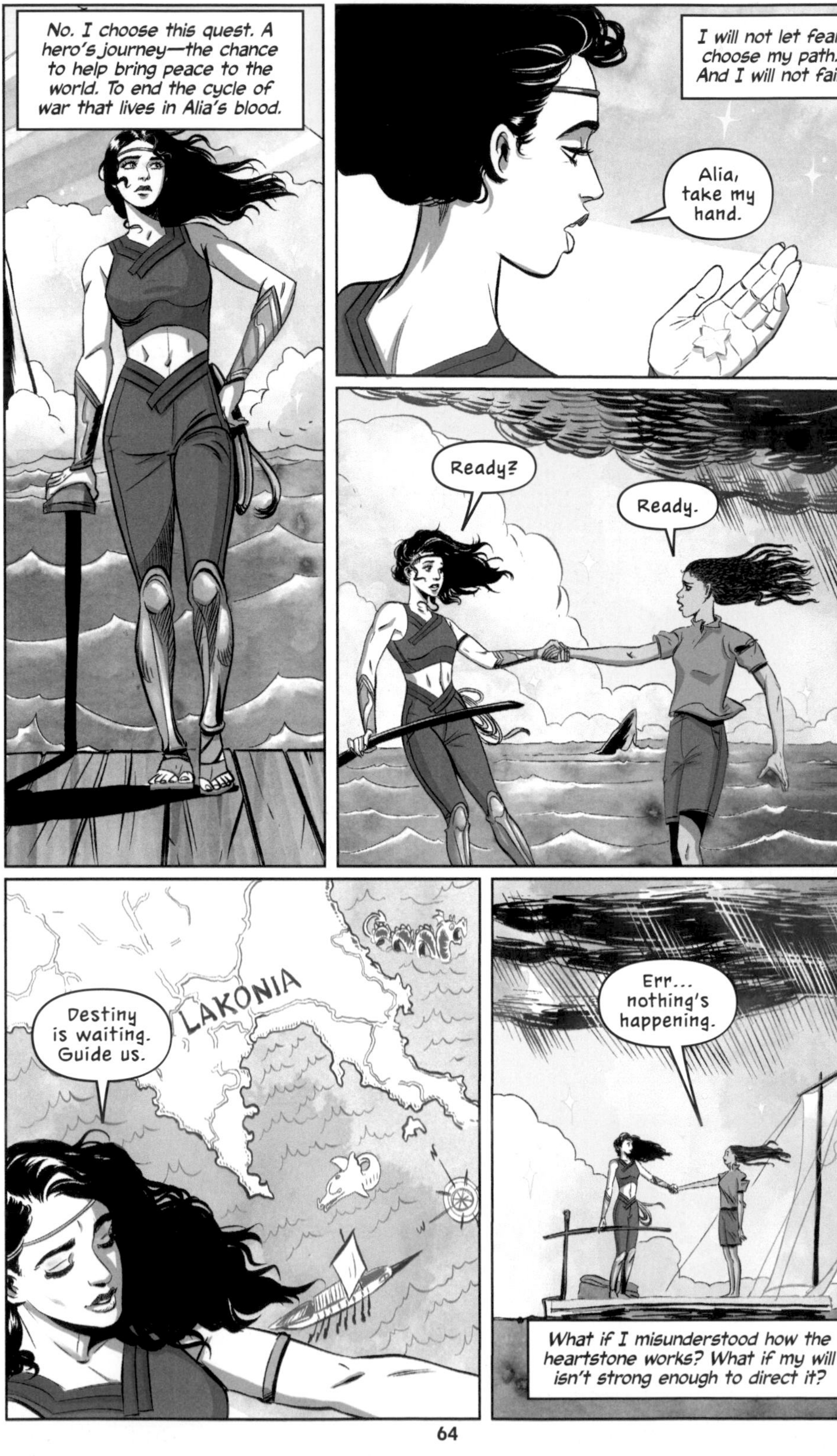
No. I choose this quest. A hero's journey—the chance to help bring peace to the world. To end the cycle of war that lives in Alia's blood.
I will not let fear choose my path. And I will not fail.
Alia, take my hand.
Ready?
Ready.
LAKONIA
Destiny is waiting. Guide us.
Err... nothing's happening.
What if I misunderstood how the heartstone works? What if my will isn't strong enough to direct it?

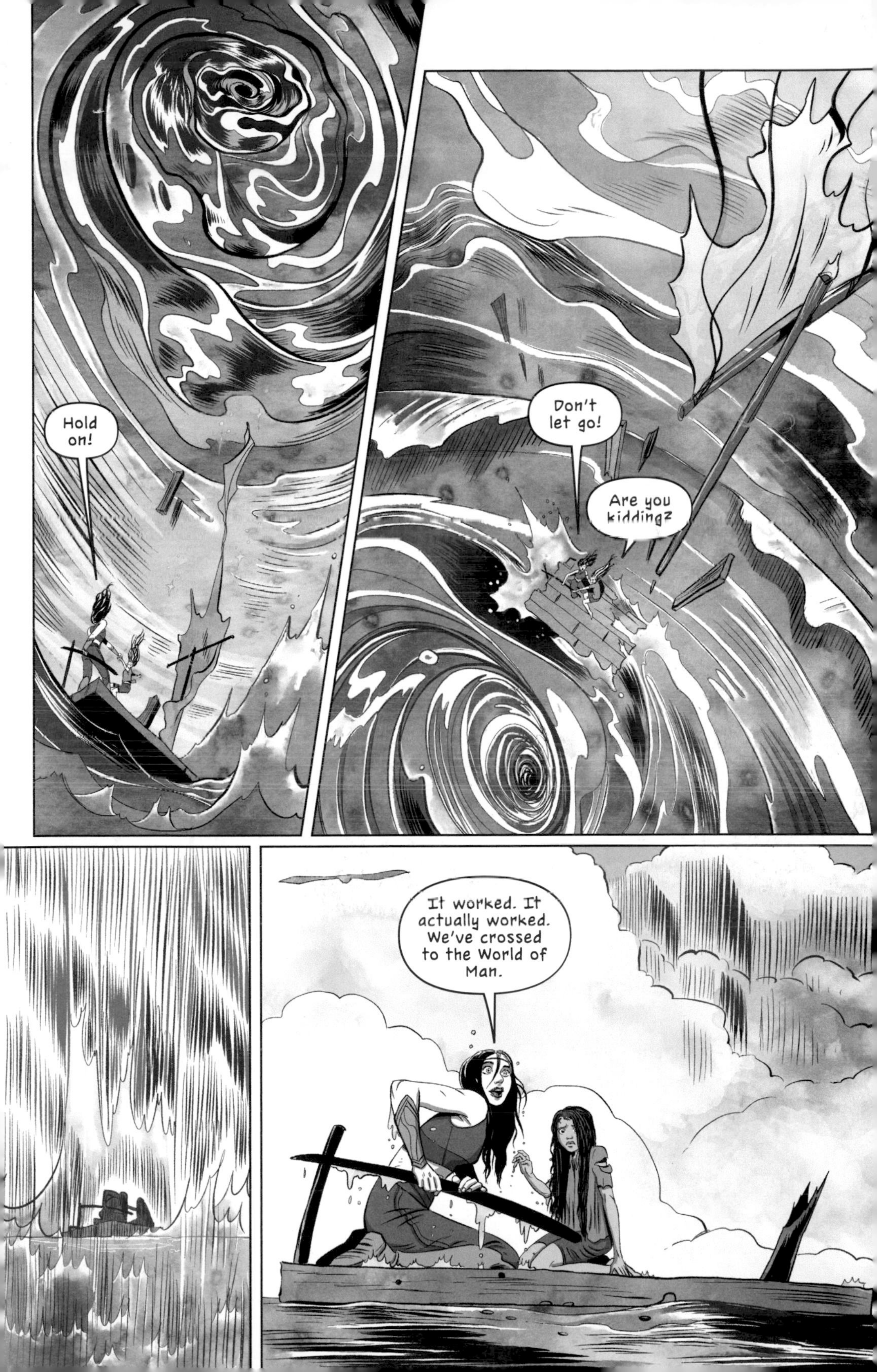
Hold on!
Don't let go!
Are you kidding?
It worked. It actually worked. We've crossed to the World of Man.

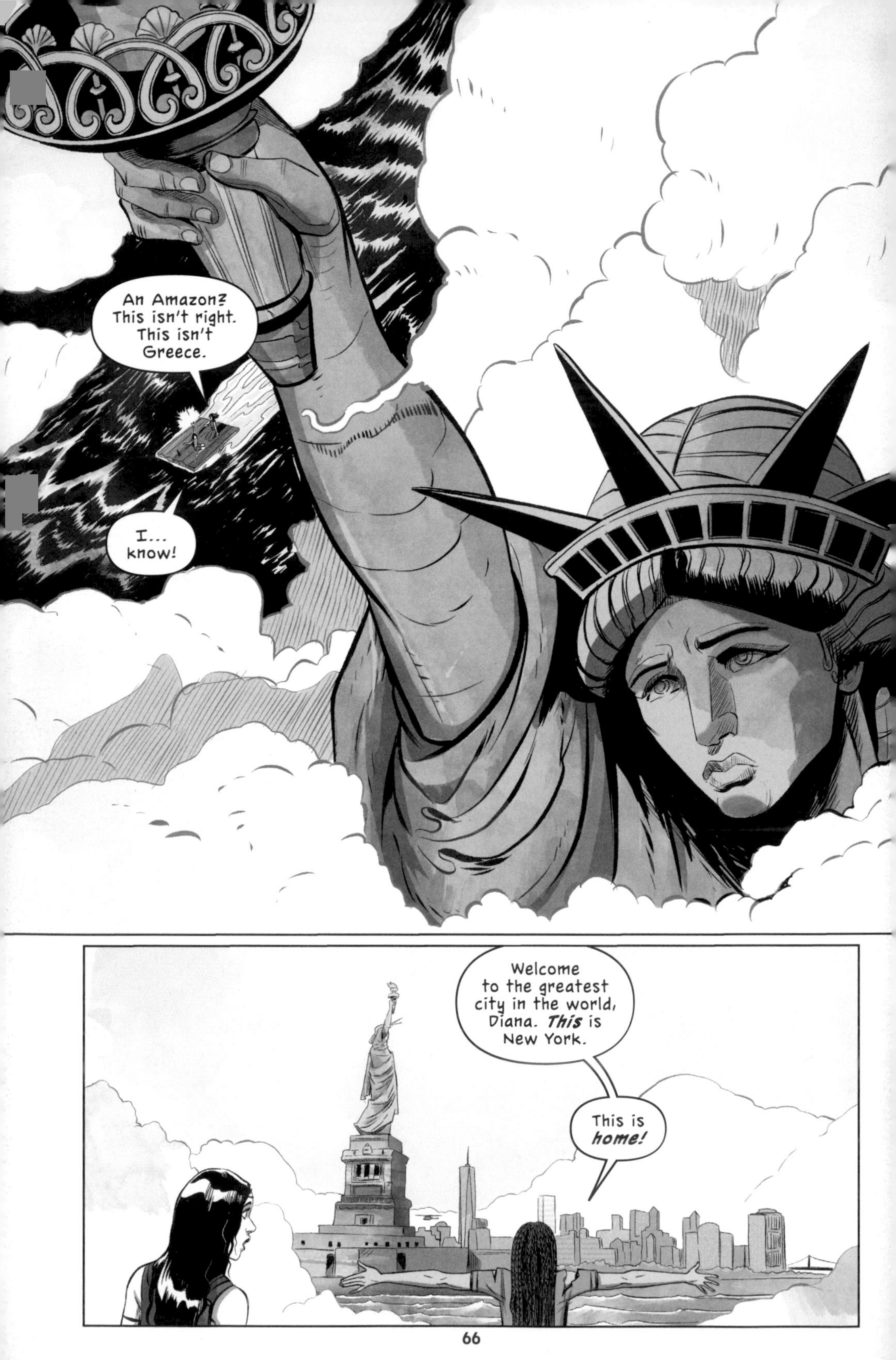
An Amazon? This isn't right. This isn't Greece.
I... know!
Welcome to the greatest city in the world, Diana. *This* is New York.
This is *home!*

PART THREE

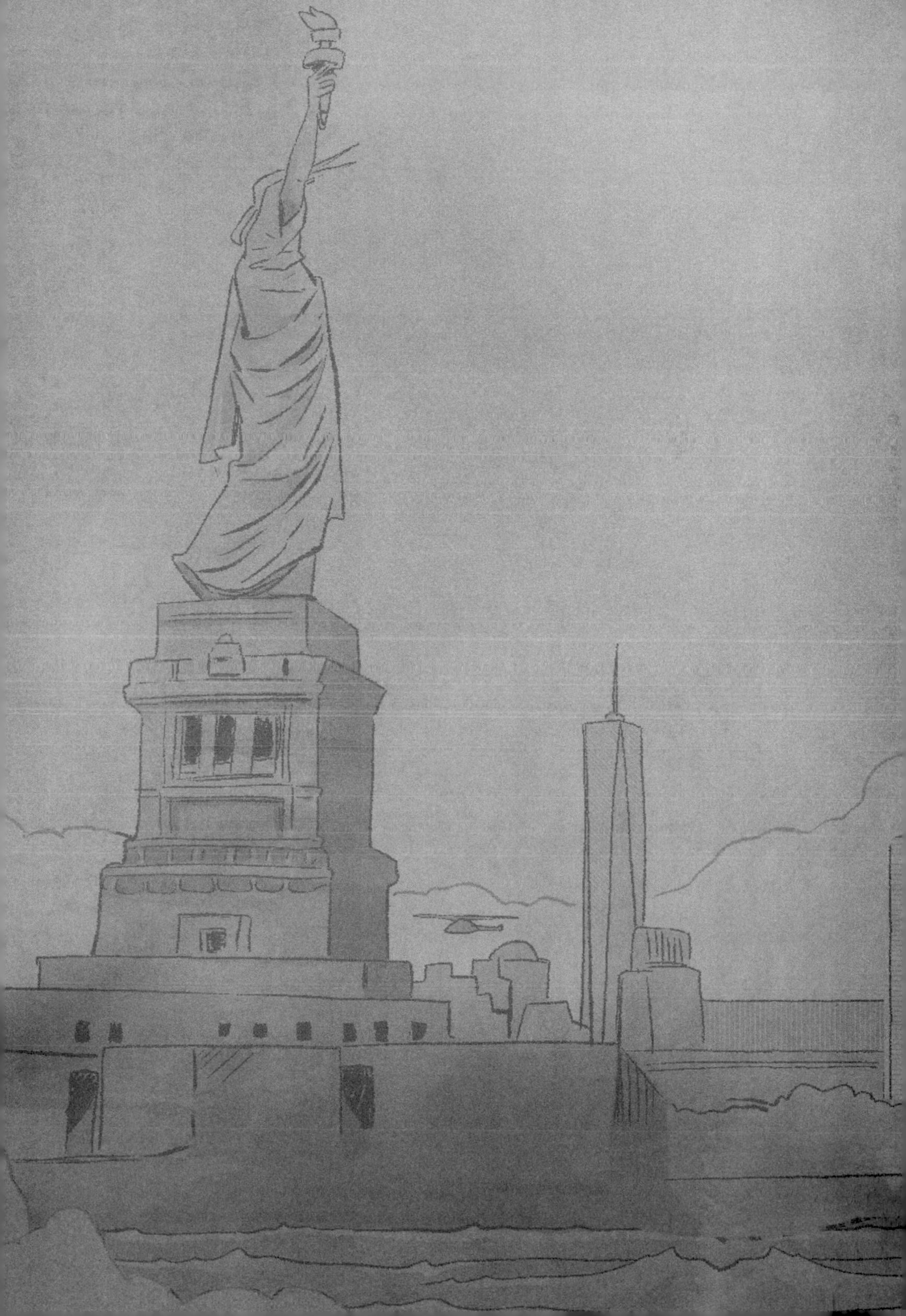

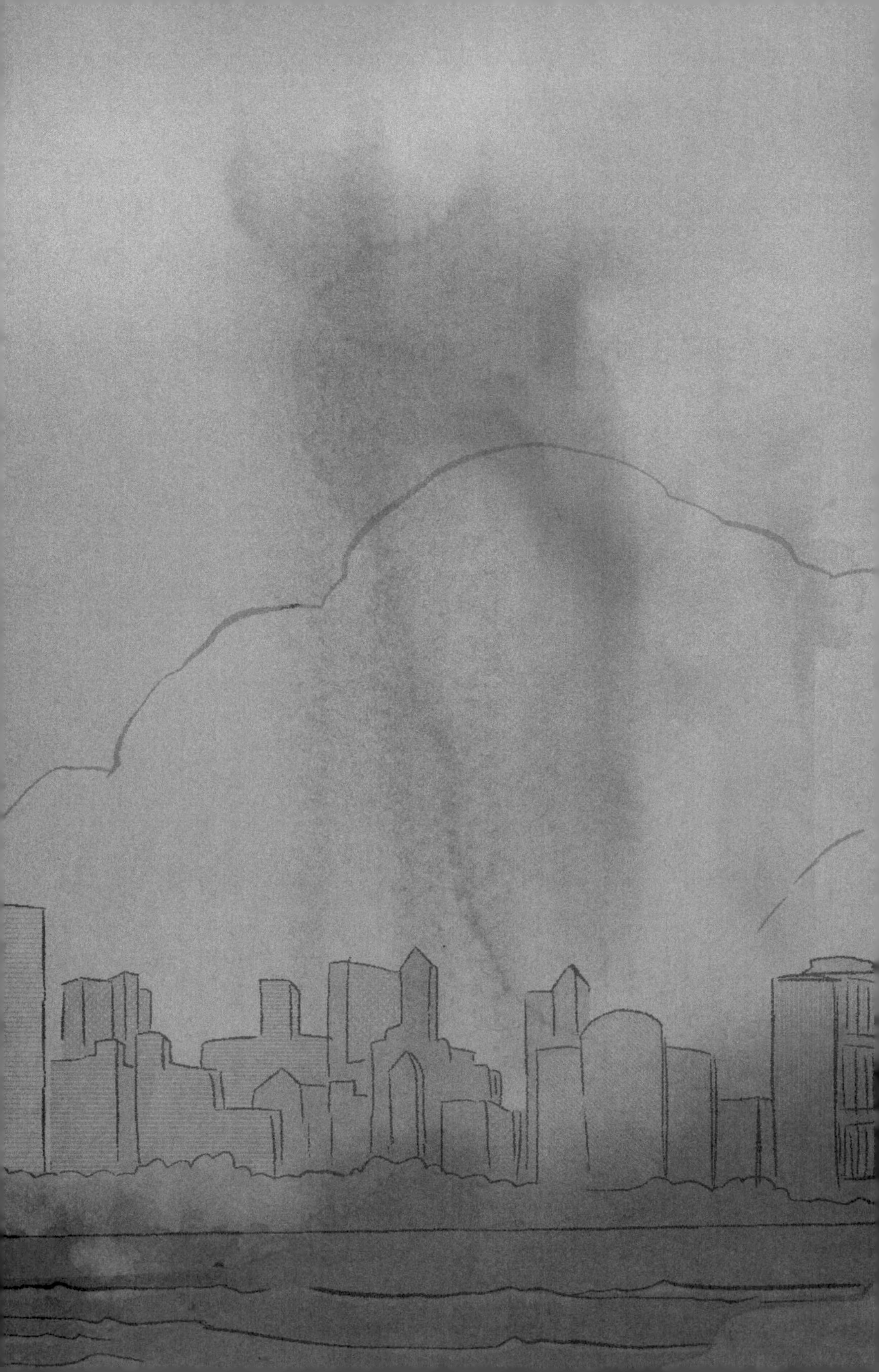

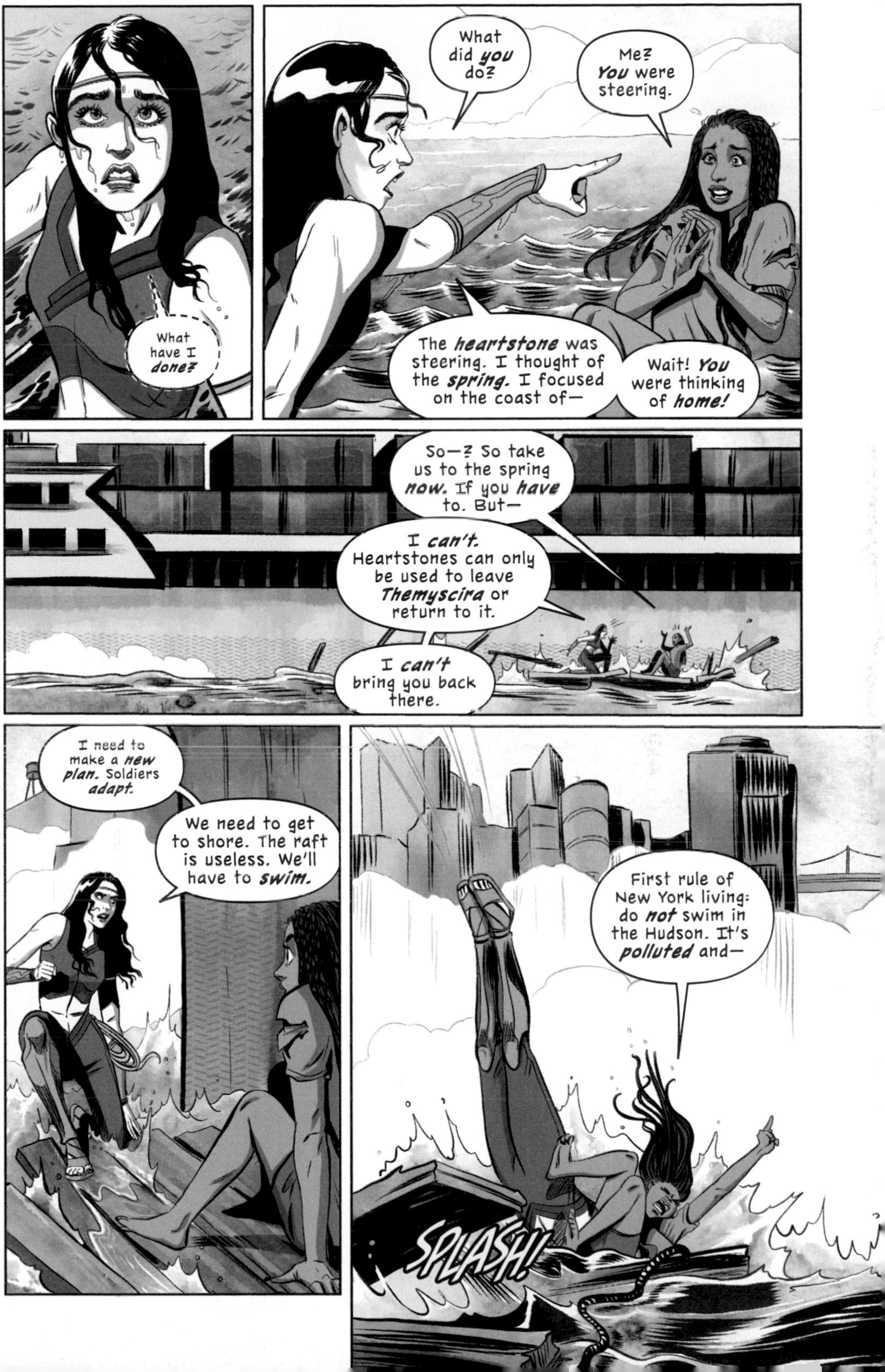
What have I done?
What did you do?
Me? You were steering.
The heartstone was steering. I thought of the spring. I focused on the coast of—
Wait! You were thinking of home!
So—? So take us to the spring now. If you have to. But—
I can't. Heartstones can only be used to leave Themyscira or return to it.
I can't bring you back there.
I need to make a new plan. Soldiers adapt.
We need to get to shore. The raft is useless. We'll have to swim.
First rule of New York living: do not swim in the Hudson. It's polluted and—
SPLASH!

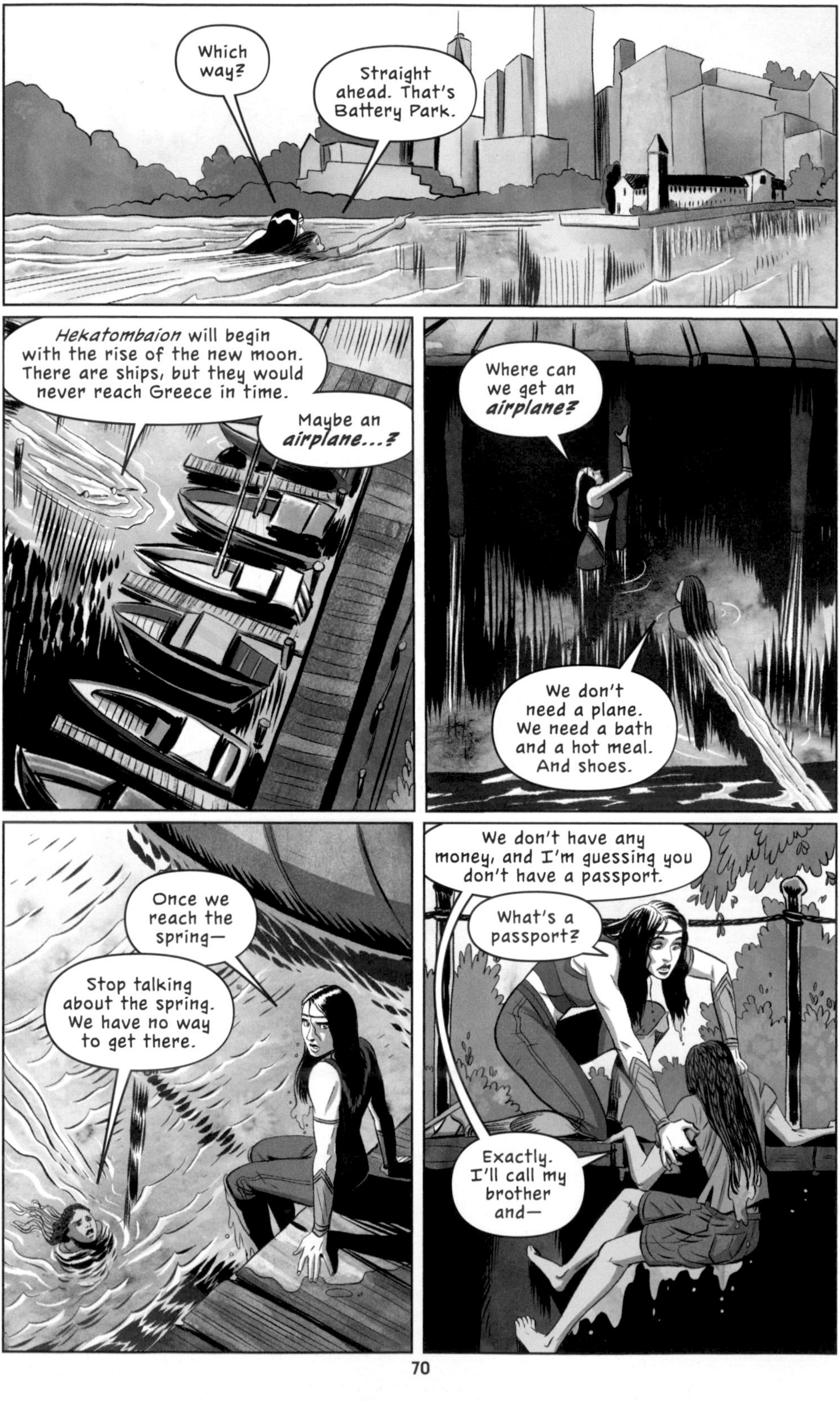

Which way?
Straight ahead. That's Battery Park.
Hekatombaion will begin with the rise of the new moon. There are ships, but they would never reach Greece in time.
Maybe an airplane...?
Where can we get an airplane?
We don't need a plane. We need a bath and a hot meal. And shoes.
Once we reach the spring—
Stop talking about the spring. We have no way to get there.
We don't have any money, and I'm guessing you don't have a passport.
What's a passport?
Exactly. I'll call my brother and—

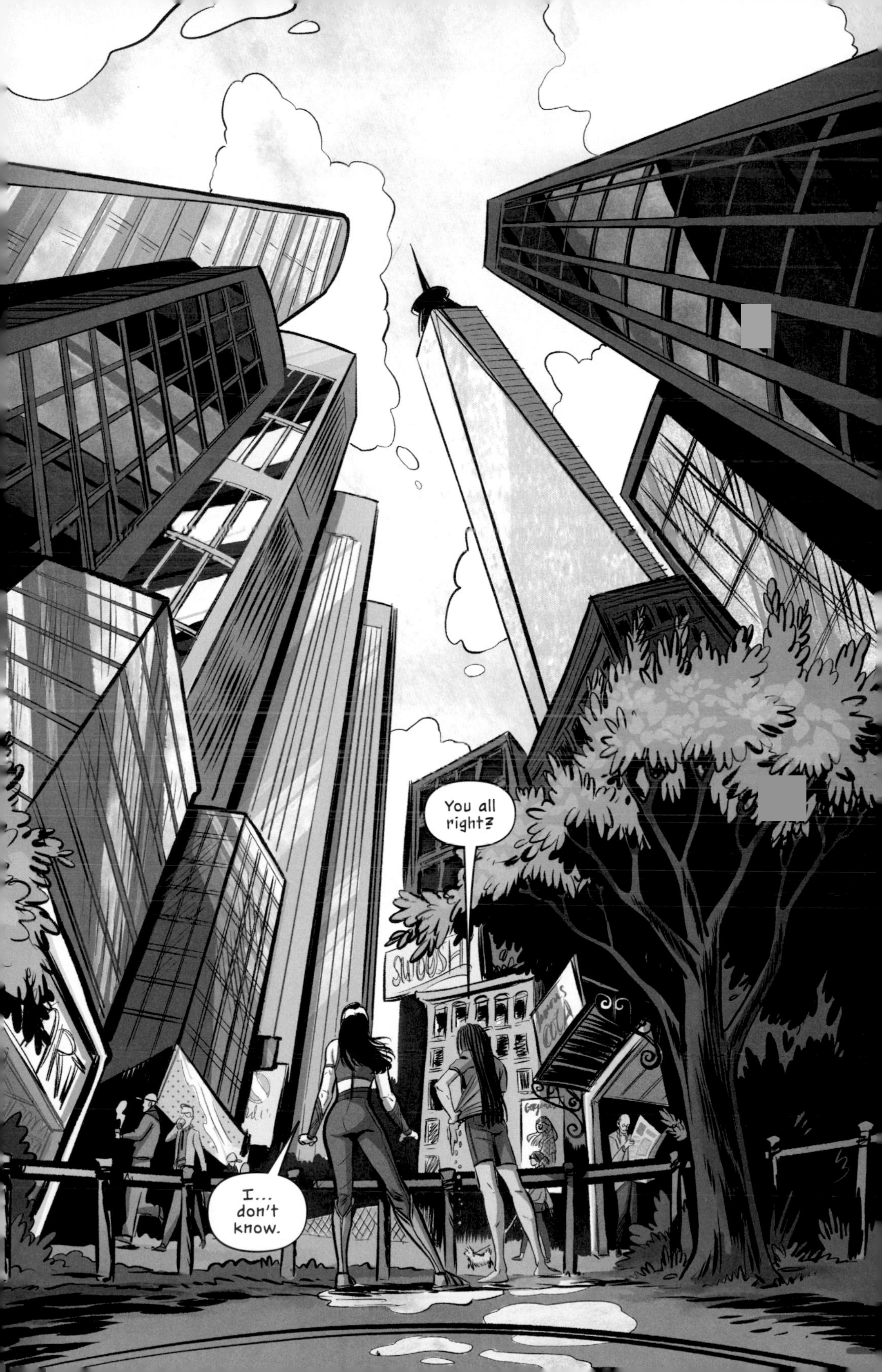
You all right?
I... don't know.

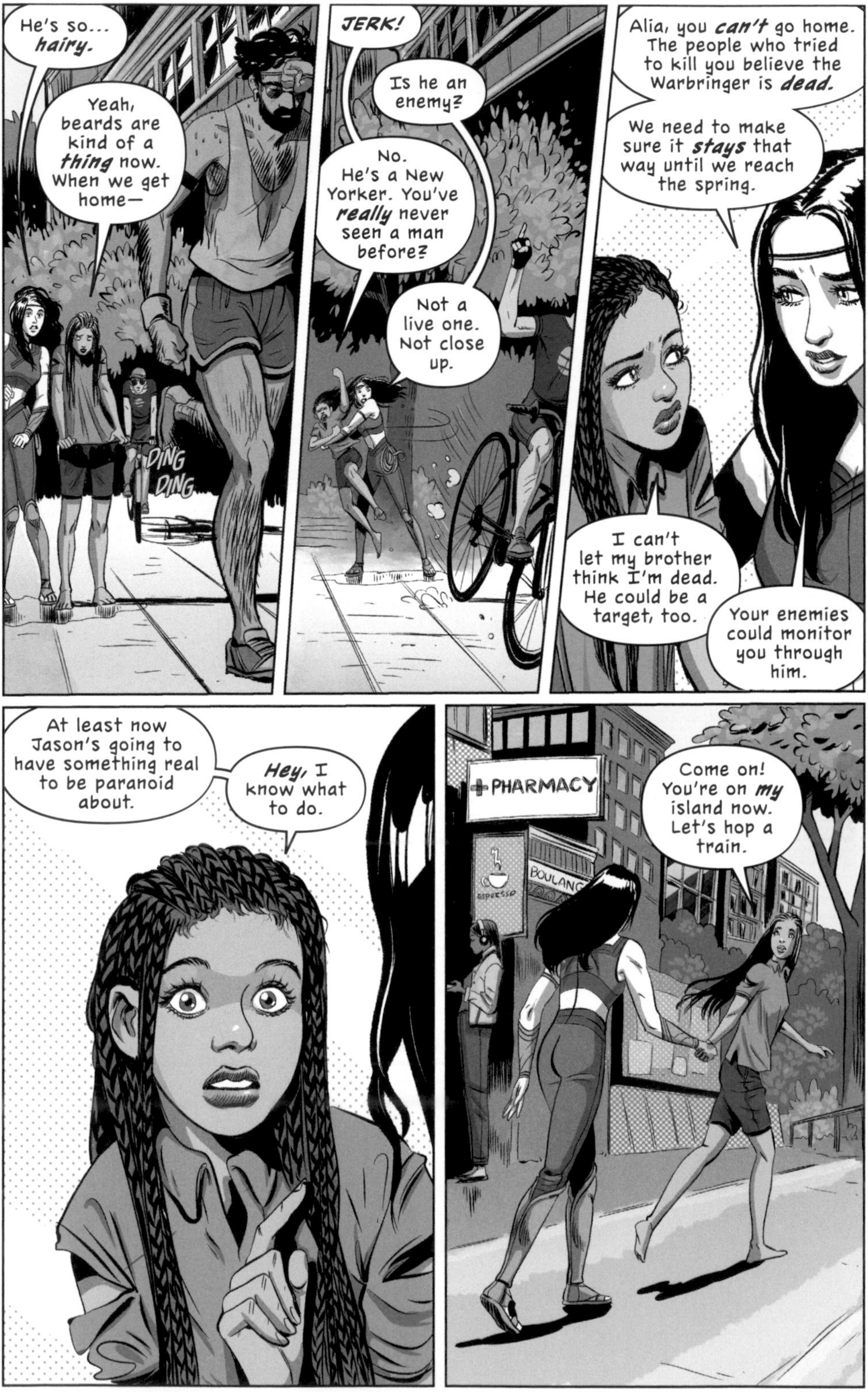
He's so... hairy.
Yeah, beards are kind of a thing now. When we get home—
DING DING
JERK!
Is he an enemy?
No. He's a New Yorker. You've really never seen a man before?
Not a live one. Not close up.
Alia, you can't go home. The people who tried to kill you believe the Warbringer is dead.
We need to make sure it stays that way until we reach the spring.
I can't let my brother think I'm dead. He could be a target, too.
Your enemies could monitor you through him.
At least now Jason's going to have something real to be paranoid about.
Hey, I know what to do.
PHARMACY
espresso
BOULANG
Come on! You're on my island now. Let's hop a train.

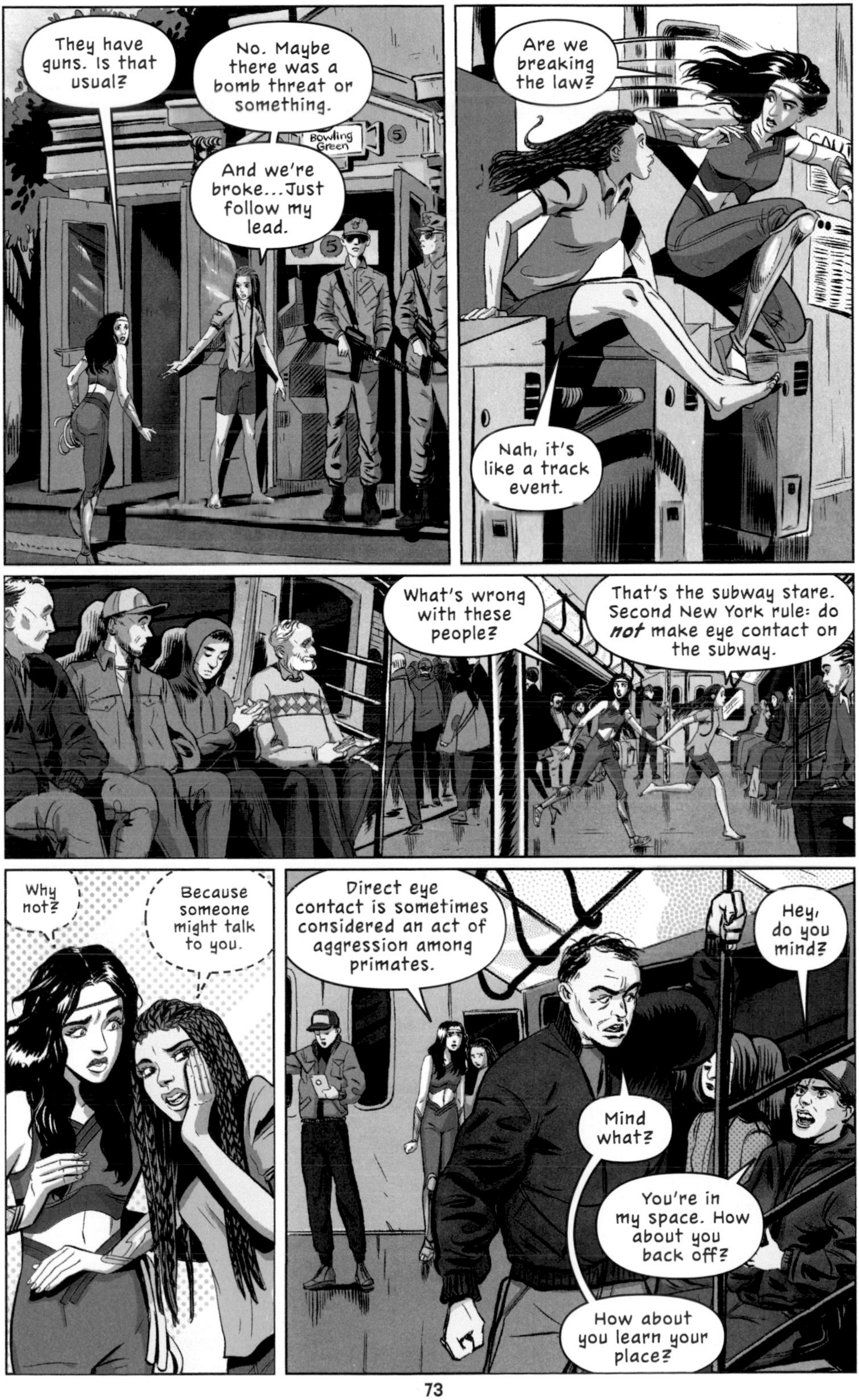
They have guns. Is that usual?
No. Maybe there was a bomb threat or something.
Bowling Green
And we're broke... Just follow my lead.
Are we breaking the law?
Nah, it's like a track event.
What's wrong with these people?
That's the subway stare. Second New York rule: do *not* make eye contact on the subway.
Why not?
Because someone might talk to you.
Direct eye contact is sometimes considered an act of aggression among primates.
Hey, do you mind?
Mind what?
You're in my space. How about you back off?
How about you learn your place?

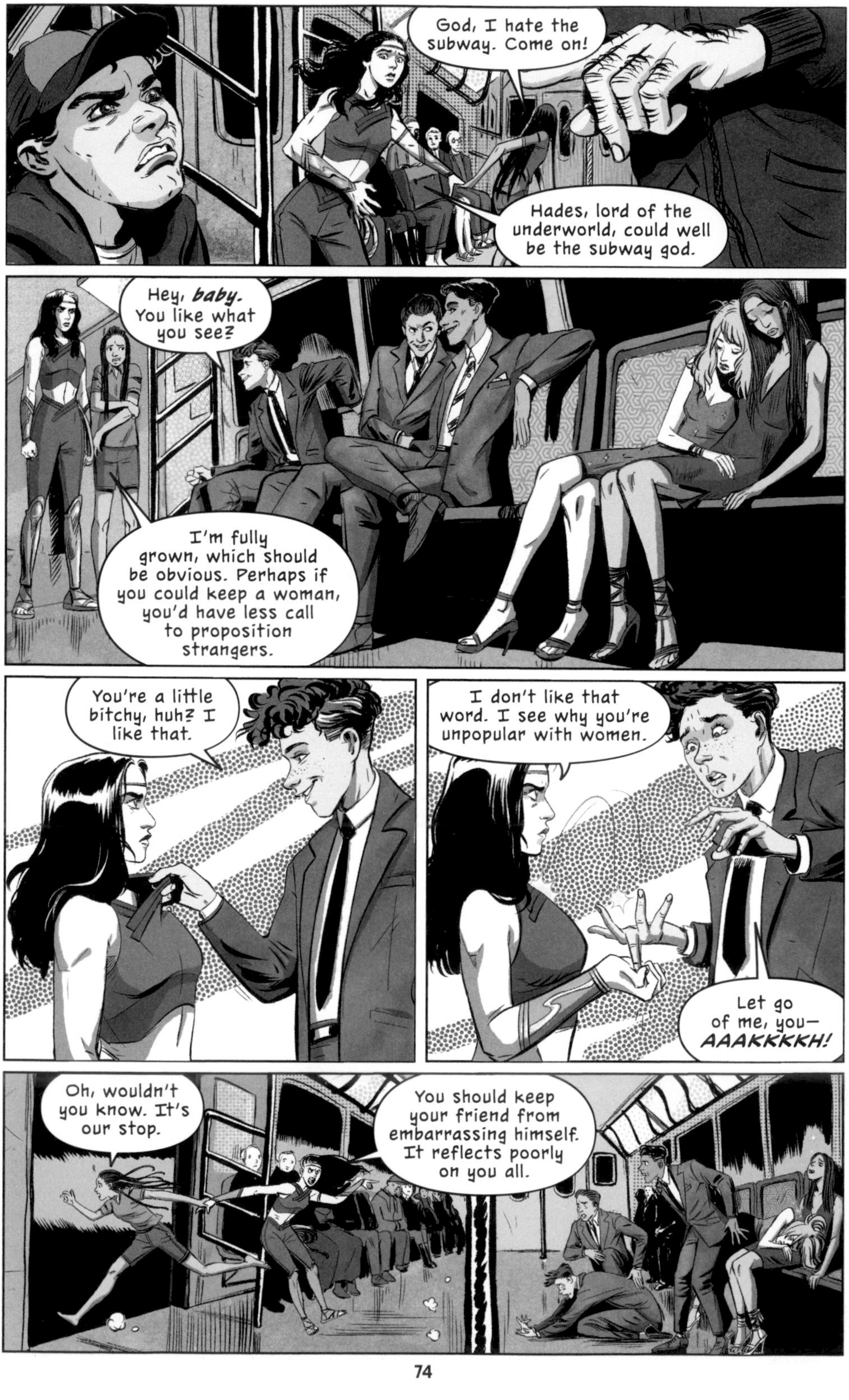
God, I hate the subway. Come on!
Hades, lord of the underworld, could well be the subway god.
Hey, *baby.* You like what you see?
I'm fully grown, which should be obvious. Perhaps if you could keep a woman, you'd have less call to proposition strangers.
You're a little bitchy, huh? I like that.
I don't like that word. I see why you're unpopular with women.
Let go of me, you— ***AAAKKKKH!***
Oh, wouldn't you know. It's our stop.
You should keep your friend from embarrassing himself. It reflects poorly on you all.

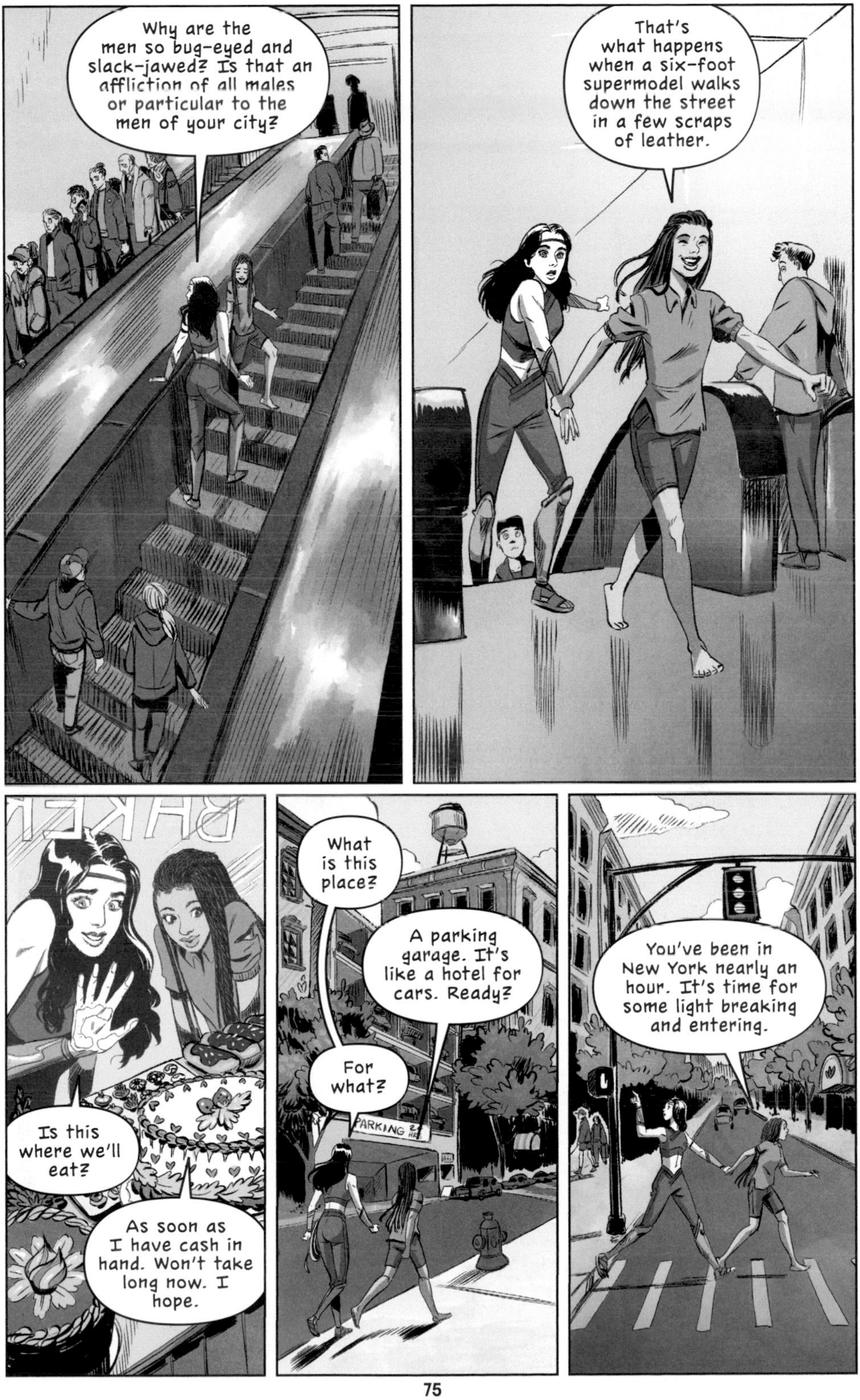

Why are the men so bug-eyed and slack-jawed? Is that an affliction of all males or particular to the men of your city?
That's what happens when a six-foot supermodel walks down the street in a few scraps of leather.
Is this where we'll eat?
As soon as I have cash in hand. Won't take long now. I hope.
What is this place?
A parking garage. It's like a hotel for cars. Ready?
For what?
PARKING
You've been in New York nearly an hour. It's time for some light breaking and entering.

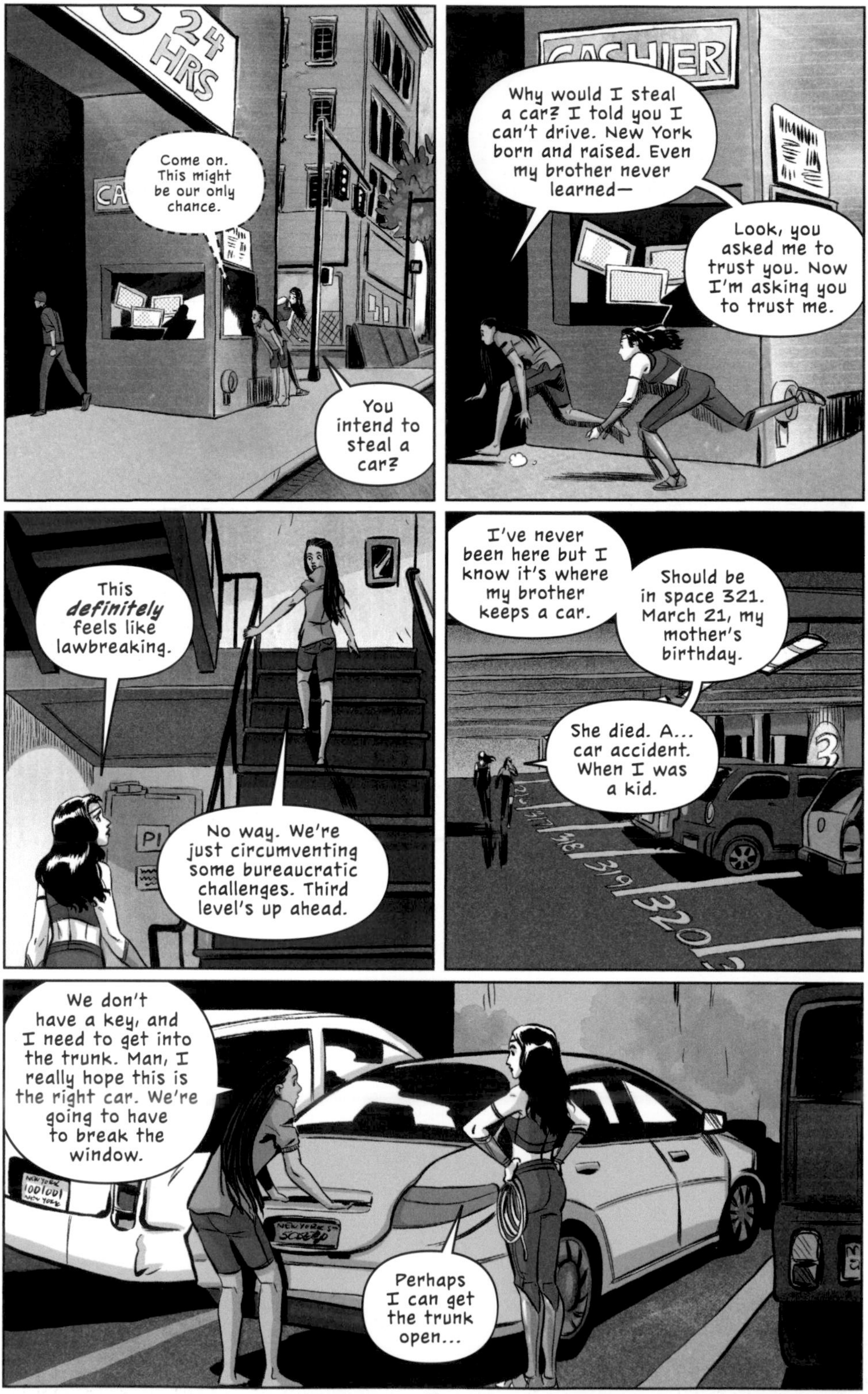
24 HRS
Come on. This might be our only chance.
You intend to steal a car?
CASHIER
Why would I steal a car? I told you I can't drive. New York born and raised. Even my brother never learned—
Look, you asked me to trust you. Now I'm asking you to trust me.
This *definitely* feels like lawbreaking.
No way. We're just circumventing some bureaucratic challenges. Third level's up ahead.
I've never been here but I know it's where my brother keeps a car.
Should be in space 321. March 21, my mother's birthday.
She died. A... car accident. When I was a kid.
319
320
We don't have a key, and I need to get into the trunk. Man, I really hope this is the right car. We're going to have to break the window.
Perhaps I can get the trunk open...

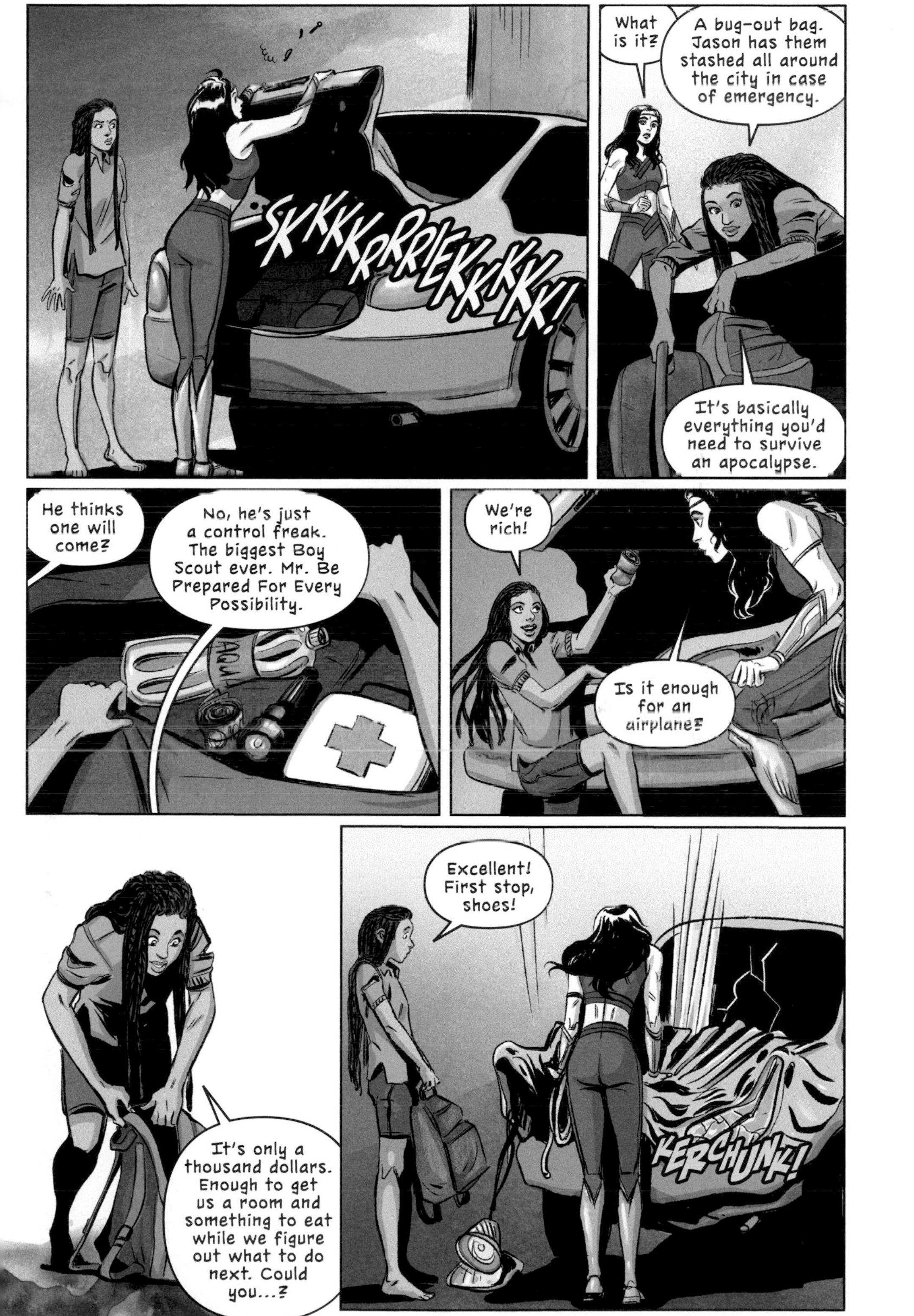
SKKKKRRRIEKKKKK!
What is it?
A bug-out bag. Jason has them stashed all around the city in case of emergency.
It's basically everything you'd need to survive an apocalypse.
He thinks one will come?
No, he's just a control freak. The biggest Boy Scout ever. Mr. Be Prepared For Every Possibility.
We're rich!
Is it enough for an airplane?
It's only a thousand dollars. Enough to get us a room and something to eat while we figure out what to do next. Could you...?
Excellent! First stop, shoes!
KERCHUNK!

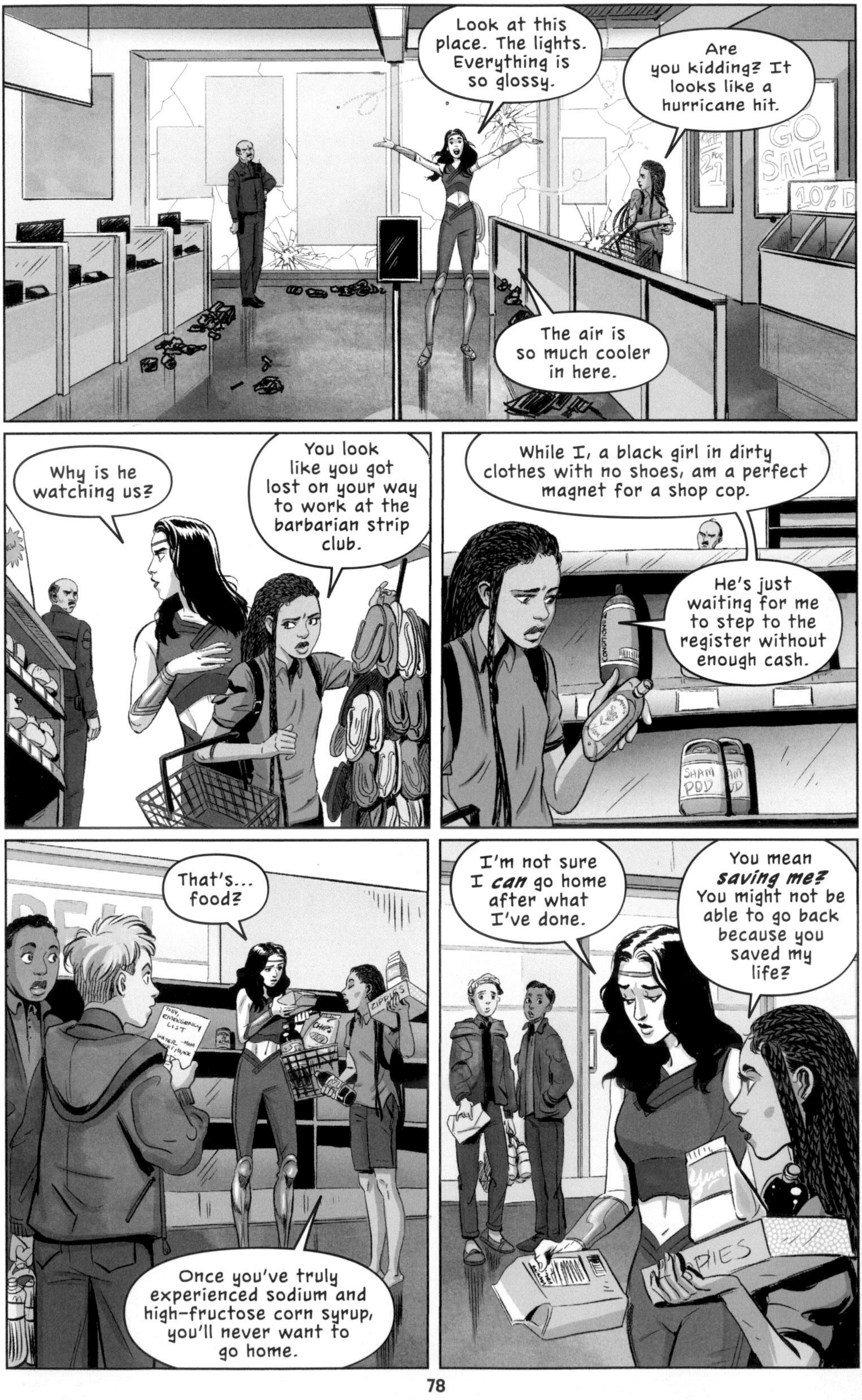
Look at this place. The lights. Everything is so glossy.
Are you kidding? It looks like a hurricane hit.
GO SALE
10% O
The air is so much cooler in here.
Why is he watching us?
You look like you got lost on your way to work at the barbarian strip club.
While I, a black girl in dirty clothes with no shoes, am a perfect magnet for a shop cop.
He's just waiting for me to step to the register without enough cash.
CONDITIONER
SHAM POO
That's... food?
CHIPS
ZIPPOS
Once you've truly experienced sodium and high-fructose corn syrup, you'll never want to go home.
I'm not sure I *can* go home after what I've done.
You mean ***saving me?*** You might not be able to go back because you saved my life?
Yum
DIES

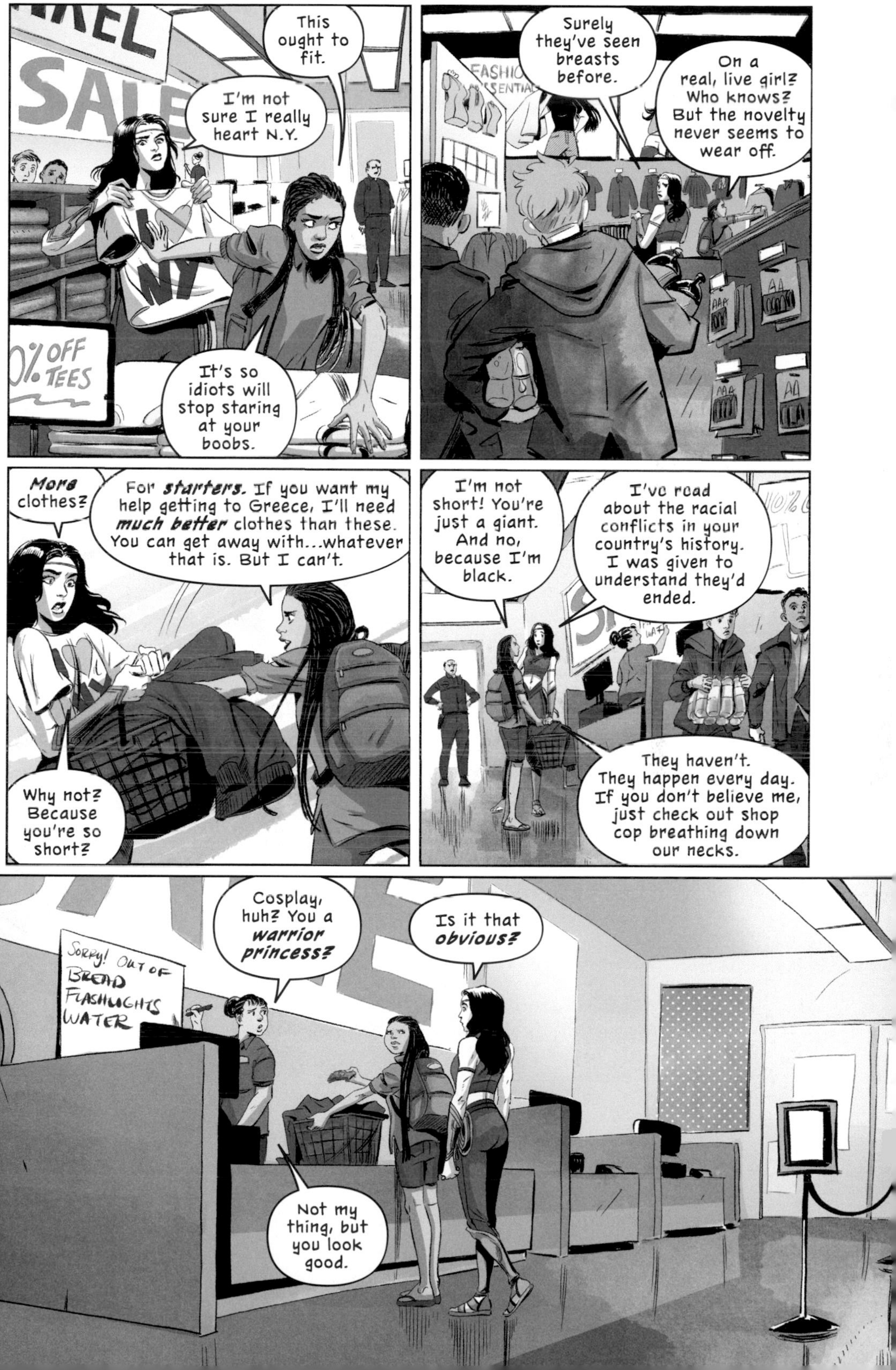

SALE
This ought to fit.
I'm not sure I really heart N.Y.
It's so idiots will stop staring at your boobs.
%OFF TEES
FASHION ESSENTIALS
Surely they've seen breasts before.
On a real, live girl? Who knows? But the novelty never seems to wear off.
More clothes?
For starters. If you want my help getting to Greece, I'll need much better clothes than these. You can get away with...whatever that is. But I can't.
Why not? Because you're so short?
I'm not short! You're just a giant. And no, because I'm black.
I've read about the racial conflicts in your country's history. I was given to understand they'd ended.
They haven't. They happen every day. If you don't believe me, just check out shop cop breathing down our necks.
SORRY! OUT OF BREAD FLASHLIGHTS WATER
Cosplay, huh? You a warrior princess?
Is it that obvious?
Not my thing, but you look good.

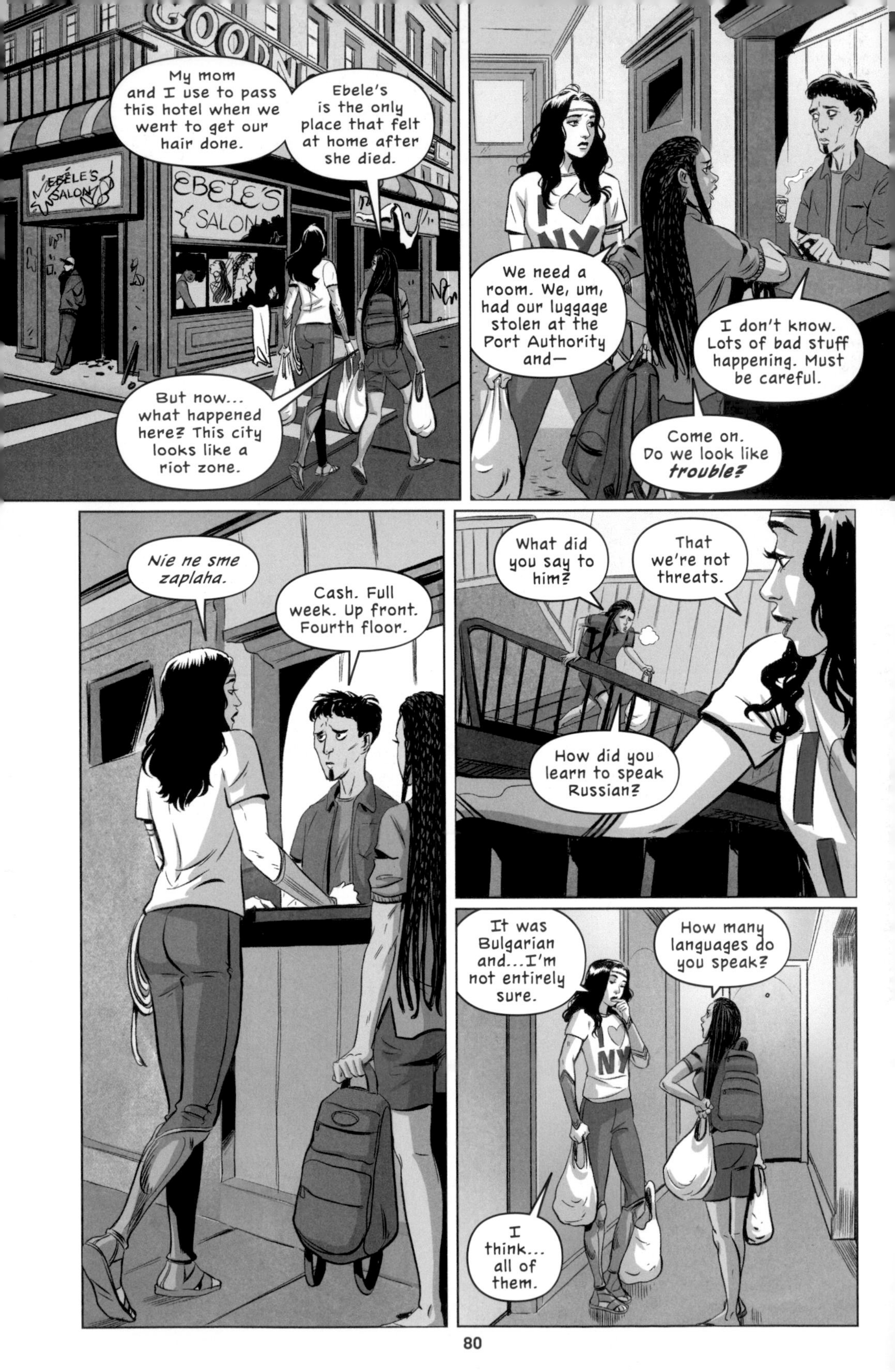
GOODN
EBELE'S SALON
EBELE'S SALON
My mom and I use to pass this hotel when we went to get our hair done.
Ebele's is the only place that felt at home after she died.
But now... what happened here? This city looks like a riot zone.
We need a room. We, um, had our luggage stolen at the Port Authority and—
I don't know. Lots of bad stuff happening. Must be careful.
Come on. Do we look like *trouble?*
Nie ne sme zaplaha.
Cash. Full week. Up front. Fourth floor.
What did you say to him?
That we're not threats.
How did you learn to speak Russian?
It was Bulgarian and...I'm not entirely sure.
How many languages do you speak?
I think... all of them.

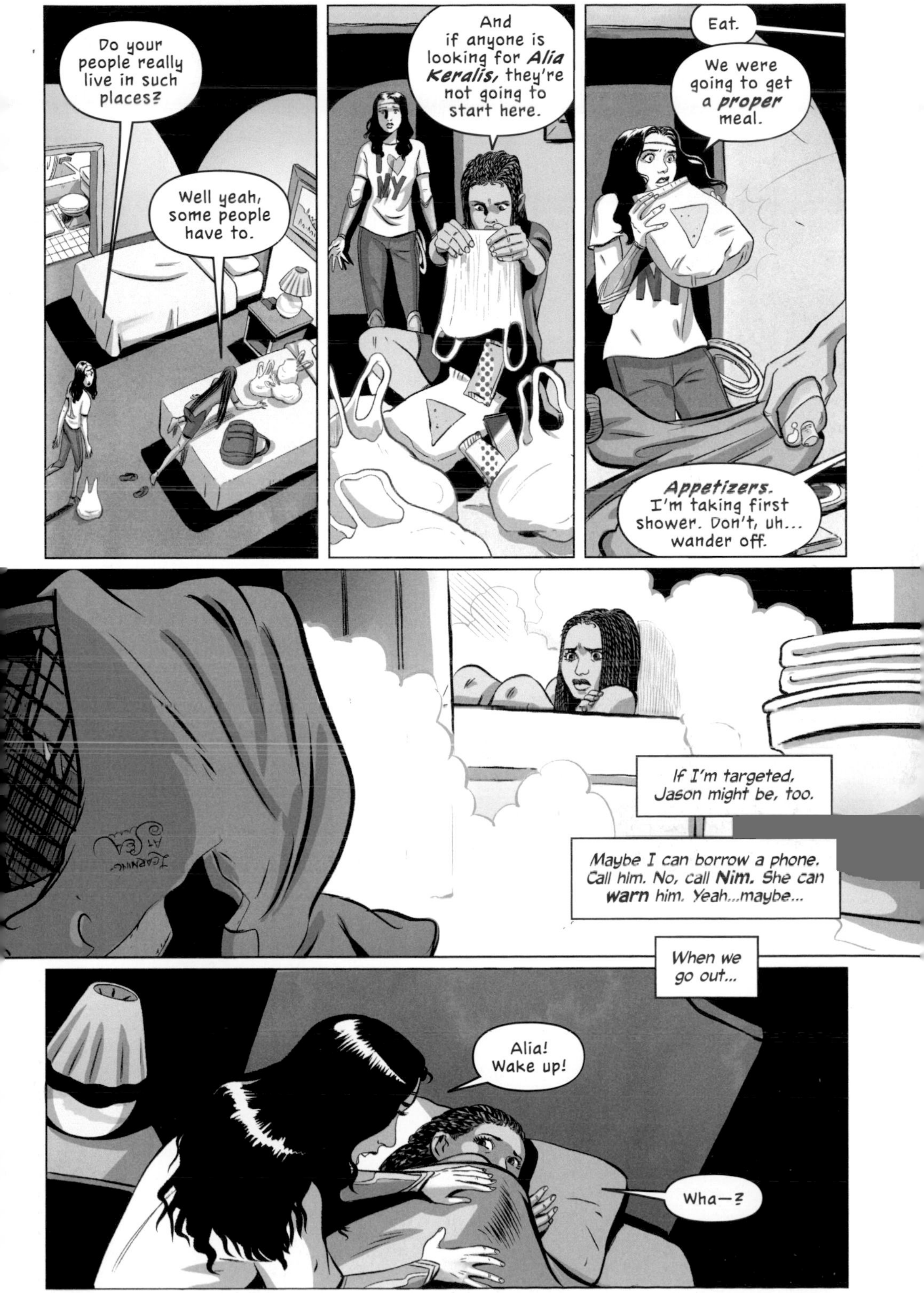
Do your people really live in such places?
Well yeah, some people have to.
And if anyone is looking for *Alia Keralis,* they're not going to start here.
Eat.
We were going to get a ***proper*** meal.
Appetizers. I'm taking first shower. Don't, uh... wander off.
If I'm targeted, Jason might be, too.
Maybe I can borrow a phone. Call him. No, call **Nim.** She can **warn** him. Yeah...maybe...
When we go out...
Alia! Wake up!
Wha—?

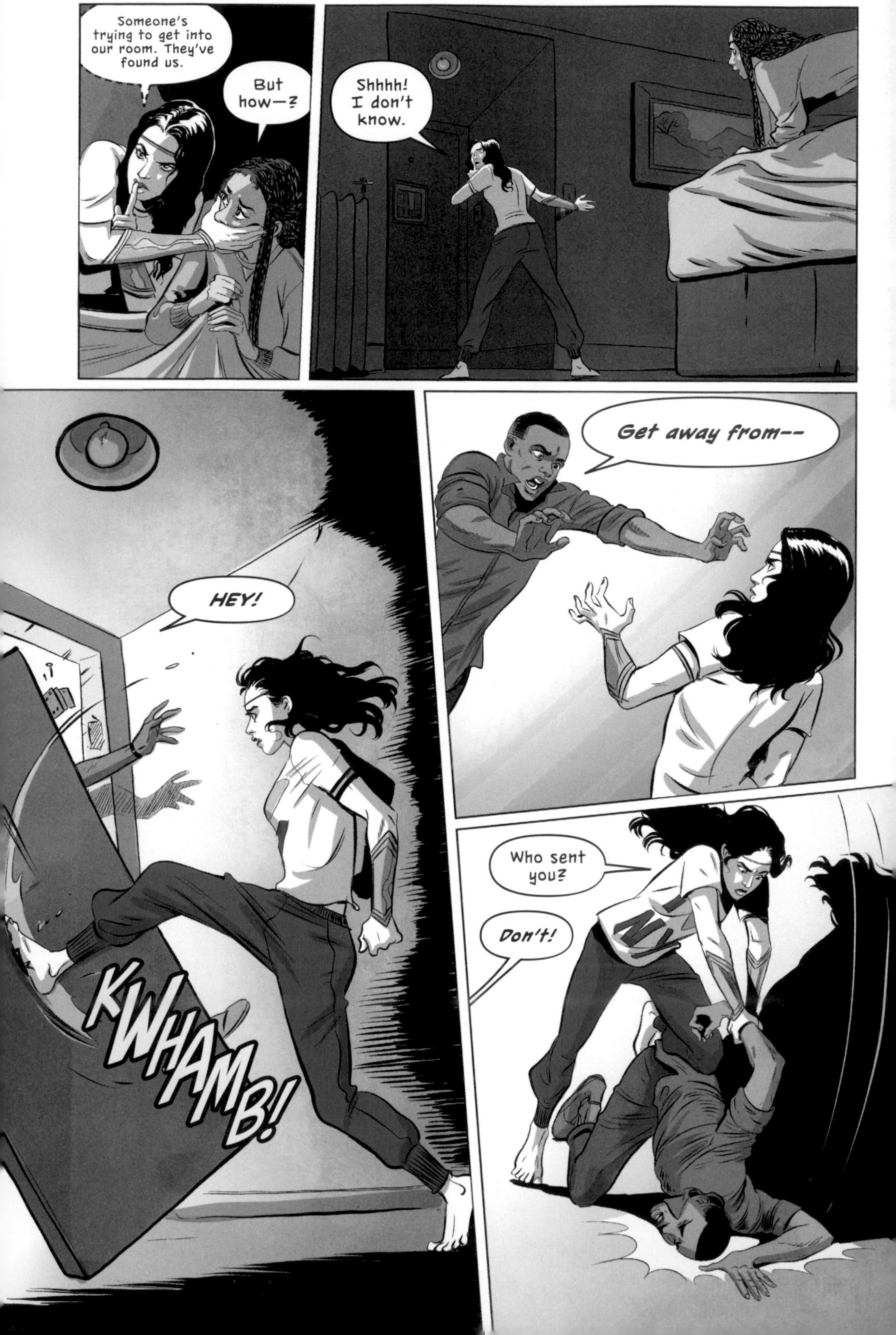
Someone's trying to get into our room. They've found us.
But how—?
Shhhh! I don't know.
HEY!
KWHAMB!
Get away from--
Who sent you?
Don't!

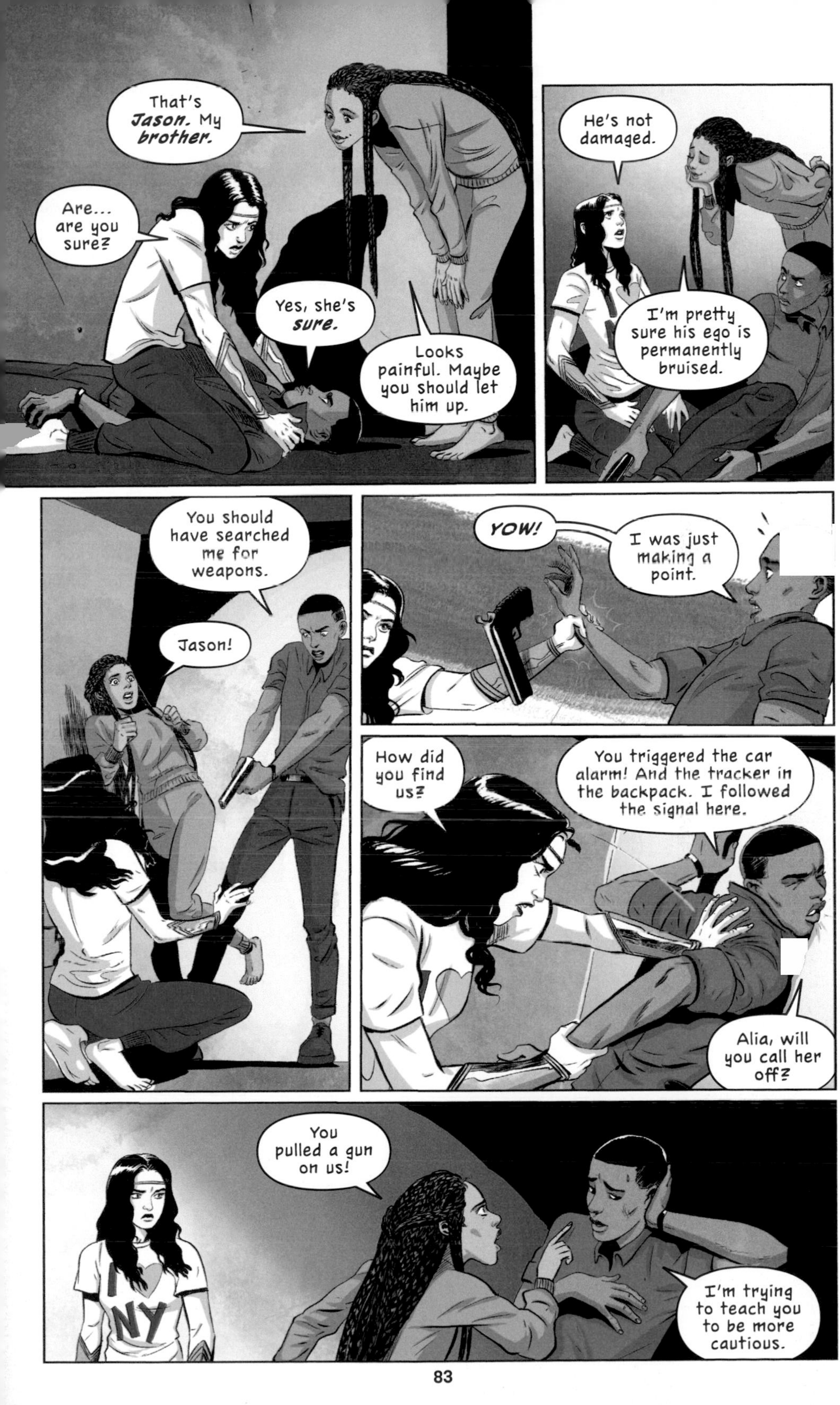

That's *Jason.* My *brother.*
Are... are you sure?
Yes, she's *sure.*
Looks painful. Maybe you should let him up.
He's not damaged.
I'm pretty sure his ego is permanently bruised.
You should have searched me for weapons.
Jason!
YOW!
I was just making a point.
How did you find us?
You triggered the car alarm! And the tracker in the backpack. I followed the signal here.
Alia, will you call her off?
You pulled a gun on us!
I'm trying to teach you to be more cautious.

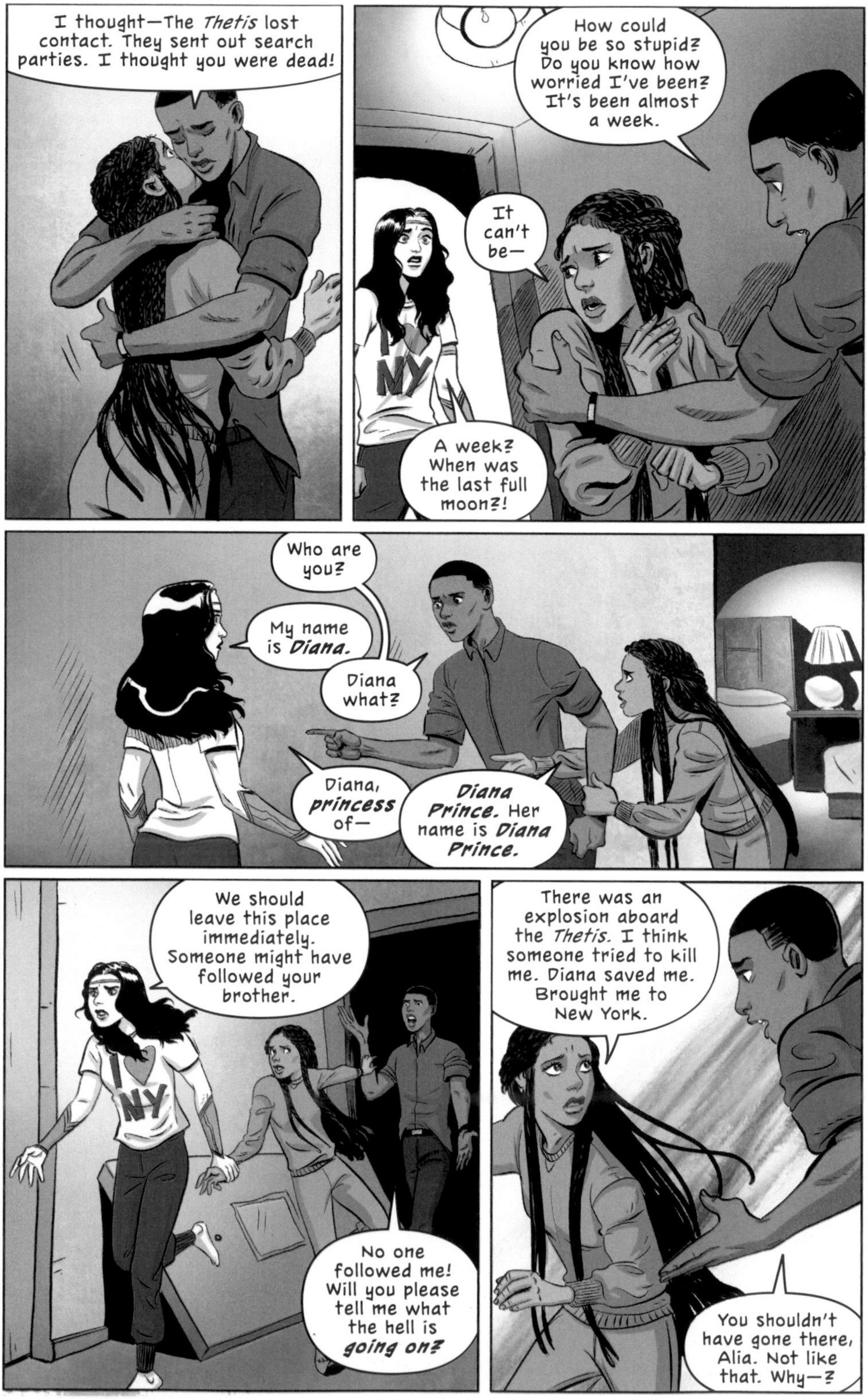
I thought—The *Thetis* lost contact. They sent out search parties. I thought you were dead!
How could you be so stupid? Do you know how worried I've been? It's been almost a week.
It can't be—
A week? When was the last full moon?!
Who are you?
My name is *Diana.*
Diana what?
Diana, *princess* of—
Diana Prince. Her name is *Diana Prince.*
We should leave this place immediately. Someone might have followed your brother.
No one followed me! Will you please tell me what the hell is *going on?*
There was an explosion aboard the *Thetis.* I think someone tried to kill me. Diana saved me. Brought me to New York.
You shouldn't have gone there, Alia. Not like that. Why—?

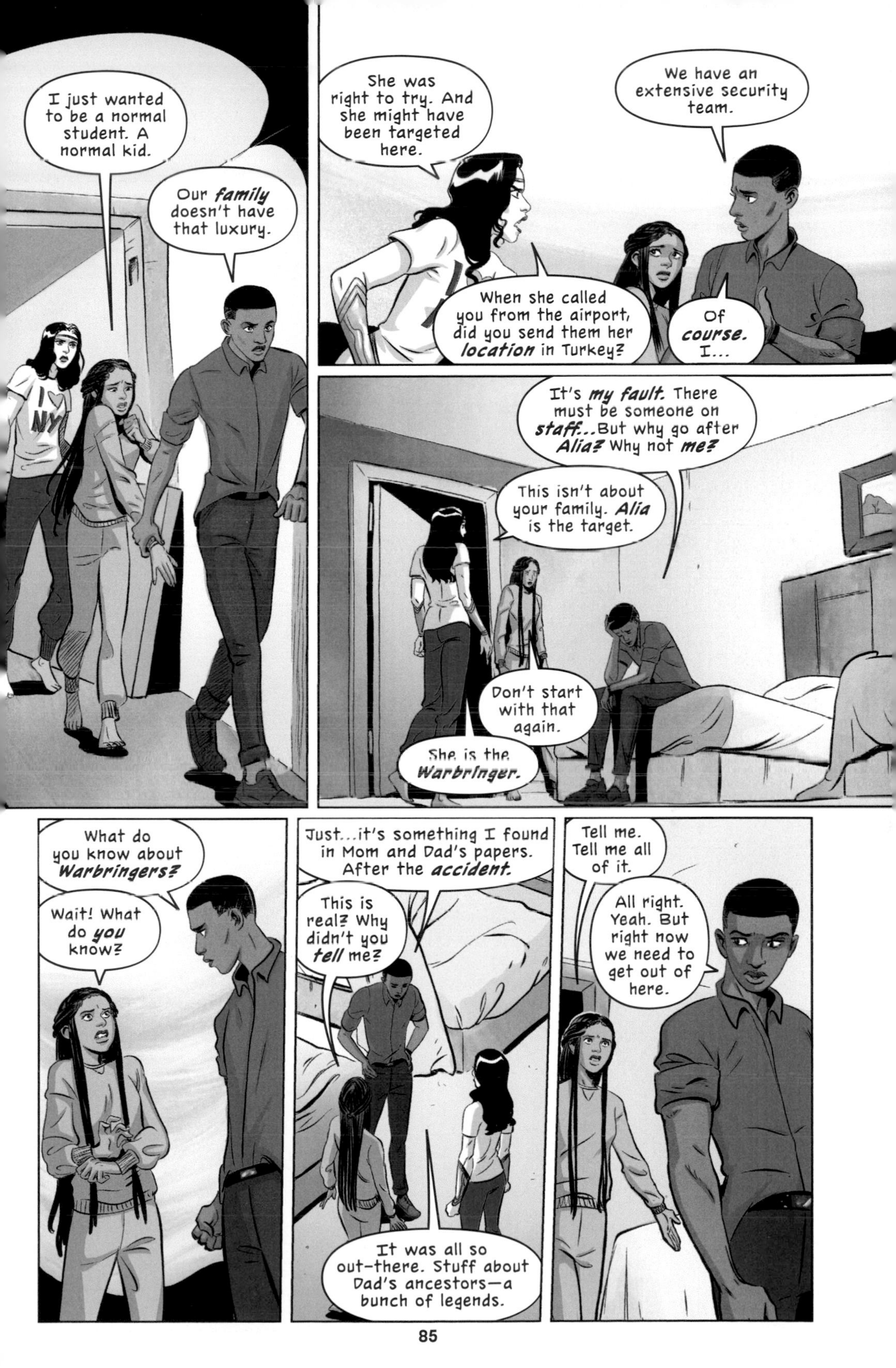
I just wanted to be a normal student. A normal kid.
Our *family* doesn't have that luxury.
She was right to try. And she might have been targeted here.
We have an extensive security team.
When she called you from the airport, did you send them her *location* in Turkey?
Of *course.* I...
It's *my fault.* There must be someone on *staff...*But why go after *Alia?* Why not *me?*
This isn't about your family. *Alia* is the target.
Don't start with that again.
She is the *Warbringer.*
What do you know about *Warbringers?*
Wait! What do *you* know?
Just...it's something I found in Mom and Dad's papers. After the *accident.*
This is real? Why didn't you *tell* me?
It was all so out-there. Stuff about Dad's ancestors—a bunch of legends.
Tell me. Tell me all of it.
All right. Yeah. But right now we need to get out of here.

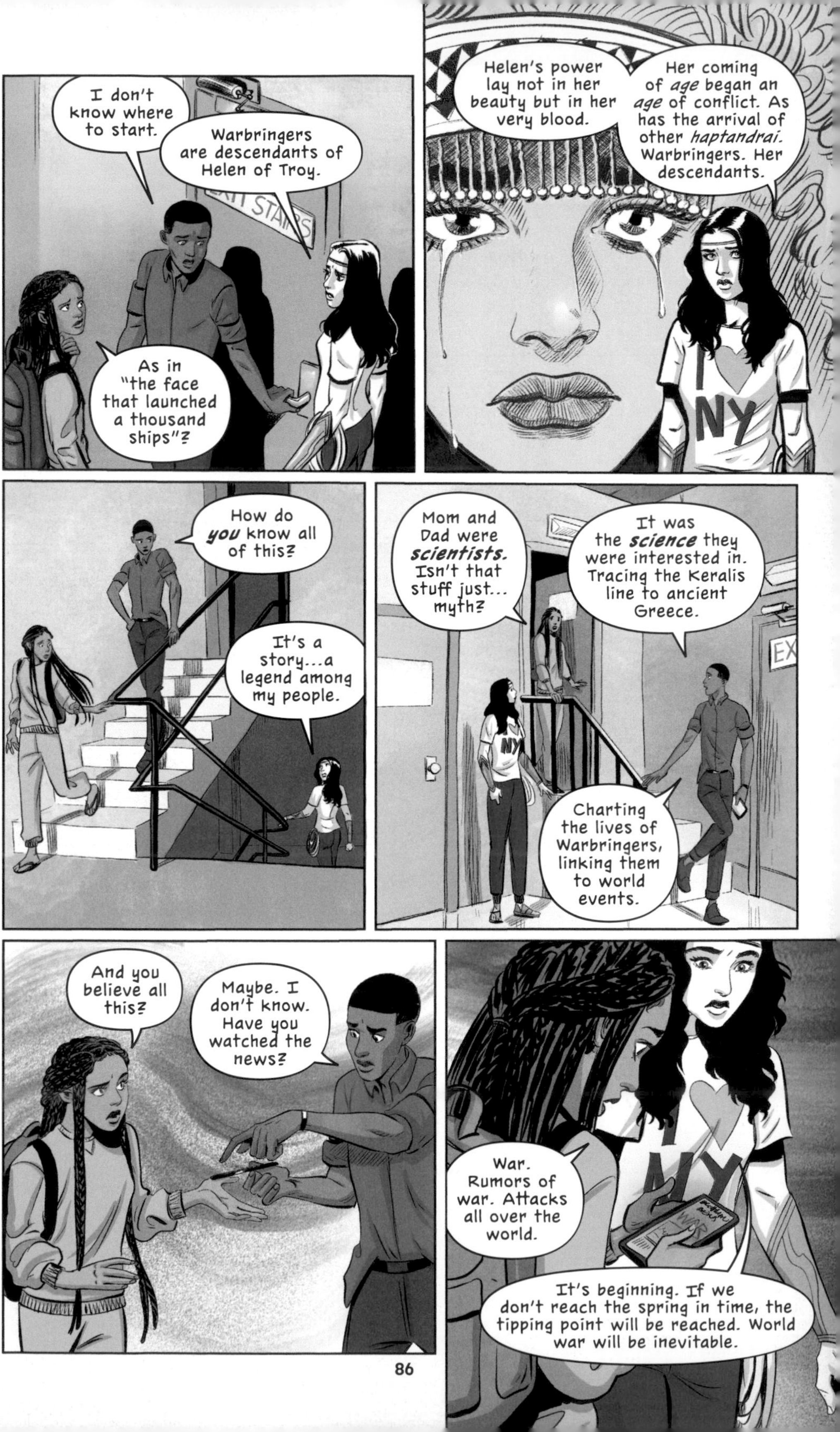

I don't know where to start.
Warbringers are descendants of Helen of Troy.
EXIT STAIRS
As in "the face that launched a thousand ships"?
Helen's power lay not in her beauty but in her very blood.
Her coming of *age* began an *age* of conflict. As has the arrival of other *haptandrai*. Warbringers. Her descendants.
I ♥ NY
How do ***you*** know all of this?
It's a story...a legend among my people.
Mom and Dad were ***scientists.*** Isn't that stuff just... myth?
It was the ***science*** they were interested in. Tracing the Keralis line to ancient Greece.
Charting the lives of Warbringers, linking them to world events.
And you believe all this?
Maybe. I don't know. Have you watched the news?
War. Rumors of war. Attacks all over the world.
It's beginning. If we don't reach the spring in time, the tipping point will be reached. World war will be inevitable.

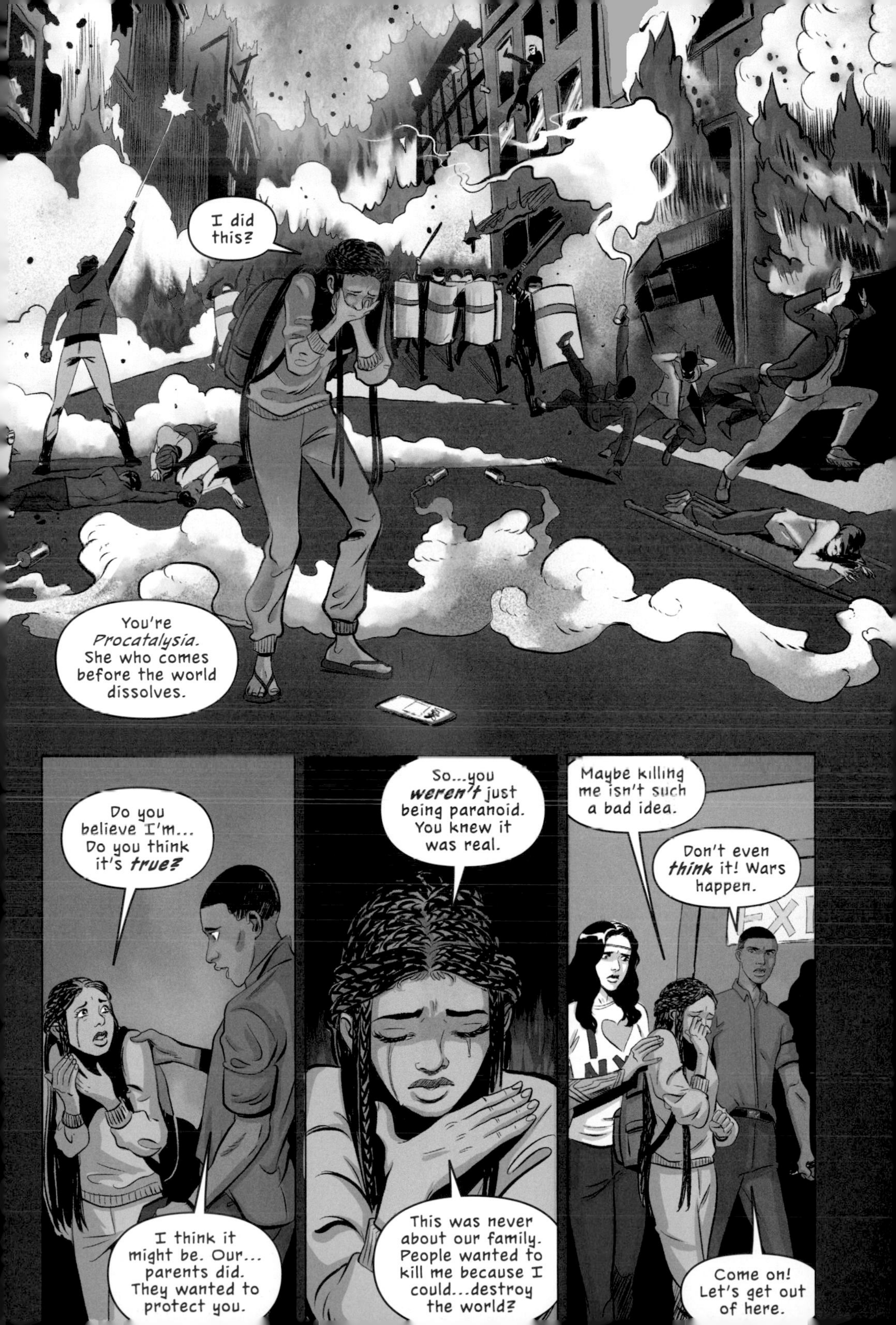
I did this?
You're *Procatalysia.* She who comes before the world dissolves.
Do you believe I'm... Do you think it's ***true?***
I think it might be. Our... parents did. They wanted to protect you.
So...you ***weren't*** just being paranoid. You knew it was real.
This was never about our family. People wanted to kill me because I could...destroy the world?
Maybe killing me isn't such a bad idea.
Don't even ***think*** it! Wars happen.
Come on! Let's get out of here.

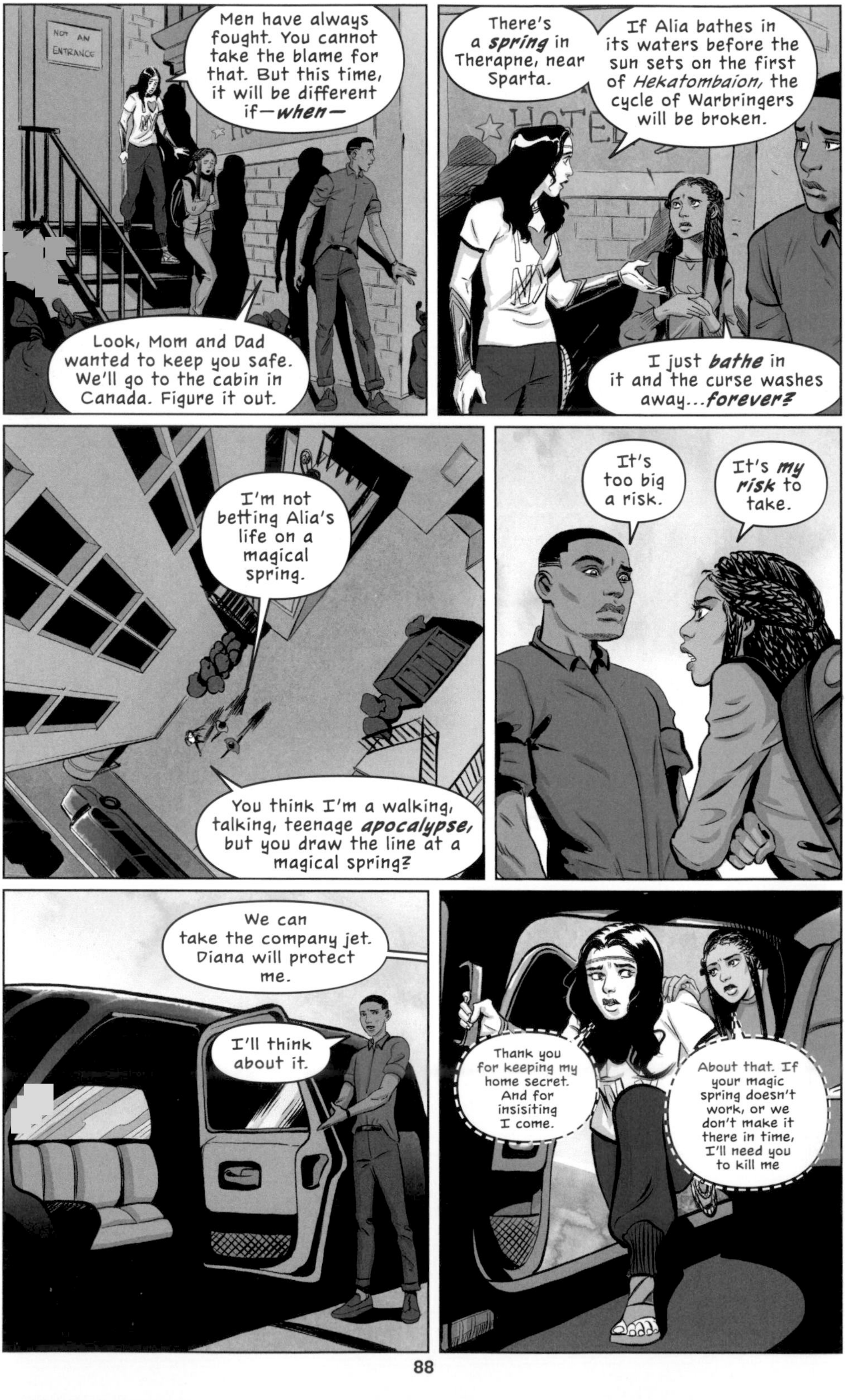
NOT AN ENTRANCE
Men have always fought. You cannot take the blame for that. But this time, it will be different if—*when*—
Look, Mom and Dad wanted to keep you safe. We'll go to the cabin in Canada. Figure it out.
There's a *spring* in Therapne, near Sparta.
If Alia bathes in its waters before the sun sets on the first of *Hekatombaion*, the cycle of Warbringers will be broken.
I just *bathe* in it and the curse washes away...*forever?*
I'm not betting Alia's life on a magical spring.
You think I'm a walking, talking, teenage *apocalypse*, but you draw the line at a magical spring?
It's too big a risk.
It's *my risk* to take.
We can take the company jet. Diana will protect me.
I'll think about it.
Thank you for keeping my home secret. And for insisiting I come.
About that. If your magic spring doesn't work, or we don't make it there in time, I'll need you to kill me

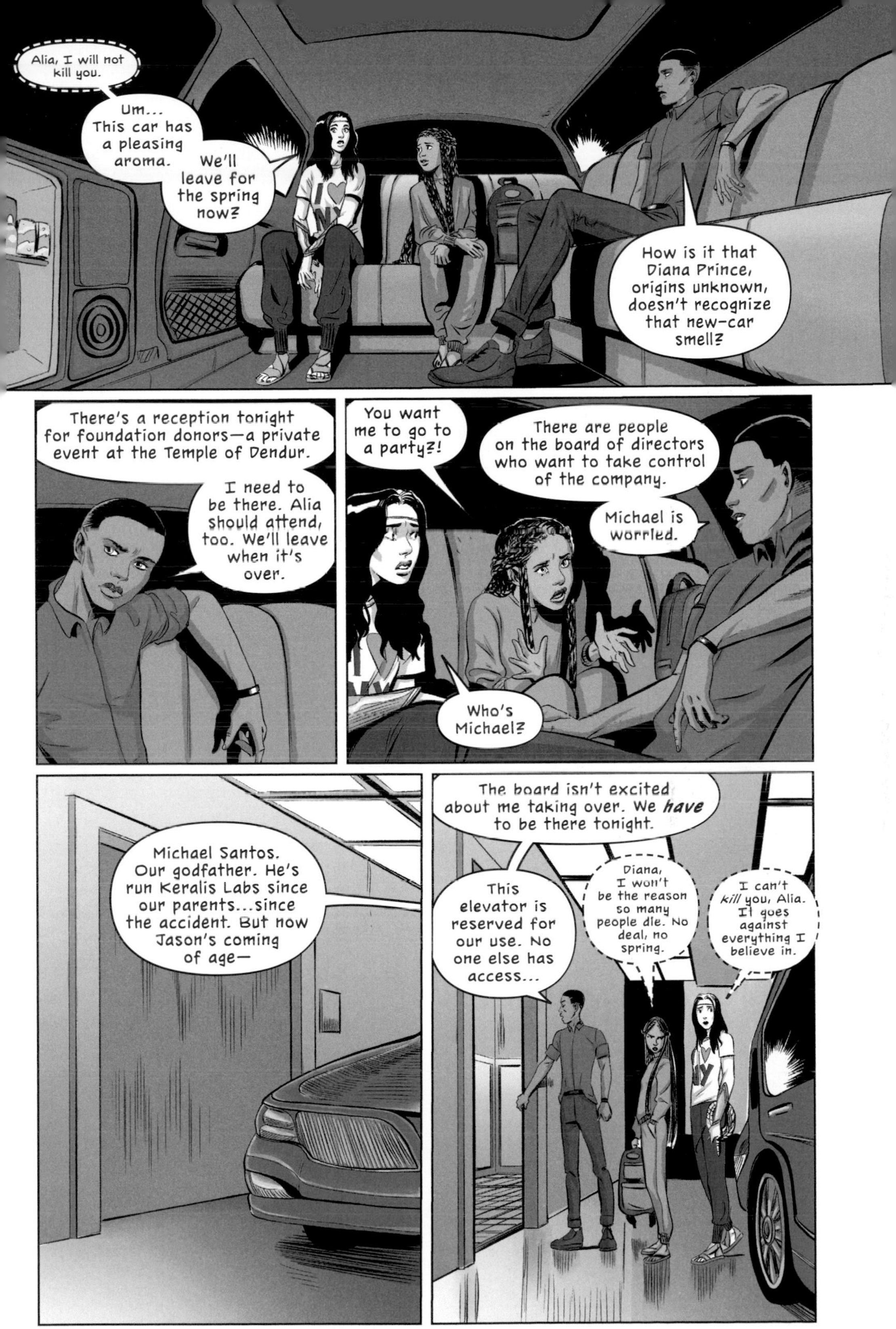
Alia, I will not kill you.
Um... This car has a pleasing aroma.
We'll leave for the spring now?
How is it that Diana Prince, origins unknown, doesn't recognize that new-car smell?
There's a reception tonight for foundation donors—a private event at the Temple of Dendur.
I need to be there. Alia should attend, too. We'll leave when it's over.
You want me to go to a party?!
There are people on the board of directors who want to take control of the company.
Michael is worried.
Who's Michael?
Michael Santos. Our godfather. He's run Keralis Labs since our parents...since the accident. But now Jason's coming of age—
The board isn't excited about me taking over. We *have* to be there tonight.
This elevator is reserved for our use. No one else has access...
Diana, I won't be the reason so many people die. No deal, no spring.
I can't *kill* you, Alia. It goes against everything I believe in.

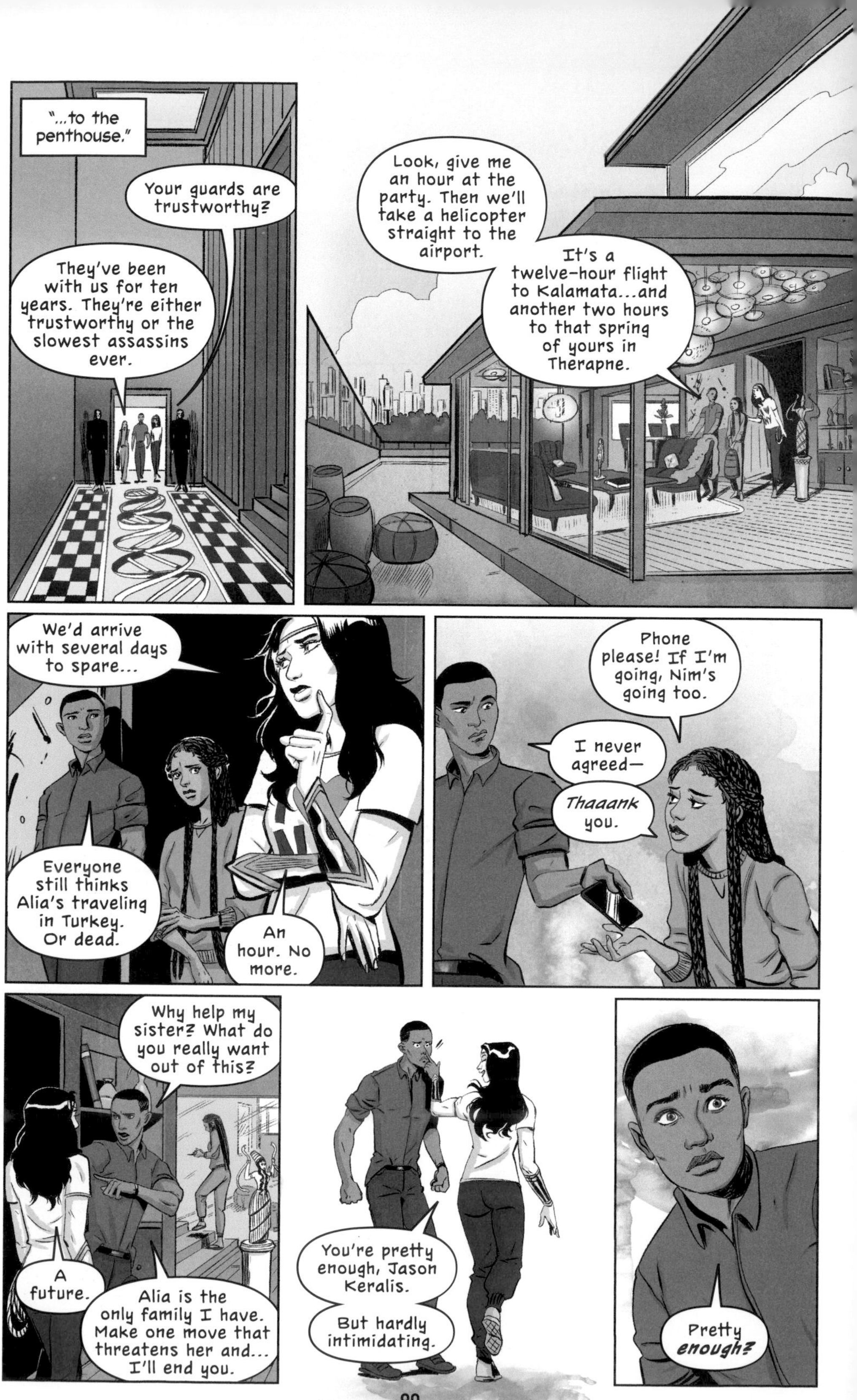
"...to the penthouse."
Your guards are trustworthy?
They've been with us for ten years. They're either trustworthy or the slowest assassins ever.
Look, give me an hour at the party. Then we'll take a helicopter straight to the airport.
It's a twelve-hour flight to Kalamata...and another two hours to that spring of yours in Therapne.
We'd arrive with several days to spare...
Everyone still thinks Alia's traveling in Turkey. Or dead.
An hour. No more.
Phone please! If I'm going, Nim's going too.
I never agreed—
Thaaank you.
Why help my sister? What do you really want out of this?
A future.
Alia is the only family I have. Make one move that threatens her and... I'll end you.
You're pretty enough, Jason Keralis.
But hardly intimidating.
Pretty ***enough?***

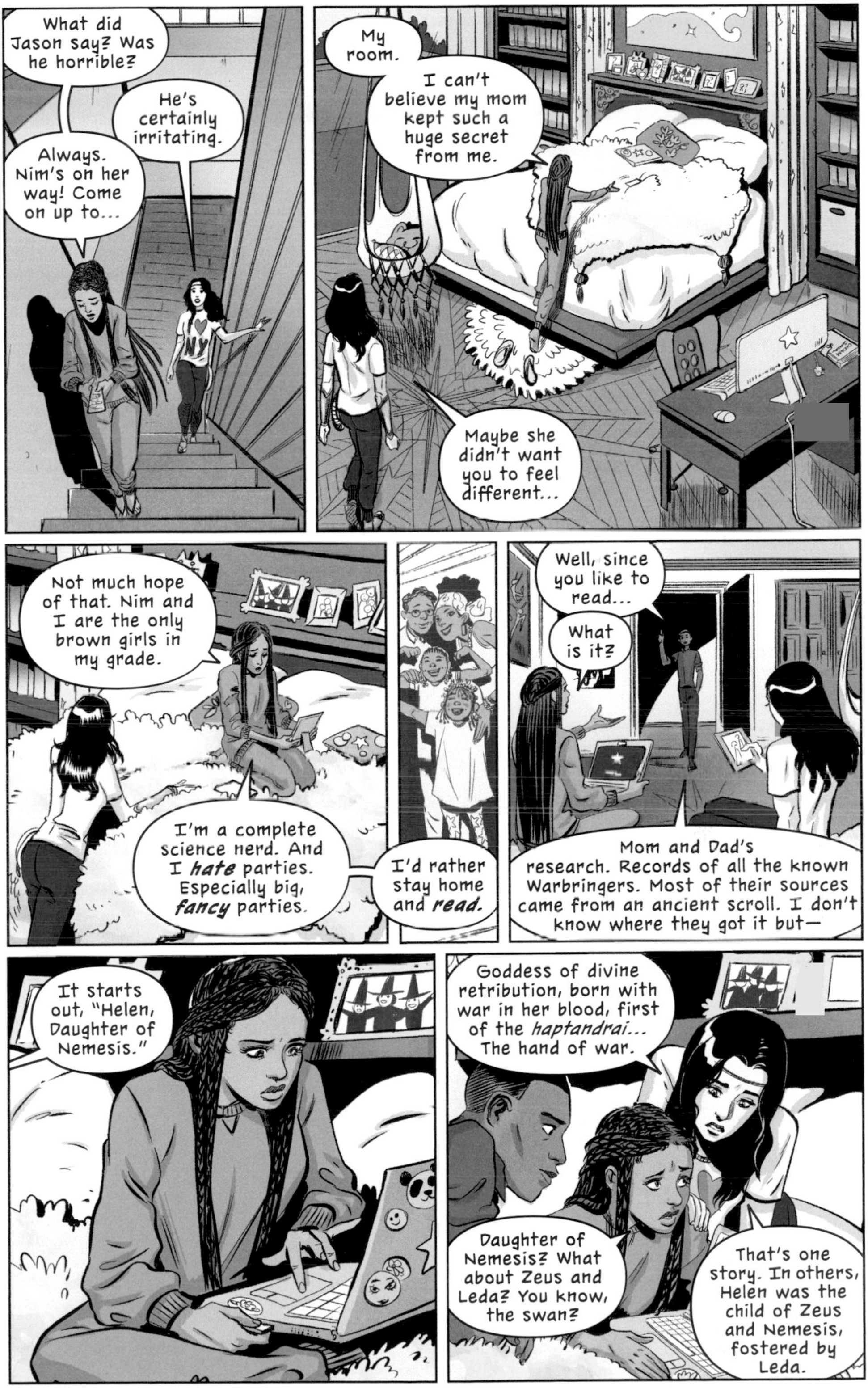
What did Jason say? Was he horrible?
He's certainly irritating.
Always. Nim's on her way! Come on up to...
My room.
I can't believe my mom kept such a huge secret from me.
Maybe she didn't want you to feel different...
Not much hope of that. Nim and I are the only brown girls in my grade.
I'm a complete science nerd. And I *hate* parties. Especially big, *fancy* parties.
I'd rather stay home and *read.*
Well, since you like to read...
What is it?
Mom and Dad's research. Records of all the known Warbringers. Most of their sources came from an ancient scroll. I don't know where they got it but—
It starts out, "Helen, Daughter of Nemesis."
Goddess of divine retribution, born with war in her blood, first of the *haptandrai...* The hand of war.
Daughter of Nemesis? What about Zeus and Leda? You know, the swan?
That's one story. In others, Helen was the child of Zeus and Nemesis, fostered by Leda.

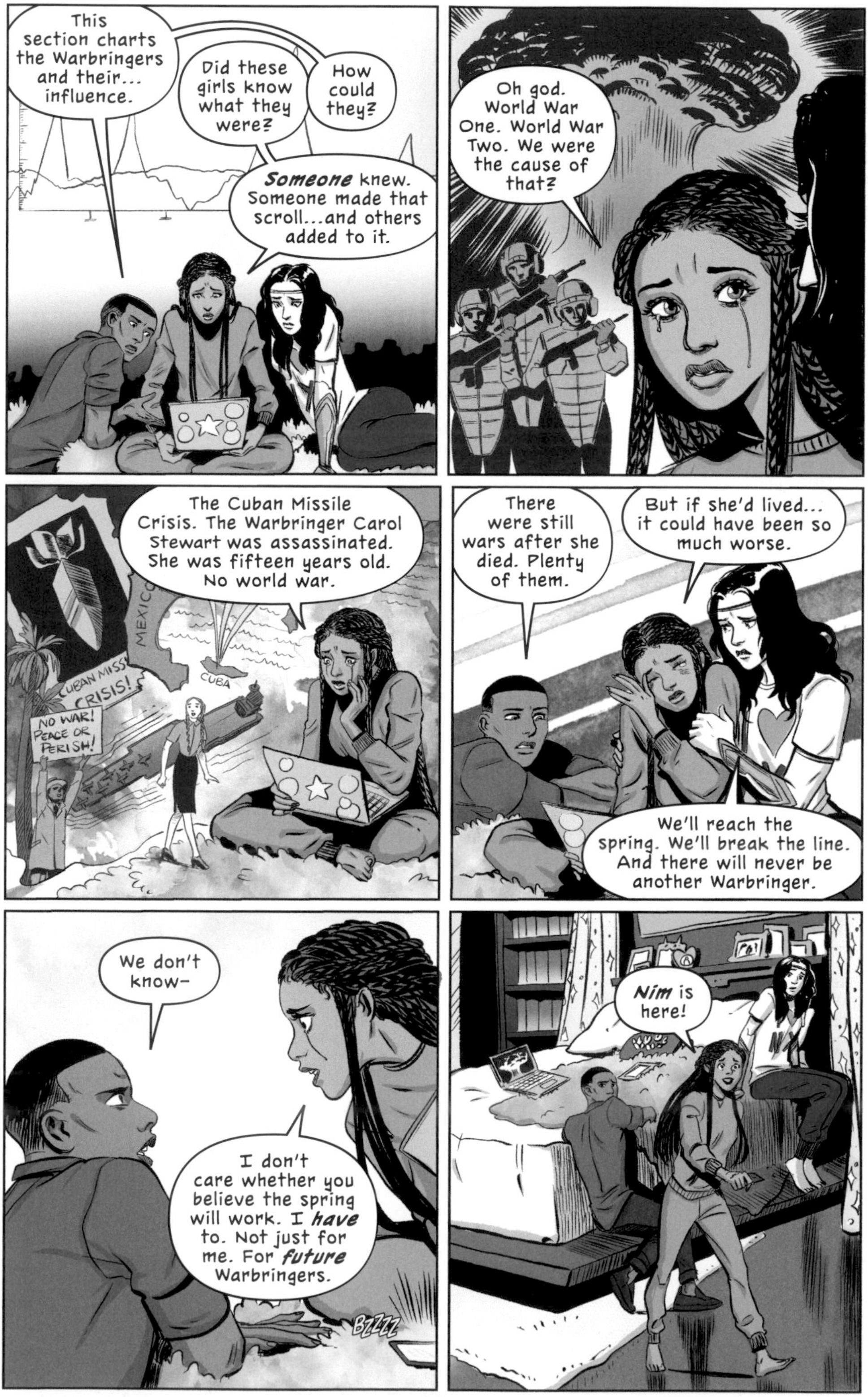

This section charts the Warbringers and their... influence.
Did these girls know what they were?
How could they?
Someone knew. Someone made that scroll...and others added to it.
Oh god. World War One. World War Two. We were the cause of that?
The Cuban Missile Crisis. The Warbringer Carol Stewart was assassinated. She was fifteen years old. No world war.
MEXICO
CUBA
CUBAN MISS CRISIS!
NO WAR! PEACE OR PERISH!
There were still wars after she died. Plenty of them.
But if she'd lived... it could have been so much worse.
We'll reach the spring. We'll break the line. And there will never be another Warbringer.
We don't know–
I don't care whether you believe the spring will work. I have to. Not just for me. For future Warbringers.
BZZZZ
Nim is here!

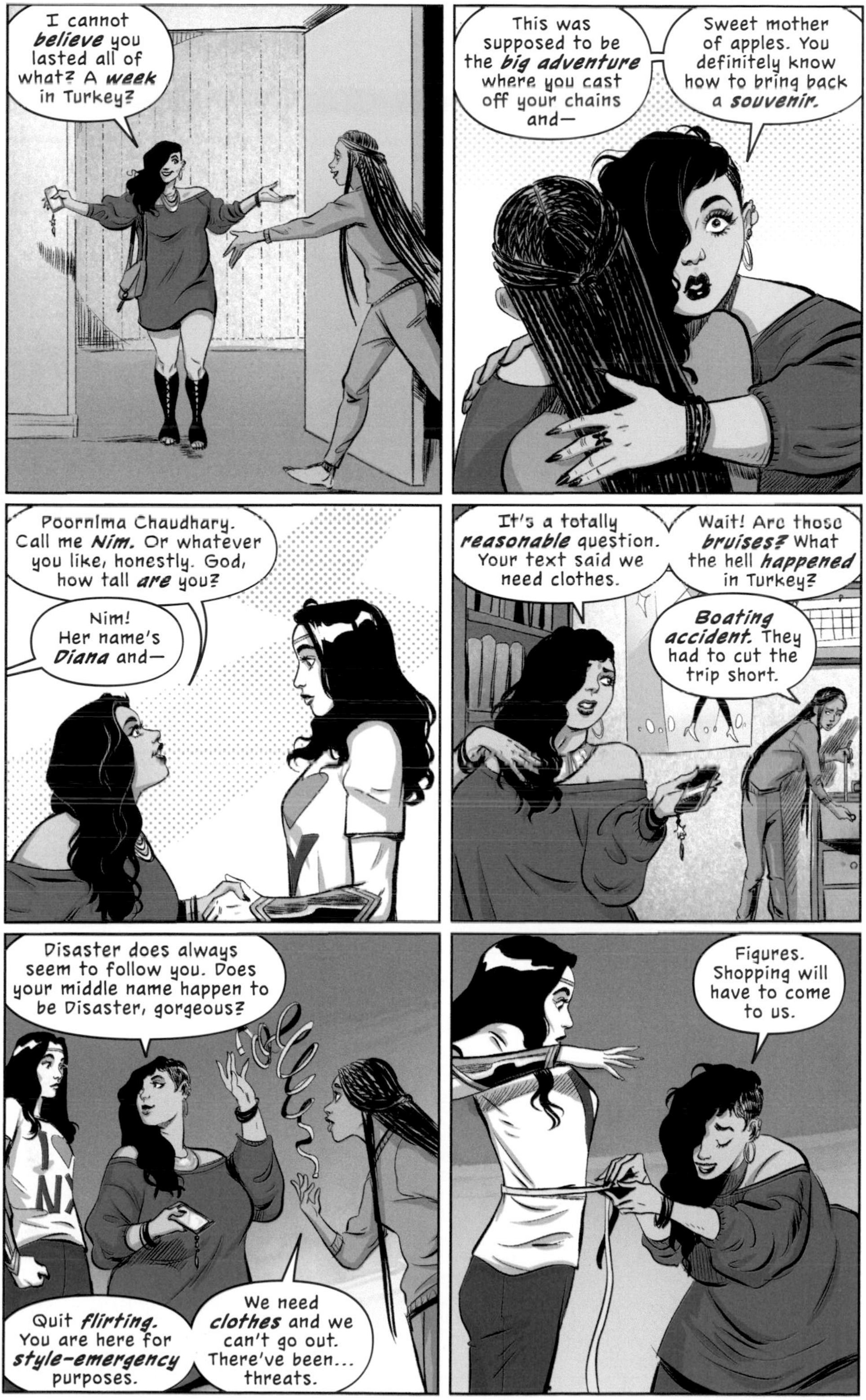
I cannot *believe* you lasted all of what? A *week* in Turkey?
This was supposed to be the *big adventure* where you cast off your chains and—
Sweet mother of apples. You definitely know how to bring back a *souvenir.*
Poornima Chaudhary. Call me *Nim.* Or whatever you like, honestly. God, how tall *are* you?
Nim! Her name's *Diana* and—
It's a totally *reasonable* question. Your text said we need clothes.
Wait! Are those *bruises?* What the hell *happened* in Turkey?
Boating accident. They had to cut the trip short.
Disaster does always seem to follow you. Does your middle name happen to be Disaster, gorgeous?
Quit *flirting.* You are here for *style-emergency* purposes.
We need *clothes* and we can't go out. There've been... threats.
Figures. Shopping will have to come to us.

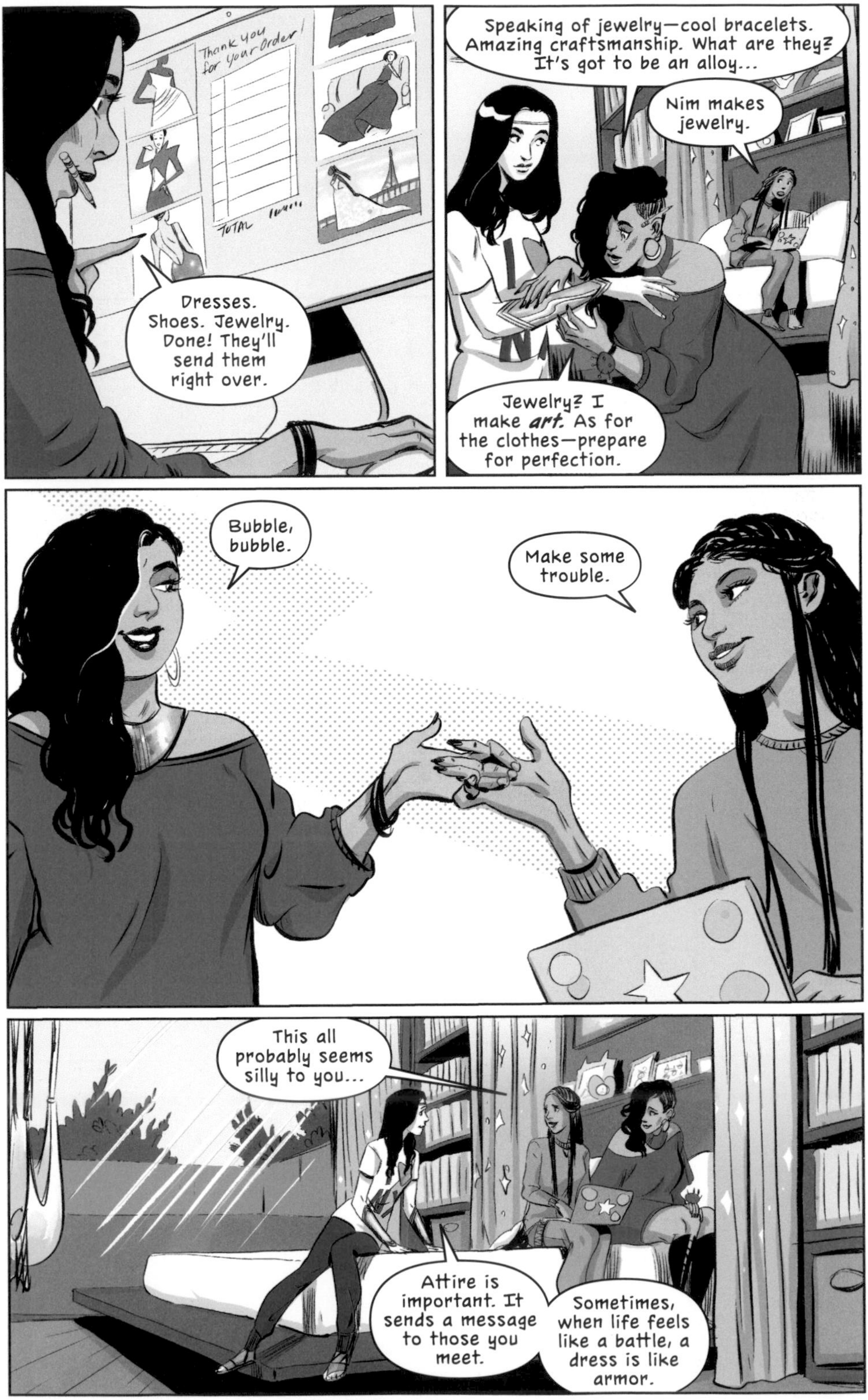
Thank you for your Order!
TOTAL
Dresses. Shoes. Jewelry. Done! They'll send them right over.
Speaking of jewelry—cool bracelets. Amazing craftsmanship. What are they? It's got to be an alloy...
Nim makes jewelry.
Jewelry? I make *art.* As for the clothes—prepare for perfection.
Bubble, bubble.
Make some trouble.
This all probably seems silly to you...
Attire is important. It sends a message to those you meet.
Sometimes, when life feels like a battle, a dress is like armor.

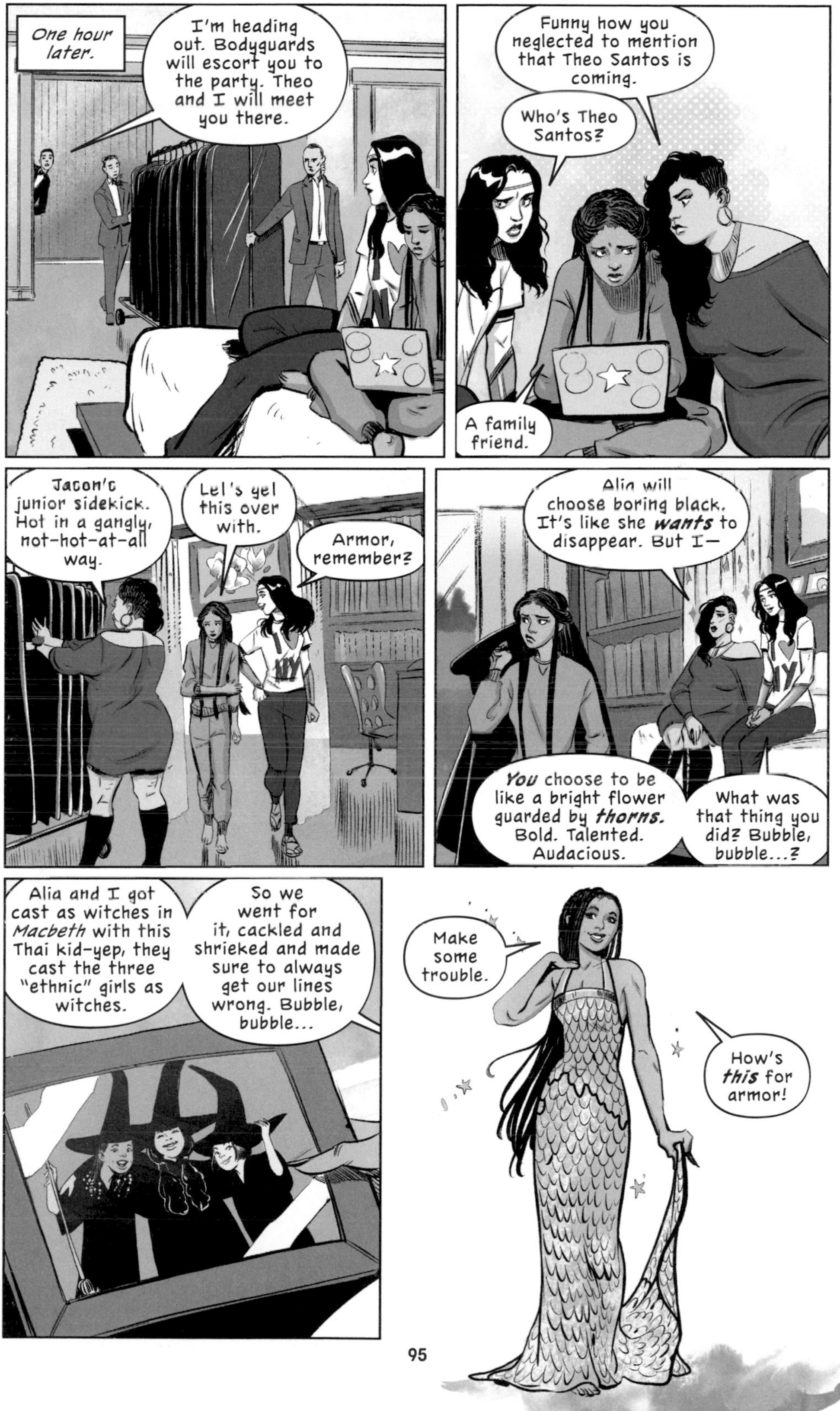
One hour later.
I'm heading out. Bodyguards will escort you to the party. Theo and I will meet you there.
Funny how you neglected to mention that Theo Santos is coming.
Who's Theo Santos?
A family friend.
Jason's junior sidekick. Hot in a gangly, not-hot-at-all way.
Let's get this over with.
Armor, remember?
Alia will choose boring black. It's like she *wants* to disappear. But I—
You choose to be like a bright flower guarded by *thorns.* Bold. Talented. Audacious.
What was that thing you did? Bubble, bubble...?
Alia and I got cast as witches in *Macbeth* with this Thai kid—yep, they cast the three "ethnic" girls as witches.
So we went for it, cackled and shrieked and made sure to always get our lines wrong. Bubble, bubble...
Make some trouble.
How's *this* for armor!

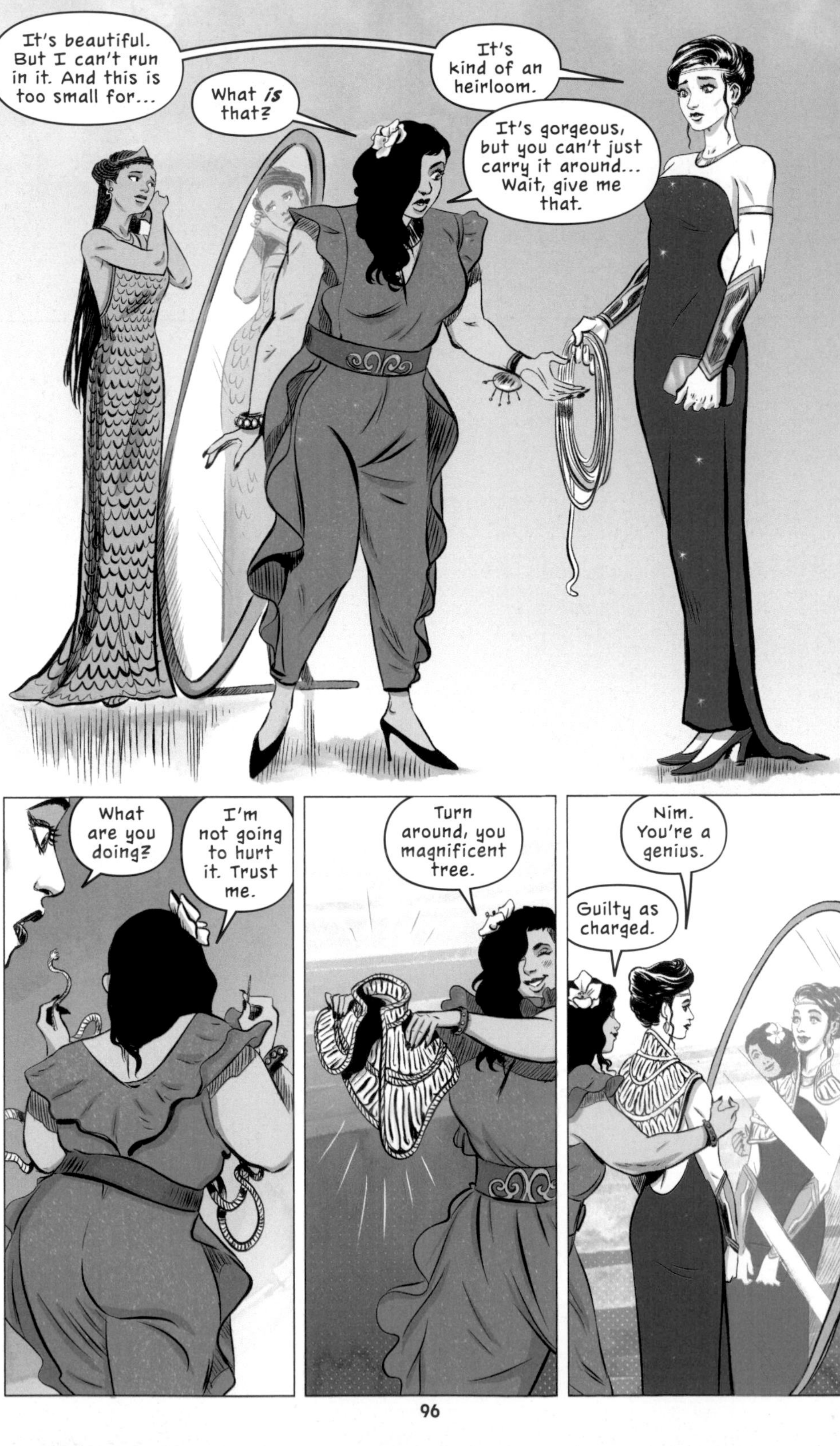
It's beautiful. But I can't run in it. And this is too small for...
It's kind of an heirloom.
What *is* that?
It's gorgeous, but you can't just carry it around... Wait, give me that.
What are you doing?
I'm not going to hurt it. Trust me.
Turn around, you magnificent tree.
Nim. You're a genius.
Guilty as charged.

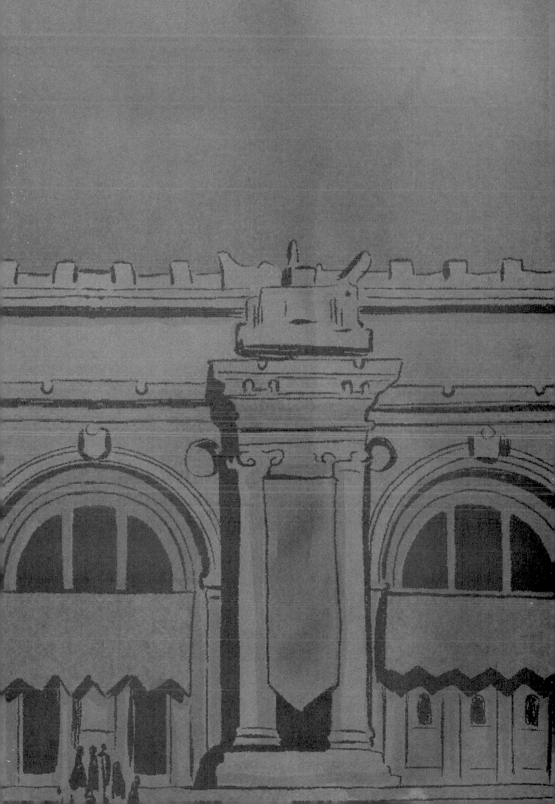

PART FOUR

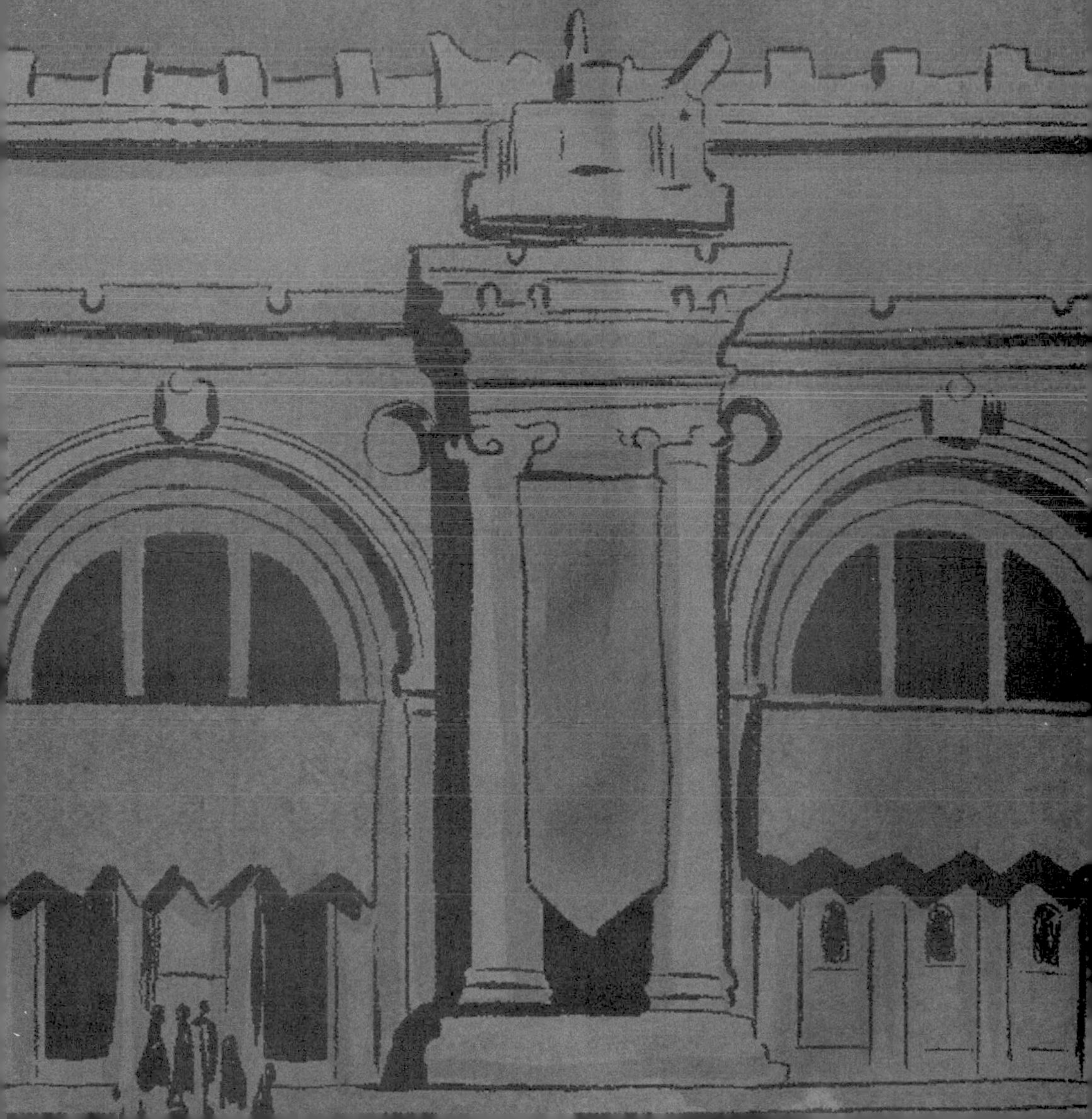

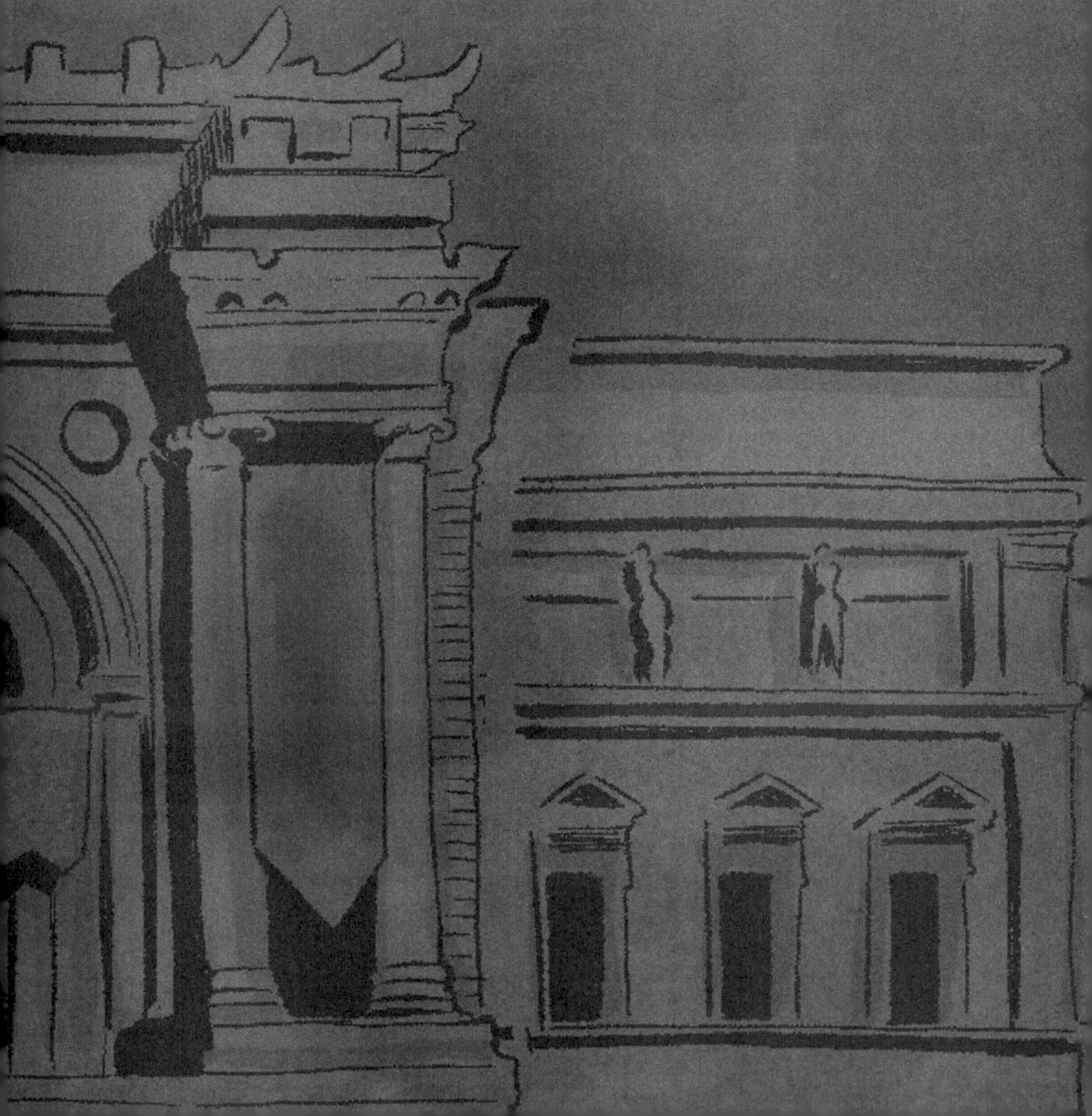

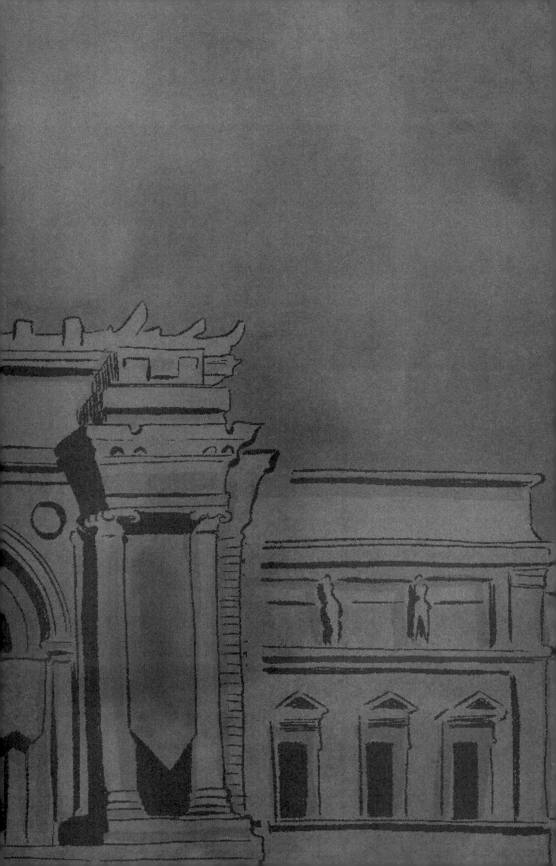

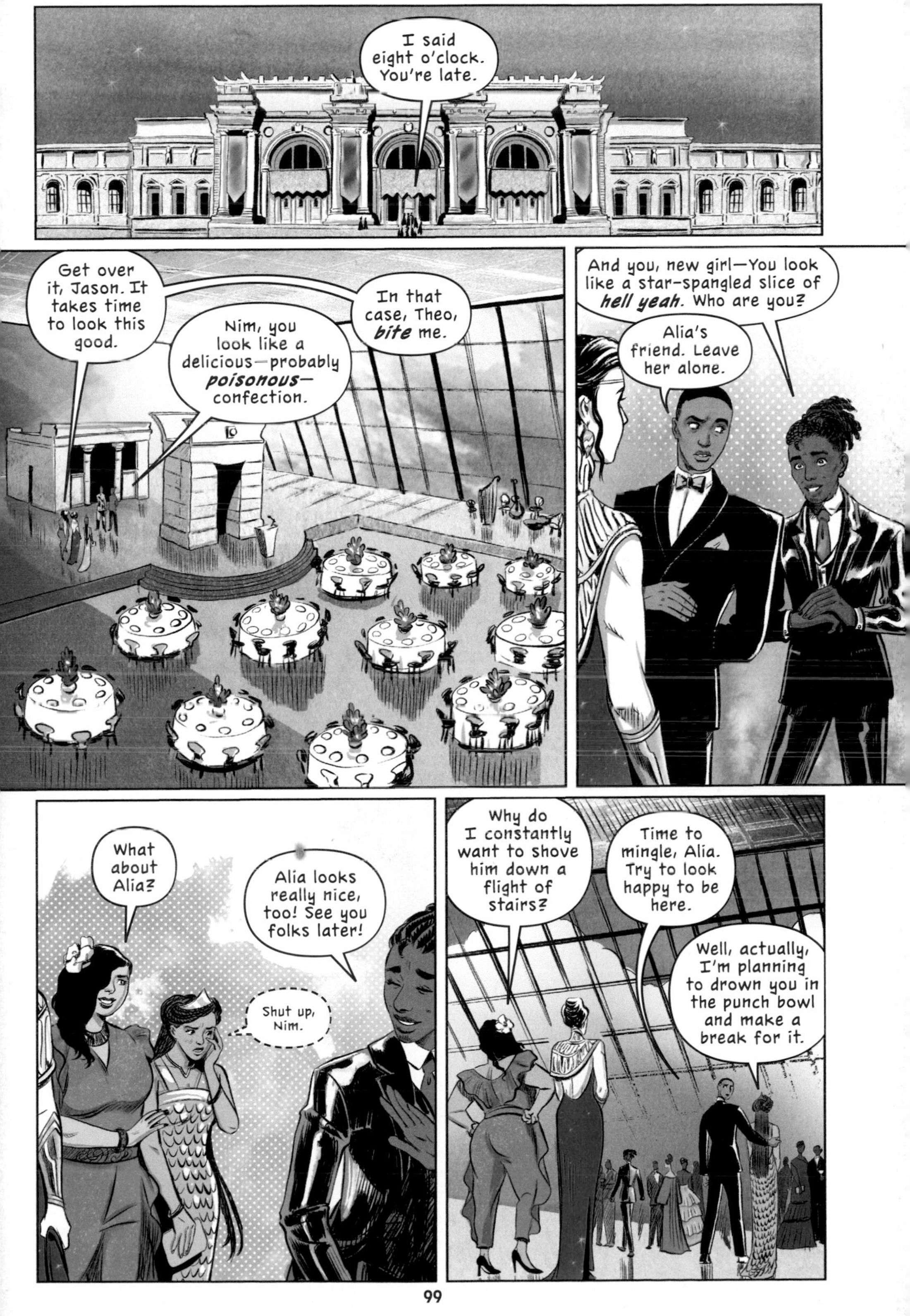
I said eight o'clock. You're late.
Get over it, Jason. It takes time to look this good.
In that case, Theo, bite me.
Nim, you look like a delicious—probably poisonous—confection.
And you, new girl—You look like a star-spangled slice of hell yeah. Who are you?
Alia's friend. Leave her alone.
What about Alia?
Alia looks really nice, too! See you folks later!
Shut up, Nim.
Why do I constantly want to shove him down a flight of stairs?
Time to mingle, Alia. Try to look happy to be here.
Well, actually, I'm planning to drown you in the punch bowl and make a break for it.

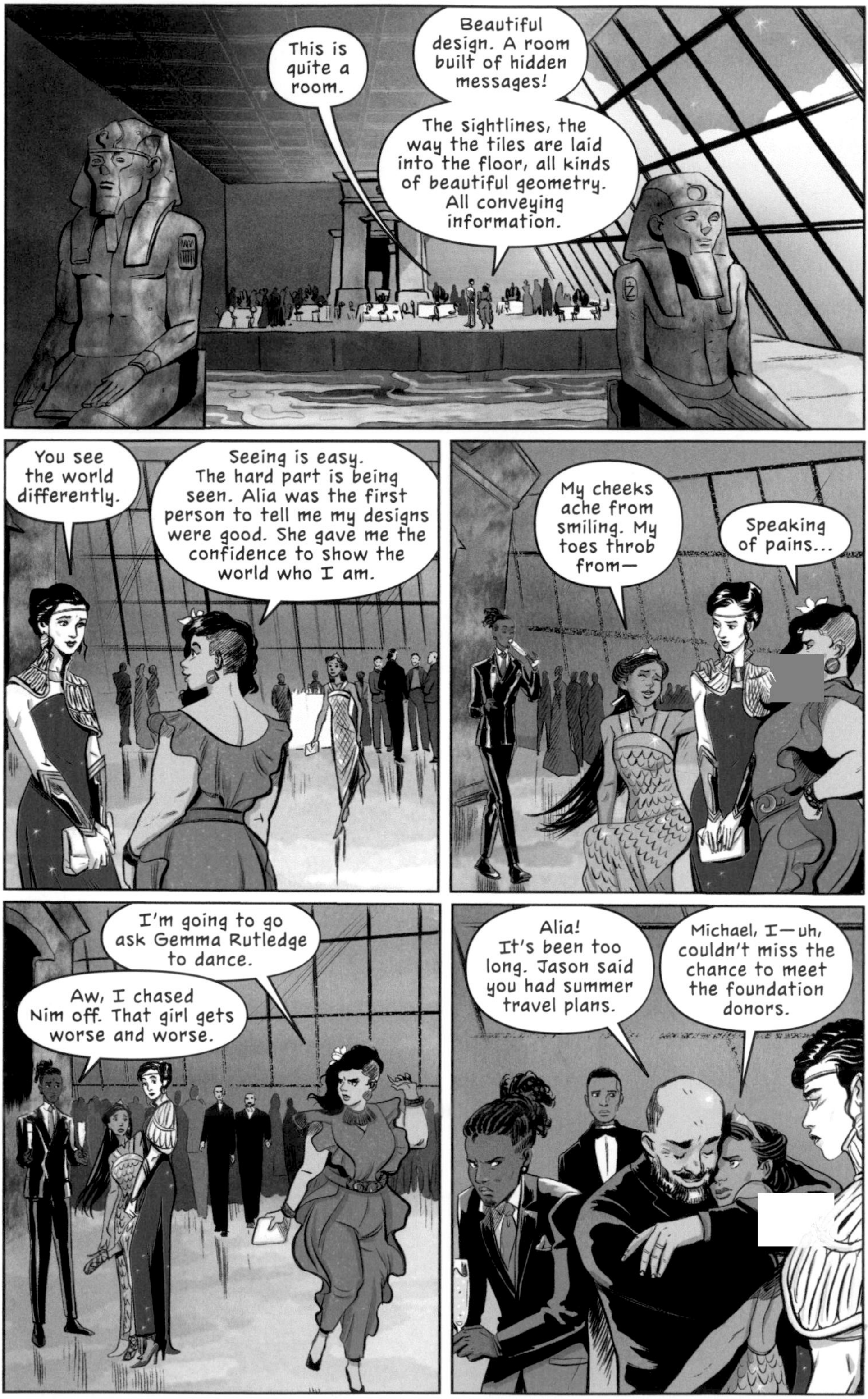
This is quite a room.
Beautiful design. A room built of hidden messages!
The sightlines, the way the tiles are laid into the floor, all kinds of beautiful geometry. All conveying information.
You see the world differently.
Seeing is easy. The hard part is being seen. Alia was the first person to tell me my designs were good. She gave me the confidence to show the world who I am.
My cheeks ache from smiling. My toes throb from—
Speaking of pains...
I'm going to go ask Gemma Rutledge to dance.
Aw, I chased Nim off. That girl gets worse and worse.
Alia! It's been too long. Jason said you had summer travel plans.
Michael, I—uh, couldn't miss the chance to meet the foundation donors.

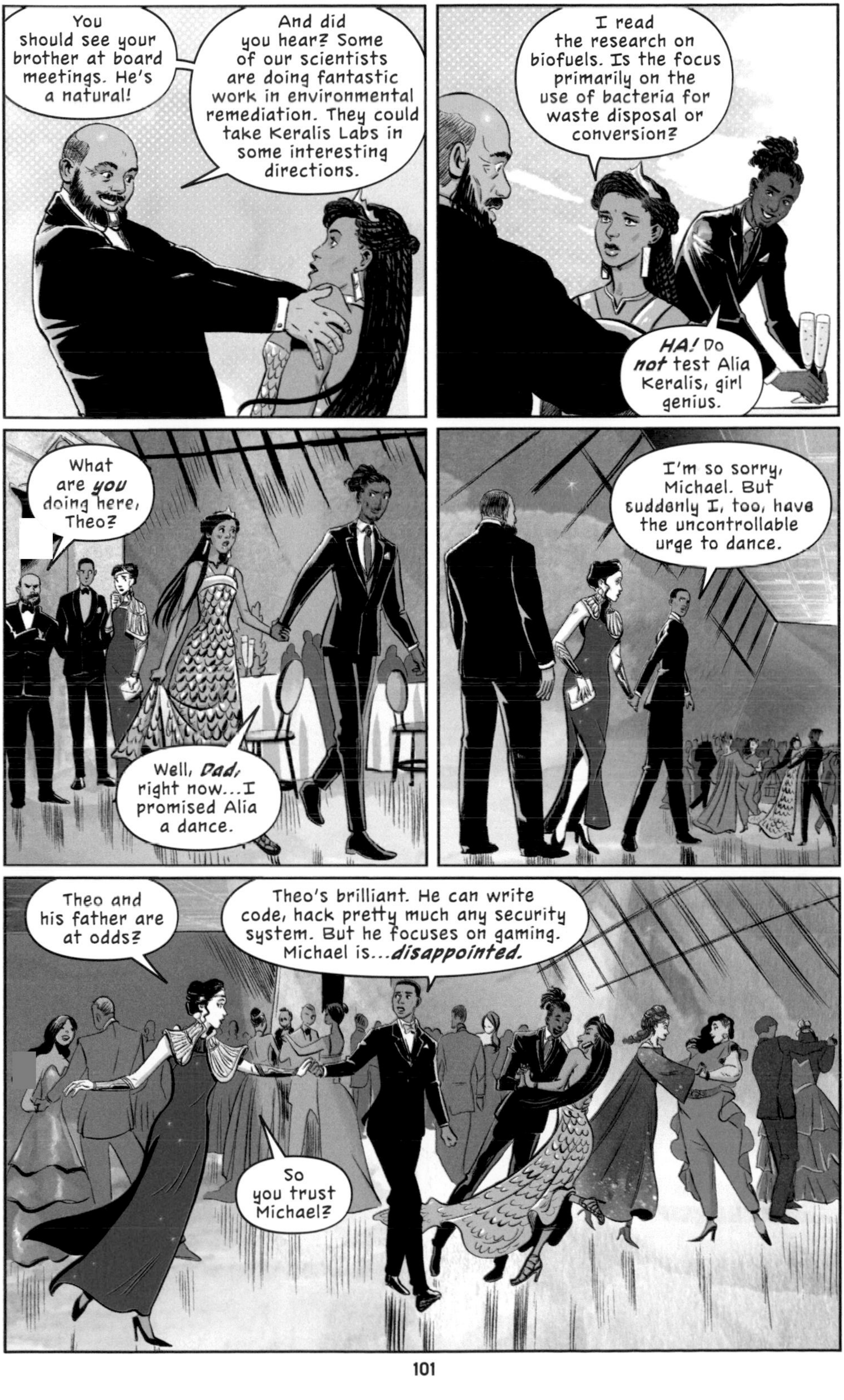
You should see your brother at board meetings. He's a natural!
And did you hear? Some of our scientists are doing fantastic work in environmental remediation. They could take Keralis Labs in some interesting directions.
I read the research on biofuels. Is the focus primarily on the use of bacteria for waste disposal or conversion?
HA! Do *not* test Alia Keralis, girl genius.
What are *you* doing here, Theo?
Well, *Dad*, right now...I promised Alia a dance.
I'm so sorry, Michael. But suddenly I, too, have the uncontrollable urge to dance.
Theo and his father are at odds?
Theo's brilliant. He can write code, hack pretty much any security system. But he focuses on gaming. Michael is...*disappointed.*
So you trust Michael?

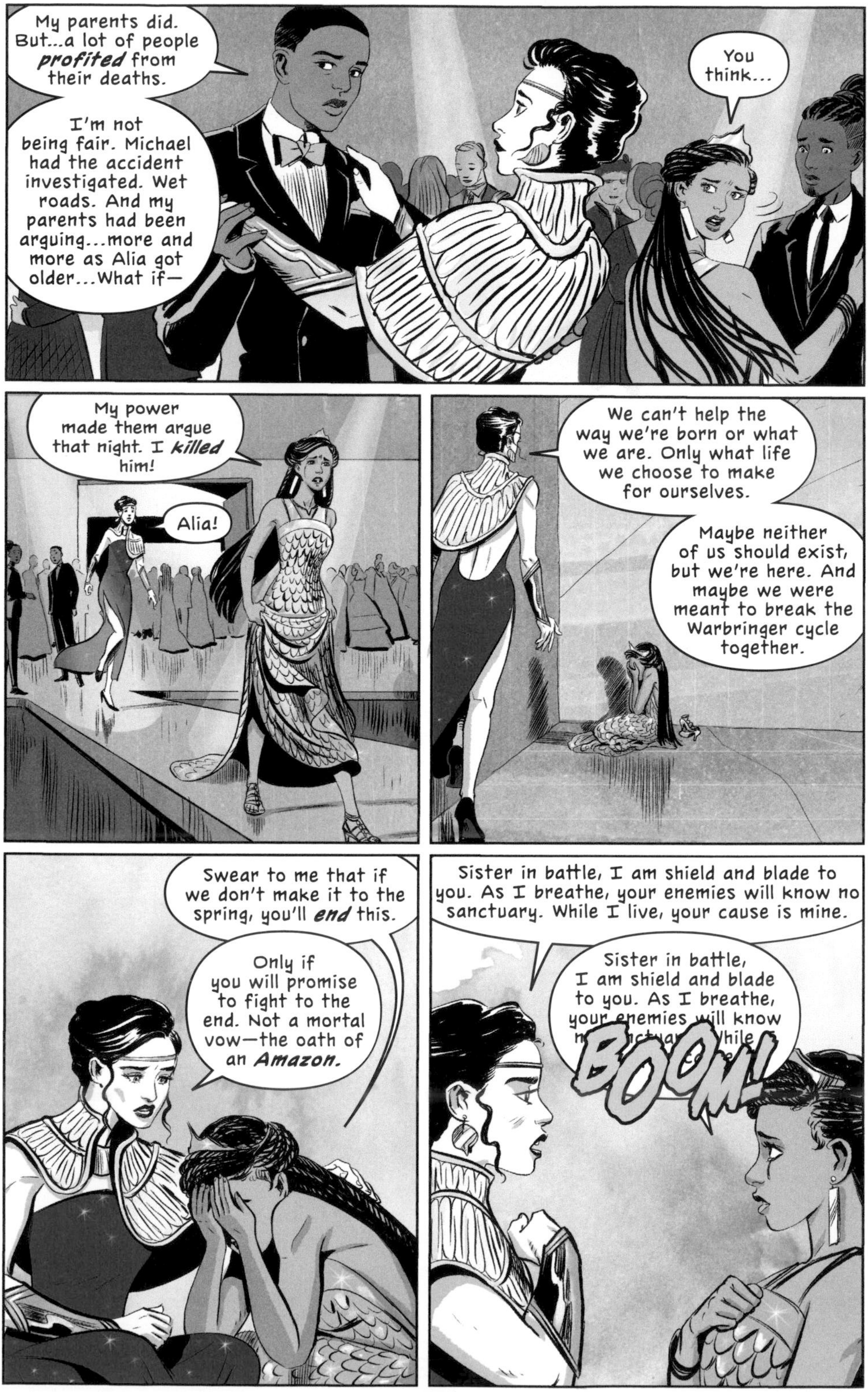
My parents did. But...a lot of people **profited** from their deaths.
I'm not being fair. Michael had the accident investigated. Wet roads. And my parents had been arguing...more and more as Alia got older...What if—
You think...
My power made them argue that night. I **killed** him!
Alia!
We can't help the way we're born or what we are. Only what life we choose to make for ourselves.
Maybe neither of us should exist, but we're here. And maybe we were meant to break the Warbringer cycle together.
Swear to me that if we don't make it to the spring, you'll **end** this.
Only if you will promise to fight to the end. Not a mortal vow—the oath of an **Amazon.**
Sister in battle, I am shield and blade to you. As I breathe, your enemies will know no sanctuary. While I live, your cause is mine.
Sister in battle, I am shield and blade to you. As I breathe, your enemies will know
BOOM!

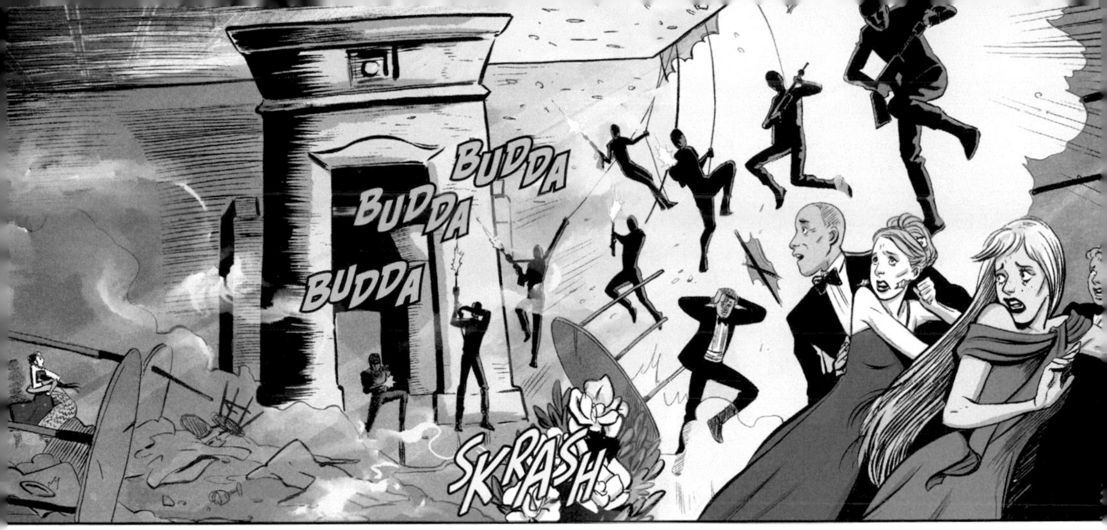
BUDDA
BUDDA
BUDDA
SKRASH

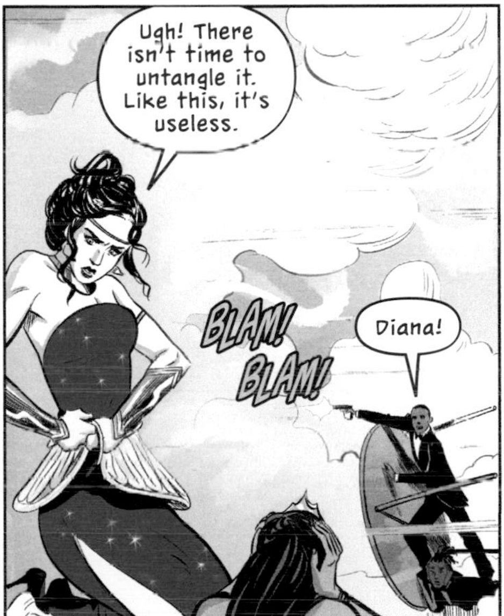
Ugh! There isn't time to untangle it. Like this, it's useless.
BLAM!
BLAM!
Diana!

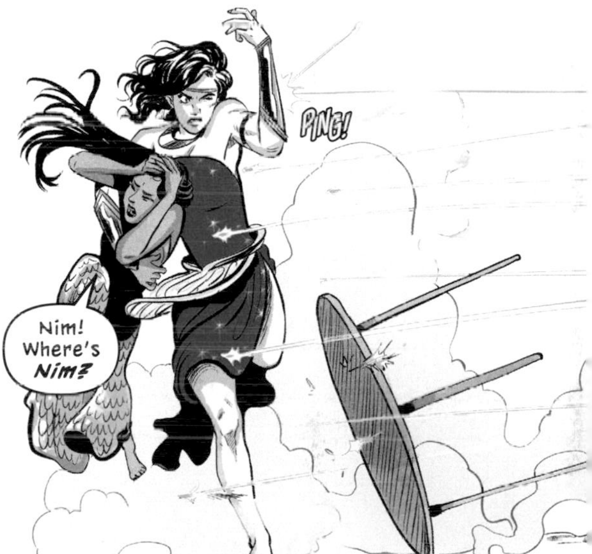
PING!
Nim! Where's *Nim?*

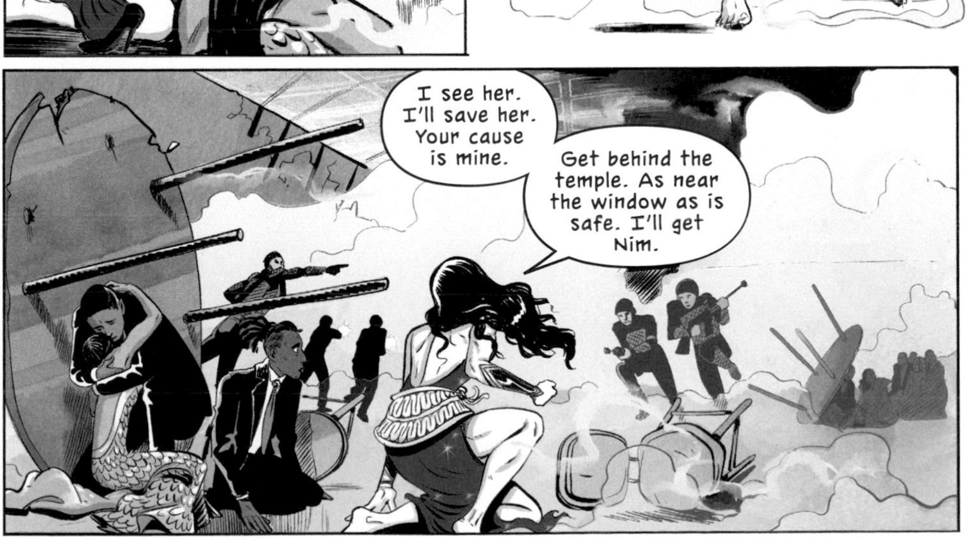
I see her. I'll save her. Your cause is mine.
Get behind the temple. As near the window as is safe. I'll get Nim.

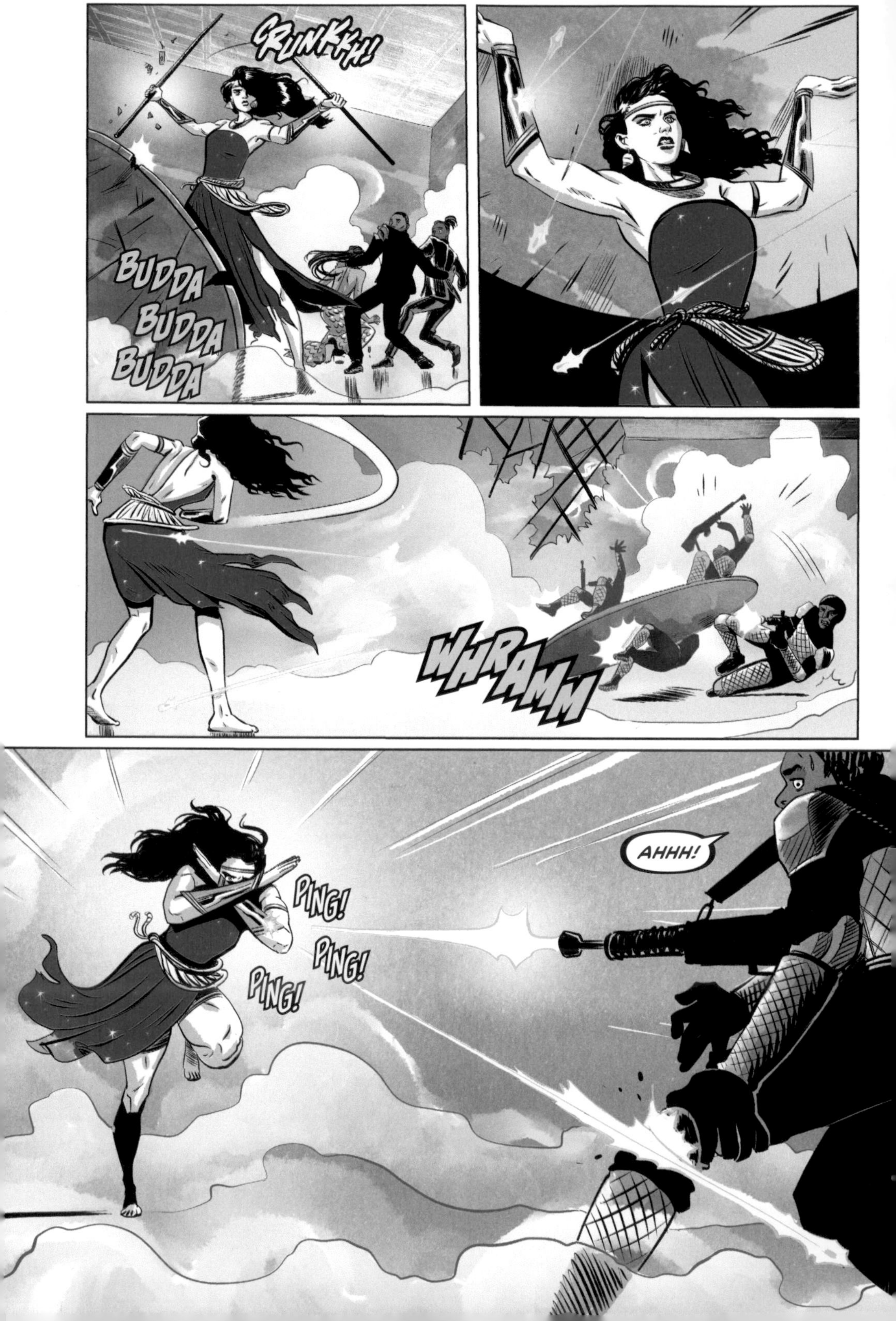
CRUNKKH!
BUDDA
BUDDA
BUDDA
WHRAMM
AHHH!
PING!
PING!
PING!

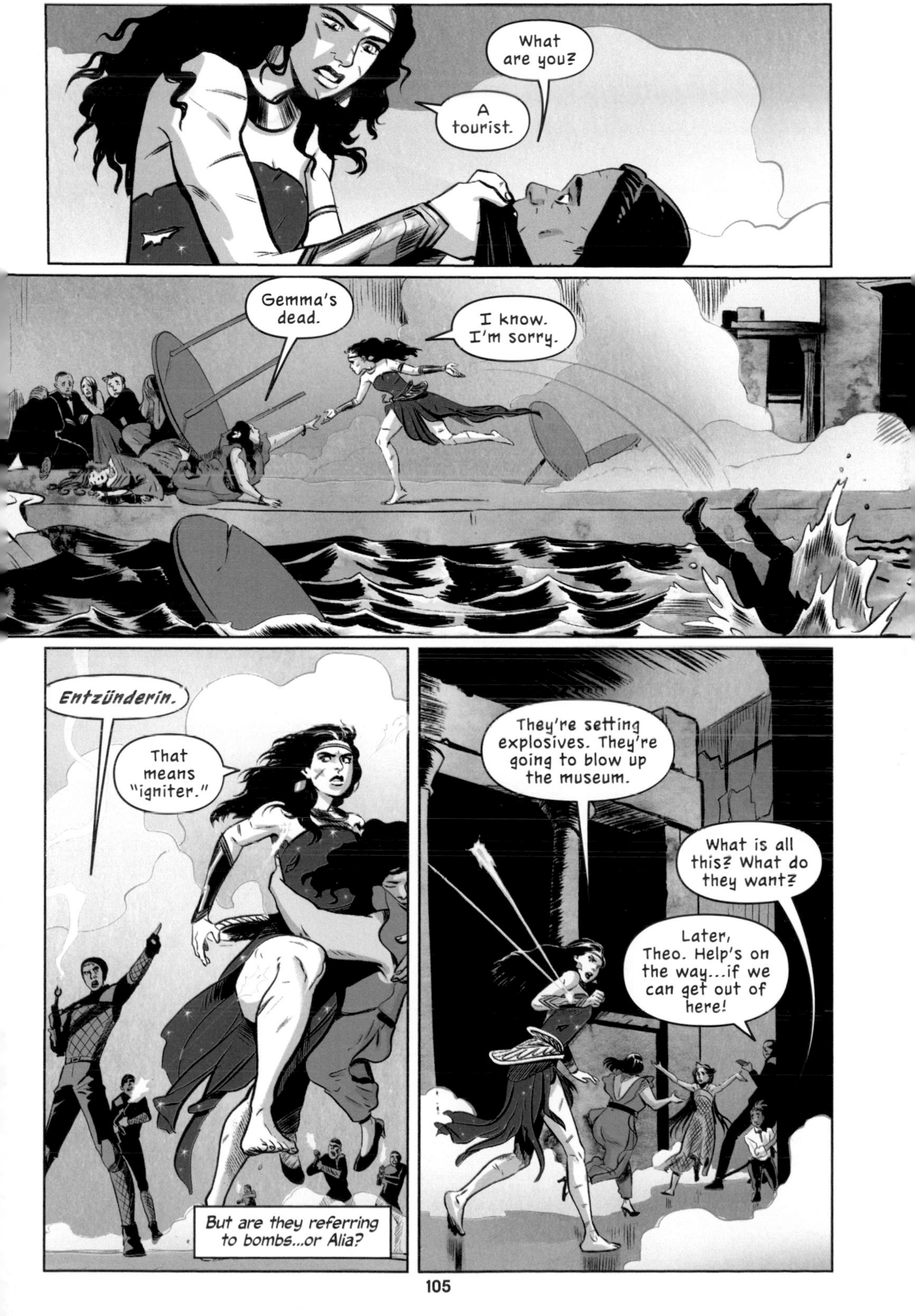
What are you?
A tourist.
Gemma's dead.
I know. I'm sorry.
Entzünderin.
That means "igniter."
But are they referring to bombs...or Alia?
They're setting explosives. They're going to blow up the museum.
What is all this? What do they want?
Later, Theo. Help's on the way...if we can get out of here!

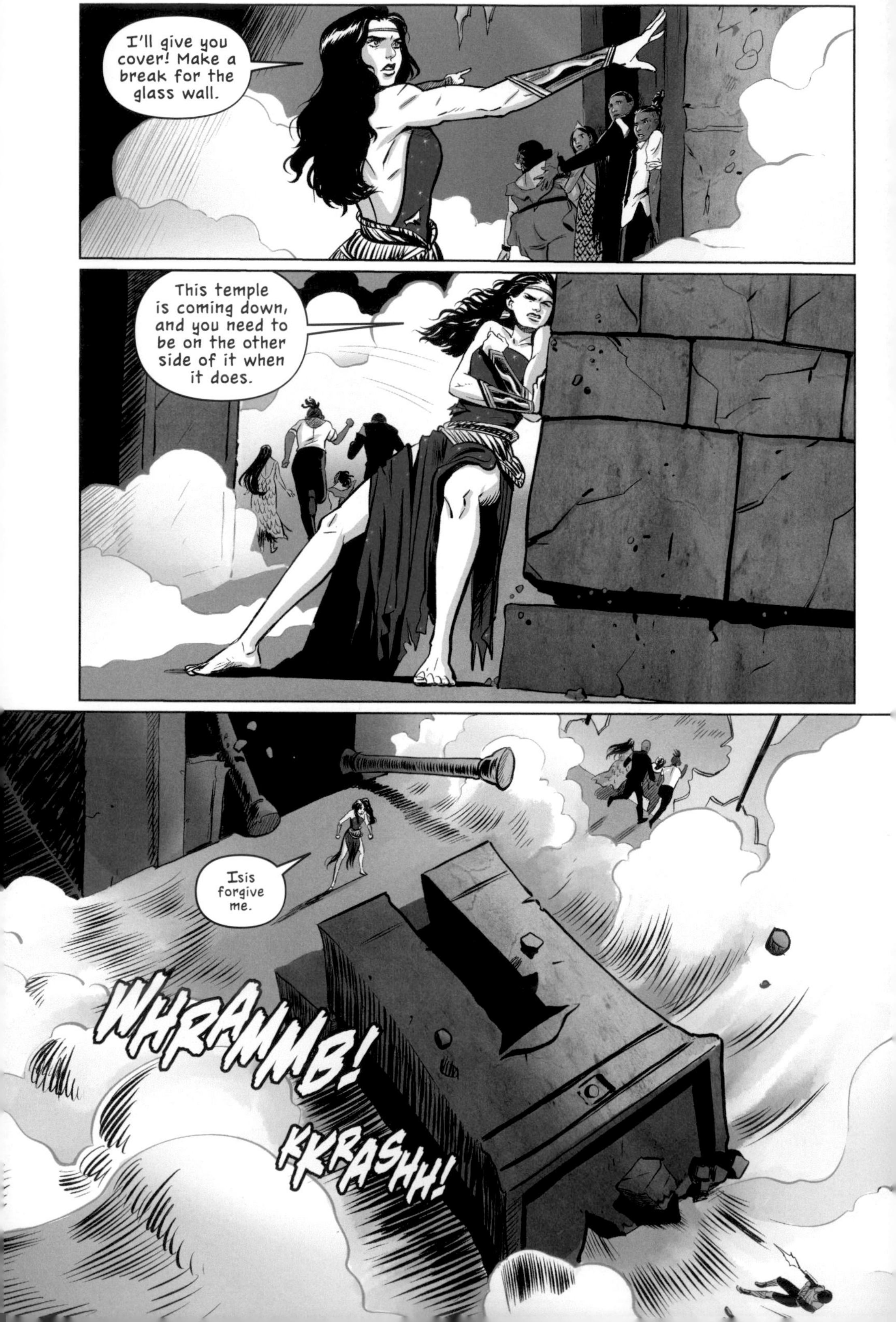
I'll give you cover! Make a break for the glass wall.
This temple is coming down, and you need to be on the other side of it when it does.
Isis forgive me.
WHRAMMB!
KKRASHH!

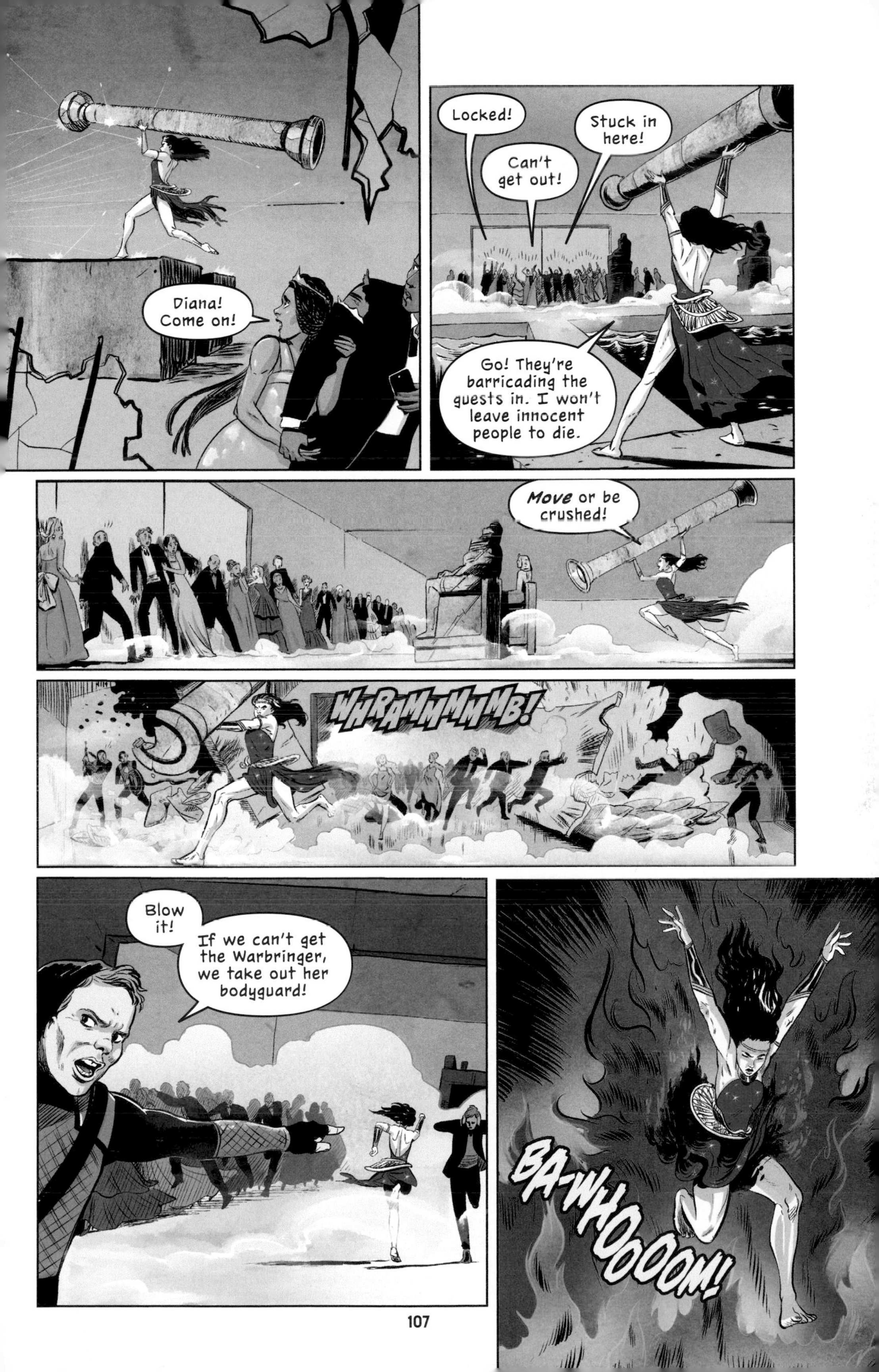

Diana! Come on!
Locked!
Can't get out!
Stuck in here!
Go! They're barricading the guests in. I won't leave innocent people to die.
Move or be crushed!
WHRAMMMMMB!
Blow it!
If we can't get the Warbringer, we take out her bodyguard!
BA-WHOOOOM!

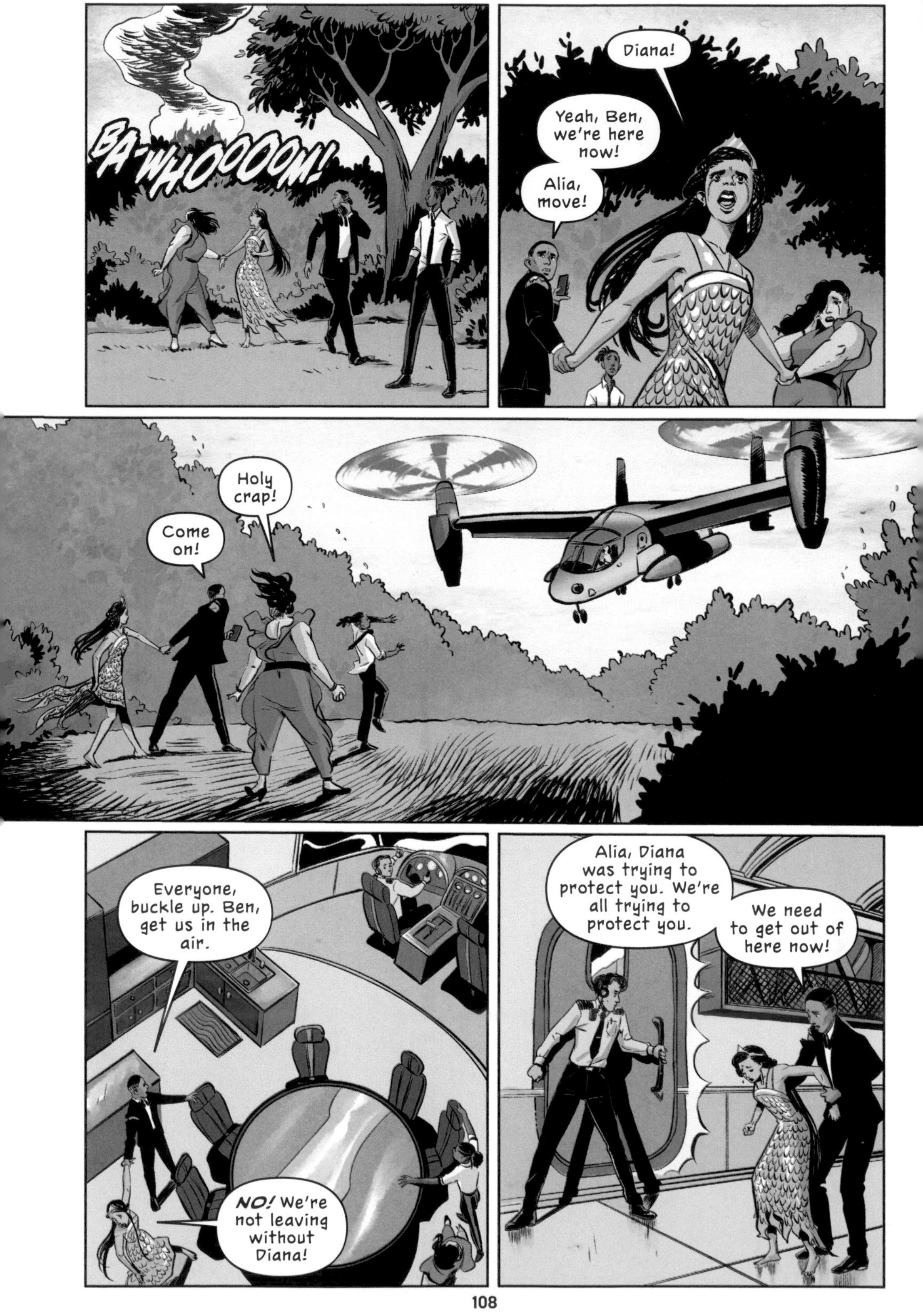
BA-WHOOOOM!
Diana!
Yeah, Ben, we're here now!
Alia, move!
Holy crap!
Come on!
Everyone, buckle up. Ben, get us in the air.
NO! We're not leaving without Diana!
Alia, Diana was trying to protect you. We're all trying to protect you.
We need to get out of here now!

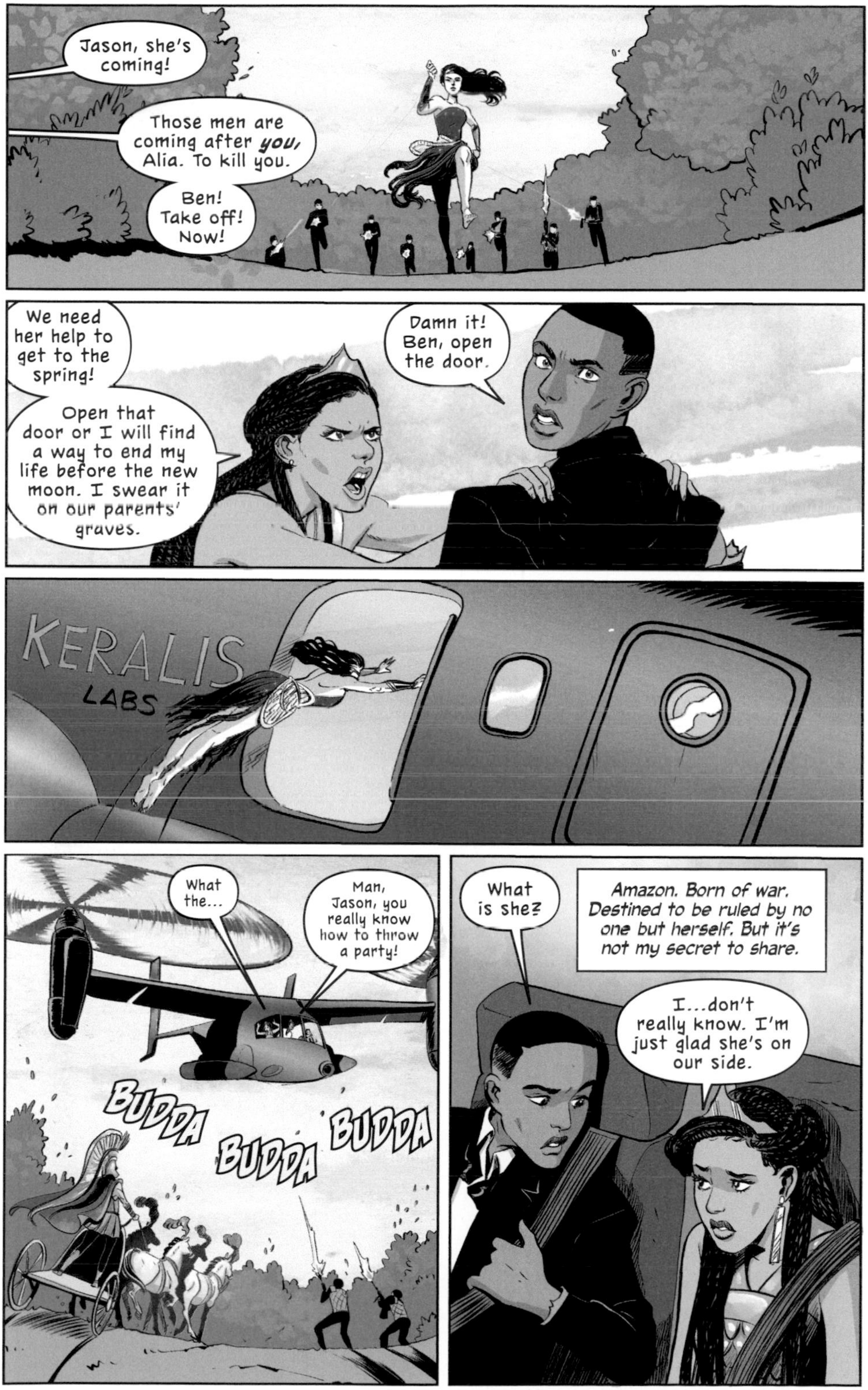
Jason, she's coming!
Those men are coming after *you,* Alia. To kill you.
Ben! Take off! Now!
We need her help to get to the spring!
Open that door or I will find a way to end my life before the new moon. I swear it on our parents' graves.
Damn it! Ben, open the door.
KERALIS LABS
What the...
Man, Jason, you really know how to throw a party!
BUDDA BUDDA BUDDA
What is she?
Amazon. Born of war. Destined to be ruled by no one but herself. But it's not my secret to share.
I...don't really know. I'm just glad she's on our side.

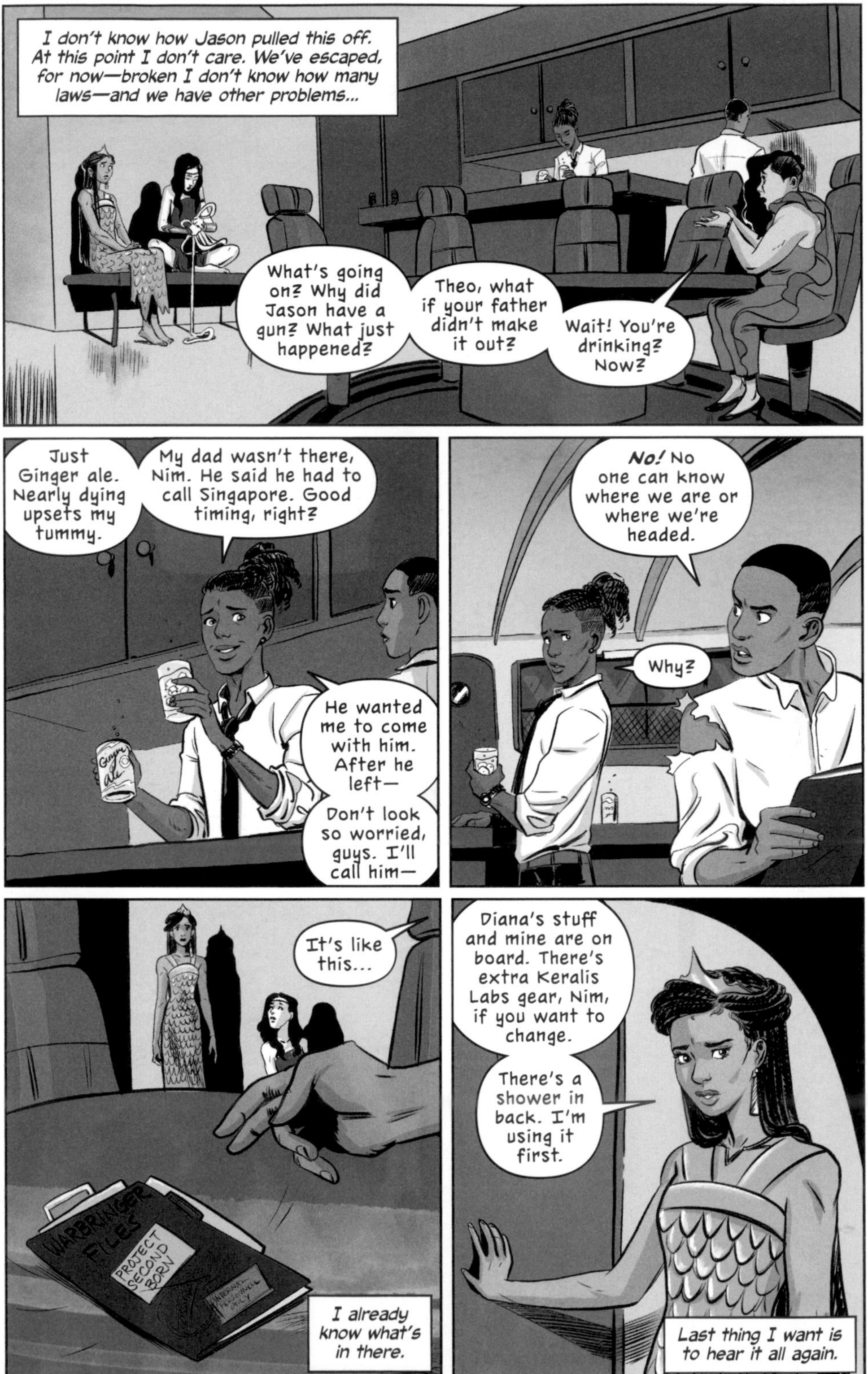

I don't know how Jason pulled this off. At this point I don't care. We've escaped, for now—broken I don't know how many laws—and we have other problems...
What's going on? Why did Jason have a gun? What just happened?
Theo, what if your father didn't make it out?
Wait! You're drinking? Now?
Just Ginger ale. Nearly dying upsets my tummy.
My dad wasn't there, Nim. He said he had to call Singapore. Good timing, right?
He wanted me to come with him. After he left—
Don't look so worried, guys. I'll call him—
No! No one can know where we are or where we're headed.
Why?
It's like this...
WARBRINGER FILES
PROJECT SECOND BORN
I already know what's in there.
Diana's stuff and mine are on board. There's extra Keralis Labs gear, Nim, if you want to change.
There's a shower in back. I'm using it first.
Last thing I want is to hear it all again.

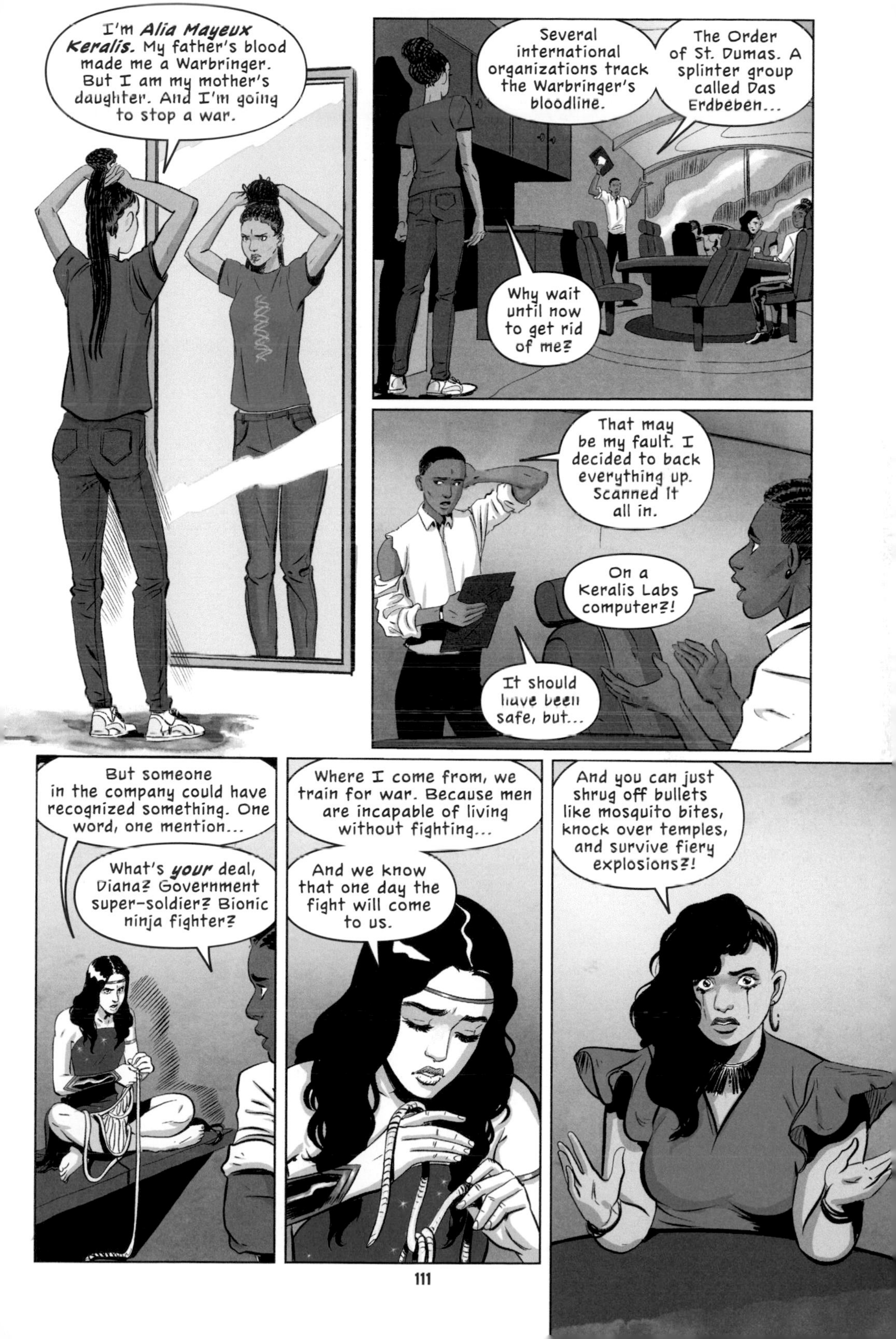
I'm *Alia Mayeux Keralis.* My father's blood made me a Warbringer. But I am my mother's daughter. And I'm going to stop a war.
Several international organizations track the Warbringer's bloodline.
The Order of St. Dumas. A splinter group called Das Erdbeben...
Why wait until now to get rid of me?
That may be my fault. I decided to back everything up. Scanned it all in.
On a Keralis Labs computer?!
It should have been safe, but...
But someone in the company could have recognized something. One word, one mention...
What's *your* deal, Diana? Government super-soldier? Bionic ninja fighter?
Where I come from, we train for war. Because men are incapable of living without fighting...
And we know that one day the fight will come to us.
And you can just shrug off bullets like mosquito bites, knock over temples, and survive fiery explosions?!

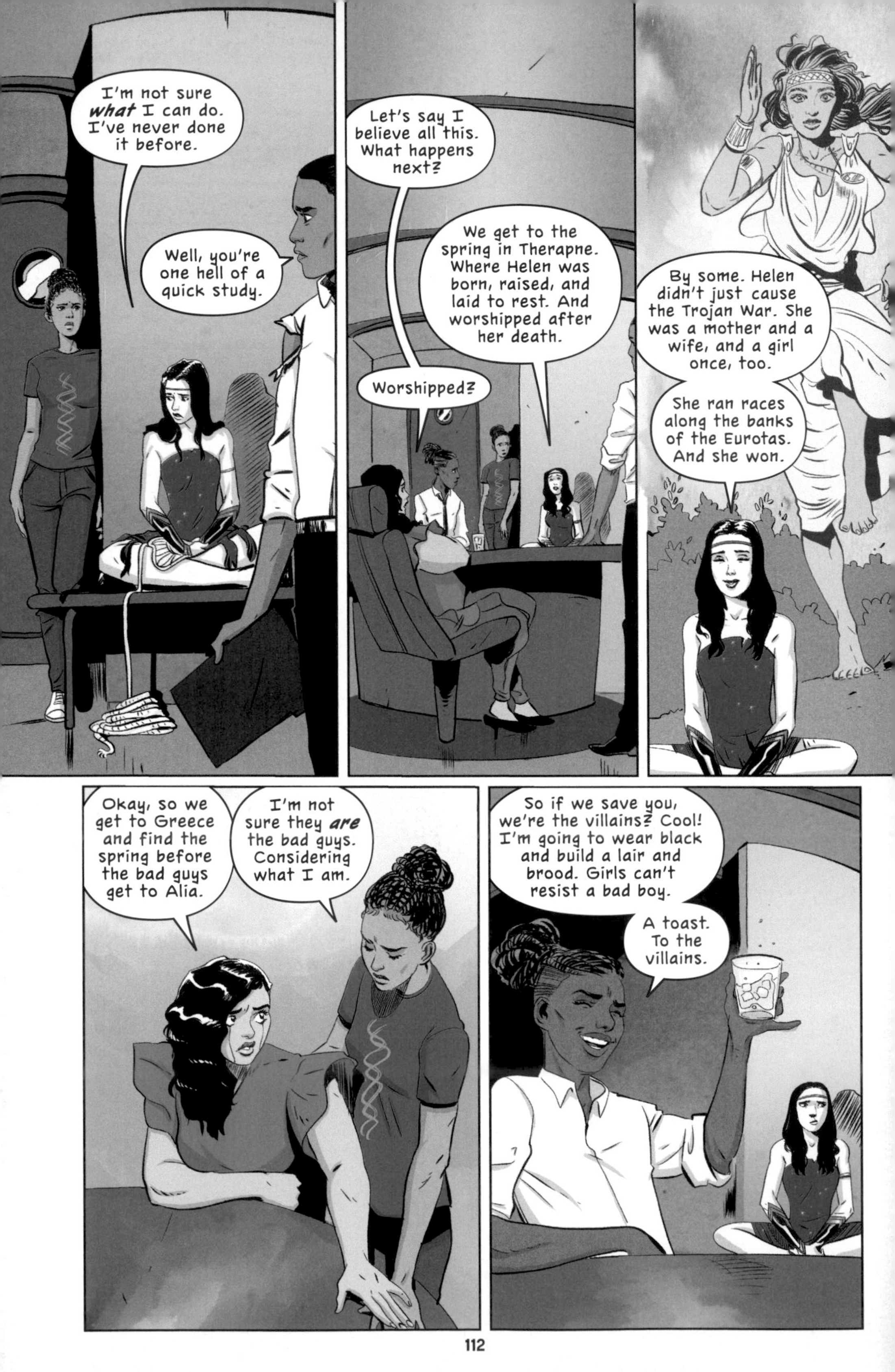

I'm not sure *what* I can do. I've never done it before.
Well, you're one hell of a quick study.
Let's say I believe all this. What happens next?
We get to the spring in Therapne. Where Helen was born, raised, and laid to rest. And worshipped after her death.
Worshipped?
By some. Helen didn't just cause the Trojan War. She was a mother and a wife, and a girl once, too.
She ran races along the banks of the Eurotas. And she won.
Okay, so we get to Greece and find the spring before the bad guys get to Alia.
I'm not sure they *are* the bad guys. Considering what I am.
So if we save you, we're the villains? Cool! I'm going to wear black and build a lair and brood. Girls can't resist a bad boy.
A toast. To the villains.

PART FIVE

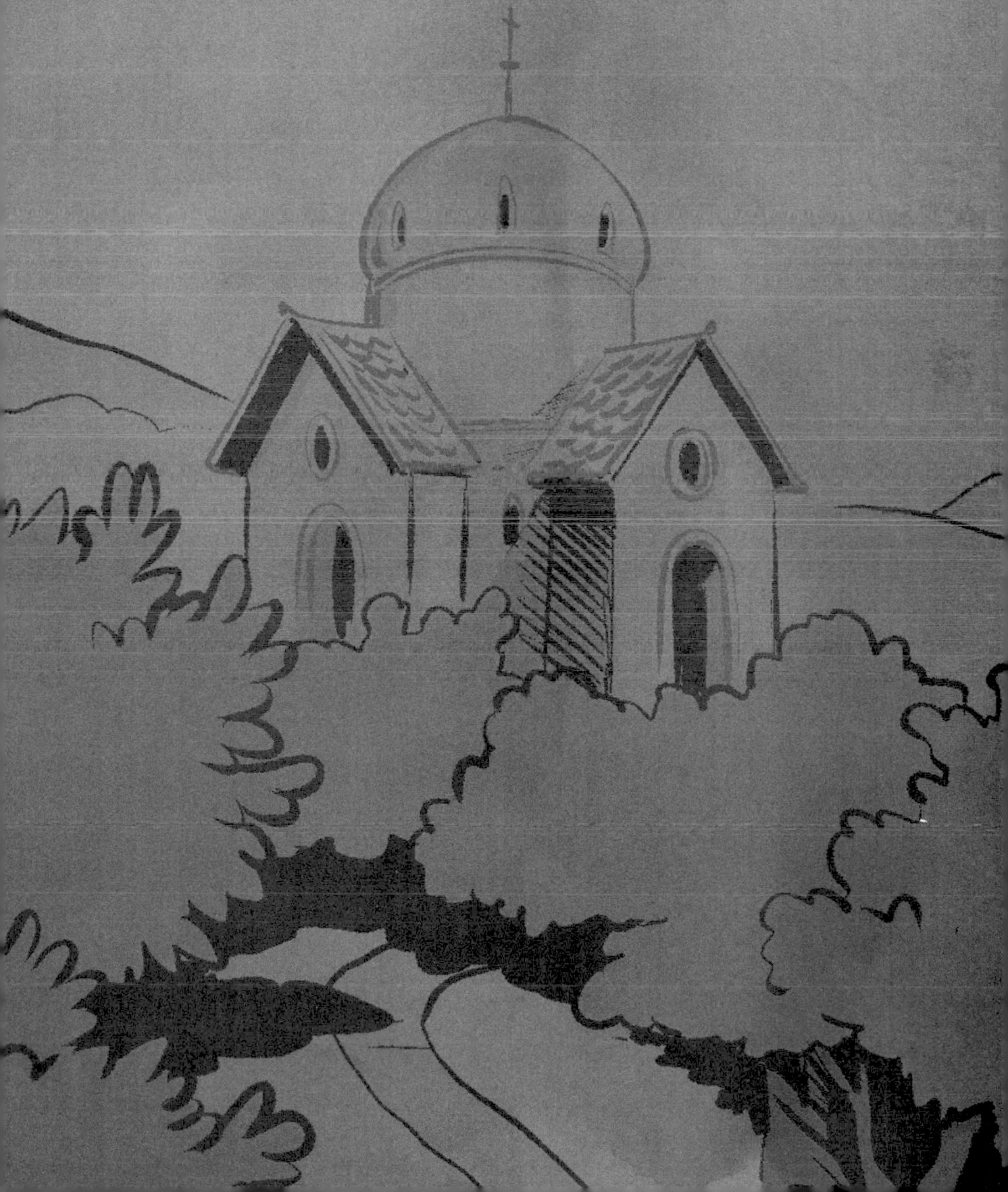

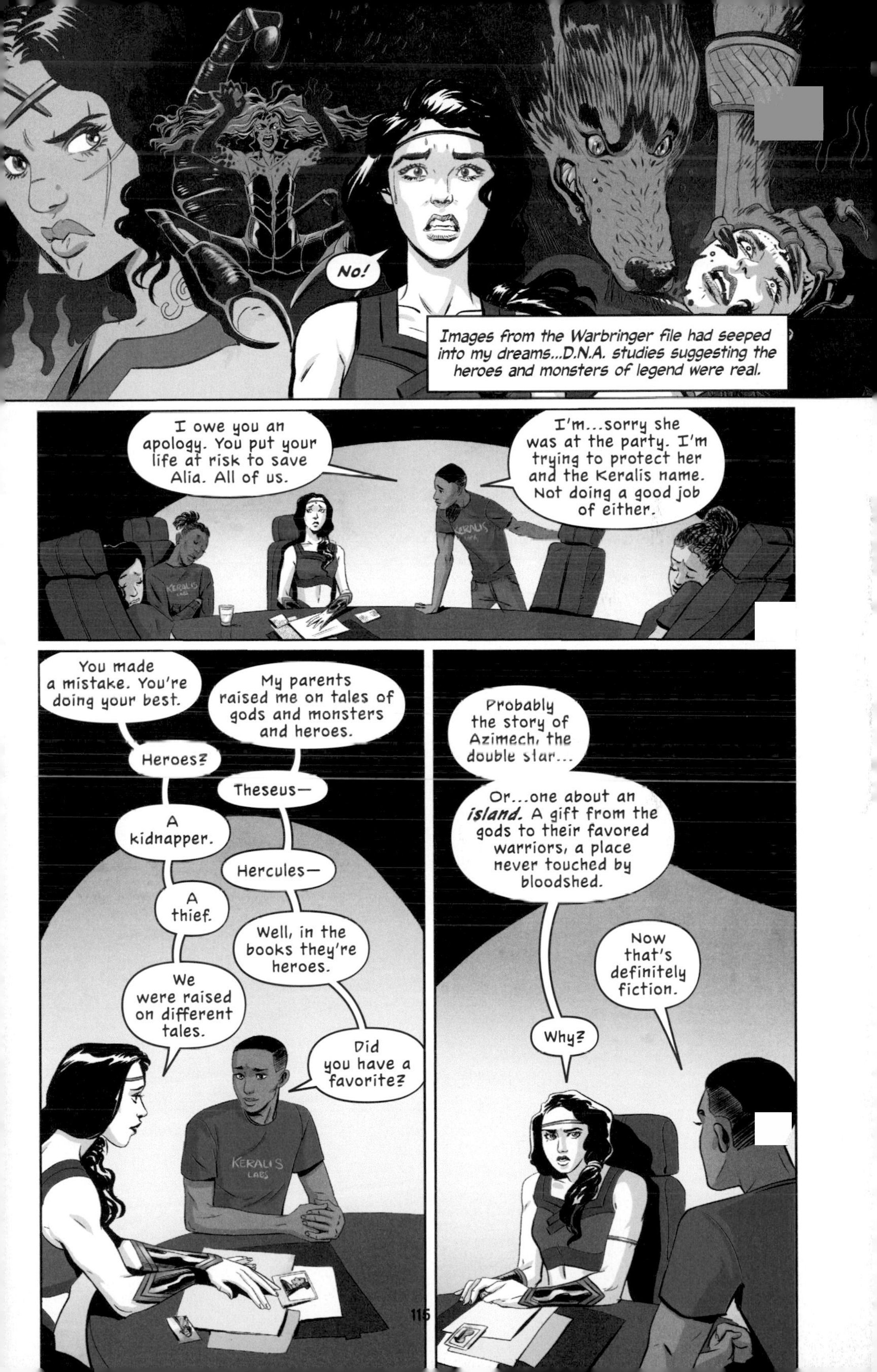
No!
Images from the Warbringer file had seeped into my dreams...D.N.A. studies suggesting the heroes and monsters of legend were real.
I owe you an apology. You put your life at risk to save Alia. All of us.
I'm...sorry she was at the party. I'm trying to protect her and the Keralis name. Not doing a good job of either.
You made a mistake. You're doing your best.
My parents raised me on tales of gods and monsters and heroes.
Heroes?
Theseus—
A kidnapper.
Hercules—
A thief.
Well, in the books they're heroes.
We were raised on different tales.
Did you have a favorite?
Probably the story of Azimech, the double star...
Or...one about an *island.* A gift from the gods to their favored warriors, a place never touched by bloodshed.
Now that's definitely fiction.
Why?

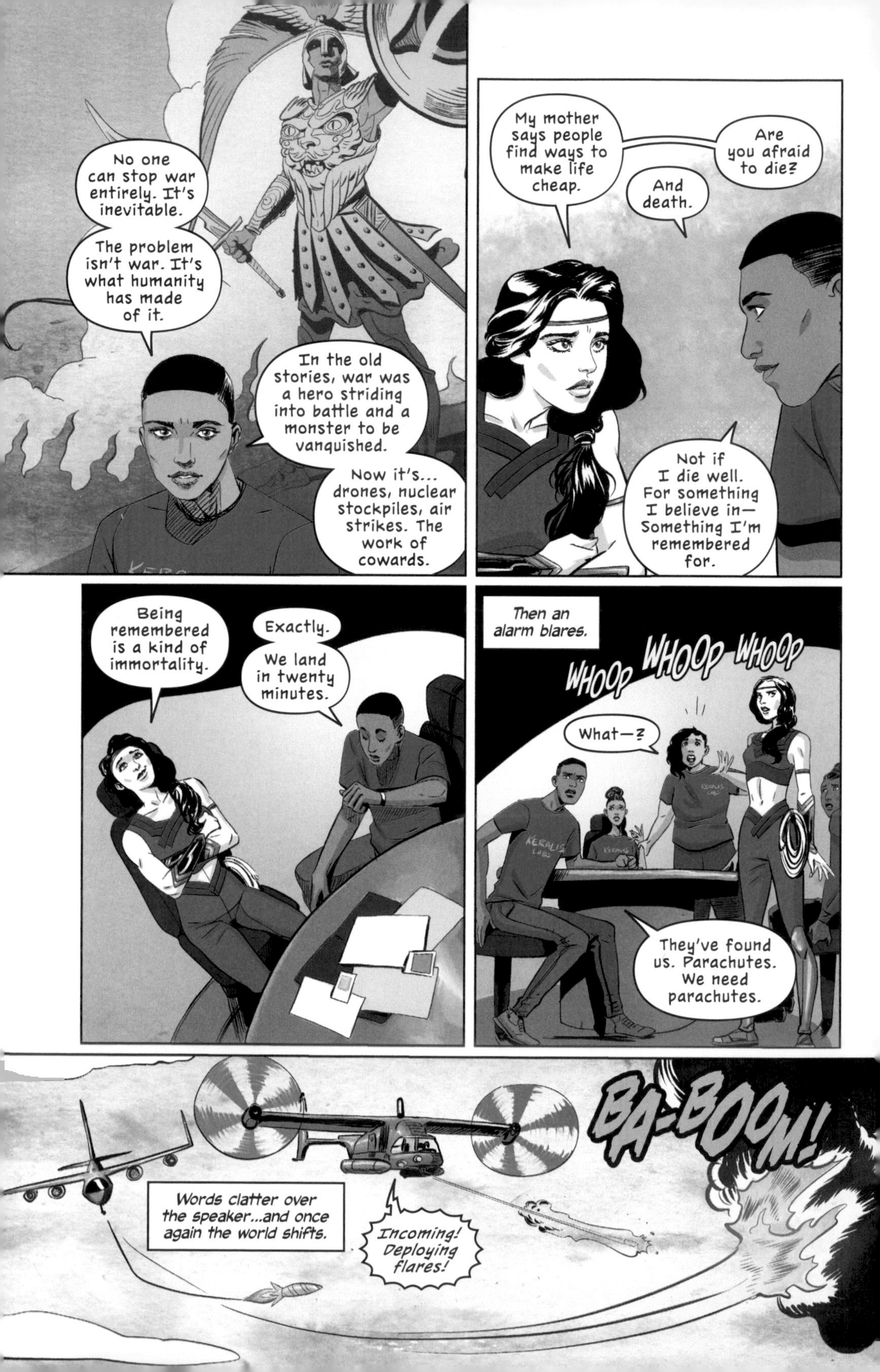
No one can stop war entirely. It's inevitable.
The problem isn't war. It's what humanity has made of it.
In the old stories, war was a hero striding into battle and a monster to be vanquished.
Now it's... drones, nuclear stockpiles, air strikes. The work of cowards.
My mother says people find ways to make life cheap.
And death.
Are you afraid to die?
Not if I die well. For something I believe in— Something I'm remembered for.
Being remembered is a kind of immortality.
Exactly.
We land in twenty minutes.
Then an alarm blares.
WHOOP WHOOP WHOOP
What—?
They've found us. Parachutes. We need parachutes.
Words clatter over the speaker...and once again the world shifts.
Incoming! Deploying flares!
BA-BOOM!

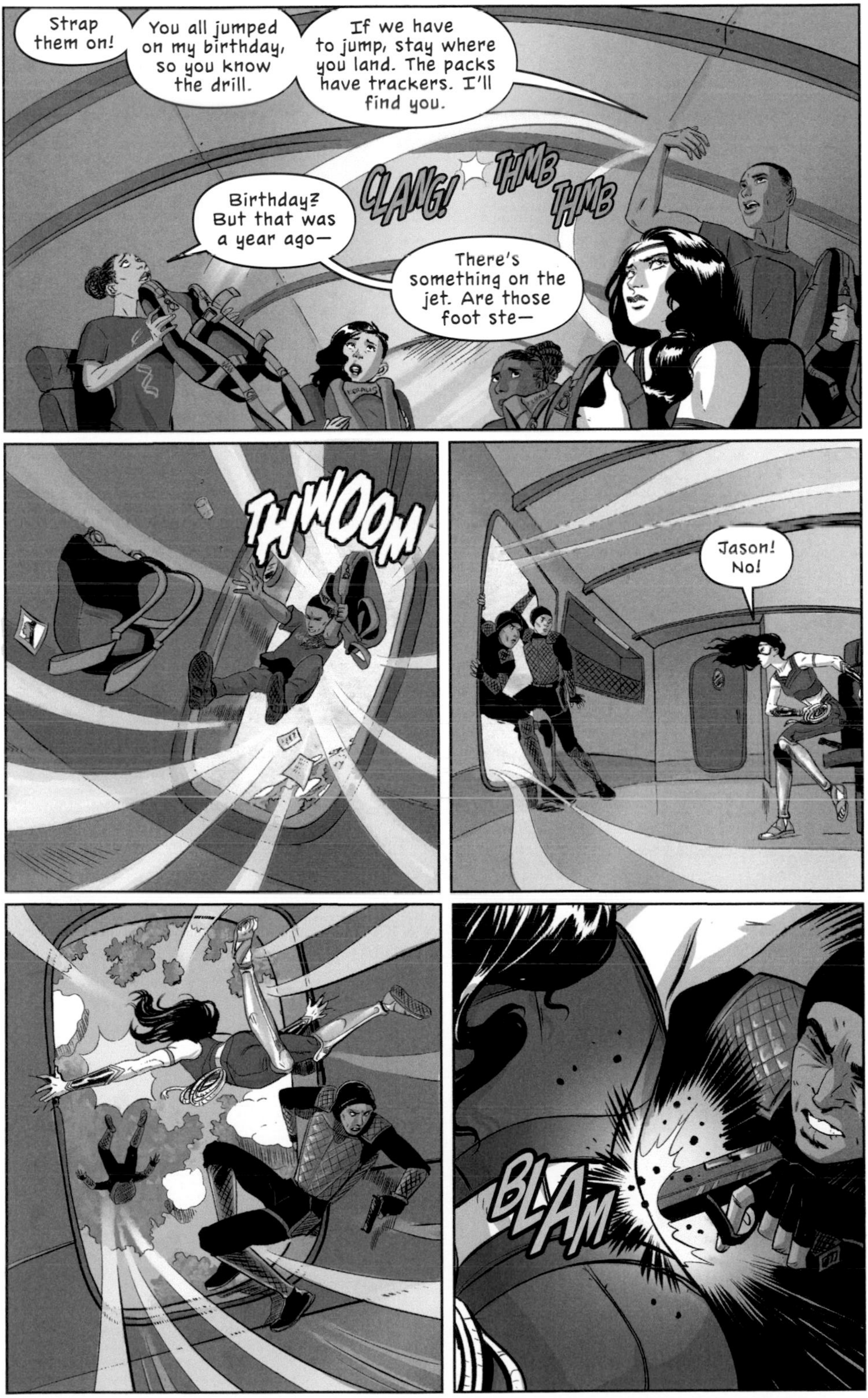
Strap them on!
You all jumped on my birthday, so you know the drill.
If we have to jump, stay where you land. The packs have trackers. I'll find you.
CLANG!
THMB THMB
Birthday? But that was a year ago—
There's something on the jet. Are those foot ste—
THWOOM
Jason! No!
BLAM

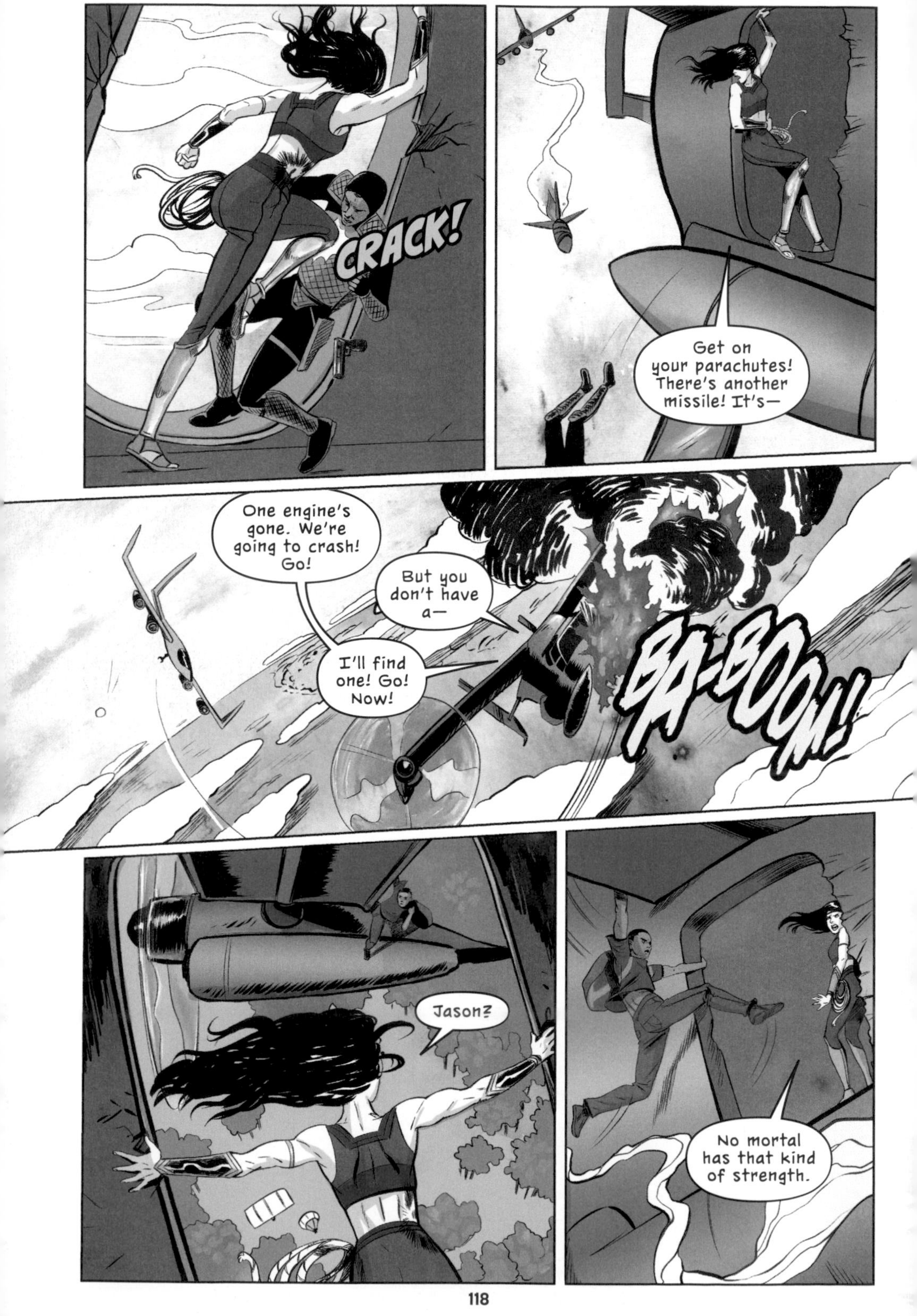
CRACK!
Get on your parachutes! There's another missile! It's—
One engine's gone. We're going to crash! Go!
But you don't have a—
I'll find one! Go! Now!
BA-BOOM!
Jason?
No mortal has that kind of strength.

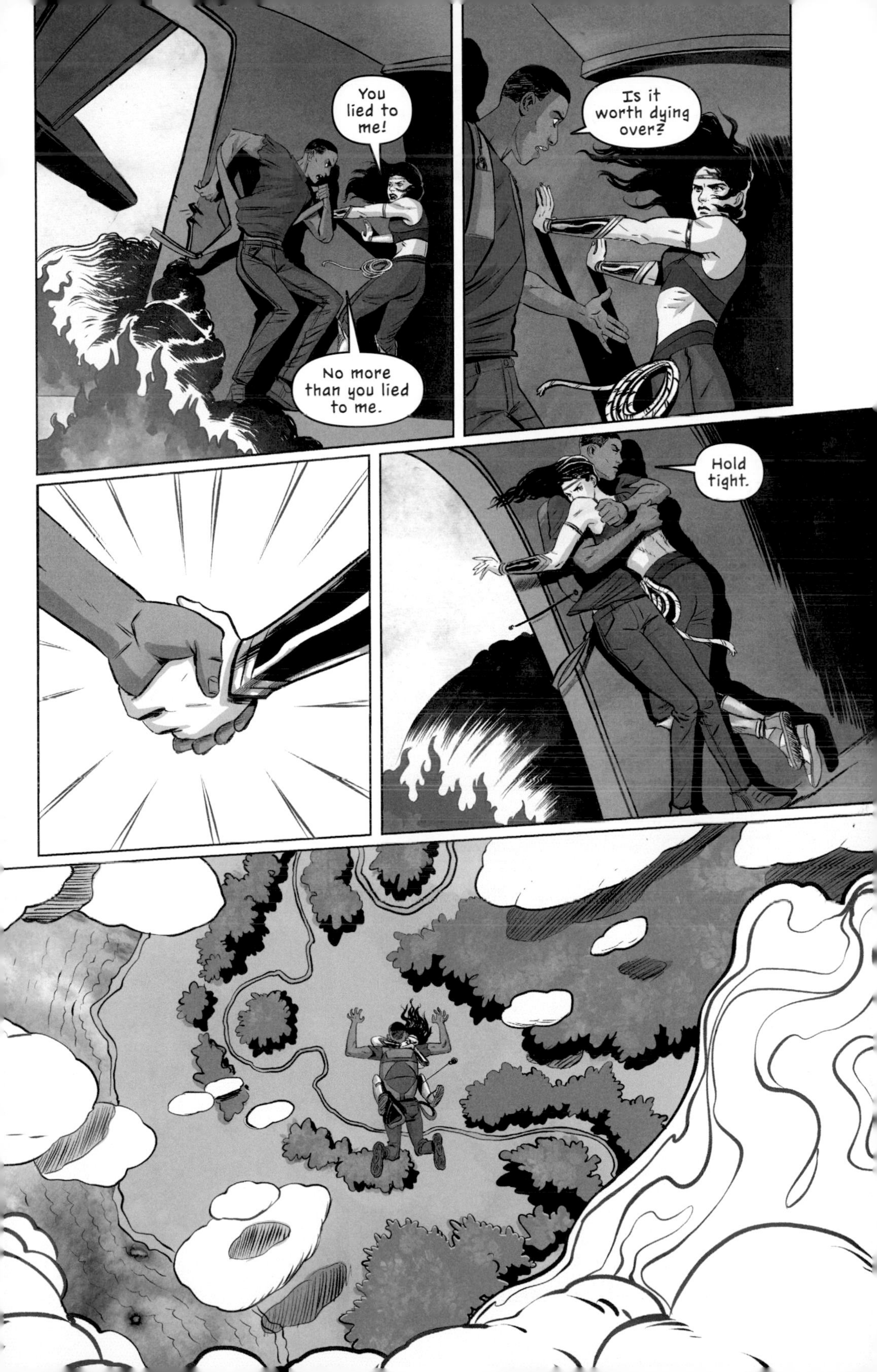
You lied to me!
No more than you lied to me.
Is it worth dying over?
Hold tight.

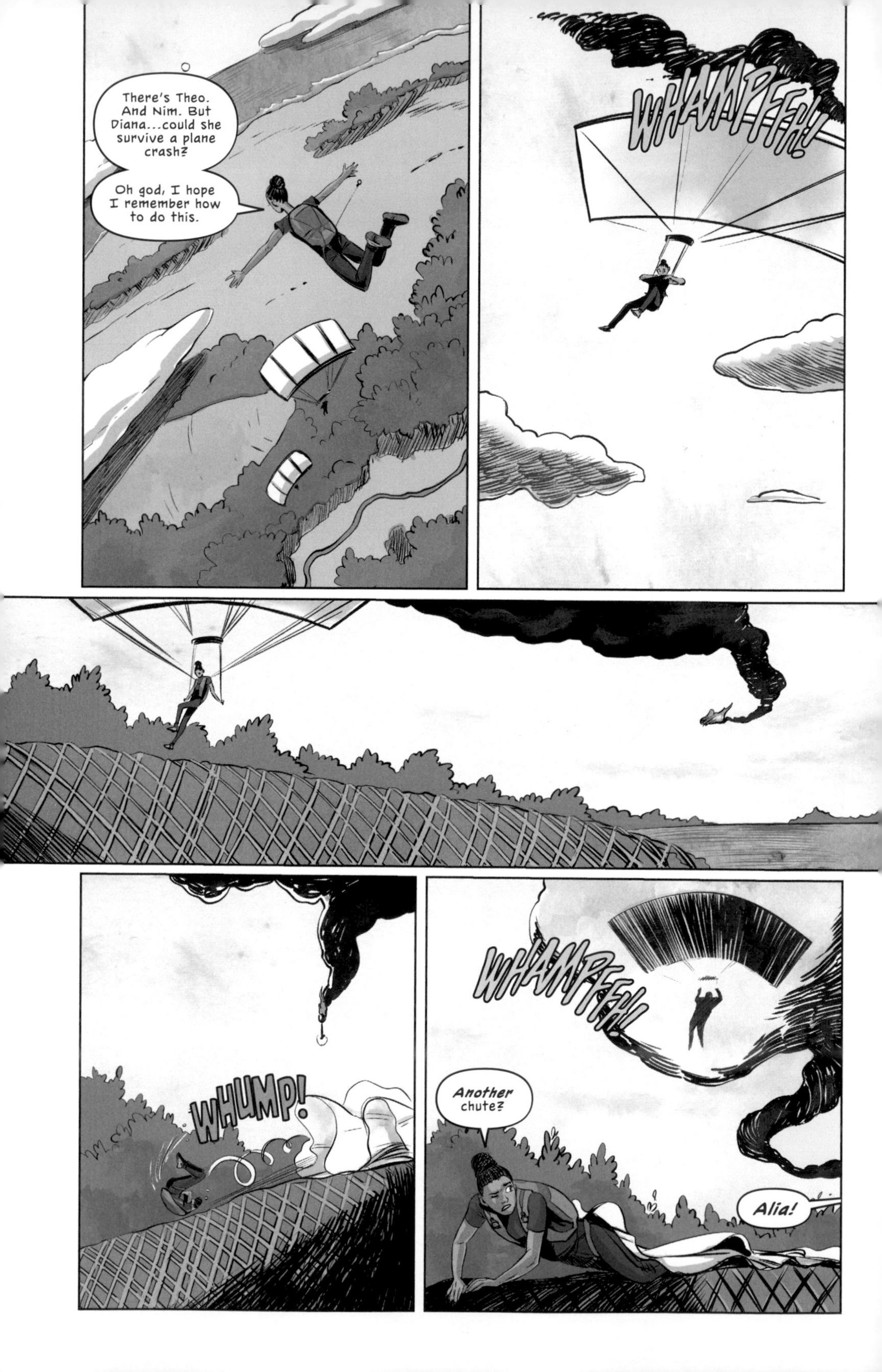
There's Theo. And Nim. But Diana...could she survive a plane crash?
Oh god, I hope I remember how to do this.
WHAMPFFH!
WHUMP!
WHAMPFFH!
Another chute?
Alia!

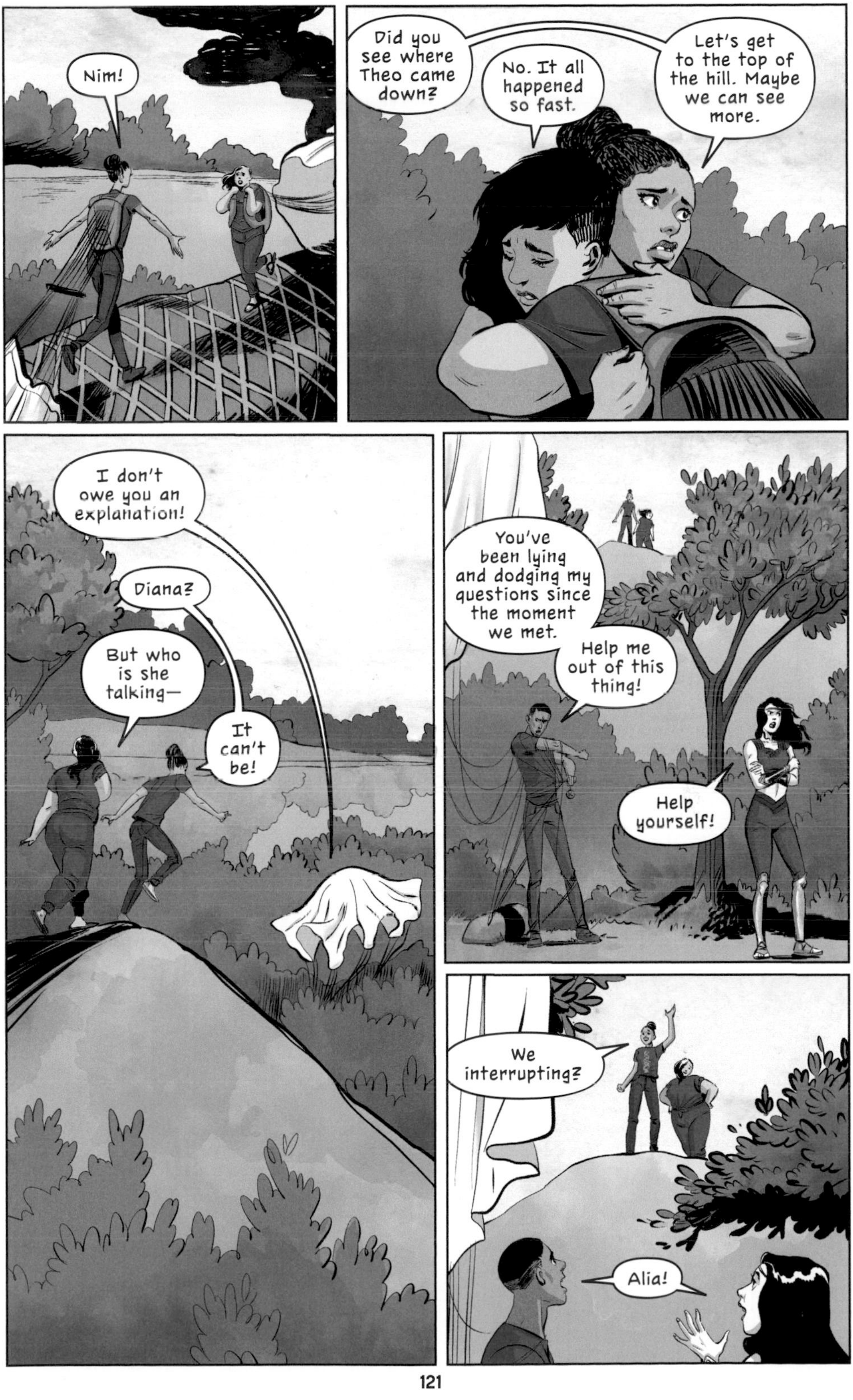
Nim!
Did you see where Theo came down?
No. It all happened so fast.
Let's get to the top of the hill. Maybe we can see more.
I don't owe you an explanation!
Diana?
But who is she talking—
It can't be!
You've been lying and dodging my questions since the moment we met.
Help me out of this thing!
Help yourself!
We interrupting?
Alia!

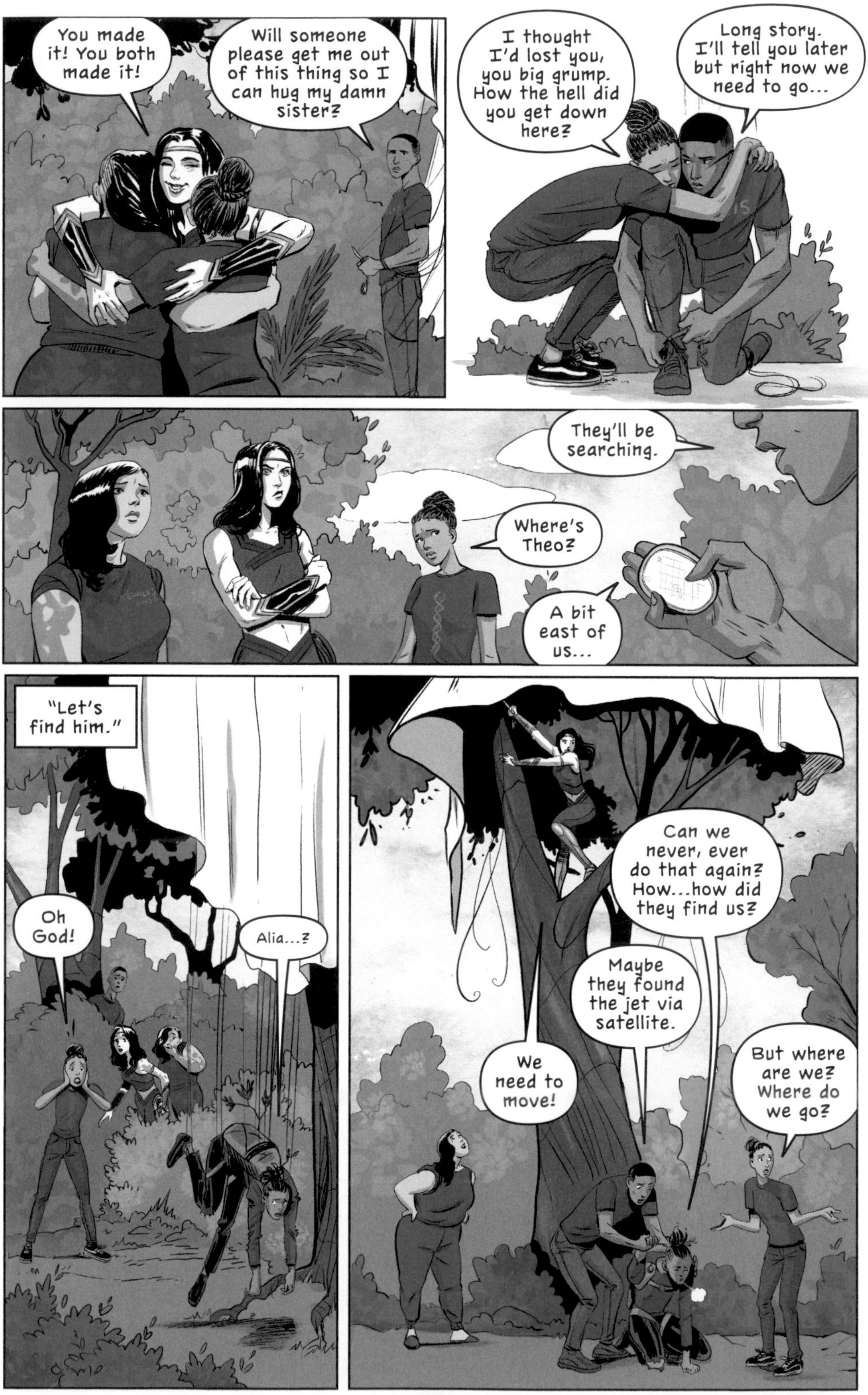
You made it! You both made it!
Will someone please get me out of this thing so I can hug my damn sister?
I thought I'd lost you, you big grump. How the hell did you get down here?
Long story. I'll tell you later but right now we need to go...
They'll be searching.
Where's Theo?
A bit east of us...
"Let's find him."
Oh God!
Alia...?
Can we never, ever do that again? How...how did they find us?
Maybe they found the jet via satellite.
We need to move!
But where are we? Where do we go?

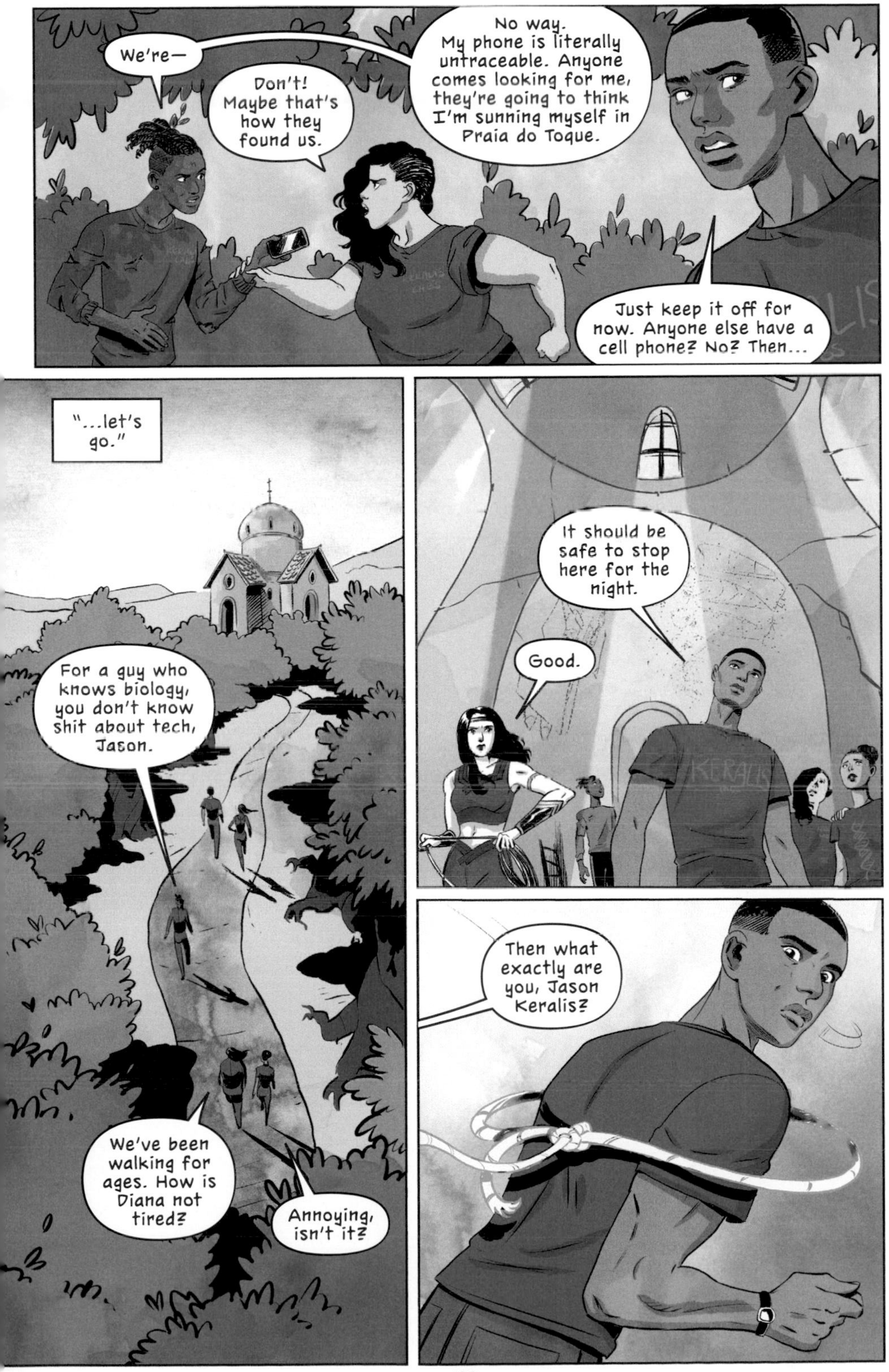
We're—
Don't! Maybe that's how they found us.
No way. My phone is literally untraceable. Anyone comes looking for me, they're going to think I'm sunning myself in Praia do Toque.
Just keep it off for now. Anyone else have a cell phone? No? Then...
"...let's go."
For a guy who knows biology, you don't know shit about tech, Jason.
We've been walking for ages. How is Diana not tired?
Annoying, isn't it?
It should be safe to stop here for the night.
Good.
Then what exactly are you, Jason Keralis?

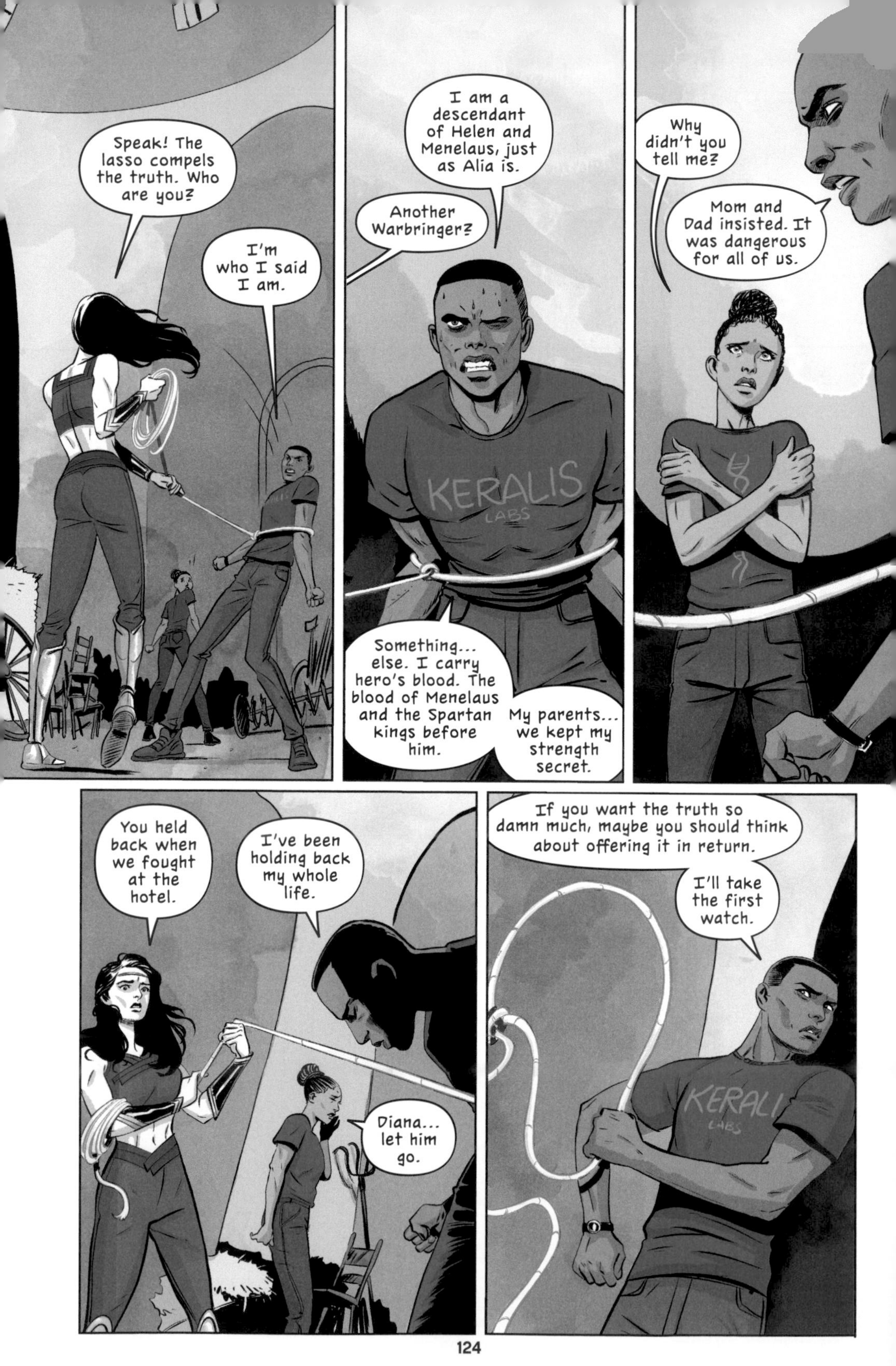

Speak! The lasso compels the truth. Who are you?
I'm who I said I am.
I am a descendant of Helen and Menelaus, just as Alia is.
Another Warbringer?
Something... else. I carry hero's blood. The blood of Menelaus and the Spartan kings before him.
My parents... we kept my strength secret.
KERALIS LABS
Why didn't you tell me?
Mom and Dad insisted. It was dangerous for all of us.
You held back when we fought at the hotel.
I've been holding back my whole life.
Diana... let him go.
If you want the truth so damn much, maybe you should think about offering it in return.
I'll take the first watch.

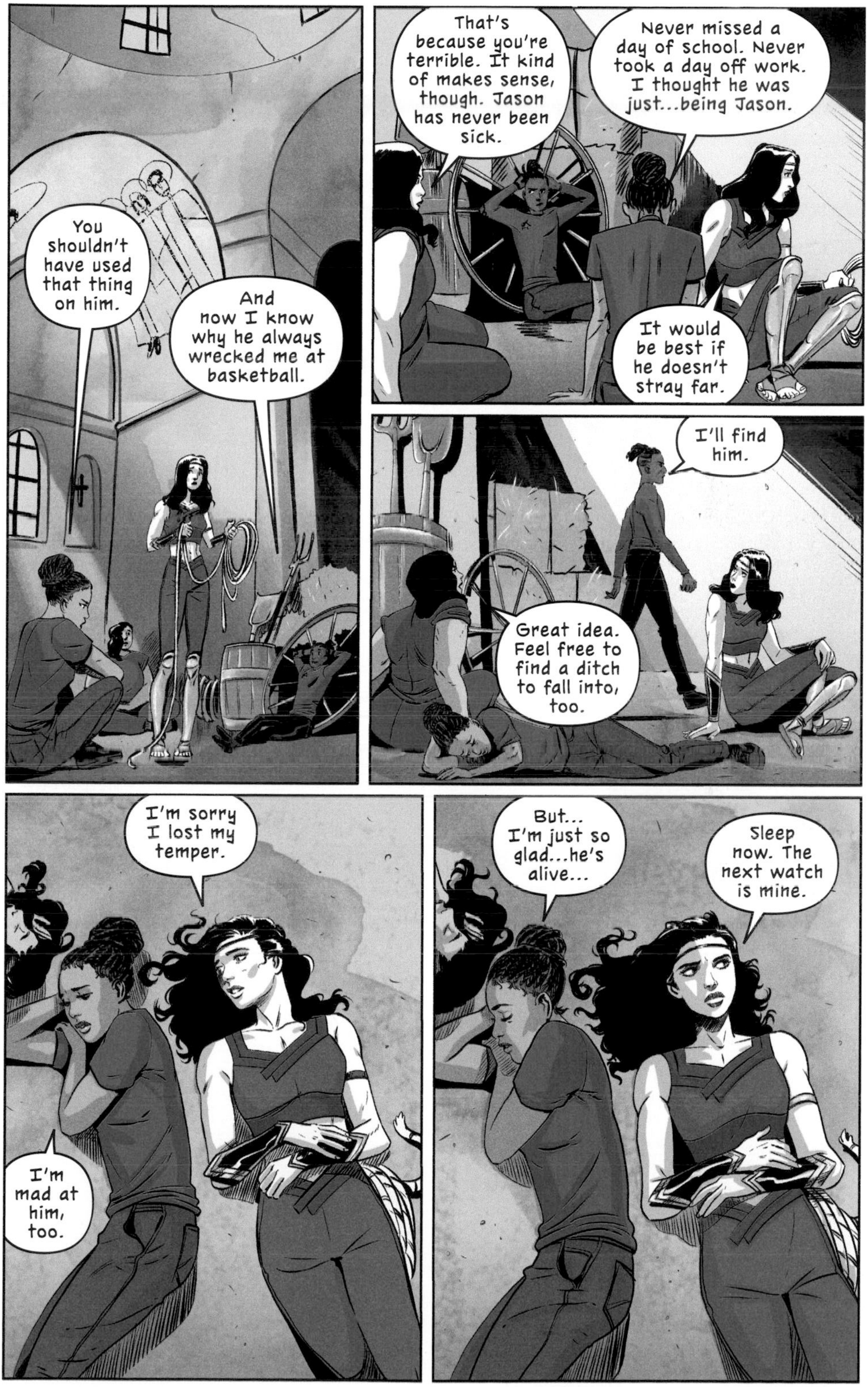

You shouldn't have used that thing on him.
And now I know why he always wrecked me at basketball.
That's because you're terrible. It kind of makes sense, though. Jason has never been sick.
Never missed a day of school. Never took a day off work. I thought he was just...being Jason.
It would be best if he doesn't stray far.
I'll find him.
Great idea. Feel free to find a ditch to fall into, too.
I'm sorry I lost my temper.
I'm mad at him, too.
But... I'm just so glad...he's alive...
Sleep now. The next watch is mine.

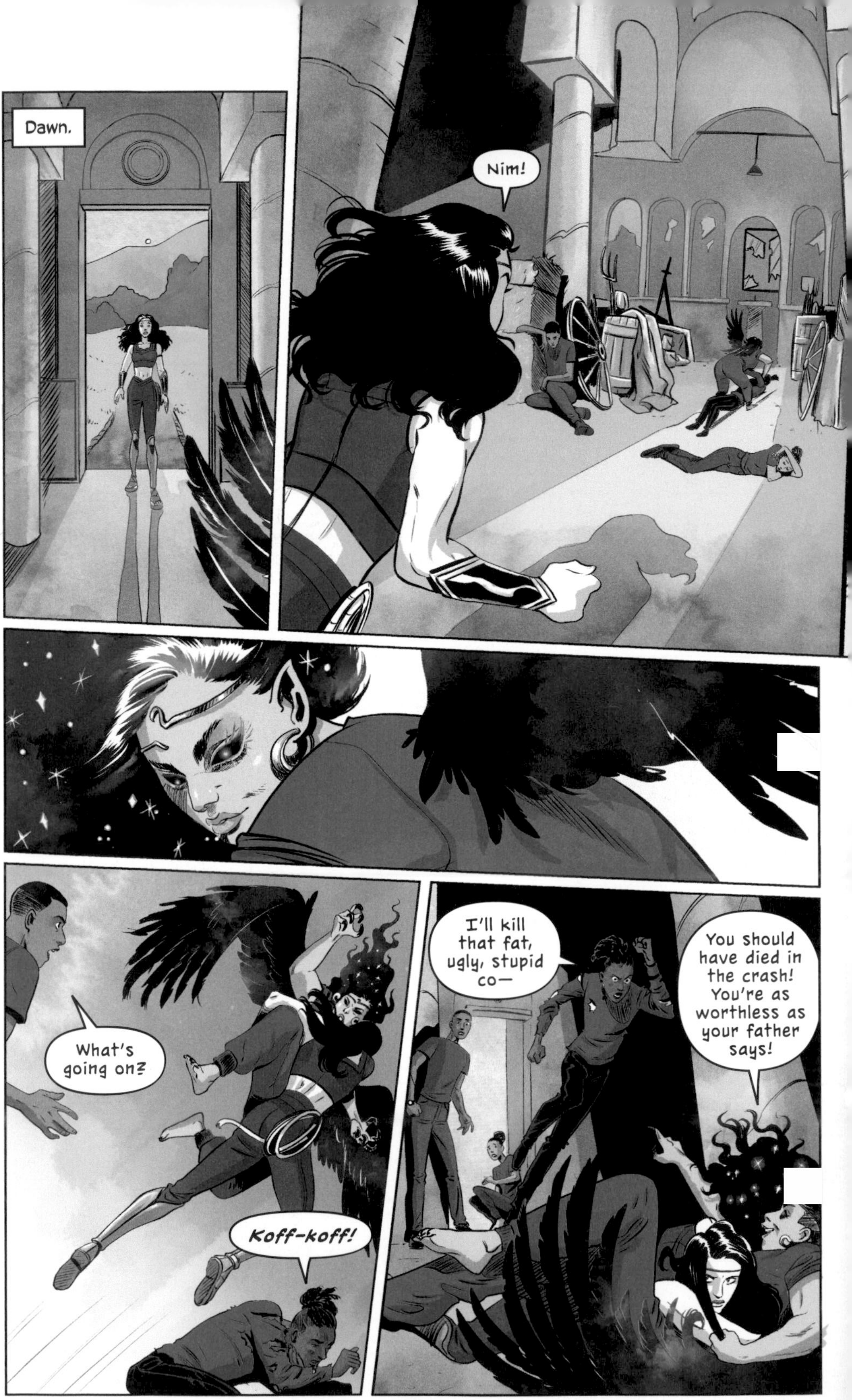
Dawn.
Nim!
What's going on?
Koff-koff!
I'll kill that fat, ugly, stupid co—
You should have died in the crash! You're as worthless as your father says!

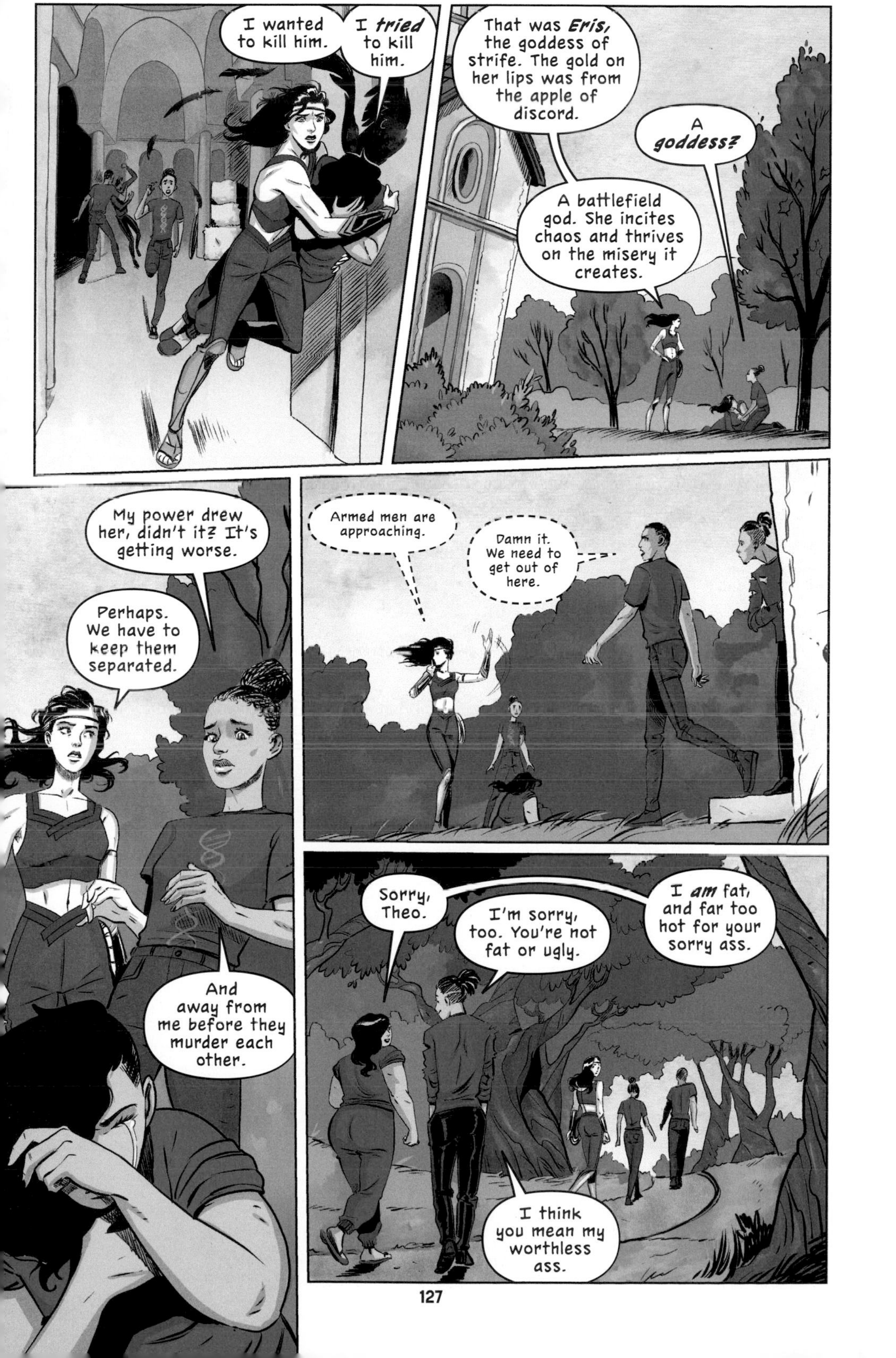

I wanted to kill him.
I *tried* to kill him.
That was *Eris,* the goddess of strife. The gold on her lips was from the apple of discord.
A *goddess?*
A battlefield god. She incites chaos and thrives on the misery it creates.
My power drew her, didn't it? It's getting worse.
Perhaps. We have to keep them separated.
And away from me before they murder each other.
Armed men are approaching.
Damn it. We need to get out of here.
Sorry, Theo.
I'm sorry, too. You're not fat or ugly.
I *am* fat, and far too hot for your sorry ass.
I think you mean my worthless ass.

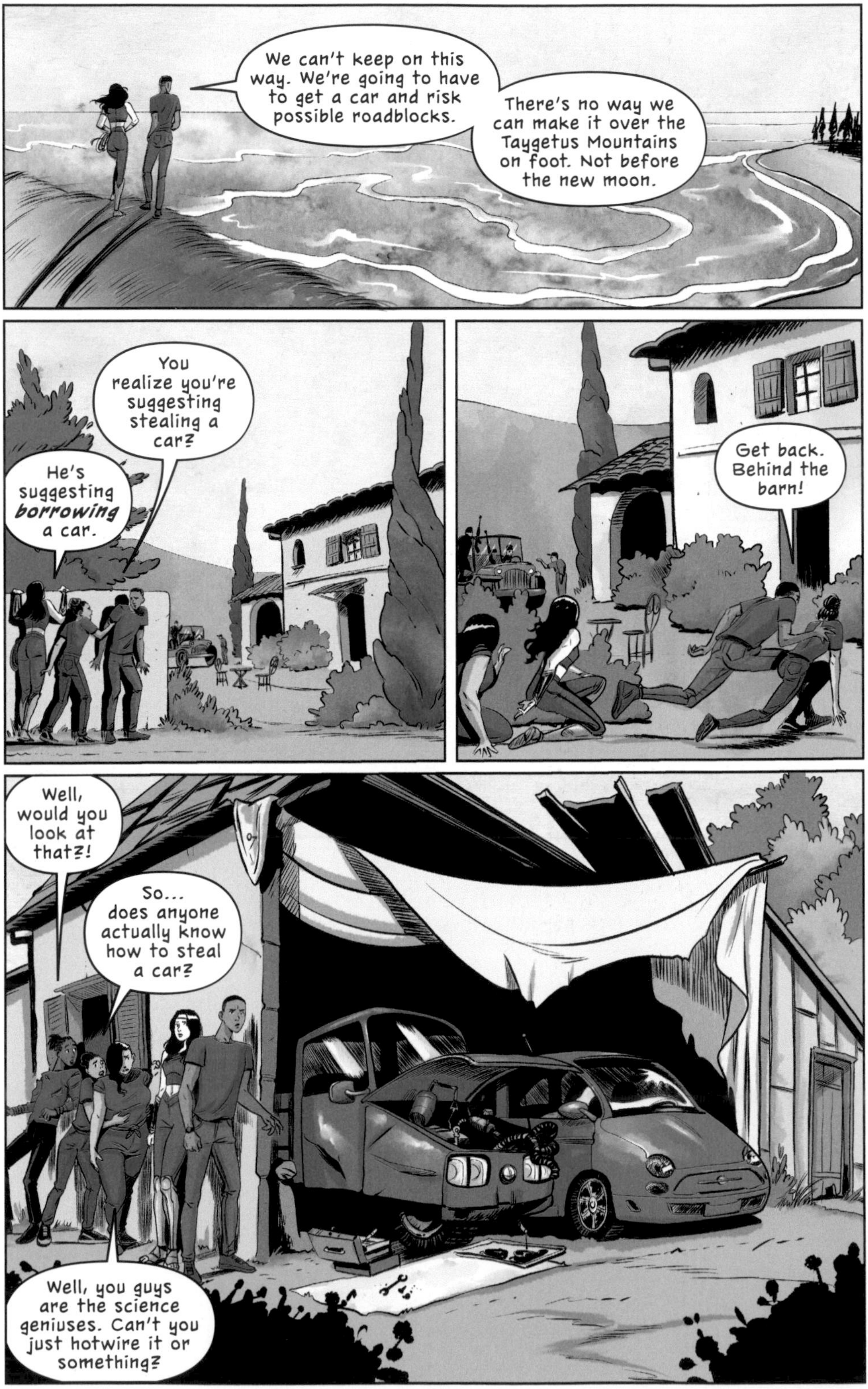
We can't keep on this way. We're going to have to get a car and risk possible roadblocks.
There's no way we can make it over the Taygetus Mountains on foot. Not before the new moon.
You realize you're suggesting stealing a car?
He's suggesting *borrowing* a car.
Get back. Behind the barn!
Well, would you look at that?!
So... does anyone actually know how to steal a car?
Well, you guys are the science geniuses. Can't you just hotwire it or something?

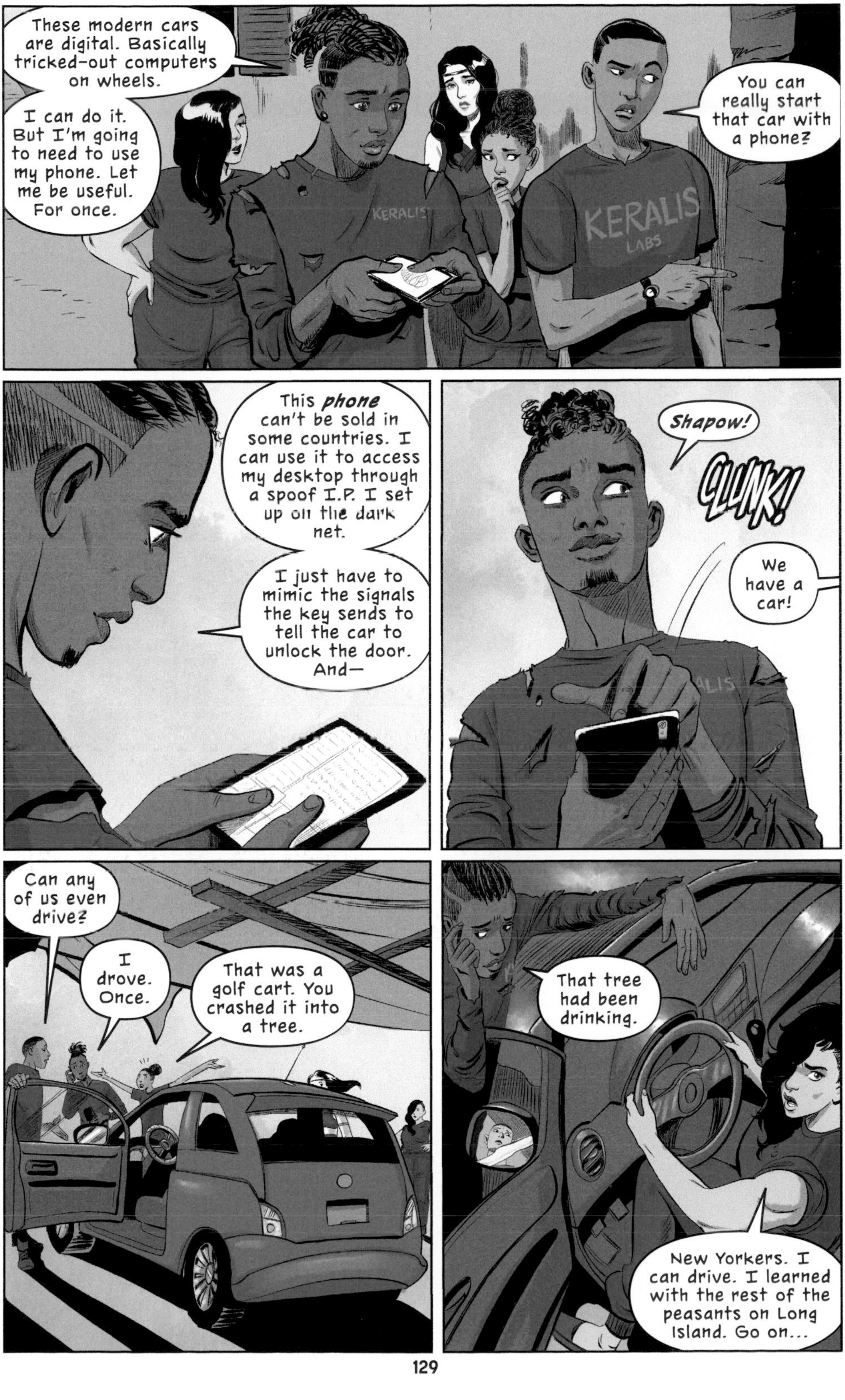
These modern cars are digital. Basically tricked-out computers on wheels.
I can do it. But I'm going to need to use my phone. Let me be useful. For once.
You can really start that car with a phone?
KERALIS LABS
This *phone* can't be sold in some countries. I can use it to access my desktop through a spoof I.P. I set up on the dark net.
I just have to mimic the signals the key sends to tell the car to unlock the door. And—
Shapow!
CLUNK!
We have a car!
Can any of us even drive?
I drove. Once.
That was a golf cart. You crashed it into a tree.
That tree had been drinking.
New Yorkers. I can drive. I learned with the rest of the peasants on Long Island. Go on...

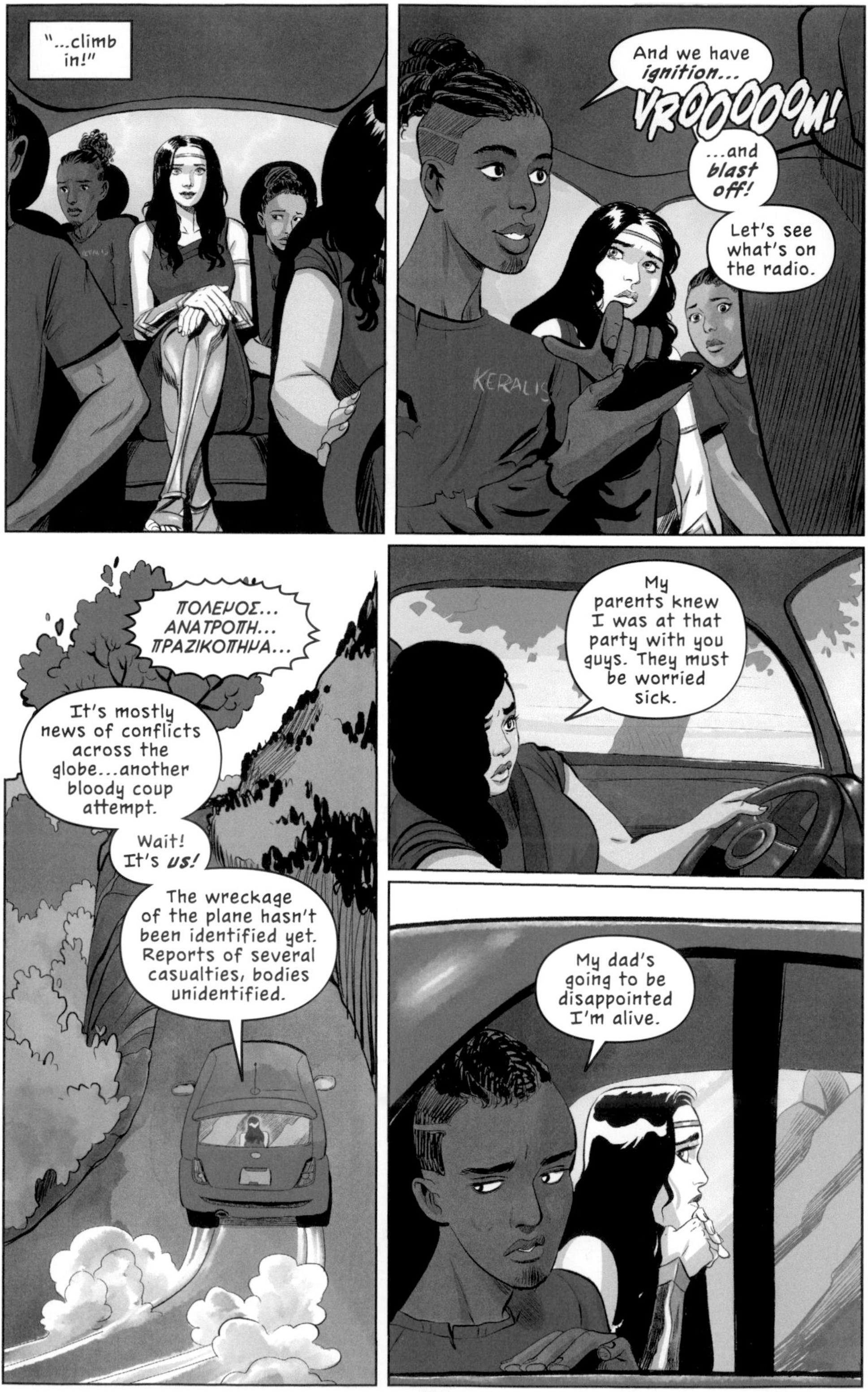
"...climb in!"
And we have *ignition*...
VROOOOOM!
...and *blast off!*
Let's see what's on the radio.
ΠΟΛΕΜΟΣ... ΑΝΑΤΡΟΠΗ... ΠΡΑΞΙΚΟΠΗΜΑ...
It's mostly news of conflicts across the globe...another bloody coup attempt.
Wait! It's *us!*
The wreckage of the plane hasn't been identified yet. Reports of several casualties, bodies unidentified.
My parents knew I was at that party with you guys. They must be worried sick.
My dad's going to be disappointed I'm alive.

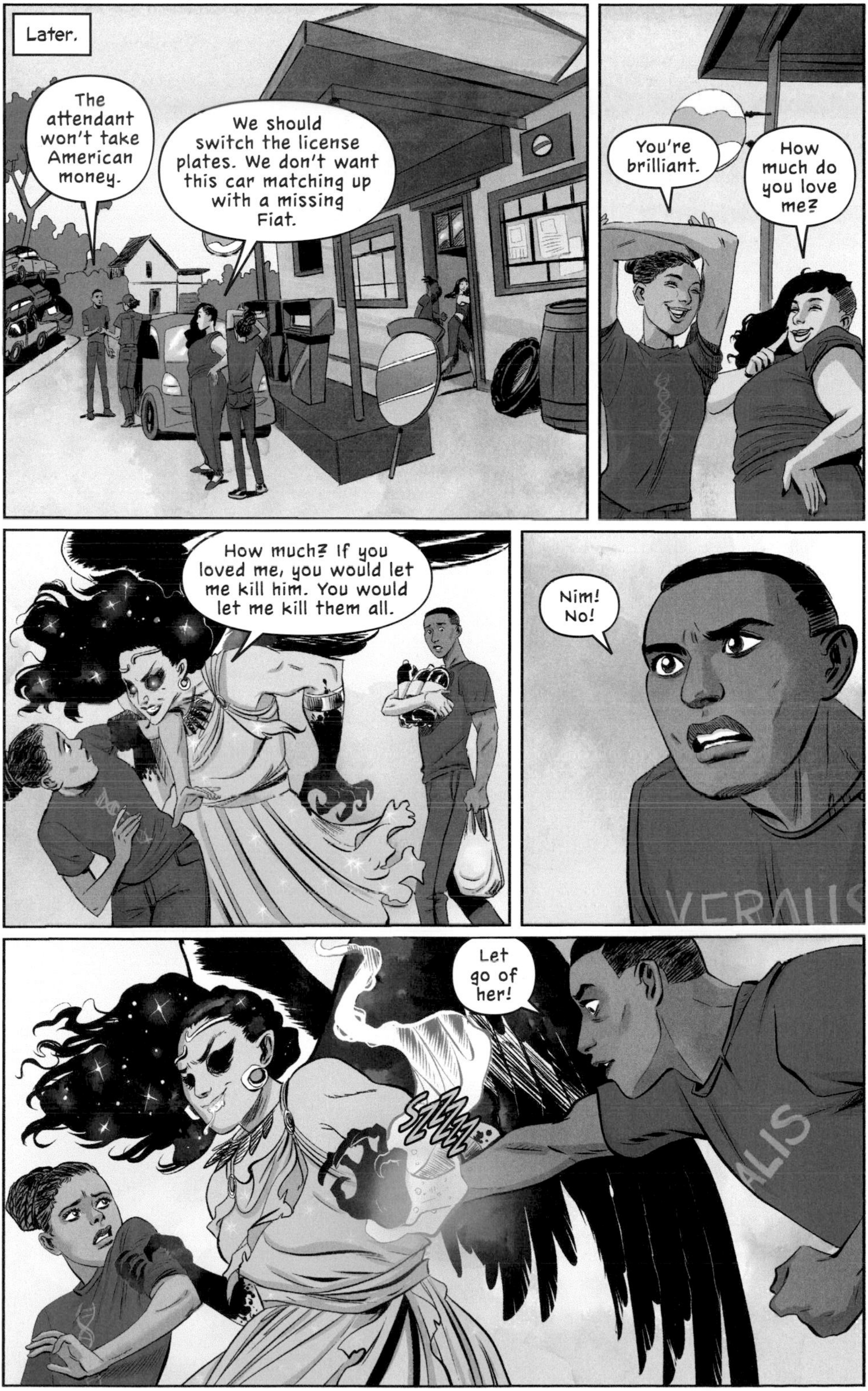
Later.
The attendant won't take American money.
We should switch the license plates. We don't want this car matching up with a missing Fiat.
You're brilliant.
How much do you love me?
How much? If you loved me, you would let me kill him. You would let me kill them all.
Nim! No!
Let go of her!
SZZZ

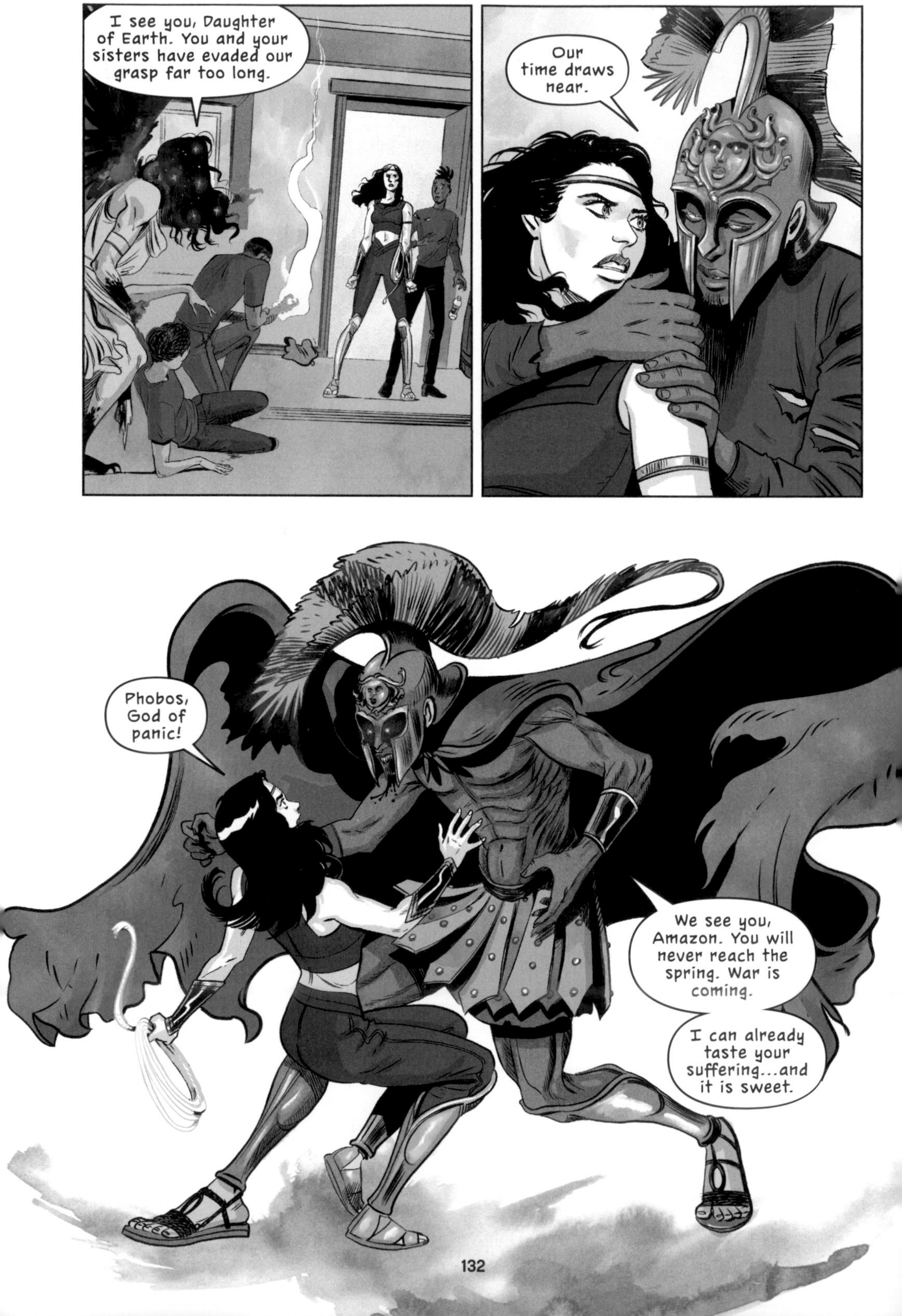
I see you, Daughter of Earth. You and your sisters have evaded our grasp far too long.
Our time draws near.
Phobos, God of panic!
We see you, Amazon. You will never reach the spring. War is coming.
I can already taste your suffering...and it is sweet.

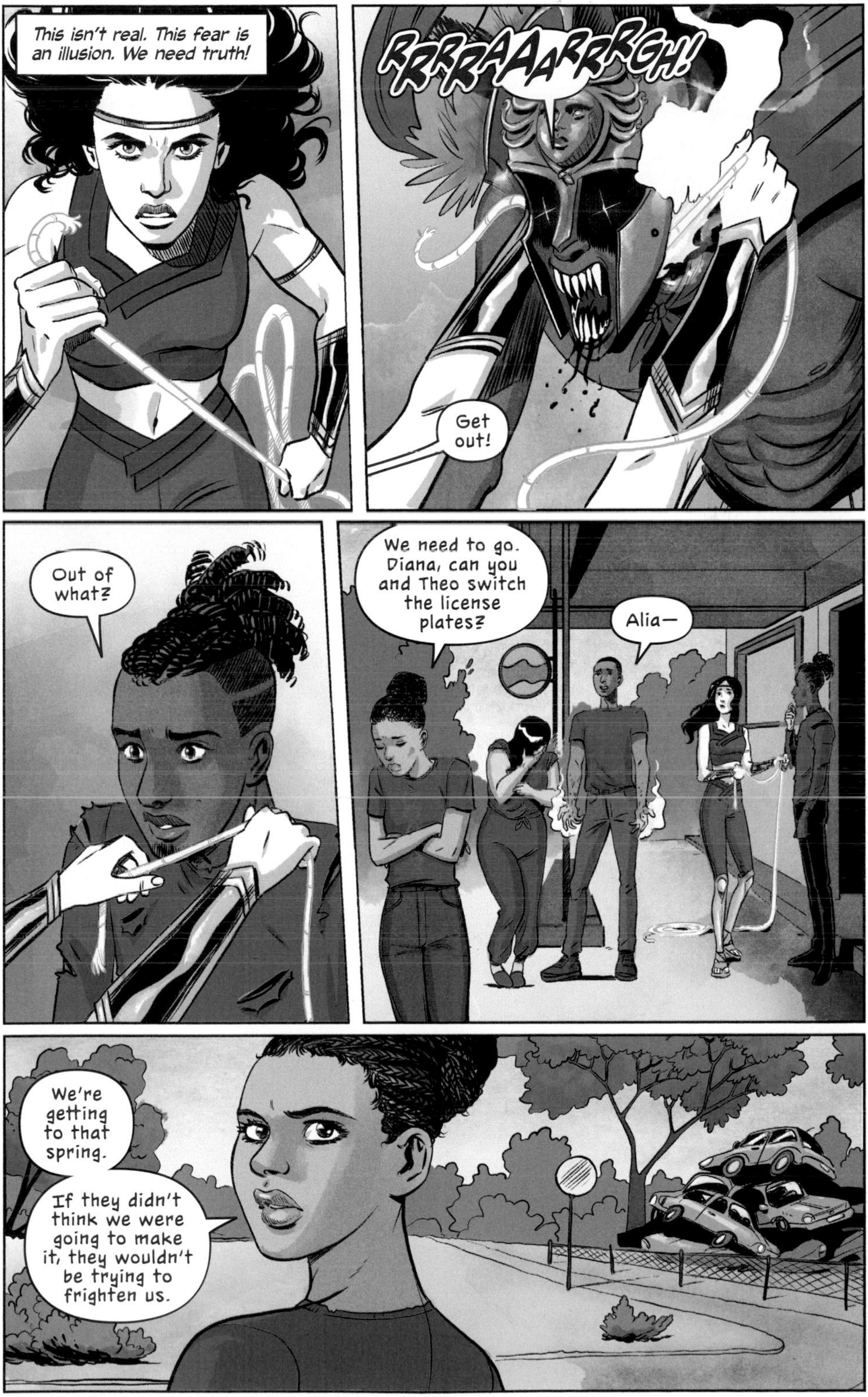
This isn't real. This fear is an illusion. We need truth!
RRRRAAARRRGH!
Get out!
Out of what?
We need to go. Diana, can you and Theo switch the license plates?
Alia—
We're getting to that spring.
If they didn't think we were going to make it, they wouldn't be trying to frighten us.

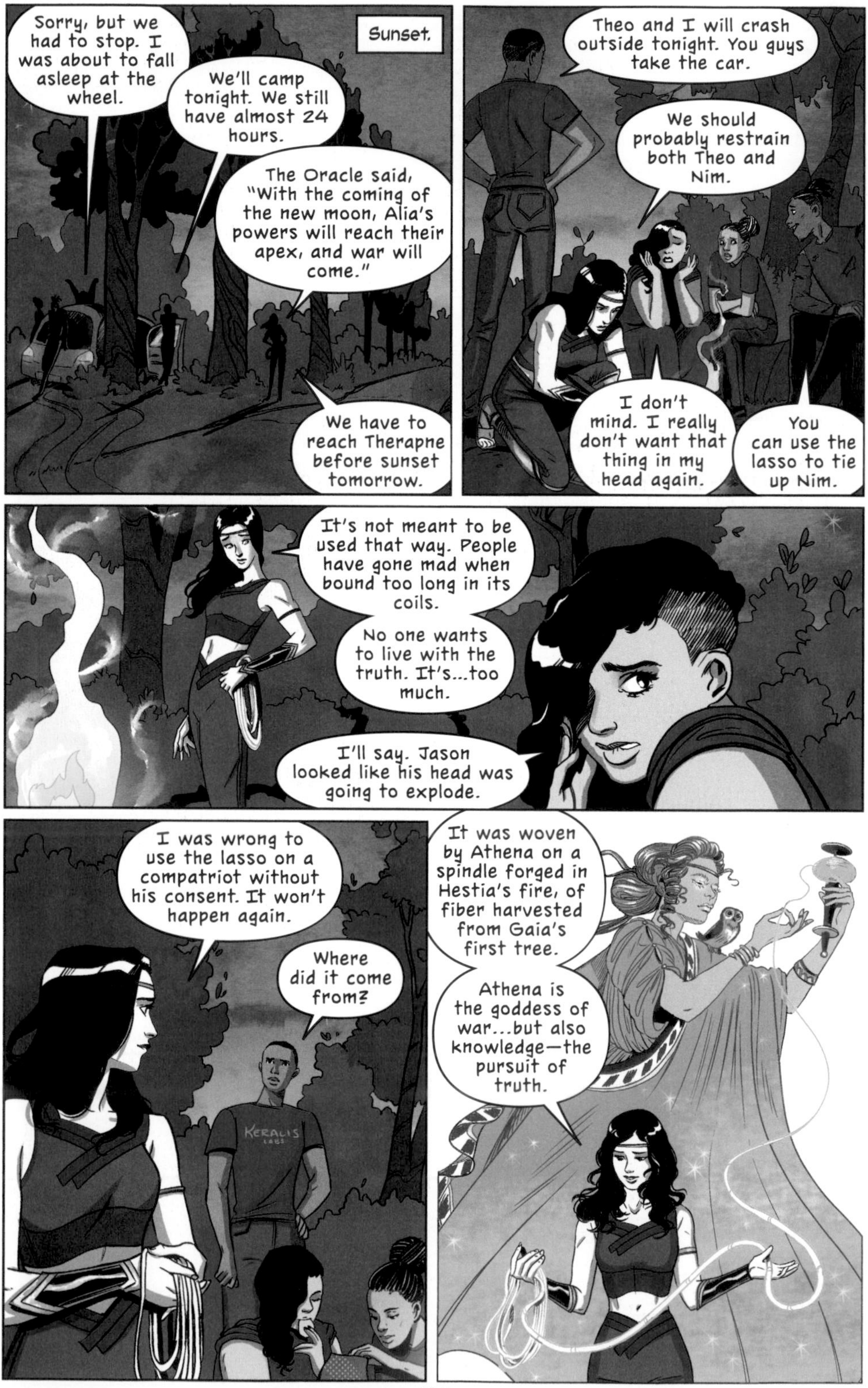
Sorry, but we had to stop. I was about to fall asleep at the wheel.
Sunset.
We'll camp tonight. We still have almost 24 hours.
The Oracle said, "With the coming of the new moon, Alia's powers will reach their apex, and war will come."
We have to reach Therapne before sunset tomorrow.
Theo and I will crash outside tonight. You guys take the car.
We should probably restrain both Theo and Nim.
I don't mind. I really don't want that thing in my head again.
You can use the lasso to tie up Nim.
It's not meant to be used that way. People have gone mad when bound too long in its coils.
No one wants to live with the truth. It's...too much.
I'll say. Jason looked like his head was going to explode.
I was wrong to use the lasso on a compatriot without his consent. It won't happen again.
Where did it come from?
It was woven by Athena on a spindle forged in Hestia's fire, of fiber harvested from Gaia's first tree.
Athena is the goddess of war...but also knowledge—the pursuit of truth.
KERALIS LABS

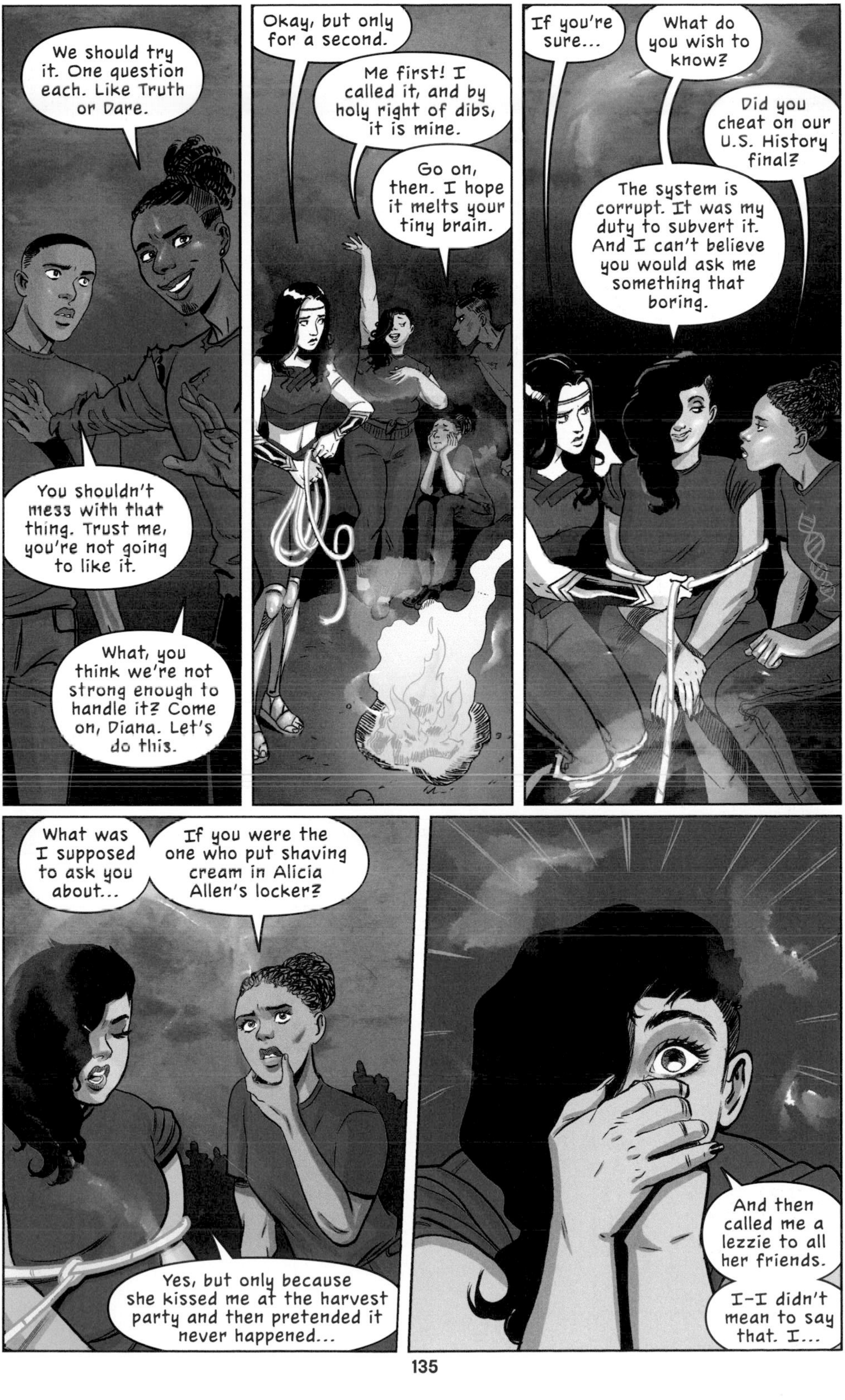
We should try it. One question each. Like Truth or Dare.
You shouldn't mess with that thing. Trust me, you're not going to like it.
What, you think we're not strong enough to handle it? Come on, Diana. Let's do this.
Okay, but only for a second.
Me first! I called it, and by holy right of dibs, it is mine.
Go on, then. I hope it melts your tiny brain.
If you're sure...
What do you wish to know?
Did you cheat on our U.S. History final?
The system is corrupt. It was my duty to subvert it. And I can't believe you would ask me something that boring.
What was I supposed to ask you about...
If you were the one who put shaving cream in Alicia Allen's locker?
Yes, but only because she kissed me at the harvest party and then pretended it never happened...
And then called me a lezzie to all her friends.
I-I didn't mean to say that. I...

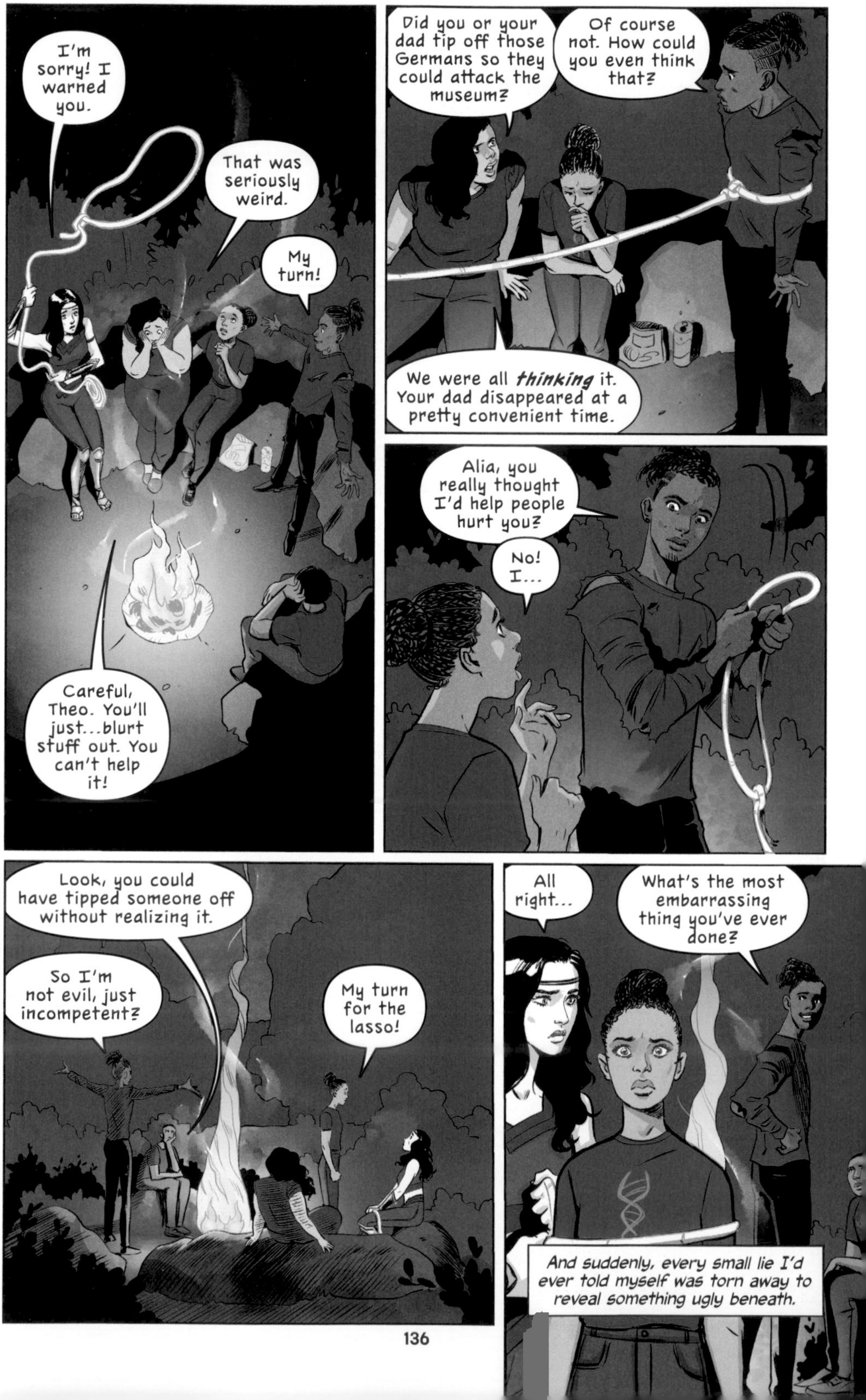
I'm sorry! I warned you.
That was seriously weird.
My turn!
Careful, Theo. You'll just...blurt stuff out. You can't help it!
Did you or your dad tip off those Germans so they could attack the museum?
Of course not. How could you even think that?
We were all *thinking* it. Your dad disappeared at a pretty convenient time.
Alia, you really thought I'd help people hurt you?
No! I...
Look, you could have tipped someone off without realizing it.
So I'm not evil, just incompetent?
My turn for the lasso!
All right...
What's the most embarrassing thing you've ever done?
And suddenly, every small lie I'd ever told myself was torn away to reveal something ugly beneath.

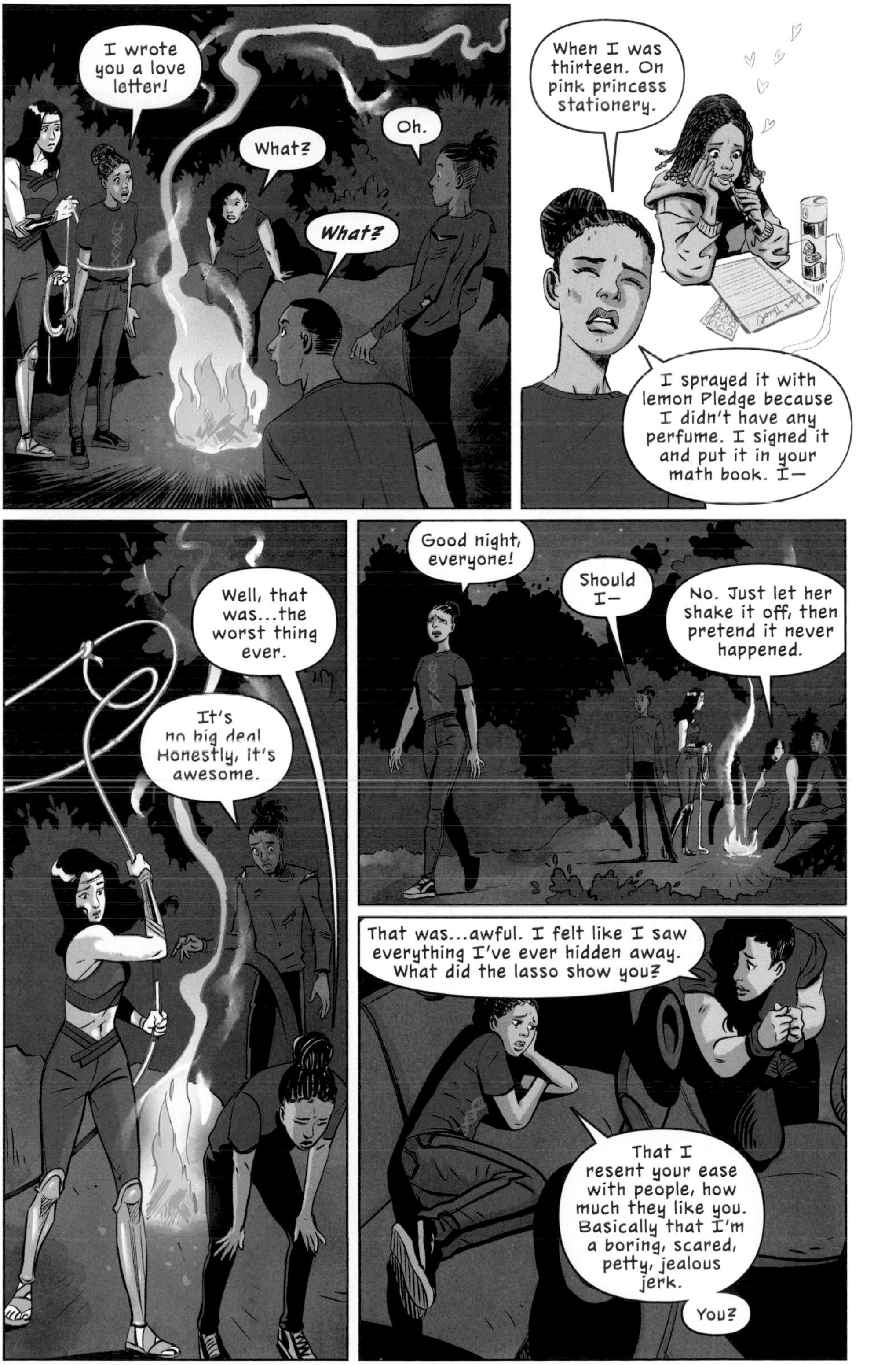
I wrote you a love letter!
What?
Oh.
What?
When I was thirteen. On pink princess stationery.
I sprayed it with lemon Pledge because I didn't have any perfume. I signed it and put it in your math book. I—
Well, that was...the worst thing ever.
It's no big deal Honestly, it's awesome.
Good night, everyone!
Should I—
No. Just let her shake it off, then pretend it never happened.
That was...awful. I felt like I saw everything I've ever hidden away. What did the lasso show you?
That I resent your ease with people, how much they like you. Basically that I'm a boring, scared, petty, jealous jerk.
You?

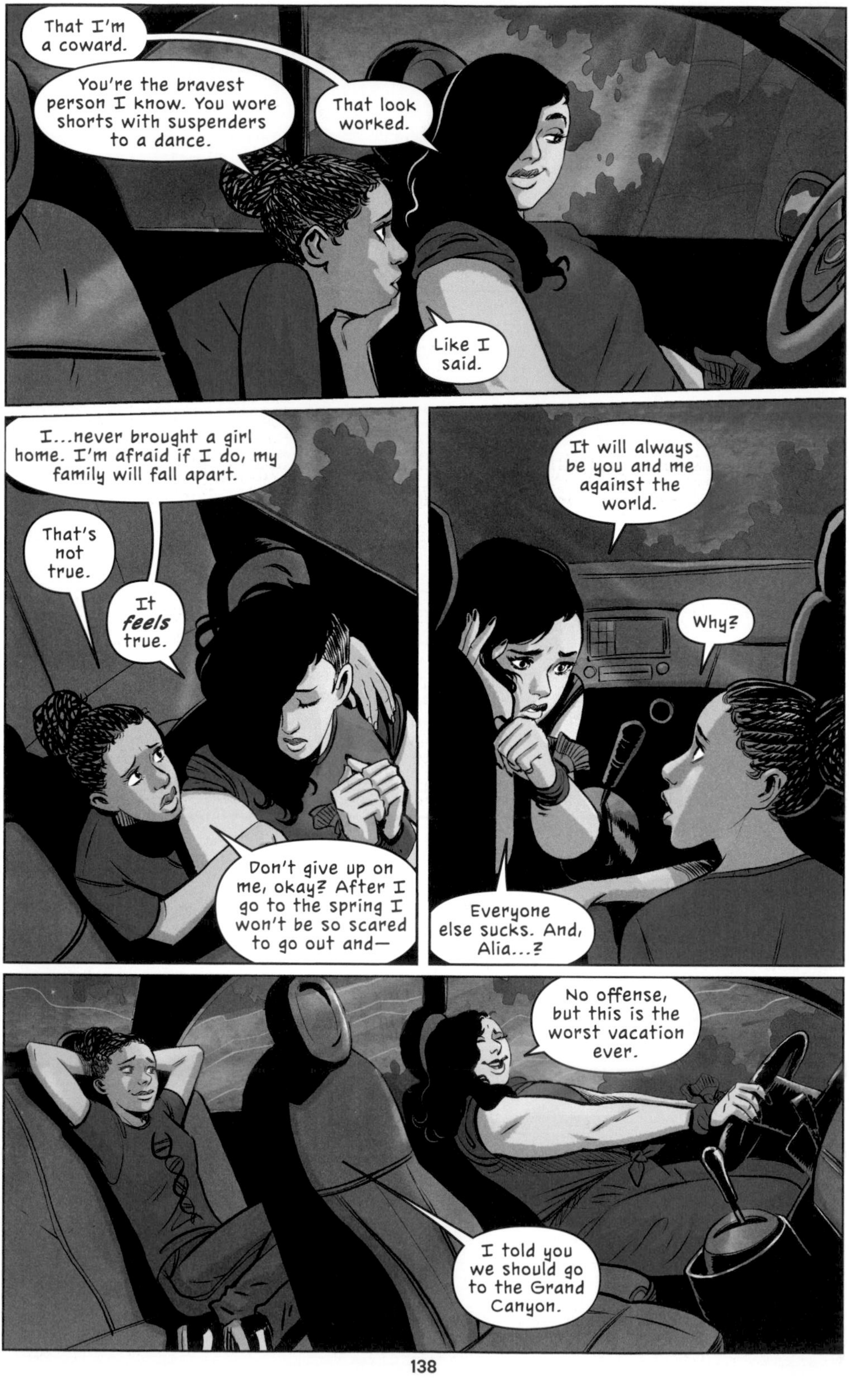
That I'm a coward.
You're the bravest person I know. You wore shorts with suspenders to a dance.
That look worked.
Like I said.
I...never brought a girl home. I'm afraid if I do, my family will fall apart.
That's not true.
It *feels* true.
Don't give up on me, okay? After I go to the spring I won't be so scared to go out and—
It will always be you and me against the world.
Why?
Everyone else sucks. And, Alia...?
No offense, but this is the worst vacation ever.
I told you we should go to the Grand Canyon.

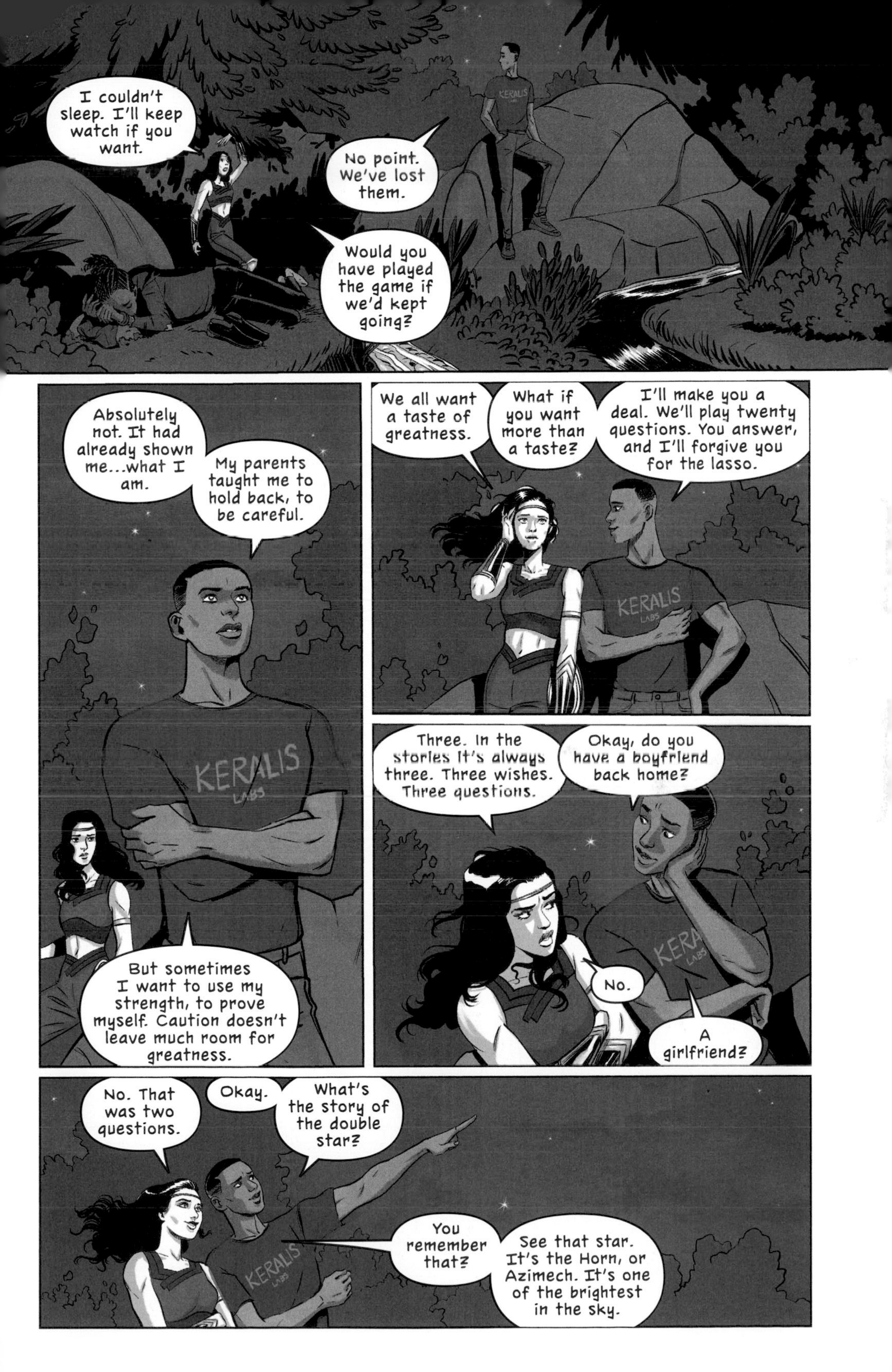
I couldn't sleep. I'll keep watch if you want.
No point. We've lost them.
Would you have played the game if we'd kept going?
Absolutely not. It had already shown me...what I am.
My parents taught me to hold back, to be careful.
But sometimes I want to use my strength, to prove myself. Caution doesn't leave much room for greatness.
We all want a taste of greatness.
What if you want more than a taste?
I'll make you a deal. We'll play twenty questions. You answer, and I'll forgive you for the lasso.
Three. In the stories it's always three. Three wishes. Three questions.
Okay, do you have a boyfriend back home?
No.
A girlfriend?
No. That was two questions.
Okay.
What's the story of the double star?
See that star. It's the Horn, or Azimech. It's one of the brightest in the sky.
You remember that?

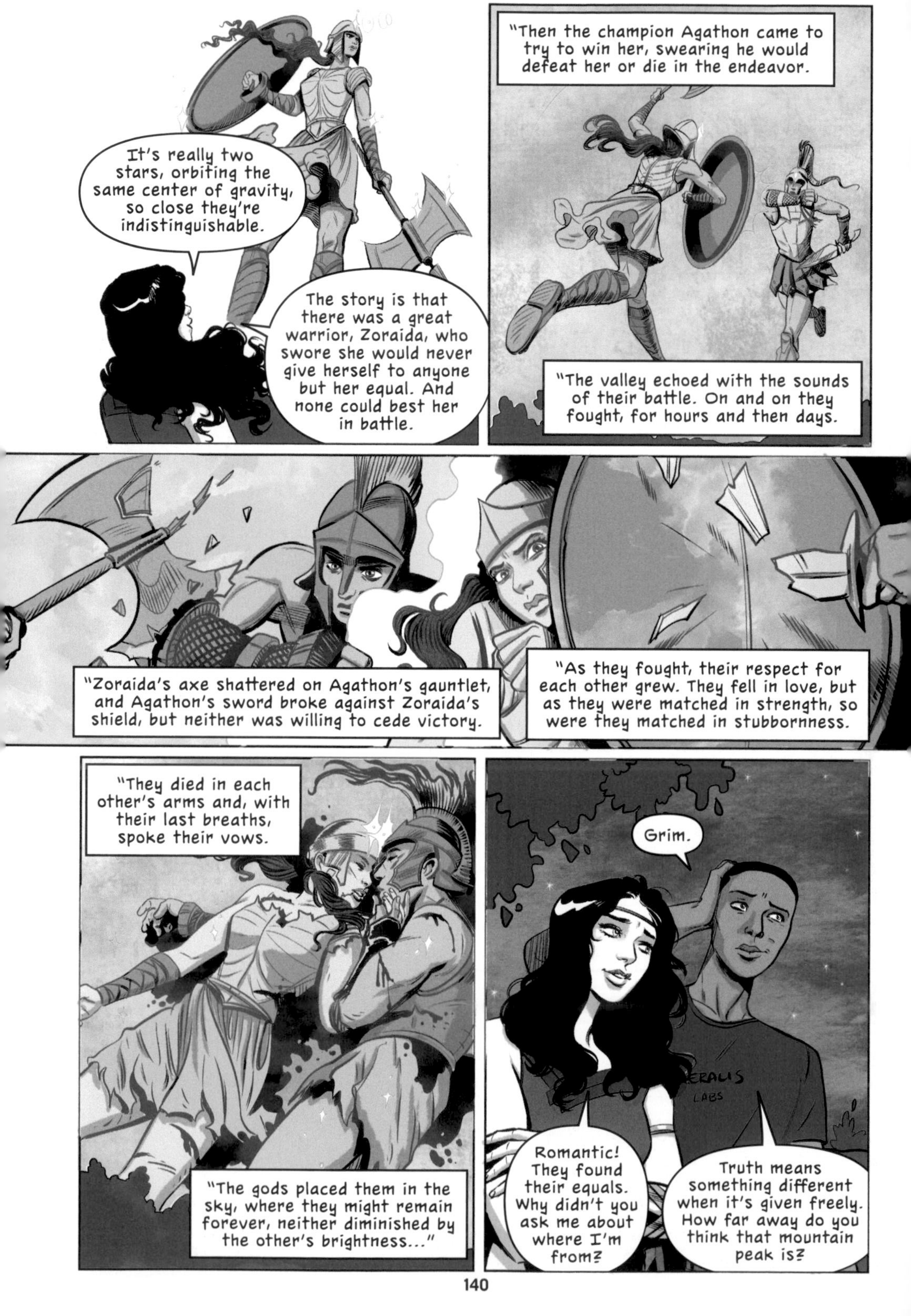

It's really two stars, orbiting the same center of gravity, so close they're indistinguishable.
The story is that there was a great warrior, Zoraida, who swore she would never give herself to anyone but her equal. And none could best her in battle.
"Then the champion Agathon came to try to win her, swearing he would defeat her or die in the endeavor.
"The valley echoed with the sounds of their battle. On and on they fought, for hours and then days.
"Zoraida's axe shattered on Agathon's gauntlet, and Agathon's sword broke against Zoraida's shield, but neither was willing to cede victory.
"As they fought, their respect for each other grew. They fell in love, but as they were matched in strength, so were they matched in stubbornness.
"They died in each other's arms and, with their last breaths, spoke their vows.
"The gods placed them in the sky, where they might remain forever, neither diminished by the other's brightness..."
Grim.
Romantic! They found their equals. Why didn't you ask me about where I'm from?
Truth means something different when it's given freely. How far away do you think that mountain peak is?

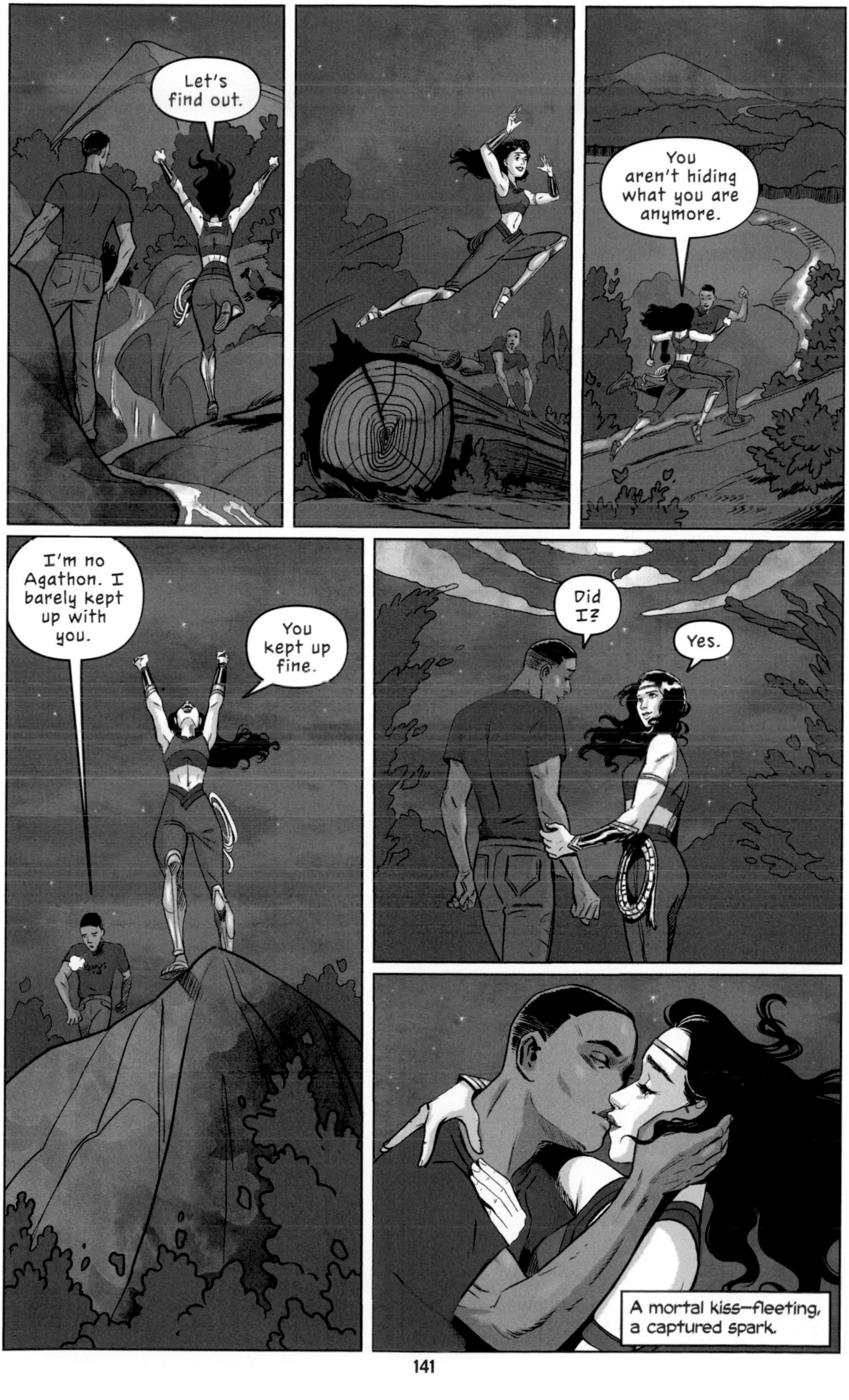
Let's find out.
You aren't hiding what you are anymore.
I'm no Agathon. I barely kept up with you.
You kept up fine.
Did I?
Yes.
A mortal kiss—fleeting, a captured spark.

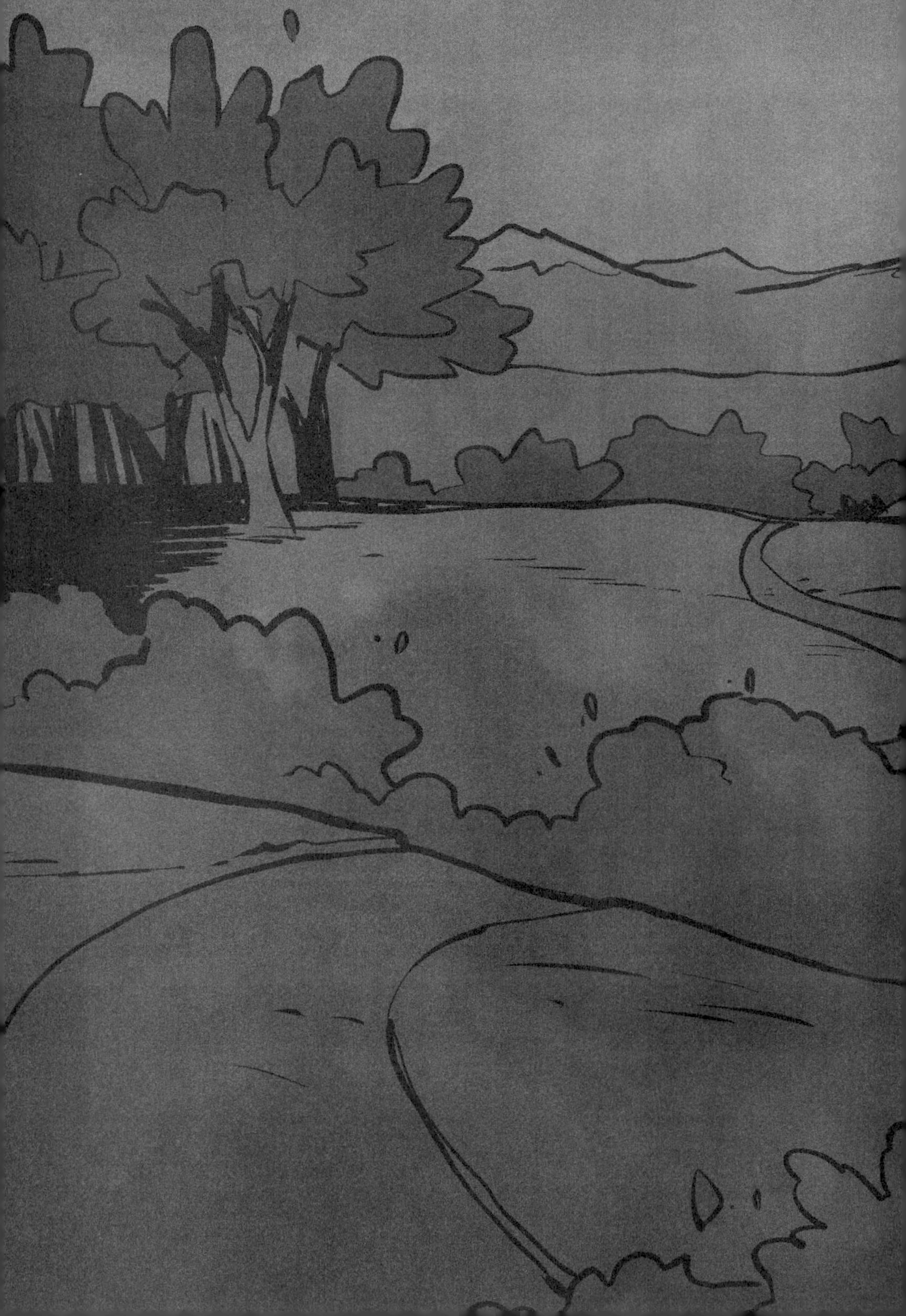

PART SIX

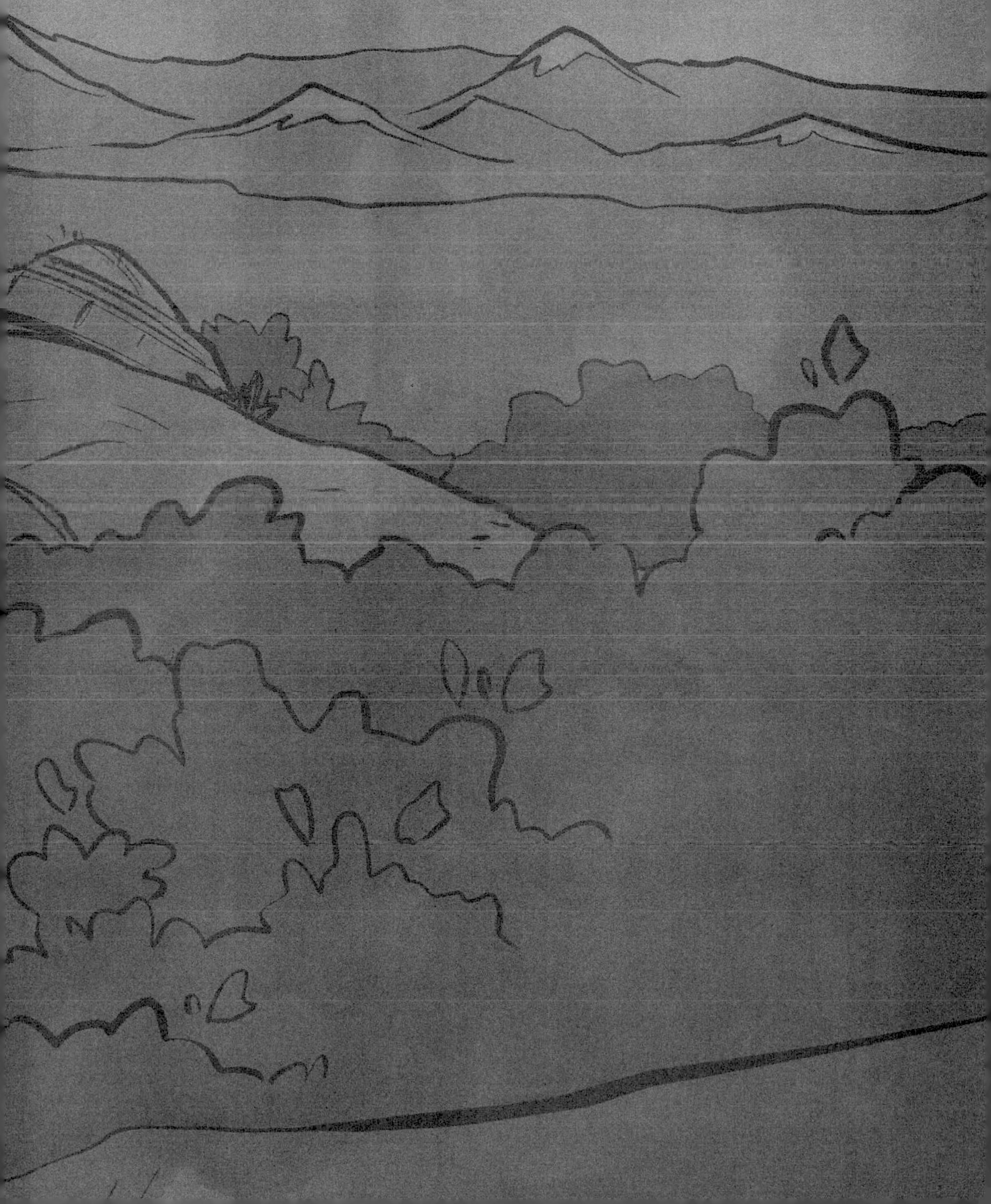

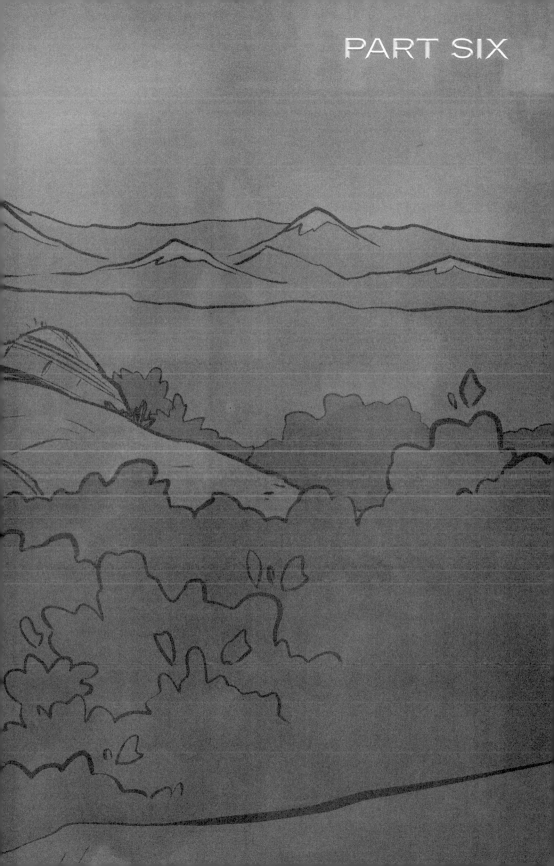

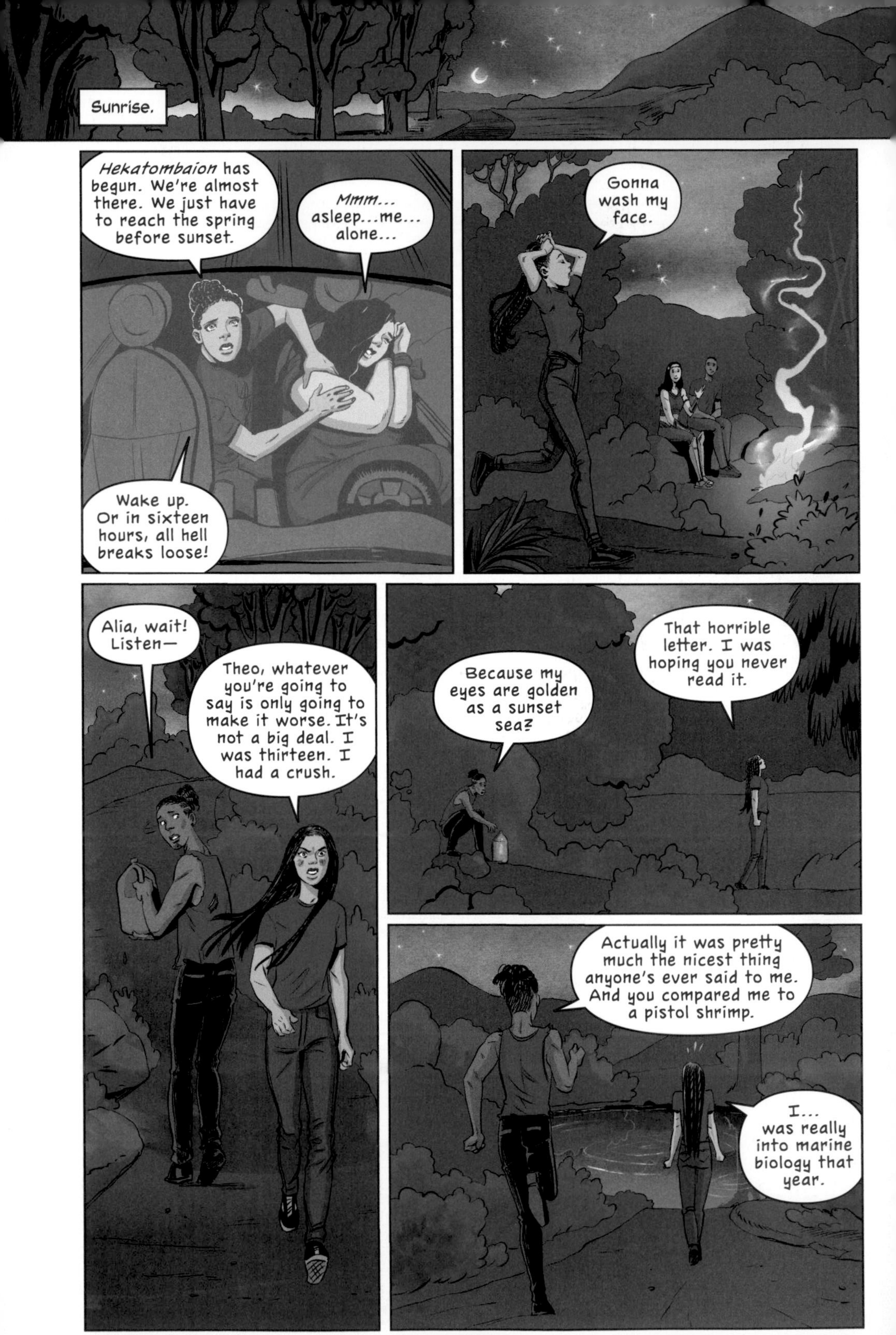
Sunrise.
Hekatombaion has begun. We're almost there. We just have to reach the spring before sunset.
Mmm... asleep...me... alone...
Wake up. Or in sixteen hours, all hell breaks loose!
Gonna wash my face.
Alia, wait! Listen—
Theo, whatever you're going to say is only going to make it worse. It's not a big deal. I was thirteen. I had a crush.
Because my eyes are golden as a sunset sea?
That horrible letter. I was hoping you never read it.
Actually it was pretty much the nicest thing anyone's ever said to me. And you compared me to a pistol shrimp.
I... was really into marine biology that year.

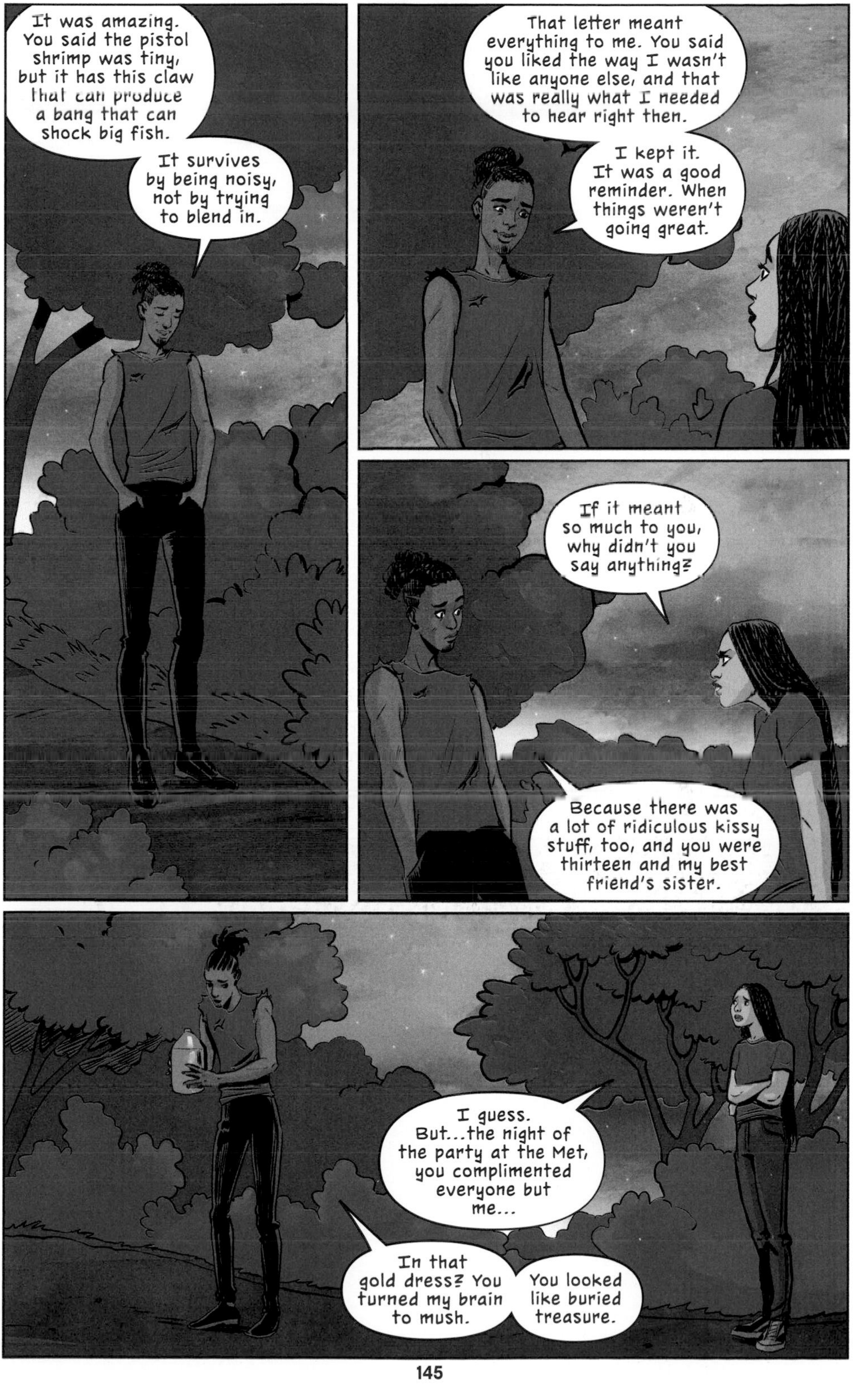
It was amazing. You said the pistol shrimp was tiny, but it has this claw that can produce a bang that can shock big fish.
It survives by being noisy, not by trying to blend in.
That letter meant everything to me. You said you liked the way I wasn't like anyone else, and that was really what I needed to hear right then.
I kept it. It was a good reminder. When things weren't going great.
If it meant so much to you, why didn't you say anything?
Because there was a lot of ridiculous kissy stuff, too, and you were thirteen and my best friend's sister.
I guess. But...the night of the party at the Met, you complimented everyone but me...
In that gold dress? You turned my brain to mush.
You looked like buried treasure.

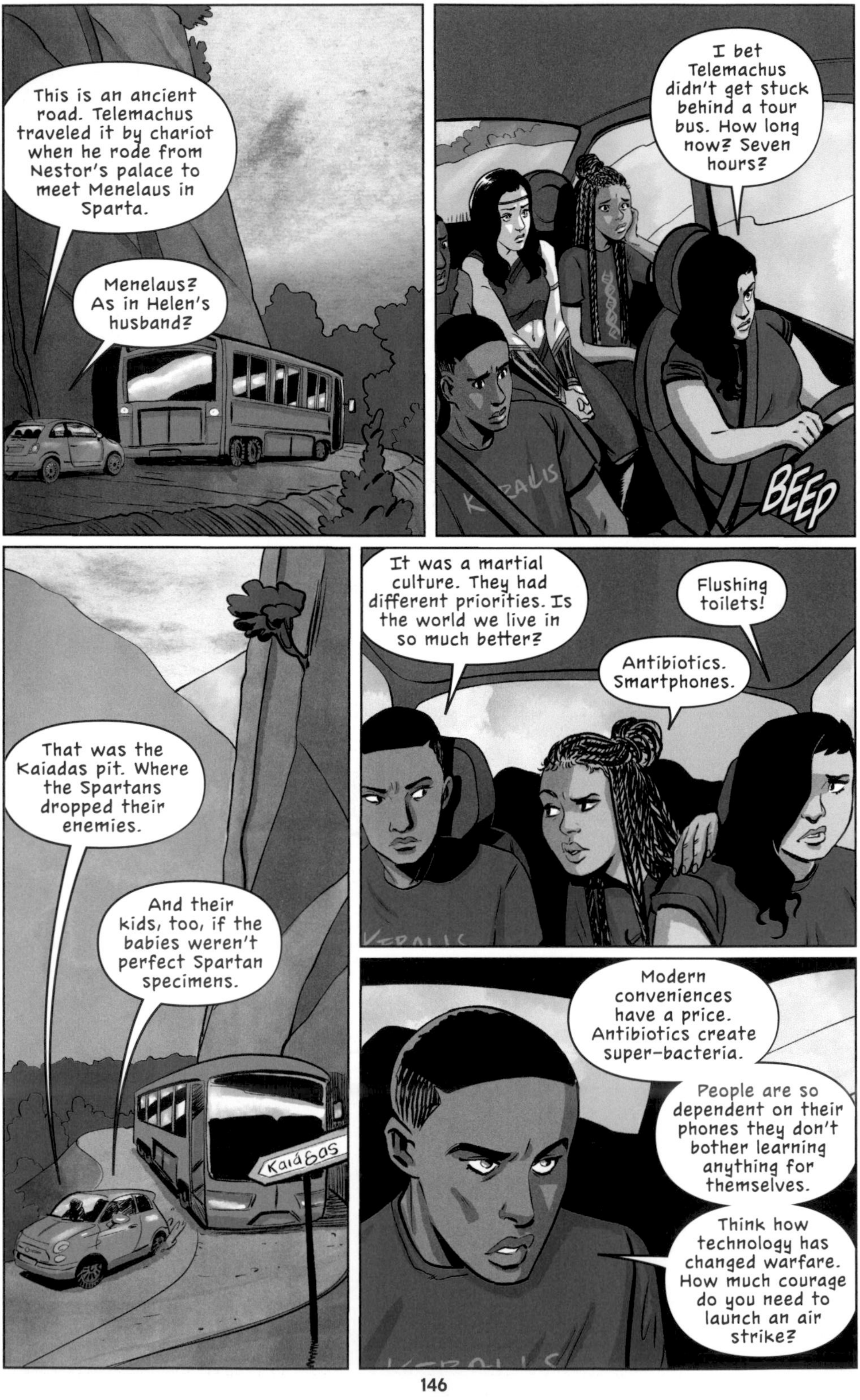
This is an ancient road. Telemachus traveled it by chariot when he rode from Nestor's palace to meet Menelaus in Sparta.
Menelaus? As in Helen's husband?
I bet Telemachus didn't get stuck behind a tour bus. How long now? Seven hours?
BEEP
That was the Kaiadas pit. Where the Spartans dropped their enemies.
And their kids, too, if the babies weren't perfect Spartan specimens.
Καιάδας
It was a martial culture. They had different priorities. Is the world we live in so much better?
Flushing toilets!
Antibiotics. Smartphones.
Modern conveniences have a price. Antibiotics create super-bacteria.
People are so dependent on their phones they don't bother learning anything for themselves.
Think how technology has changed warfare. How much courage do you need to launch an air strike?

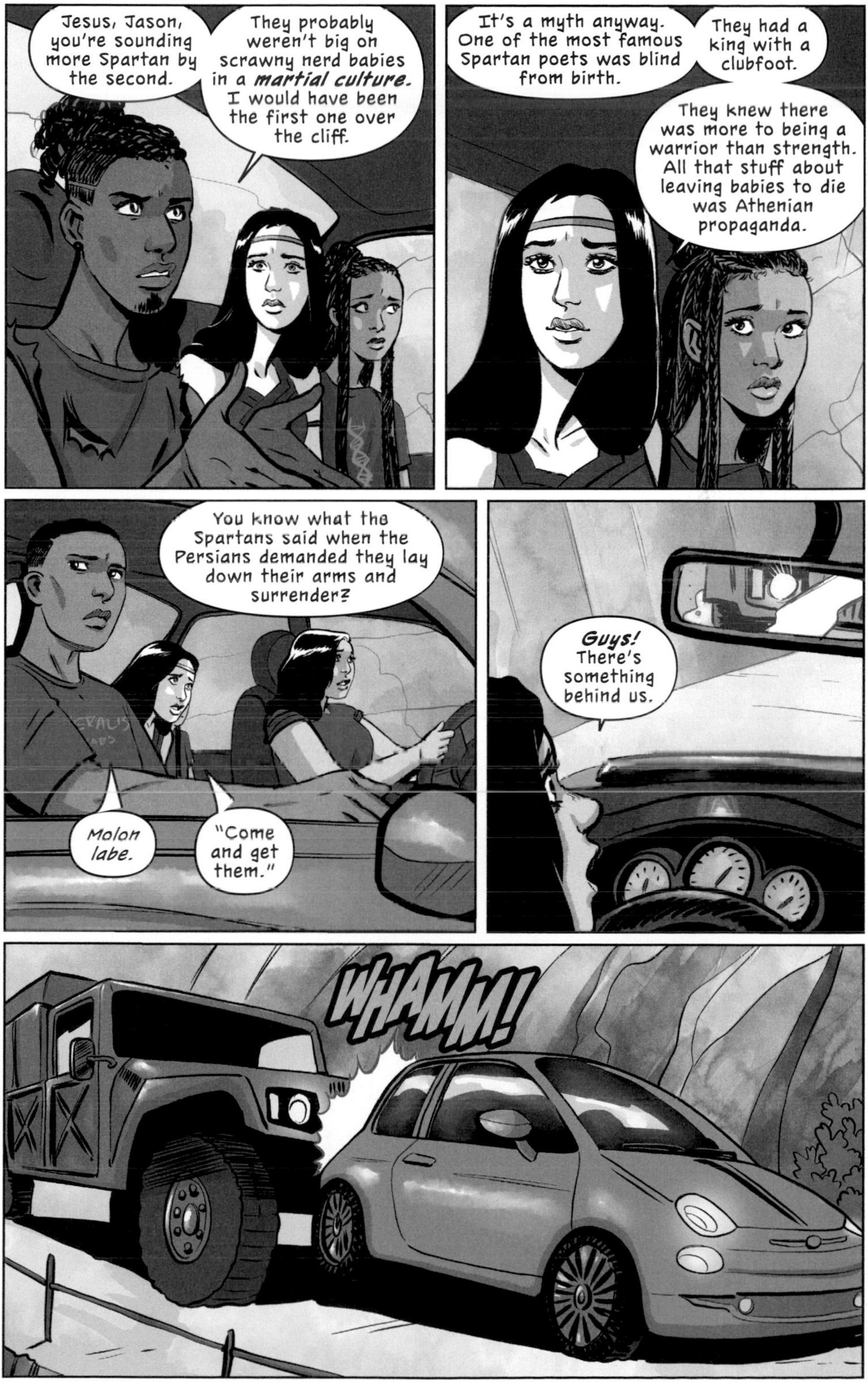
Jesus, Jason, you're sounding more Spartan by the second.
They probably weren't big on scrawny nerd babies in a *martial culture.* I would have been the first one over the cliff.
It's a myth anyway. One of the most famous Spartan poets was blind from birth.
They had a king with a clubfoot.
They knew there was more to being a warrior than strength. All that stuff about leaving babies to die was Athenian propaganda.
You know what the Spartans said when the Persians demanded they lay down their arms and surrender?
Molon labe.
"Come and get them."
Guys! There's something behind us.
WHAMM!

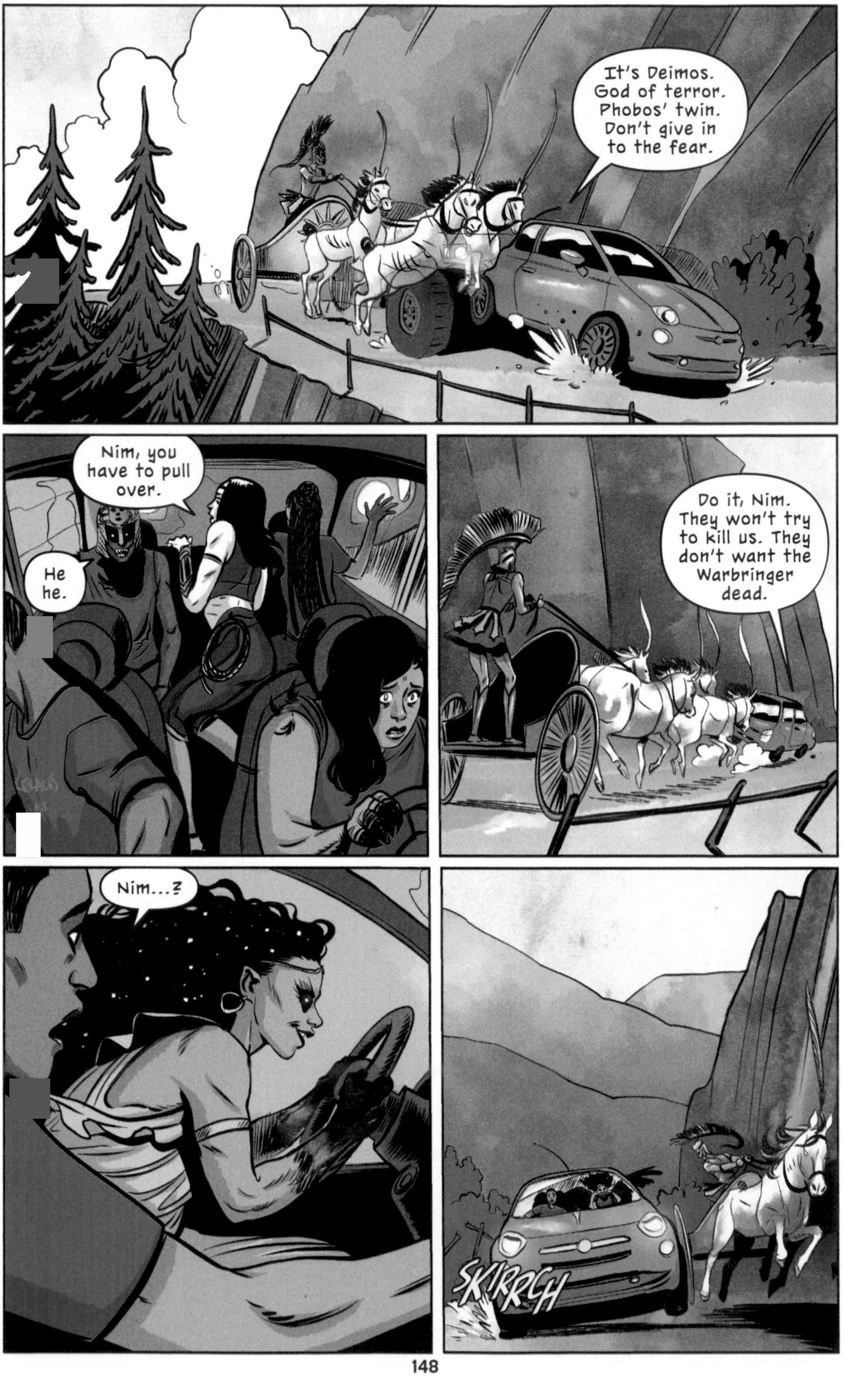
It's Deimos. God of terror. Phobos' twin. Don't give in to the fear.
Nim, you have to pull over.
He he.
Do it, Nim. They won't try to kill us. They don't want the Warbringer dead.
Nim...?
SKIRRCH

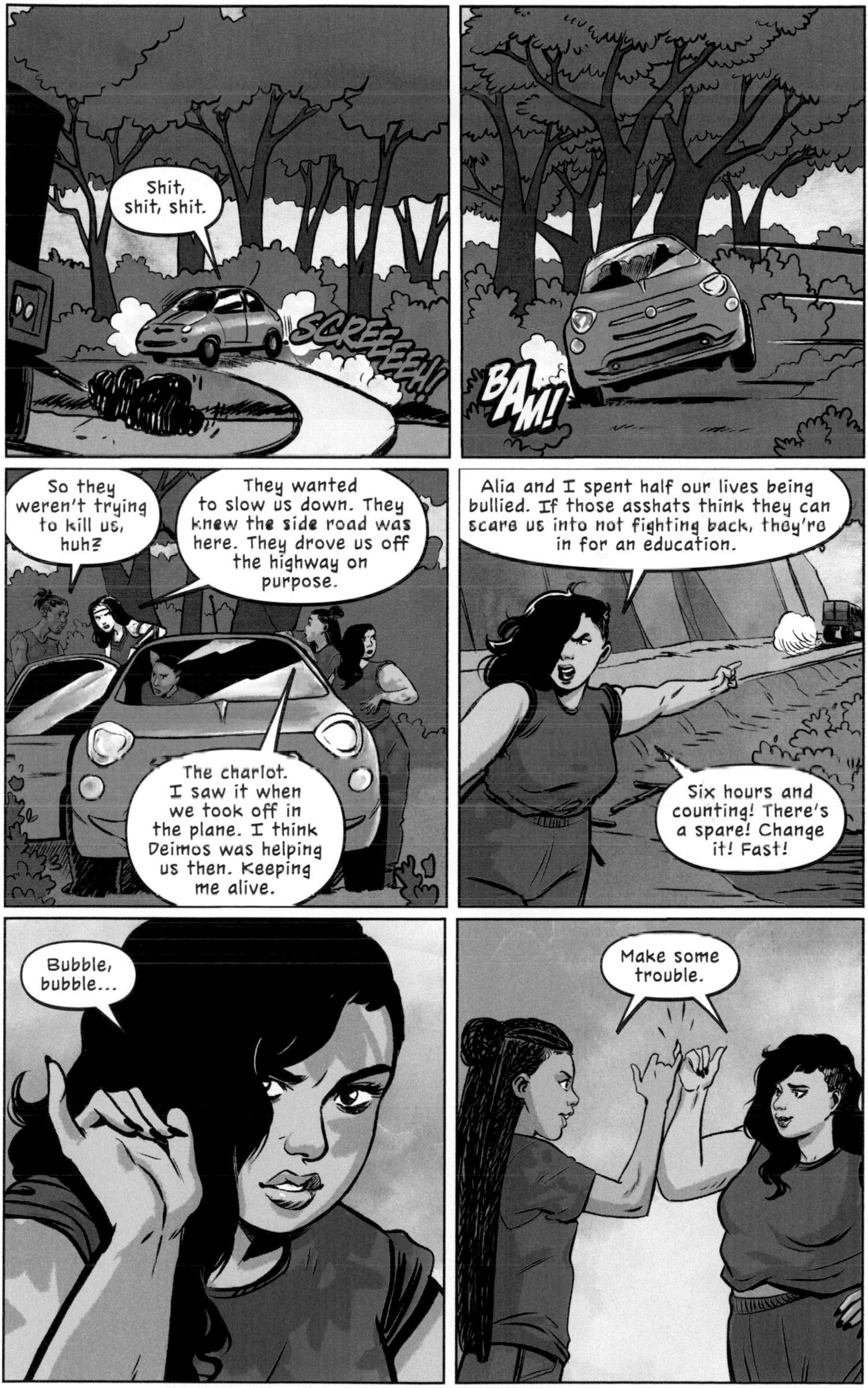
Shit, shit, shit.
SCREEEEEH!
BAM!
So they weren't trying to kill us, huh?
They wanted to slow us down. They knew the side road was here. They drove us off the highway on purpose.
The chariot. I saw it when we took off in the plane. I think Deimos was helping us then. Keeping me alive.
Alia and I spent half our lives being bullied. If those asshats think they can scare us into not fighting back, they're in for an education.
Six hours and counting! There's a spare! Change it! Fast!
Bubble, bubble...
Make some trouble.

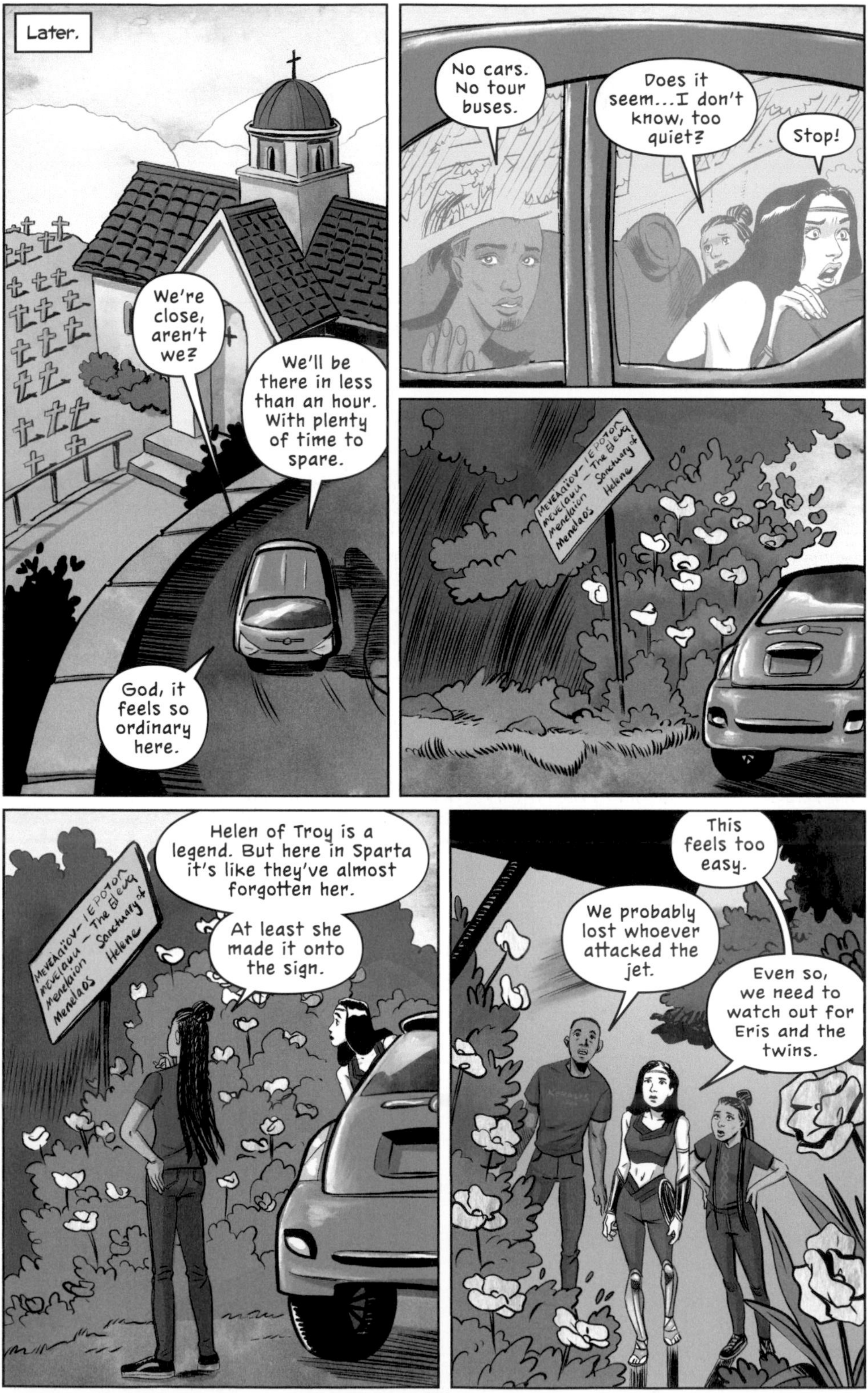

Later.
We're close, aren't we?
We'll be there in less than an hour. With plenty of time to spare.
God, it feels so ordinary here.
No cars. No tour buses.
Does it seem...I don't know, too quiet?
Stop!
Helen of Troy is a legend. But here in Sparta it's like they've almost forgotten her.
At least she made it onto the sign.
This feels too easy.
We probably lost whoever attacked the jet.
Even so, we need to watch out for Eris and the twins.

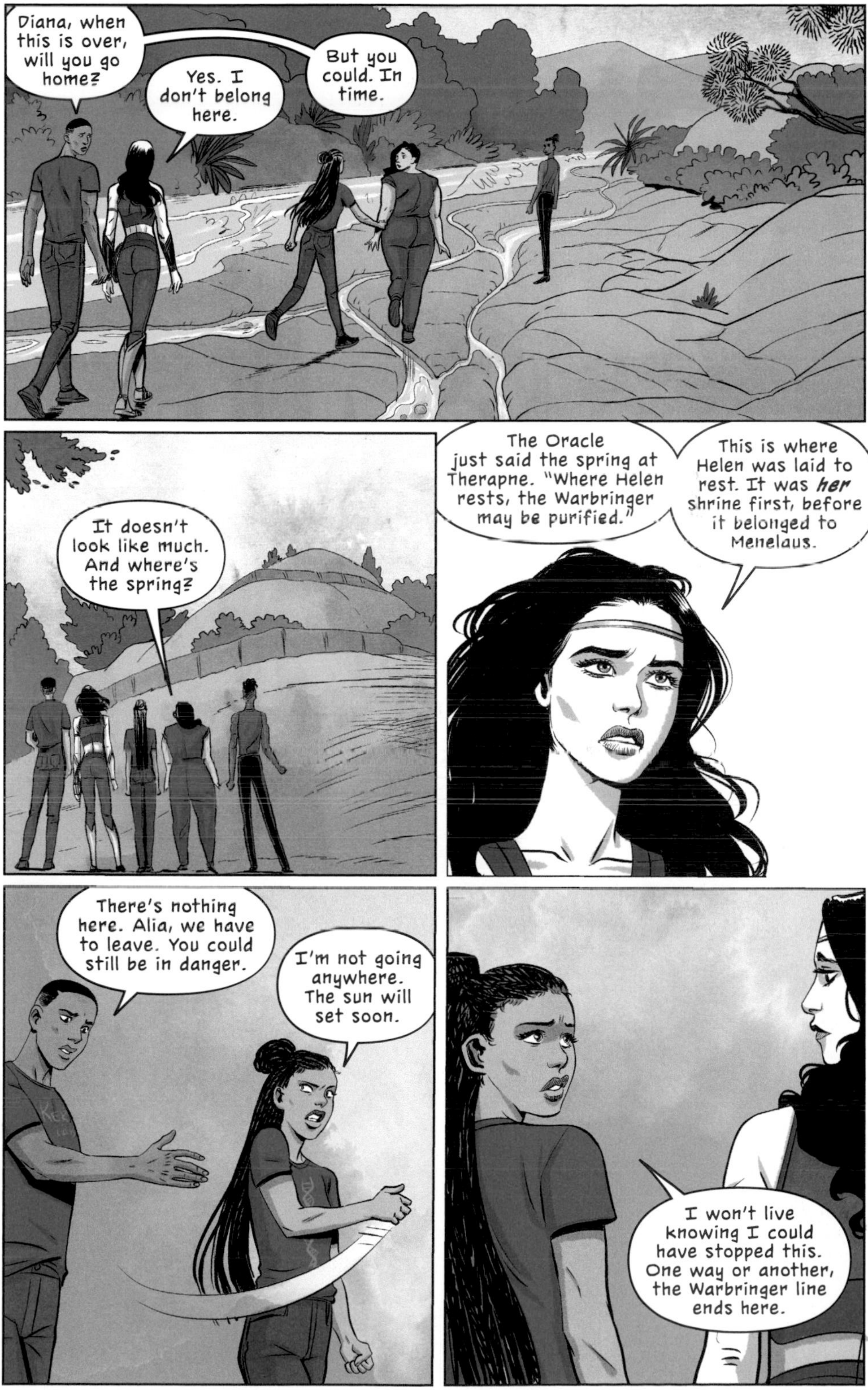
Diana, when this is over, will you go home?
Yes. I don't belong here.
But you could. In time.
It doesn't look like much. And where's the spring?
The Oracle just said the spring at Therapne. "Where Helen rests, the Warbringer may be purified."
This is where Helen was laid to rest. It was *her* shrine first, before it belonged to Menelaus.
There's nothing here. Alia, we have to leave. You could still be in danger.
I'm not going anywhere. The sun will set soon.
I won't live knowing I could have stopped this. One way or another, the Warbringer line ends here.

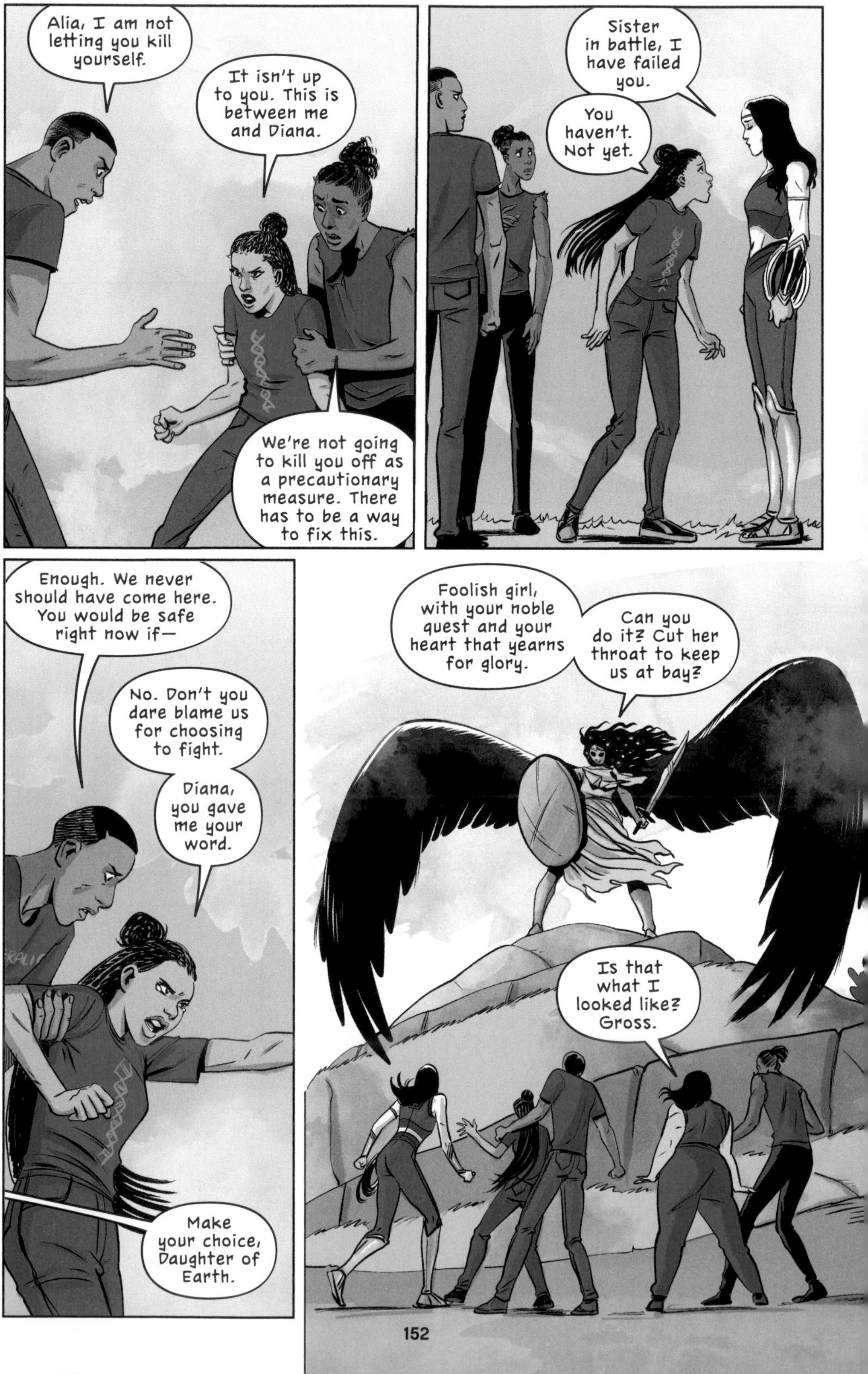
Alia, I am not letting you kill yourself.
It isn't up to you. This is between me and Diana.
We're not going to kill you off as a precautionary measure. There has to be a way to fix this.
Sister in battle, I have failed you.
You haven't. Not yet.
Enough. We never should have come here. You would be safe right now if—
No. Don't you dare blame us for choosing to fight.
Diana, you gave me your word.
Make your choice, Daughter of Earth.
Foolish girl, with your noble quest and your heart that yearns for glory.
Can you do it? Cut her throat to keep us at bay?
Is that what I looked like? Gross.

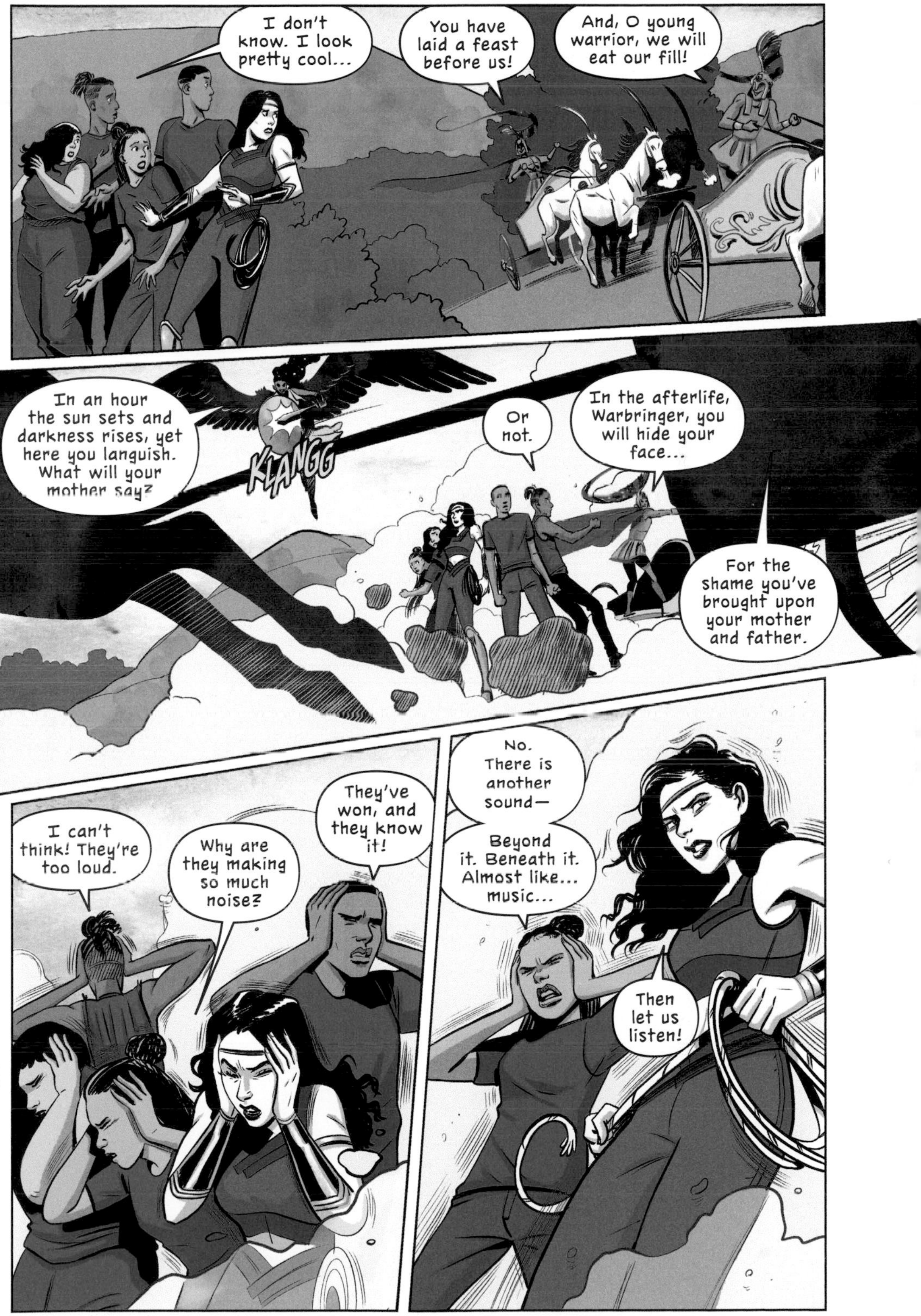
I don't know. I look pretty cool...
You have laid a feast before us!
And, O young warrior, we will eat our fill!
In an hour the sun sets and darkness rises, yet here you languish. What will your mother say?
KLANGG
Or not.
In the afterlife, Warbringer, you will hide your face...
For the shame you've brought upon your mother and father.
I can't think! They're too loud.
Why are they making so much noise?
They've won, and they know it!
No. There is another sound—
Beyond it. Beneath it. Almost like... music...
Then let us listen!

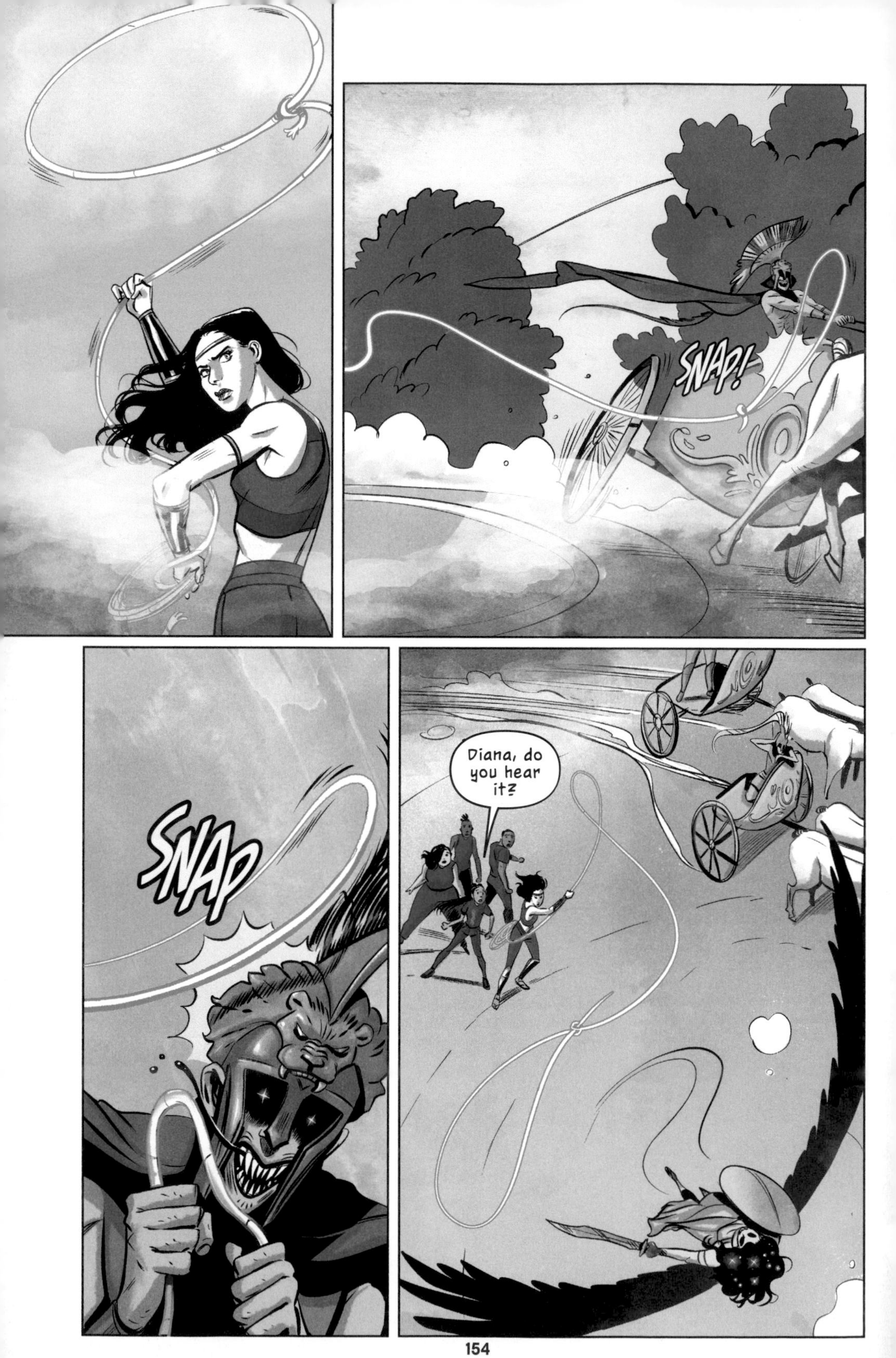
SNAP!
SNAP
Diana, do you hear it?

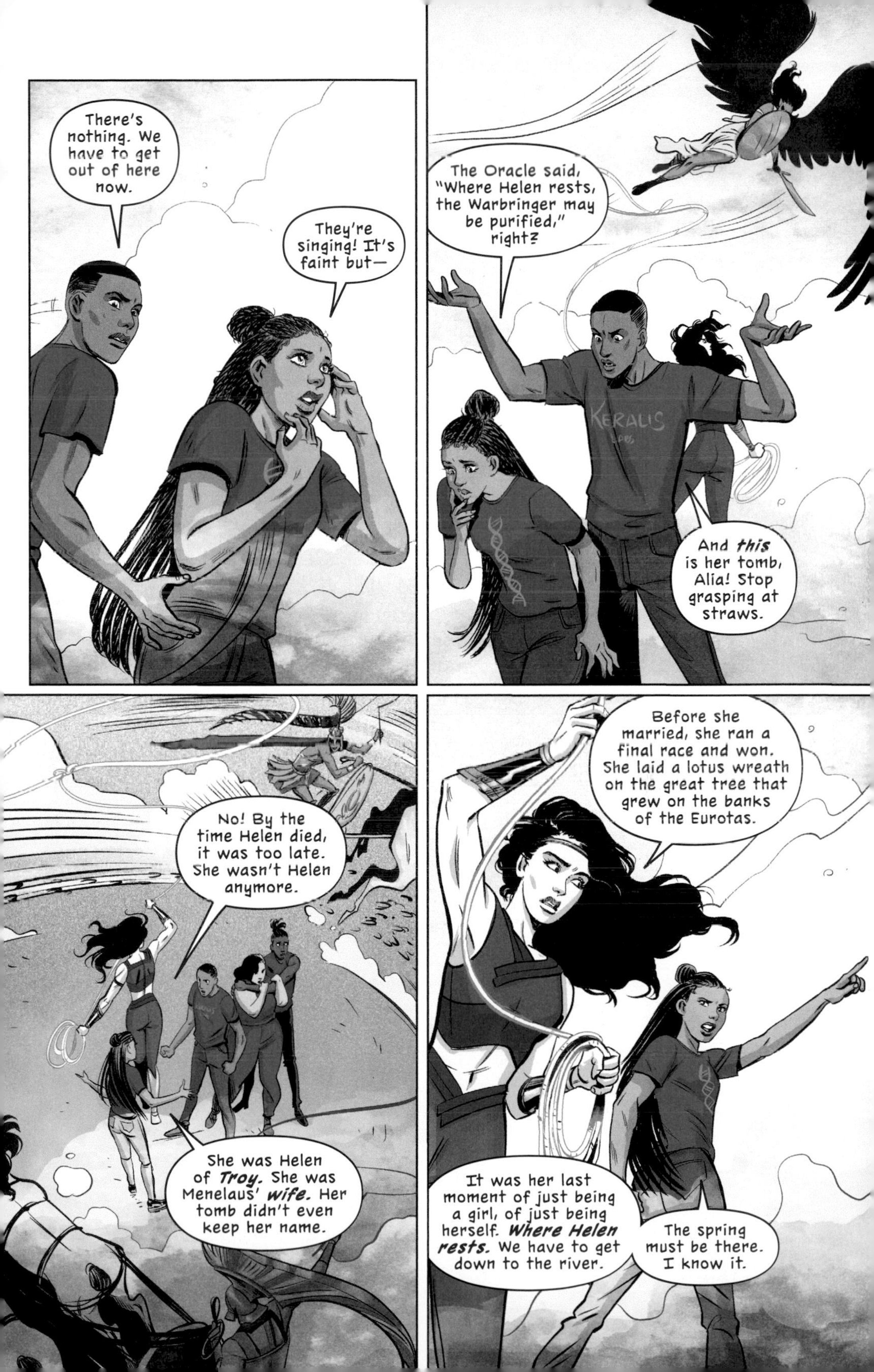
There's nothing. We have to get out of here now.
They're singing! It's faint but—
The Oracle said, "Where Helen rests, the Warbringer may be purified," right?
And *this* is her tomb, Alia! Stop grasping at straws.
No! By the time Helen died, it was too late. She wasn't Helen anymore.
She was Helen of *Troy.* She was Menelaus' *wife.* Her tomb didn't even keep her name.
Before she married, she ran a final race and won. She laid a lotus wreath on the great tree that grew on the banks of the Eurotas.
It was her last moment of just being a girl, of just being herself. *Where Helen rests.* We have to get down to the river.
The spring must be there. I know it.

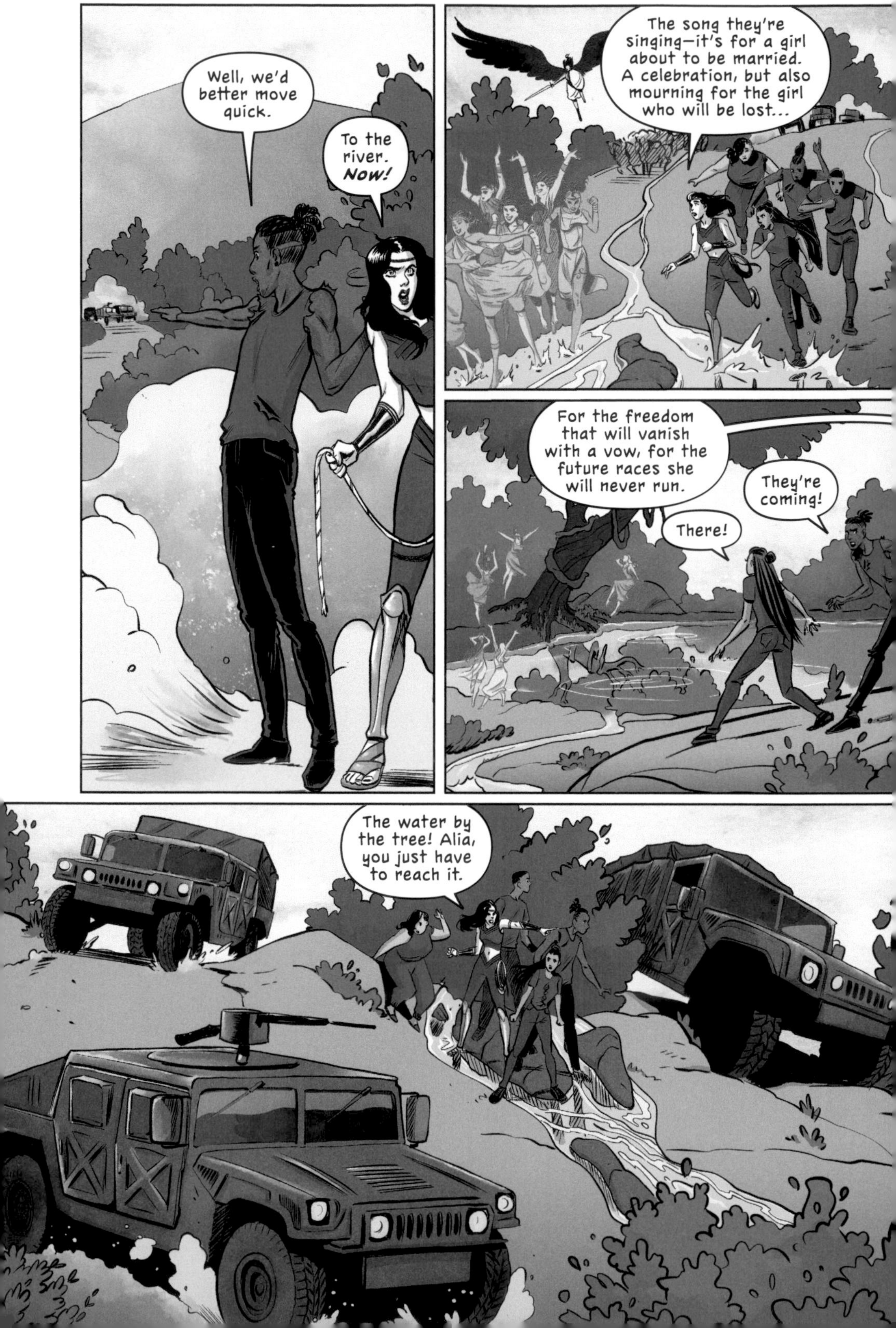
Well, we'd better move quick.
To the river. ***Now!***
The song they're singing—it's for a girl about to be married. A celebration, but also mourning for the girl who will be lost...
For the freedom that will vanish with a vow, for the future races she will never run.
There!
They're coming!
The water by the tree! Alia, you just have to reach it.

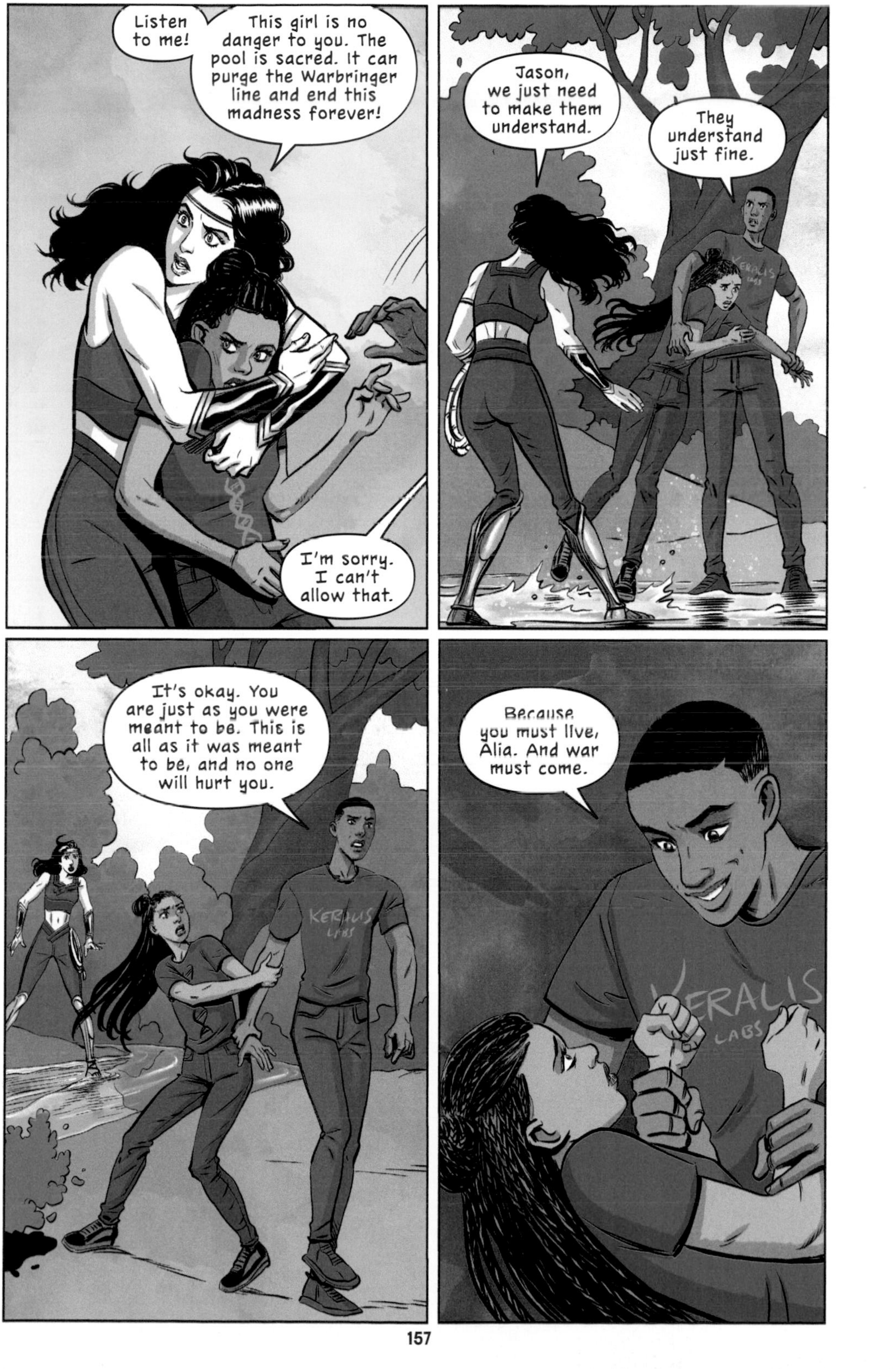
Listen to me!
This girl is no danger to you. The pool is sacred. It can purge the Warbringer line and end this madness forever!
I'm sorry. I can't allow that.
Jason, we just need to make them understand.
They understand just fine.
It's okay. You are just as you were meant to be. This is all as it was meant to be, and no one will hurt you.
Because you must live, Alia. And war must come.

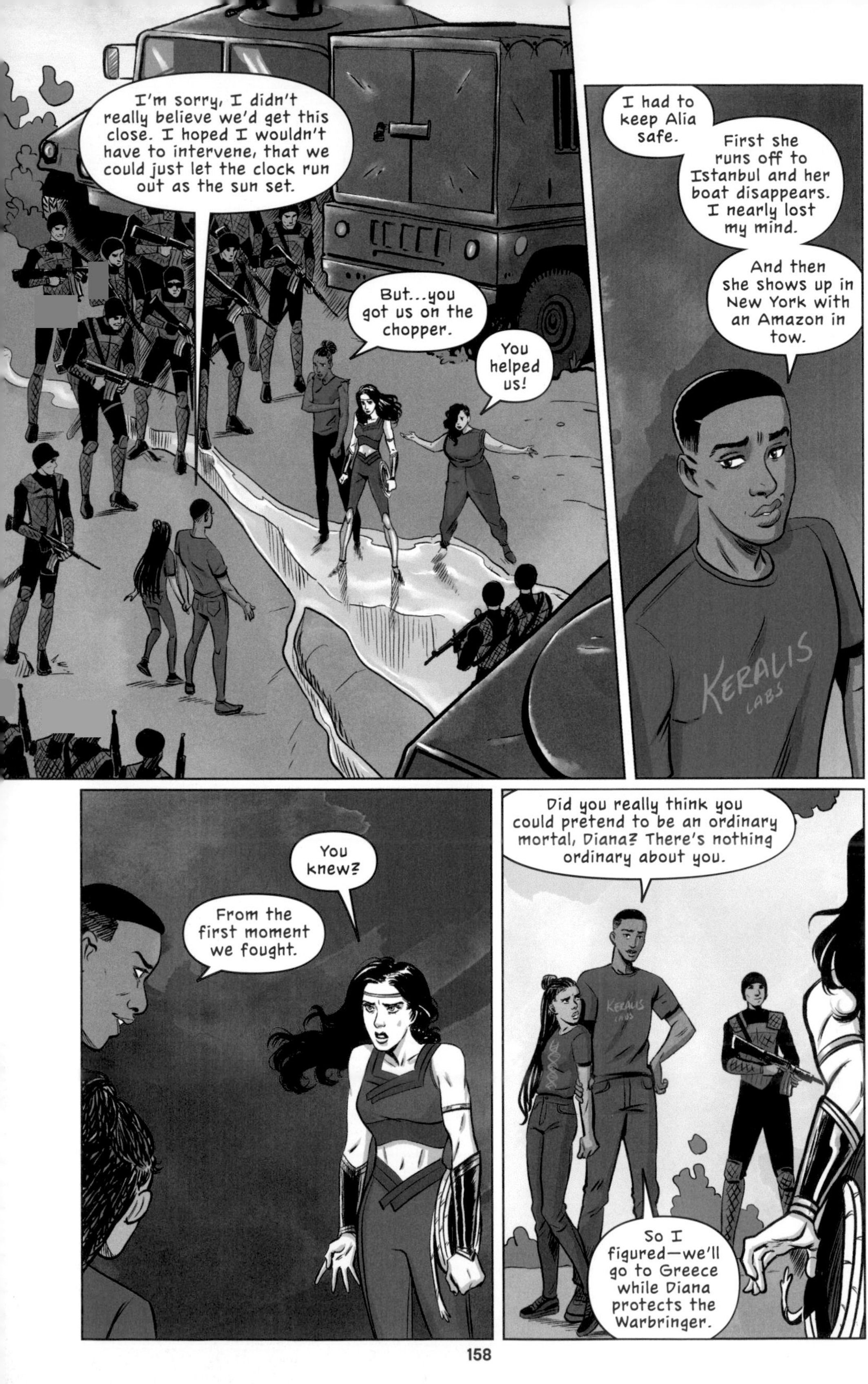
I'm sorry, I didn't really believe we'd get this close. I hoped I wouldn't have to intervene, that we could just let the clock run out as the sun set.
But...you got us on the chopper.
You helped us!
I had to keep Alia safe.
First she runs off to Istanbul and her boat disappears. I nearly lost my mind.
And then she shows up in New York with an Amazon in tow.
KERALIS LABS
You knew?
From the first moment we fought.
Did you really think you could pretend to be an ordinary mortal, Diana? There's nothing ordinary about you.
KERALIS LABS
So I figured—we'll go to Greece while Diana protects the Warbringer.

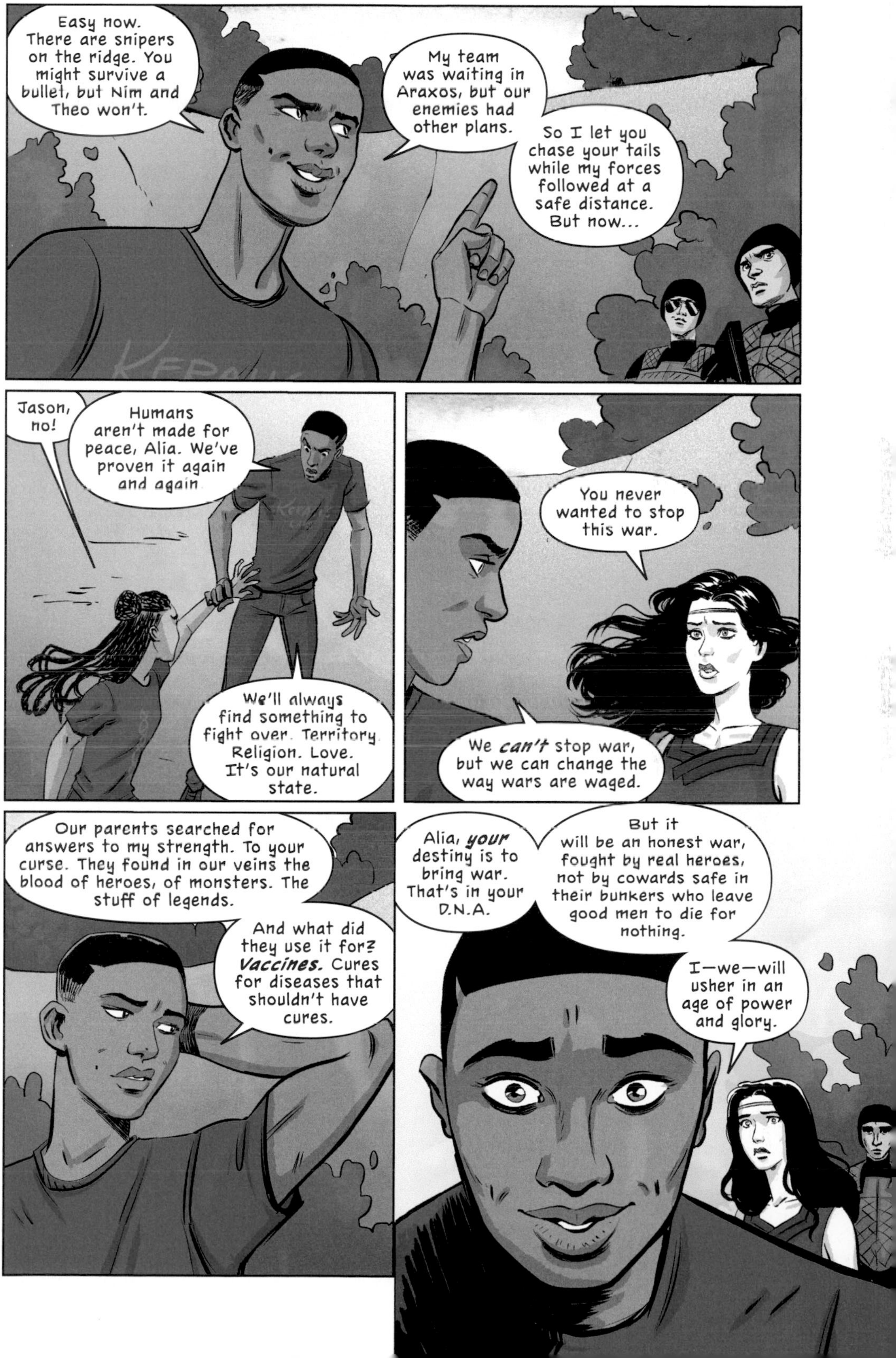
Easy now. There are snipers on the ridge. You might survive a bullet, but Nim and Theo won't.
My team was waiting in Araxos, but our enemies had other plans.
So I let you chase your tails while my forces followed at a safe distance. But now...
Jason, no!
Humans aren't made for peace, Alia. We've proven it again and again.
We'll always find something to fight over. Territory. Religion. Love. It's our natural state.
You never wanted to stop this war.
We *can't* stop war, but we can change the way wars are waged.
Our parents searched for answers to my strength. To your curse. They found in our veins the blood of heroes, of monsters. The stuff of legends.
And what did they use it for? *Vaccines.* Cures for diseases that shouldn't have cures.
Alia, *your* destiny is to bring war. That's in your D.N.A.
But it will be an honest war, fought by real heroes, not by cowards safe in their bunkers who leave good men to die for nothing.
I—we—will usher in an age of power and glory.

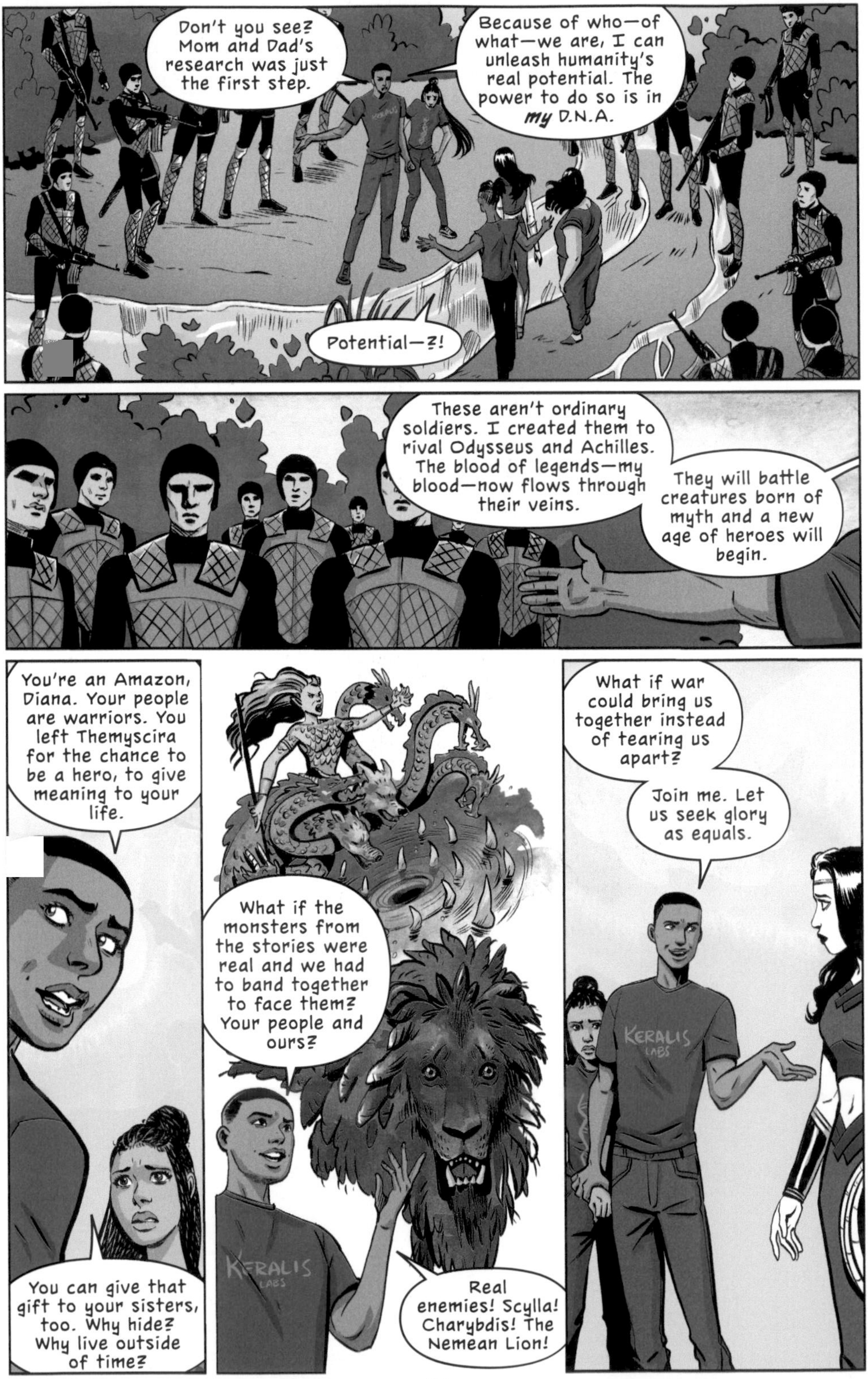
Don't you see? Mom and Dad's research was just the first step.
Because of who—of what—we are, I can unleash humanity's real potential. The power to do so is in *my* D.N.A.
Potential—?!
These aren't ordinary soldiers. I created them to rival Odysseus and Achilles. The blood of legends—my blood—now flows through their veins.
They will battle creatures born of myth and a new age of heroes will begin.
You're an Amazon, Diana. Your people are warriors. You left Themyscira for the chance to be a hero, to give meaning to your life.
You can give that gift to your sisters, too. Why hide? Why live outside of time?
What if the monsters from the stories were real and we had to band together to face them? Your people and ours?
Real enemies! Scylla! Charybdis! The Nemean Lion!
KERALIS LABS
What if war could bring us together instead of tearing us apart?
Join me. Let us seek glory as equals.
KERALIS LABS

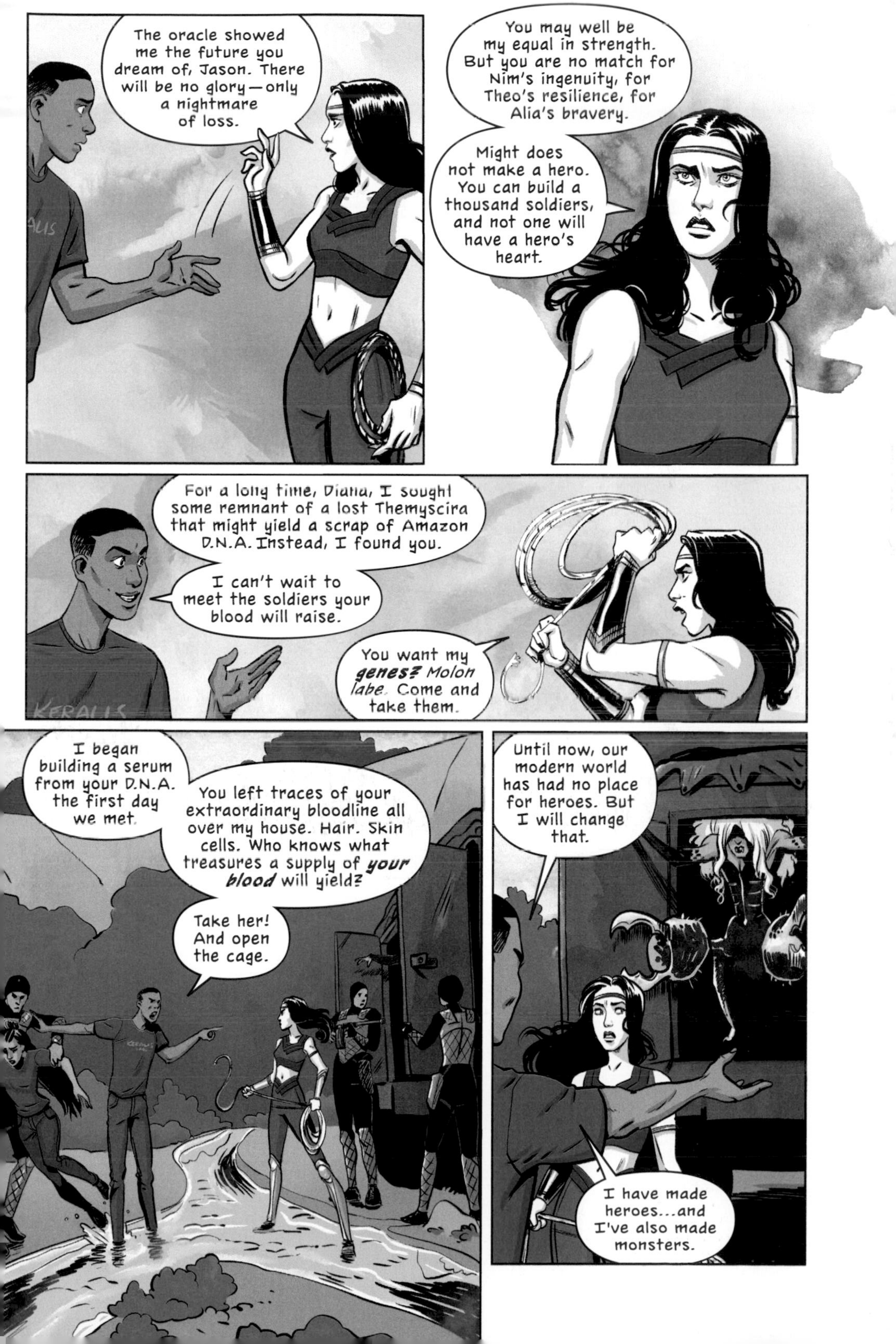
The oracle showed me the future you dream of, Jason. There will be no glory—only a nightmare of loss.
You may well be my equal in strength. But you are no match for Nim's ingenuity, for Theo's resilience, for Alia's bravery.
Might does not make a hero. You can build a thousand soldiers, and not one will have a hero's heart.
For a long time, Diana, I sought some remnant of a lost Themyscira that might yield a scrap of Amazon D.N.A. Instead, I found you.
I can't wait to meet the soldiers your blood will raise.
You want my genes? Molon labe. Come and take them.
I began building a serum from your D.N.A. the first day we met.
You left traces of your extraordinary bloodline all over my house. Hair. Skin cells. Who knows what treasures a supply of your blood will yield?
Take her! And open the cage.
Until now, our modern world has had no place for heroes. But I will change that.
I have made heroes...and I've also made monsters.

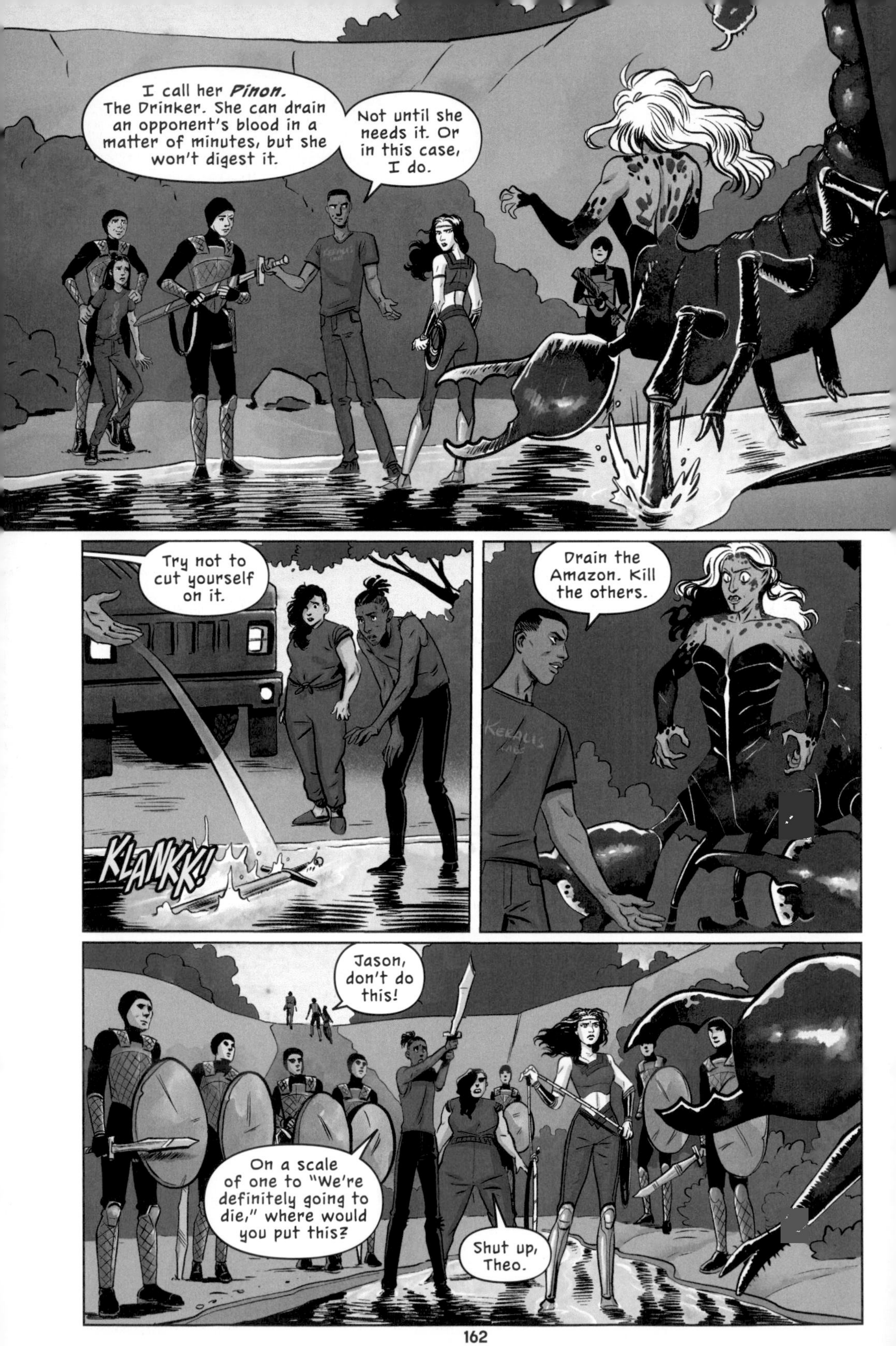
I call her *Pinon.* The Drinker. She can drain an opponent's blood in a matter of minutes, but she won't digest it.
Not until she needs it. Or in this case, I do.
Try not to cut yourself on it.
KLANKK!
Drain the Amazon. Kill the others.
Jason, don't do this!
On a scale of one to "We're definitely going to die," where would you put this?
Shut up, Theo.

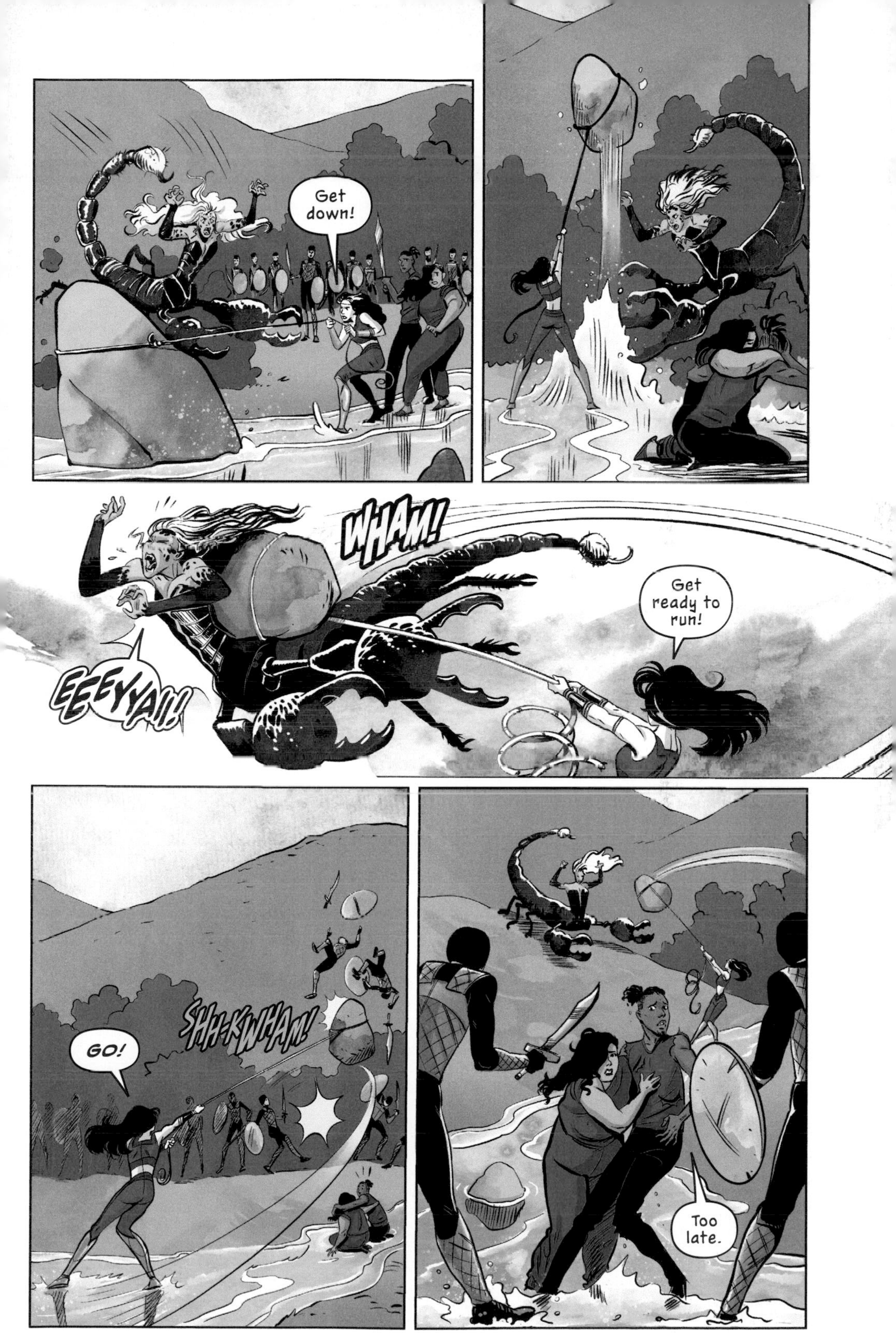
Get down!
WHAM!
EEEYYAII!
Get ready to run!
SHH-KWHAM!
GO!
Too late.

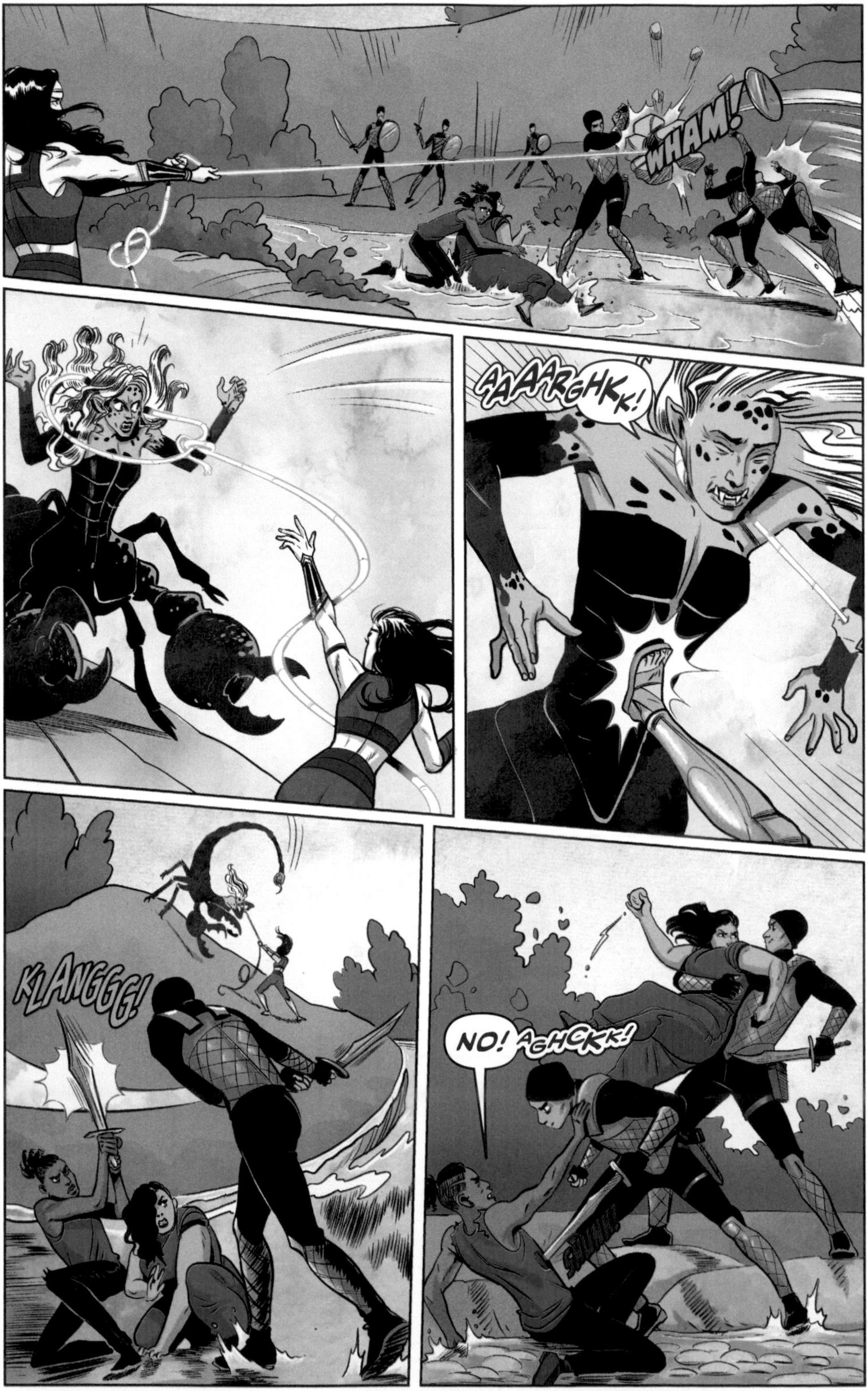
WHAM!
AAAARGHKK!
KLANGGG!
NO!
AGHCKK!

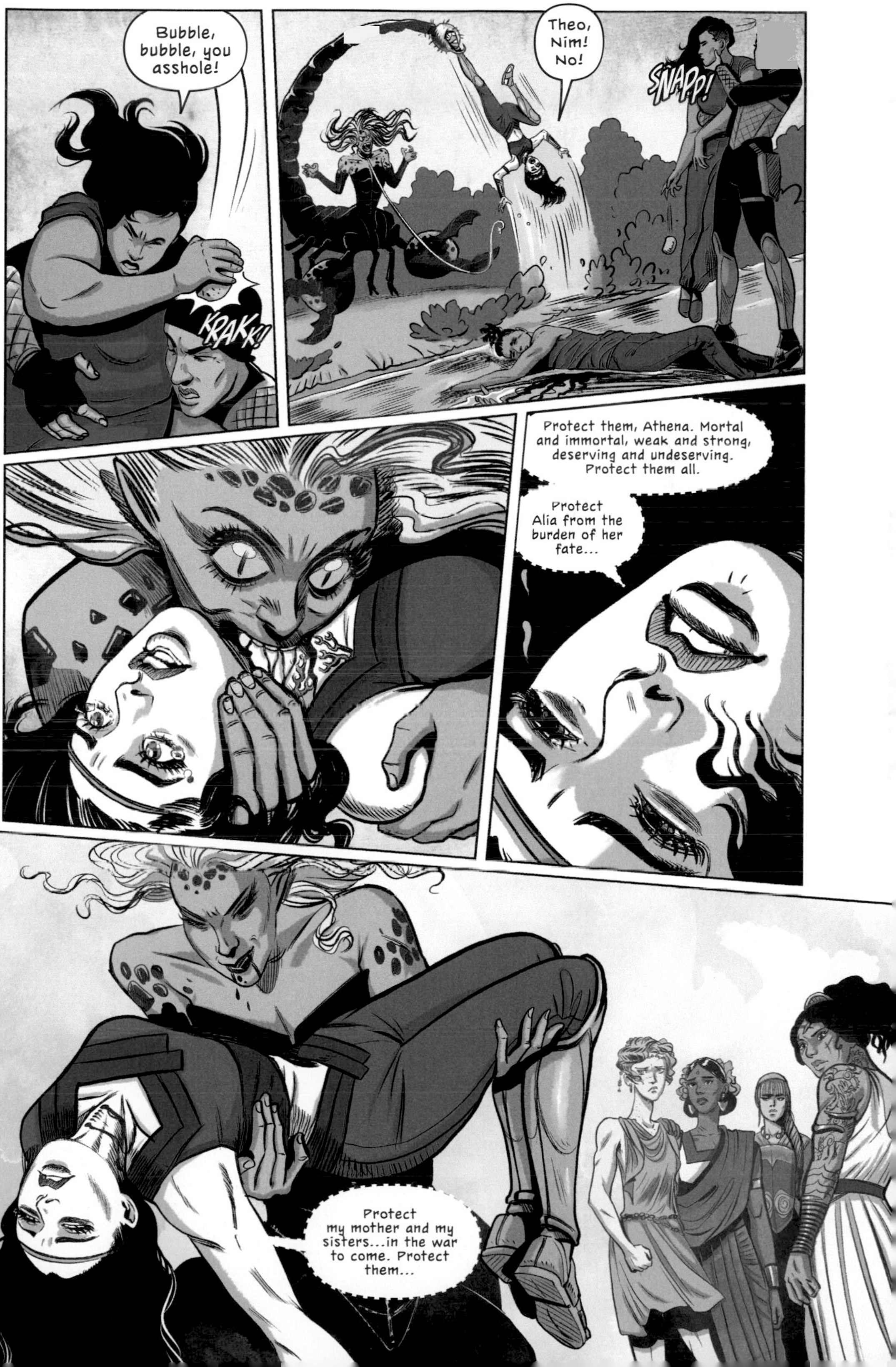

Bubble, bubble, you asshole!
KRAKK!
Theo, Nim! No!
SNAPP!
Protect them, Athena. Mortal and immortal, weak and strong, deserving and undeserving. Protect them all.
Protect Alia from the burden of her fate...
Protect my mother and my sisters...in the war to come. Protect them...

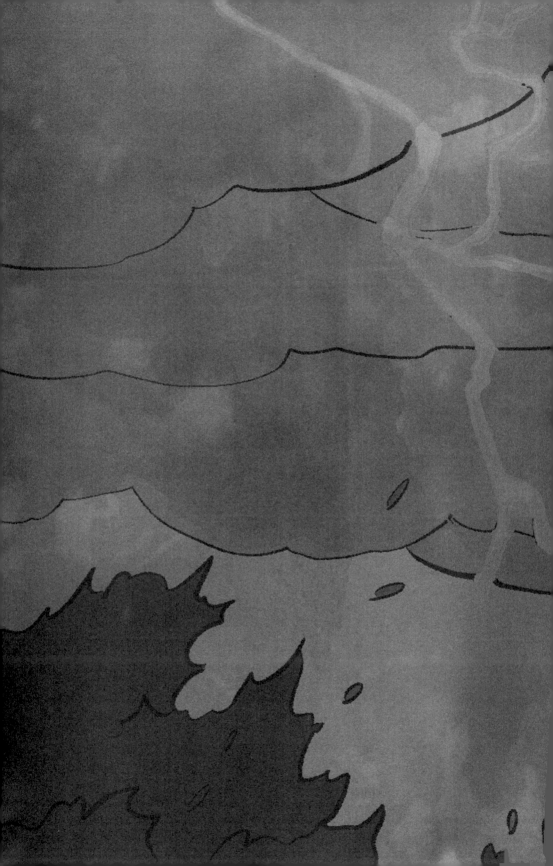

PART SEVEN

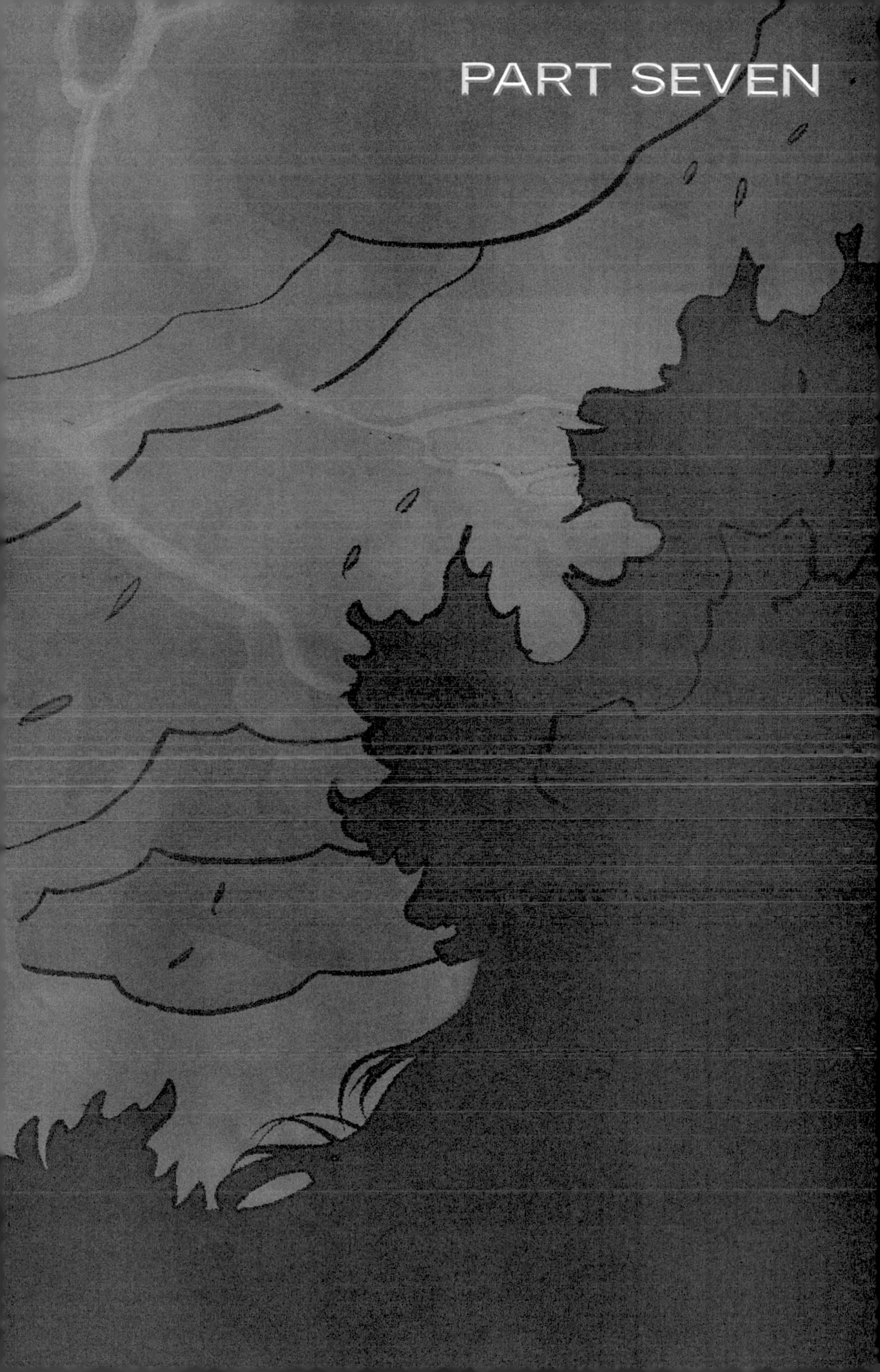

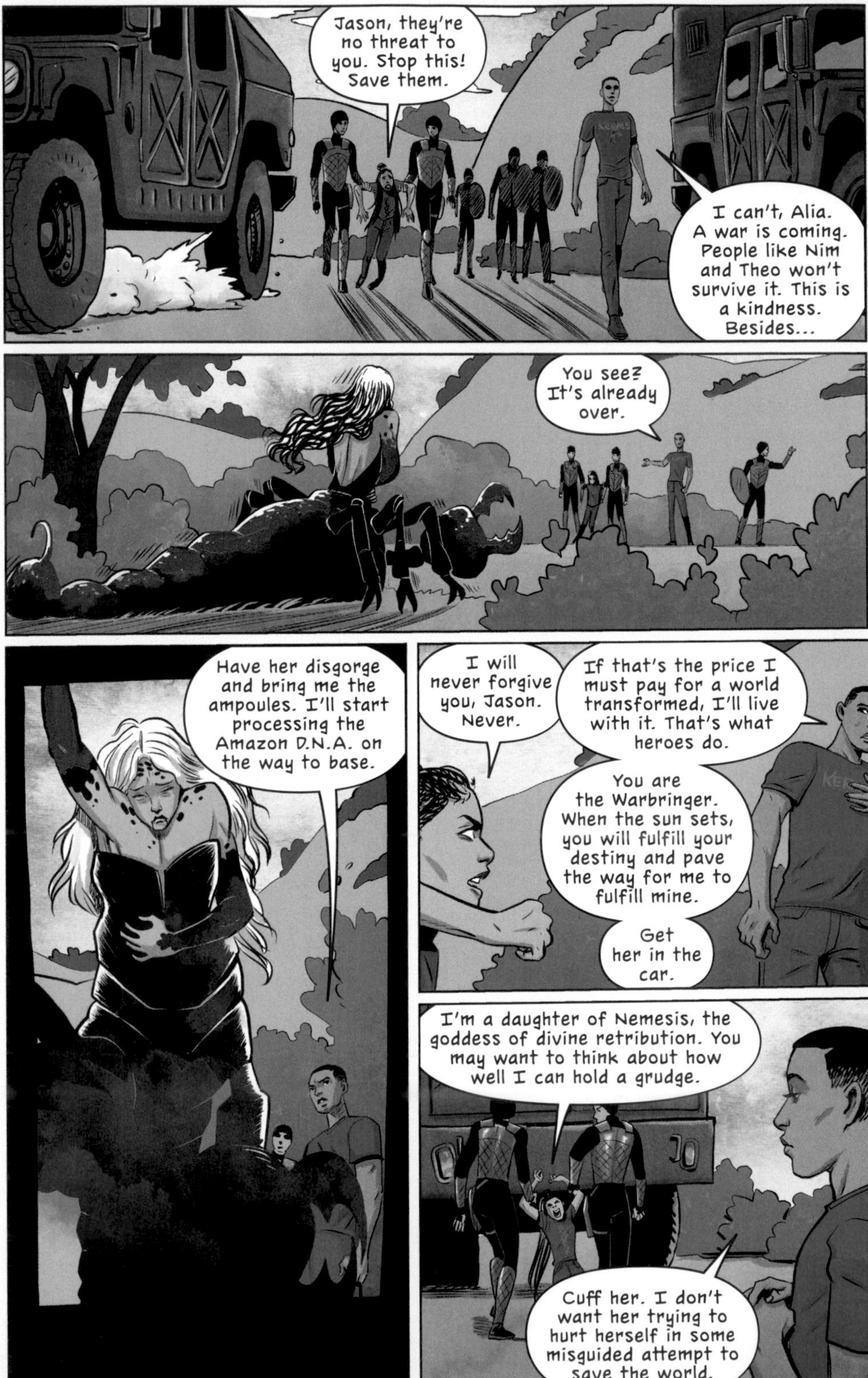

Jason, they're no threat to you. Stop this! Save them.
I can't, Alia. A war is coming. People like Nim and Theo won't survive it. This is a kindness. Besides...
You see? It's already over.
Have her disgorge and bring me the ampoules. I'll start processing the Amazon D.N.A. on the way to base.
I will never forgive you, Jason. Never.
If that's the price I must pay for a world transformed, I'll live with it. That's what heroes do.
You are the Warbringer. When the sun sets, you will fulfill your destiny and pave the way for me to fulfill mine.
Get her in the car.
I'm a daughter of Nemesis, the goddess of divine retribution. You may want to think about how well I can hold a grudge.
Cuff her. I don't want her trying to hurt herself in some misguided attempt to save the world.

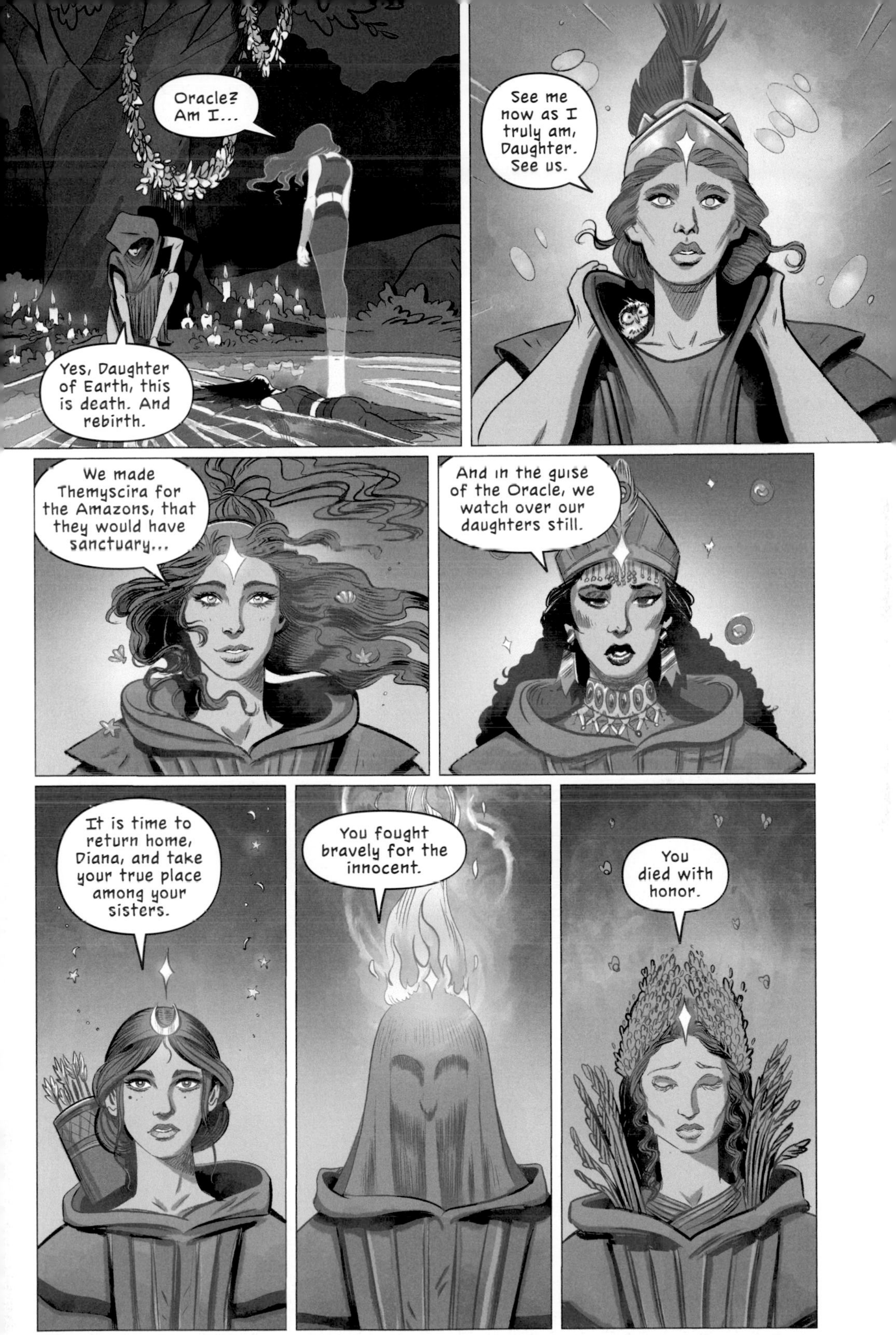
Oracle? Am I...
Yes, Daughter of Earth, this is death. And rebirth.
See me now as I truly am, Daughter. See us.
We made Themyscira for the Amazons, that they would have sanctuary...
And in the guise of the Oracle, we watch over our daughters still.
It is time to return home, Diana, and take your true place among your sisters.
You fought bravely for the innocent.
You died with honor.

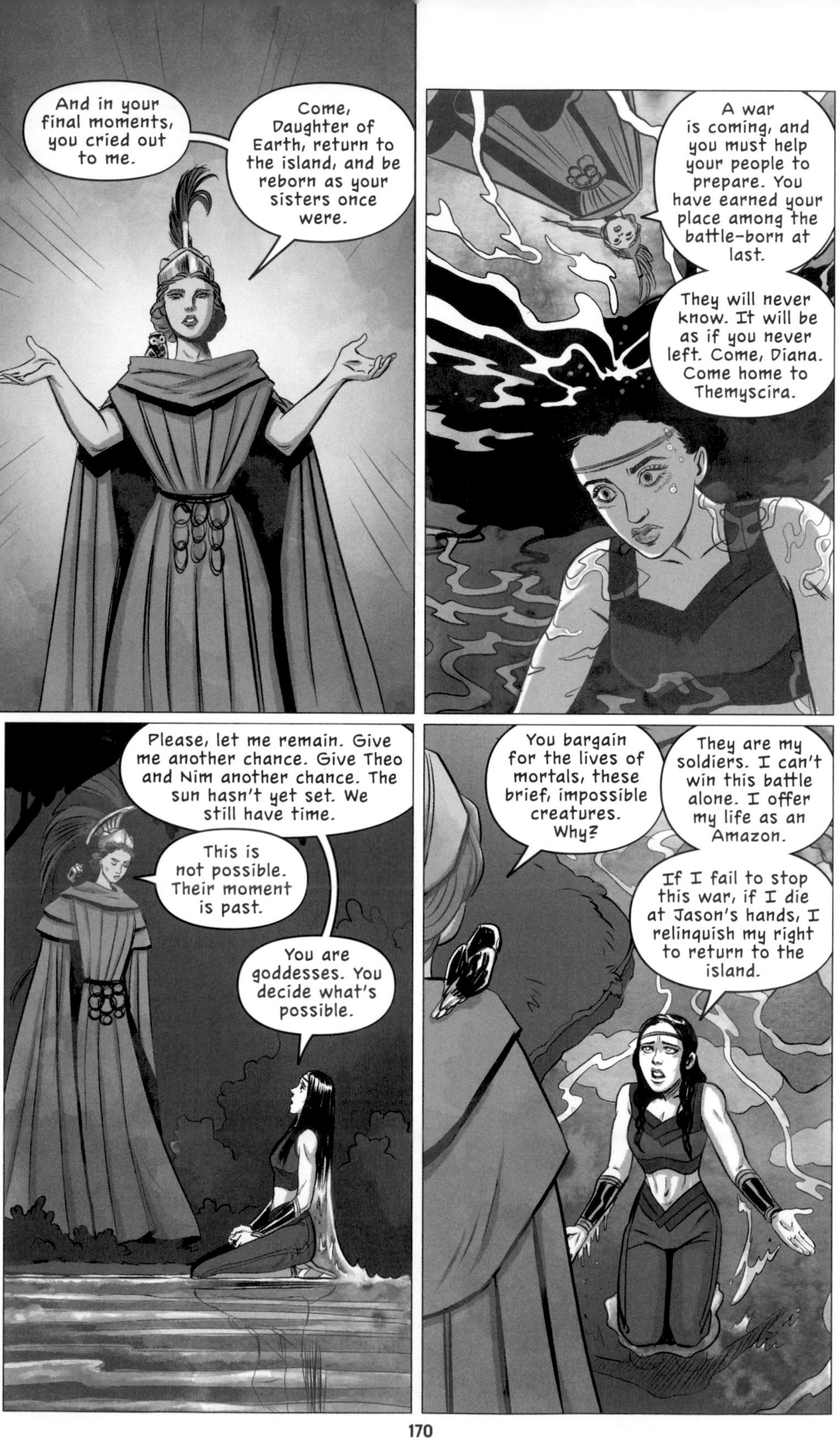
And in your final moments, you cried out to me.
Come, Daughter of Earth, return to the island, and be reborn as your sisters once were.
A war is coming, and you must help your people to prepare. You have earned your place among the battle-born at last.
They will never know. It will be as if you never left. Come, Diana. Come home to Themyscira.
Please, let me remain. Give me another chance. Give Theo and Nim another chance. The sun hasn't yet set. We still have time.
This is not possible. Their moment is past.
You are goddesses. You decide what's possible.
You bargain for the lives of mortals, these brief, impossible creatures. Why?
They are my soldiers. I can't win this battle alone. I offer my life as an Amazon.
If I fail to stop this war, if I die at Jason's hands, I relinquish my right to return to the island.

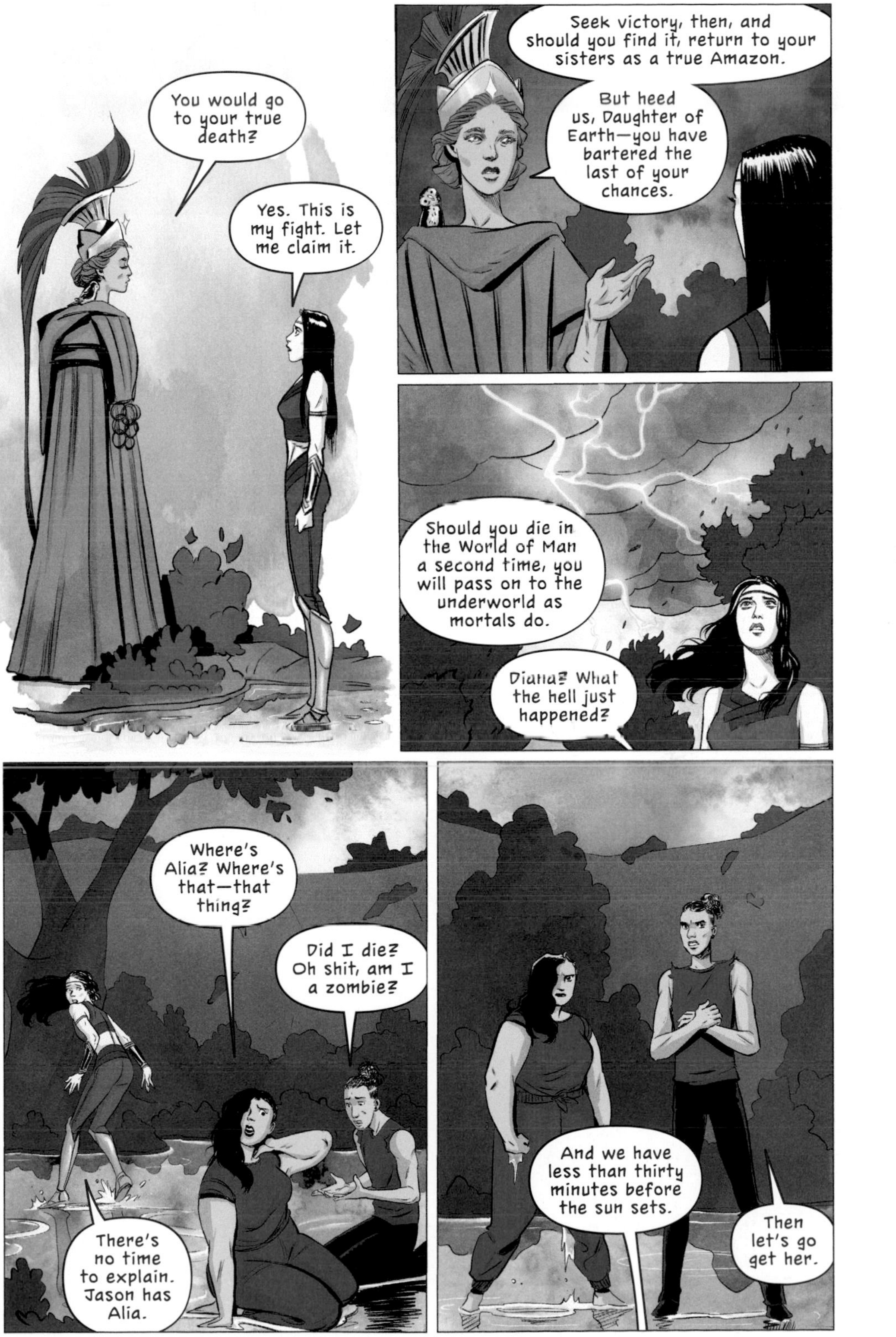

You would go to your true death?
Yes. This is my fight. Let me claim it.
Seek victory, then, and should you find it, return to your sisters as a true Amazon.
But heed us, Daughter of Earth—you have bartered the last of your chances.
Should you die in the World of Man a second time, you will pass on to the underworld as mortals do.
Diana? What the hell just happened?
Where's Alia? Where's that—that thing?
Did I die? Oh shit, am I a zombie?
There's no time to explain. Jason has Alia.
And we have less than thirty minutes before the sun sets.
Then let's go get her.

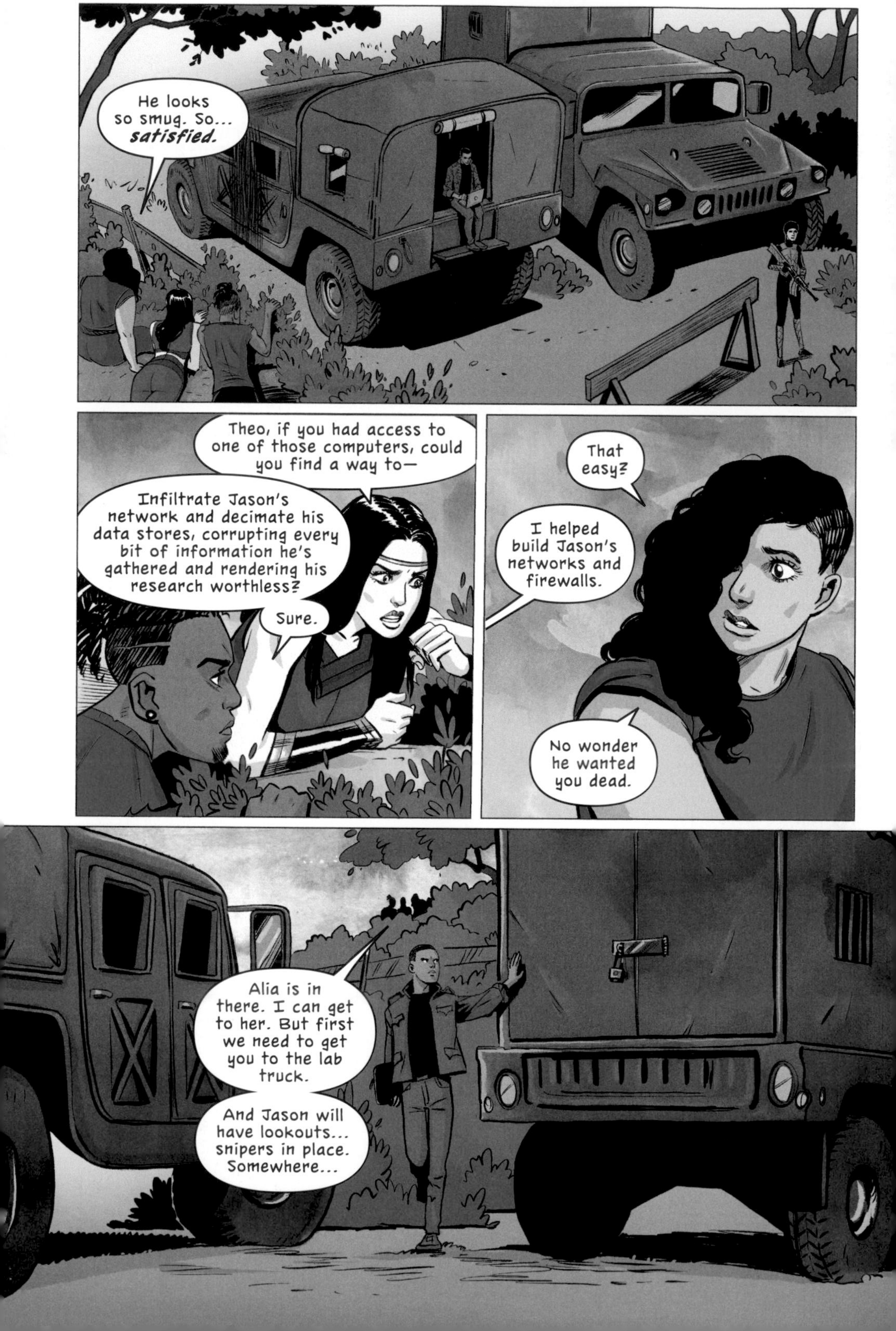
He looks so smug. So... *satisfied.*
Theo, if you had access to one of those computers, could you find a way to—
Infiltrate Jason's network and decimate his data stores, corrupting every bit of information he's gathered and rendering his research worthless?
Sure.
That easy?
I helped build Jason's networks and firewalls.
No wonder he wanted you dead.
Alia is in there. I can get to her. But first we need to get you to the lab truck.
And Jason will have lookouts... snipers in place. Somewhere...

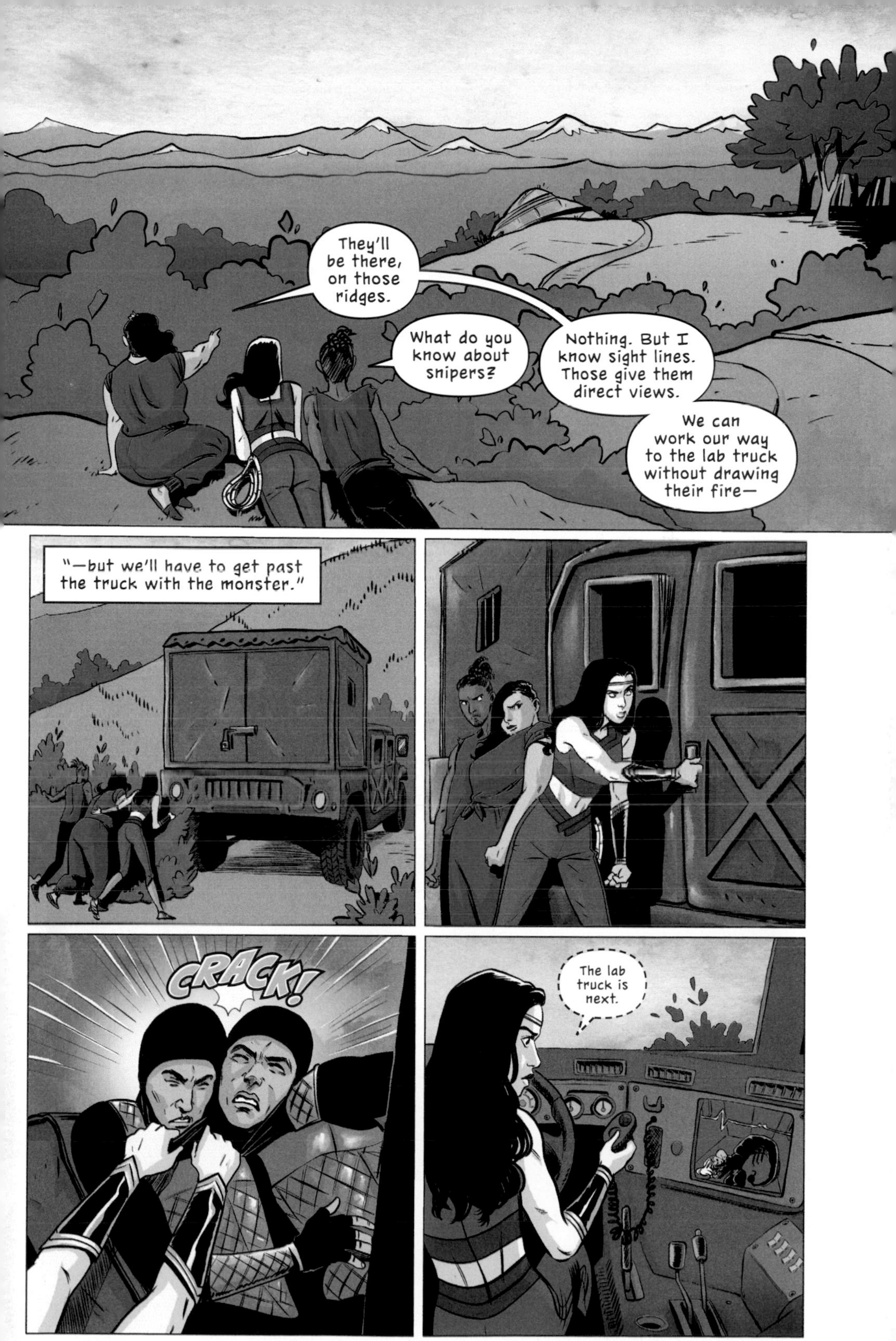
They'll be there, on those ridges.
What do you know about snipers?
Nothing. But I know sight lines. Those give them direct views.
We can work our way to the lab truck without drawing their fire—
"—but we'll have to get past the truck with the monster."
CRACK!
The lab truck is next.

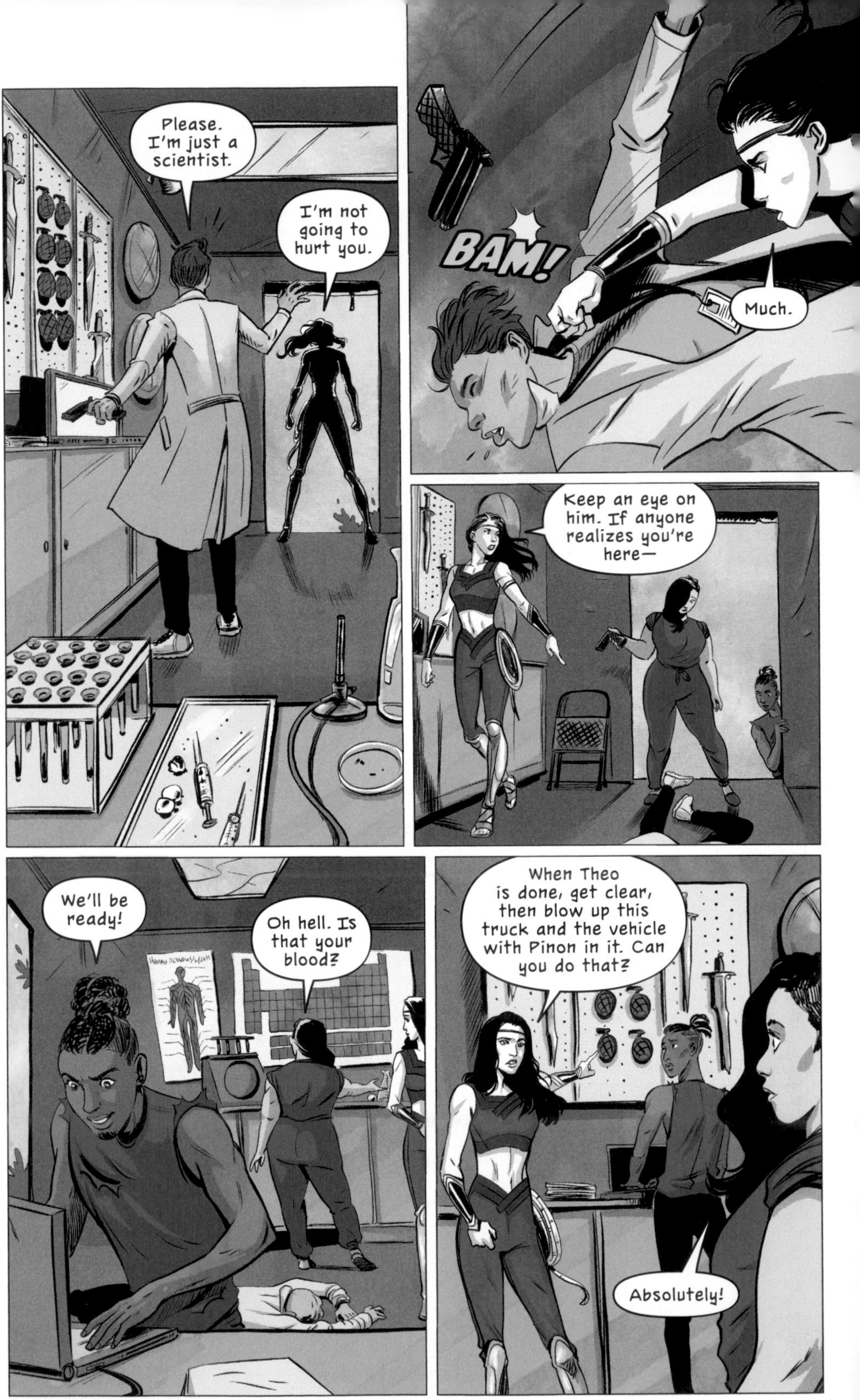
Please. I'm just a scientist.
I'm not going to hurt you.
BAM!
Much.
Keep an eye on him. If anyone realizes you're here—
We'll be ready!
Oh hell. Is that your blood?
When Theo is done, get clear, then blow up this truck and the vehicle with Pinon in it. Can you do that?
Absolutely!

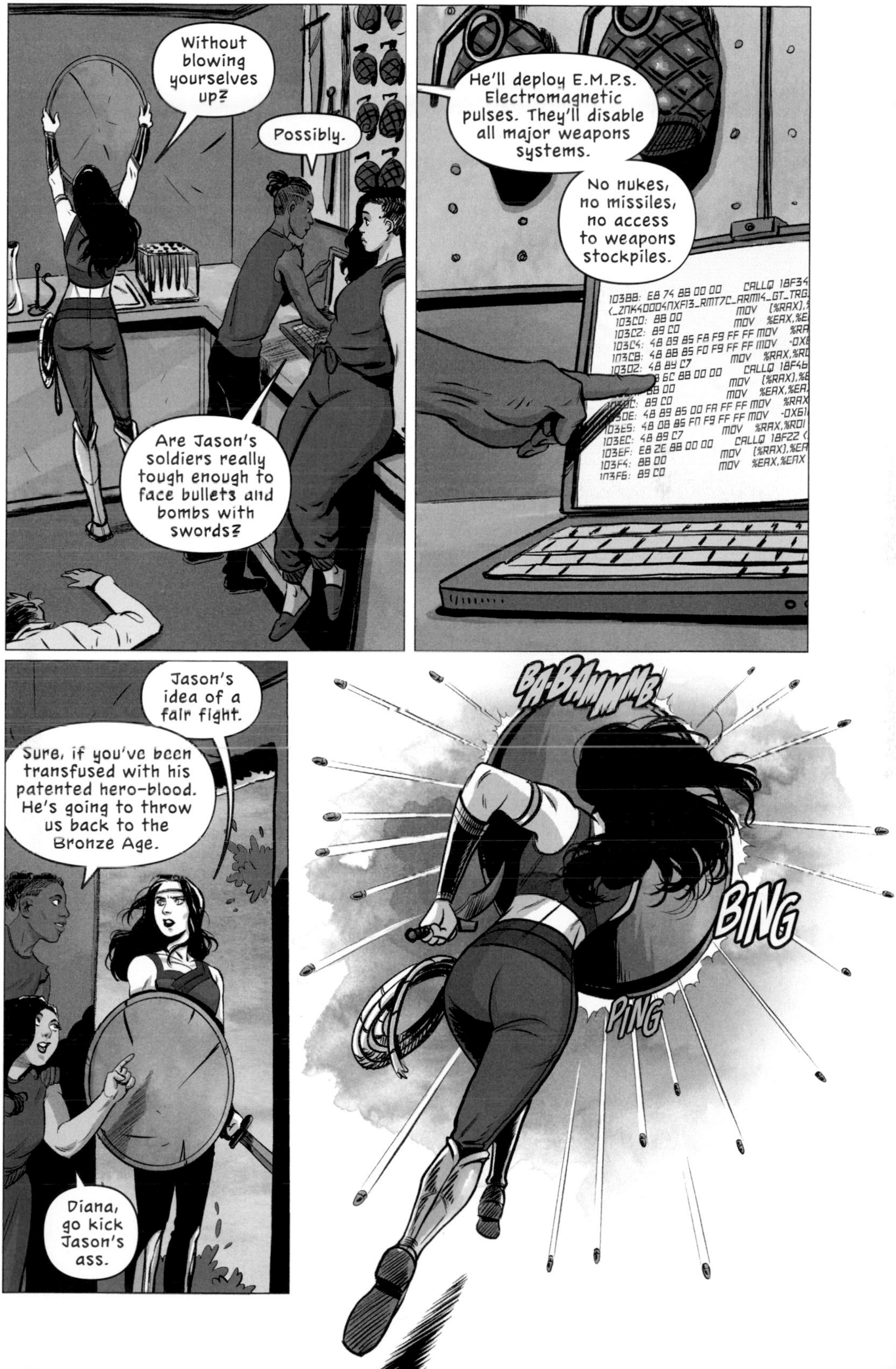
Without blowing yourselves up?
Possibly.
Are Jason's soldiers really tough enough to face bullets and bombs with swords?
He'll deploy E.M.P.s. Electromagnetic pulses. They'll disable all major weapons systems.
No nukes, no missiles, no access to weapons stockpiles.
Jason's idea of a fair fight.
Sure, if you've been transfused with his patented hero-blood. He's going to throw us back to the Bronze Age.
Diana, go kick Jason's ass.
BA-BAMMMB
BING
PING

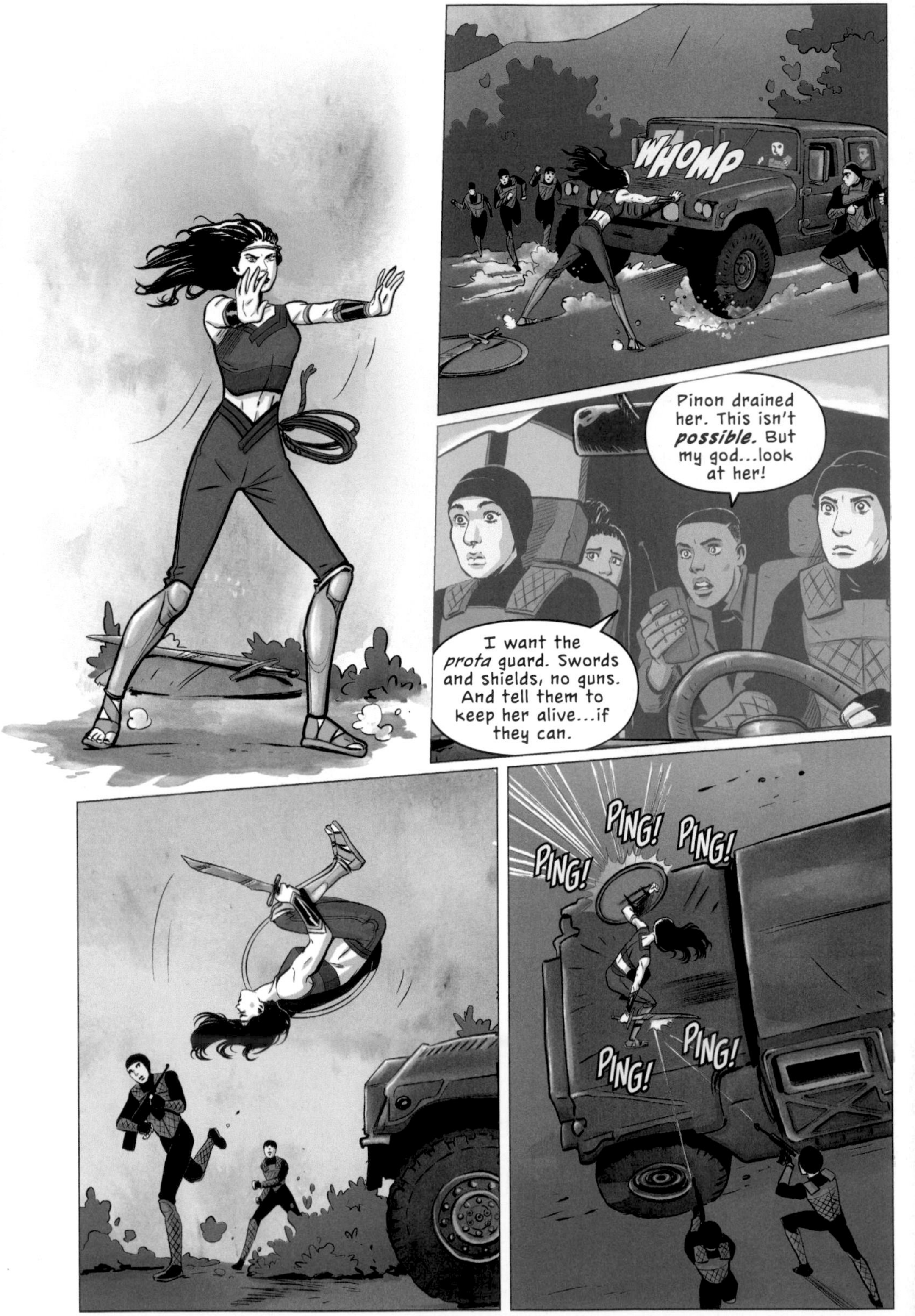
WHOMP
Pinon drained her. This isn't *possible.* But my god...look at her!
I want the *prota* guard. Swords and shields, no guns. And tell them to keep her alive...if they can.
PING! PING! PING!
PING! PING!

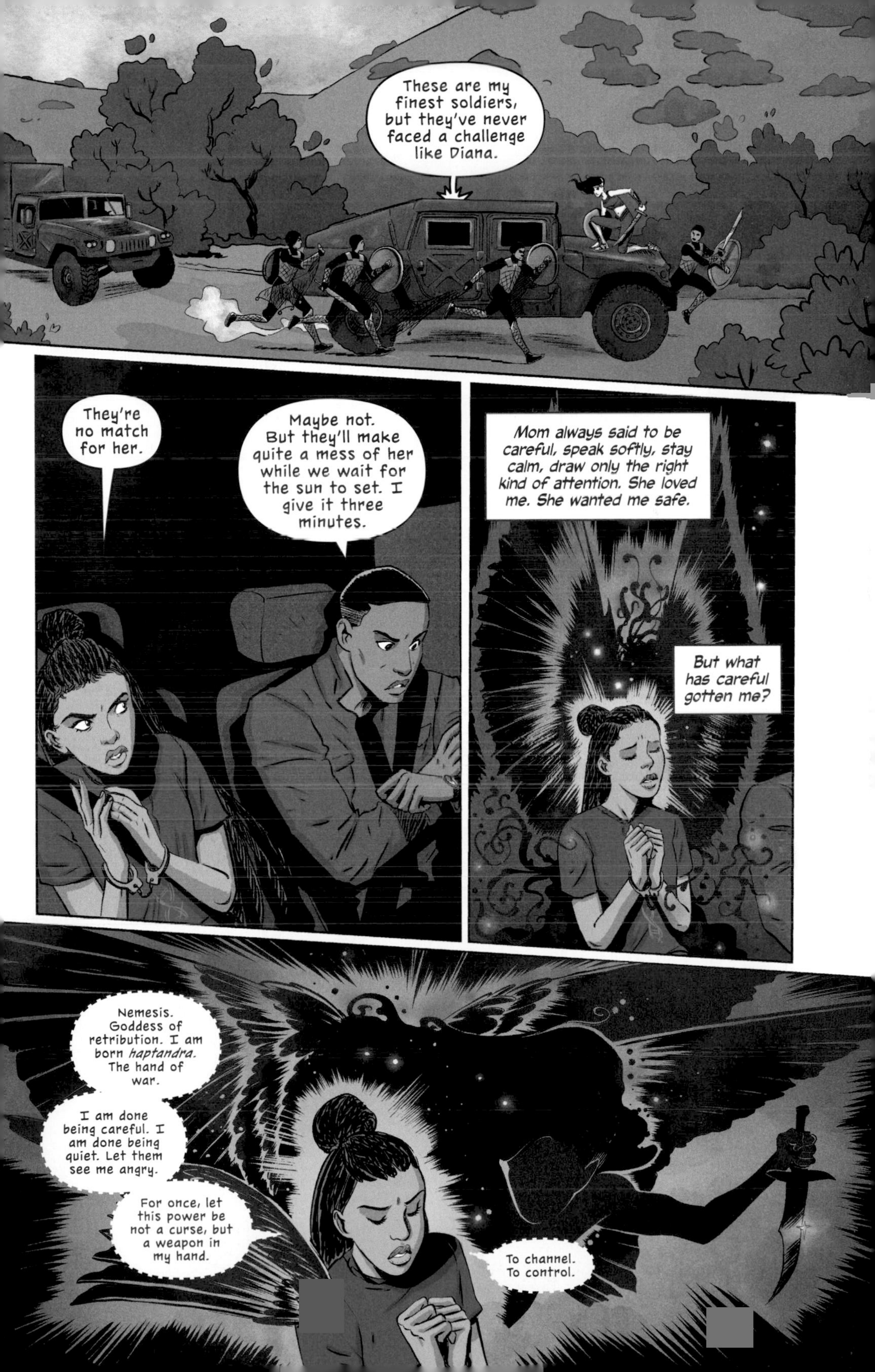
These are my finest soldiers, but they've never faced a challenge like Diana.
They're no match for her.
Maybe not. But they'll make quite a mess of her while we wait for the sun to set. I give it three minutes.
Mom always said to be careful, speak softly, stay calm, draw only the right kind of attention. She loved me. She wanted me safe.
But what has careful gotten me?
Nemesis. Goddess of retribution. I am born haptandra. The hand of war.
I am done being careful. I am done being quiet. Let them see me angry.
For once, let this power be not a curse, but a weapon in my hand.
To channel. To control.

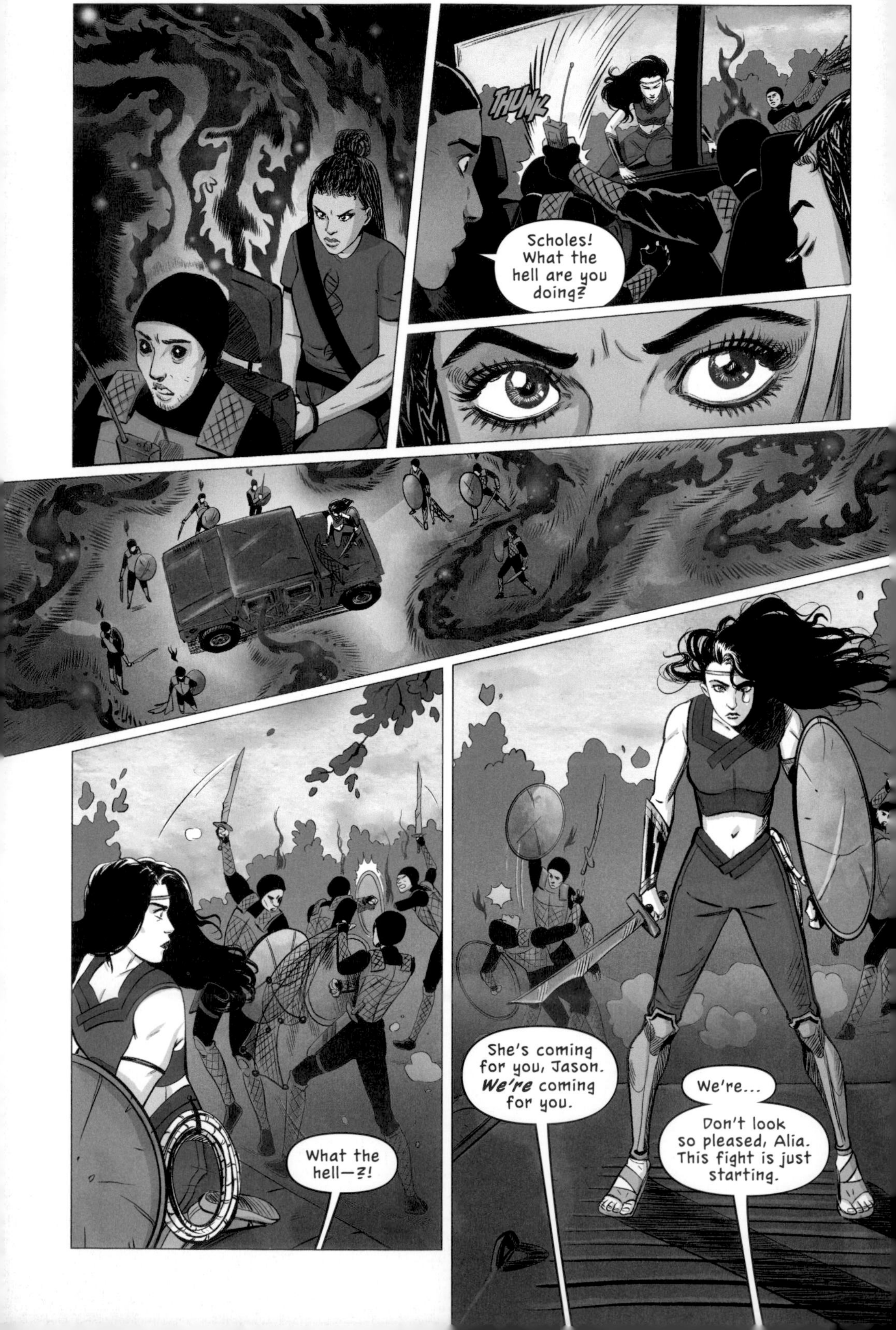
THUNK
Scholes! What the hell are you doing?
What the hell—?!
She's coming for you, Jason. *We're* coming for you.
We're...
Don't look so pleased, Alia. This fight is just starting.

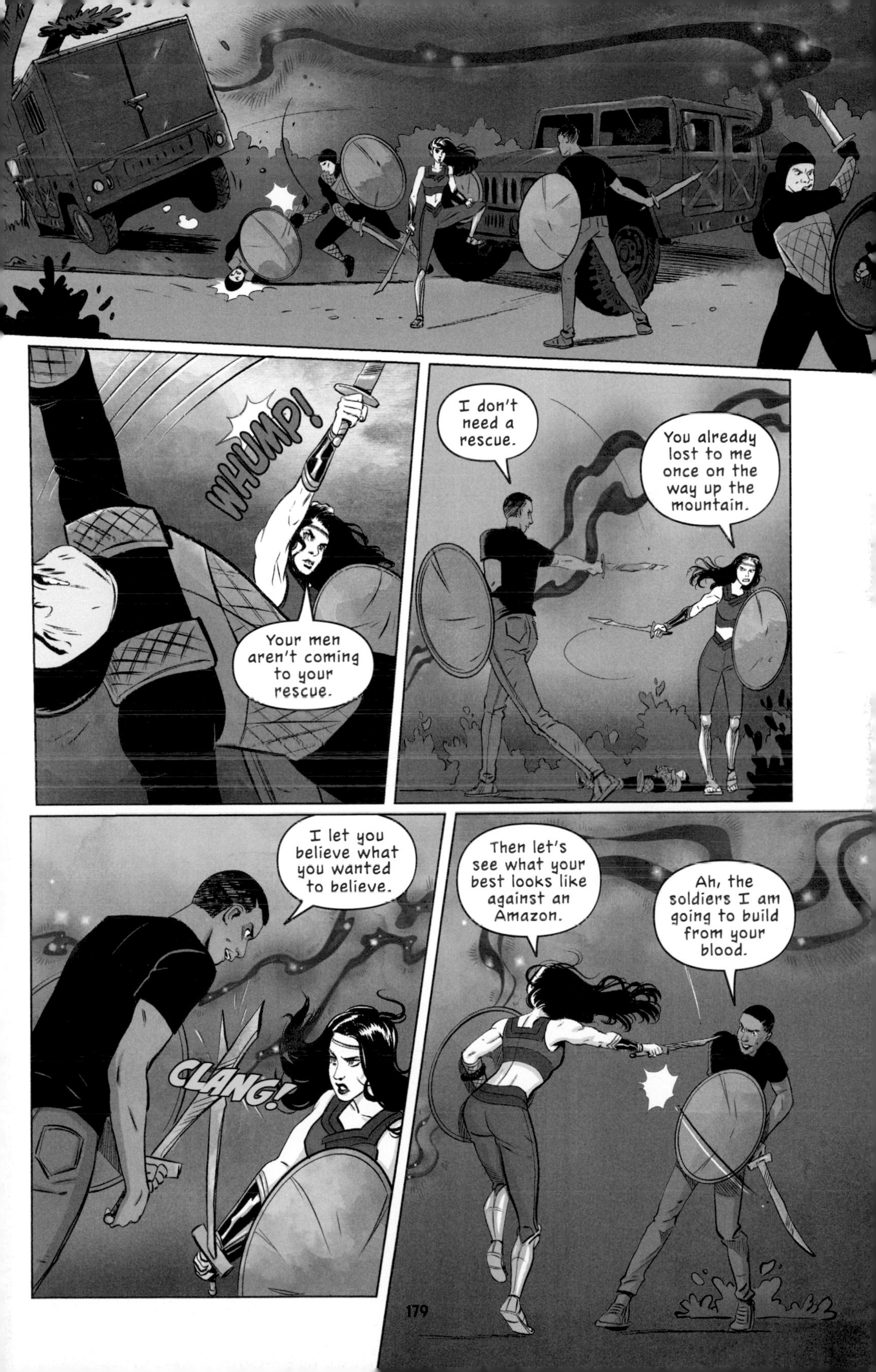
WHUMP!
Your men aren't coming to your rescue.
I don't need a rescue.
You already lost to me once on the way up the mountain.
I let you believe what you wanted to believe.
CLANG!
Then let's see what your best looks like against an Amazon.
Ah, the soldiers I am going to build from your blood.

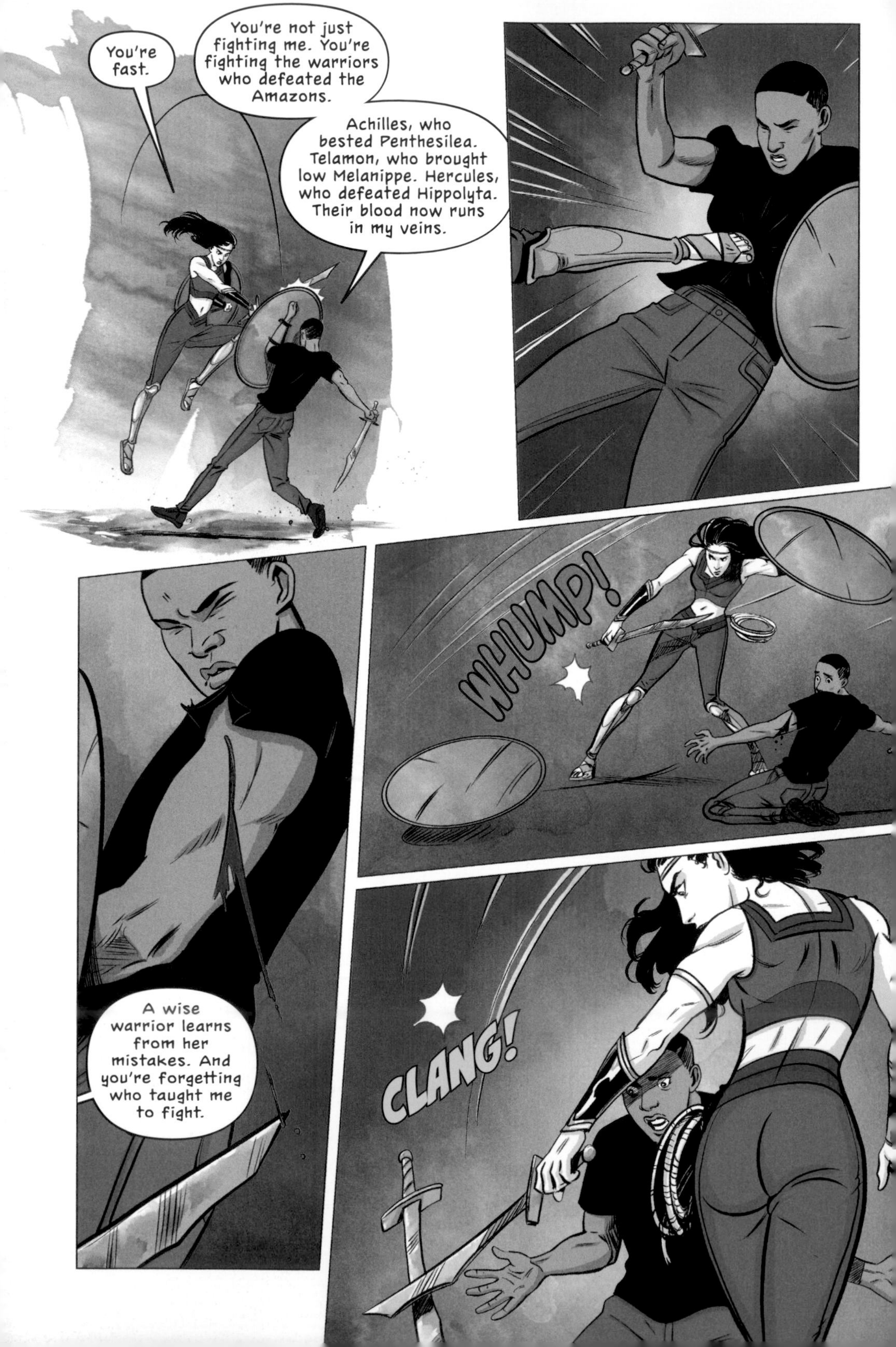
You're fast.
You're not just fighting me. You're fighting the warriors who defeated the Amazons.
Achilles, who bested Penthesilea. Telamon, who brought low Melanippe. Hercules, who defeated Hippolyta. Their blood now runs in my veins.
A wise warrior learns from her mistakes. And you're forgetting who taught me to fight.
WHUMP!
CLANG!

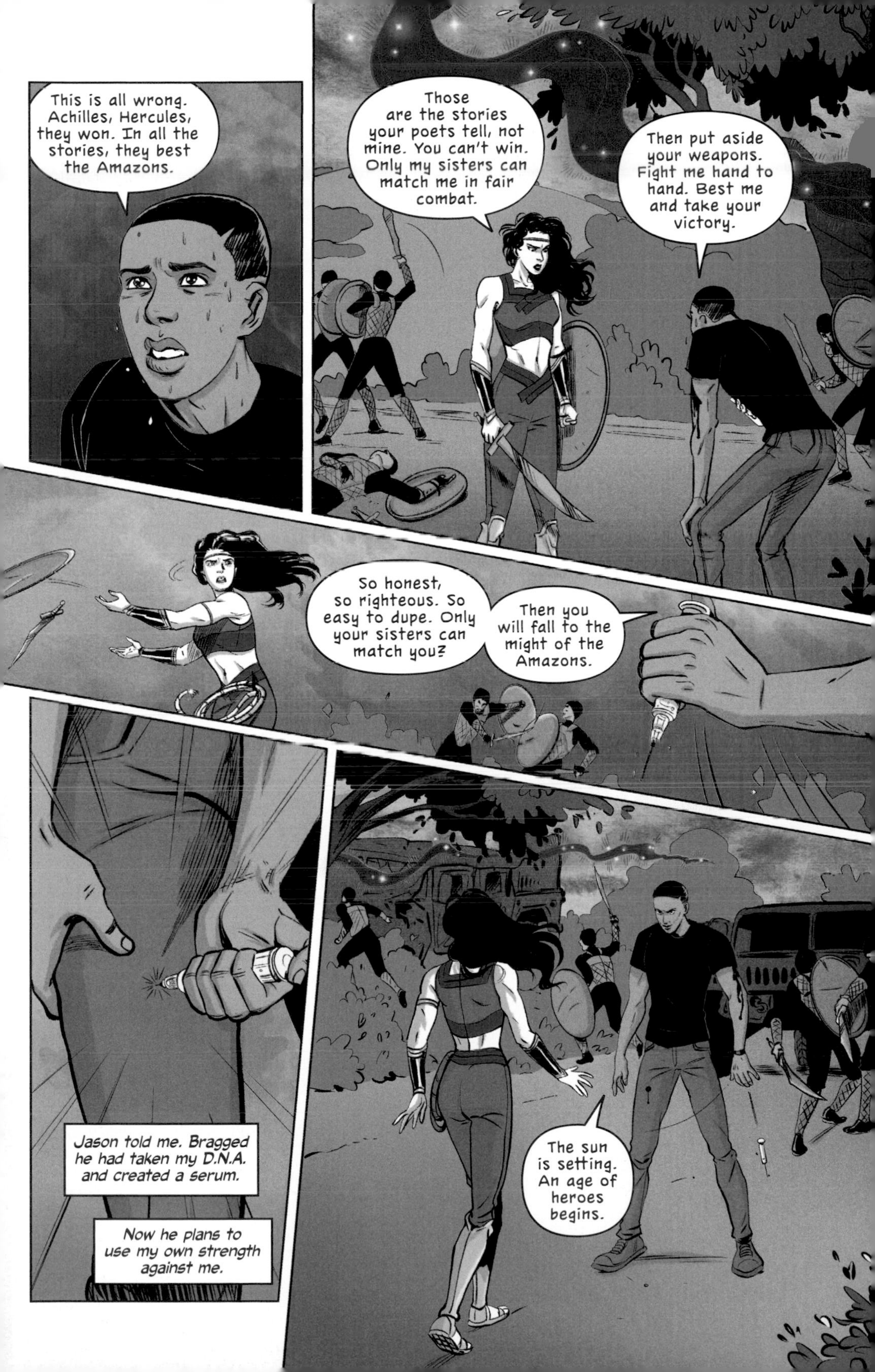
This is all wrong. Achilles, Hercules, they won. In all the stories, they best the Amazons.
Those are the stories your poets tell, not mine. You can't win. Only my sisters can match me in fair combat.
Then put aside your weapons. Fight me hand to hand. Best me and take your victory.
So honest, so righteous. So easy to dupe. Only your sisters can match you?
Then you will fall to the might of the Amazons.
Jason told me. Bragged he had taken my D.N.A. and created a serum.
Now he plans to use my own strength against me.
The sun is setting. An age of heroes begins.

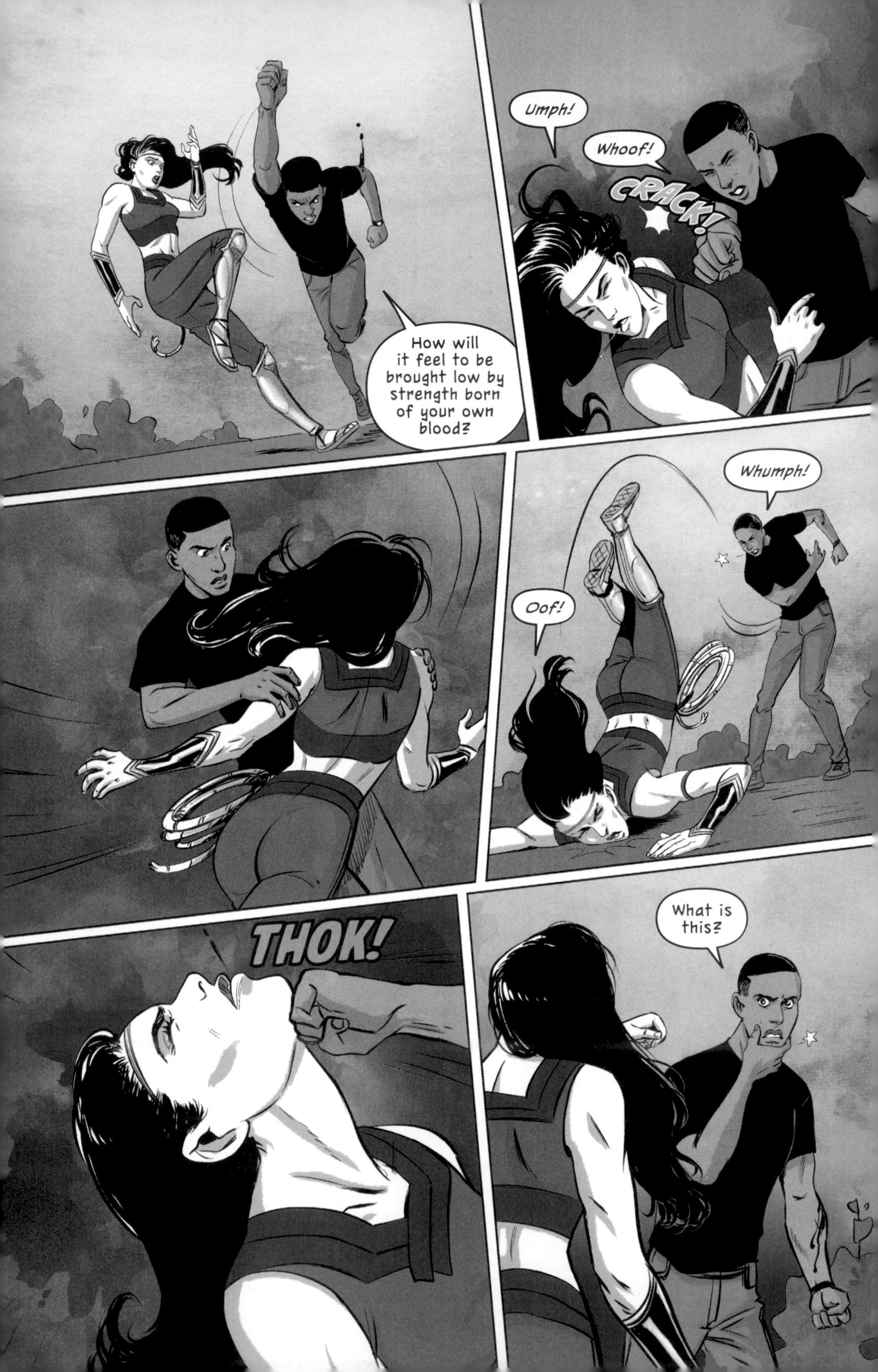
How will it feel to be brought low by strength born of your own blood?
Umph!
Whoof!
CRACK!
Whumph!
Oof!
THOK!
What is this?

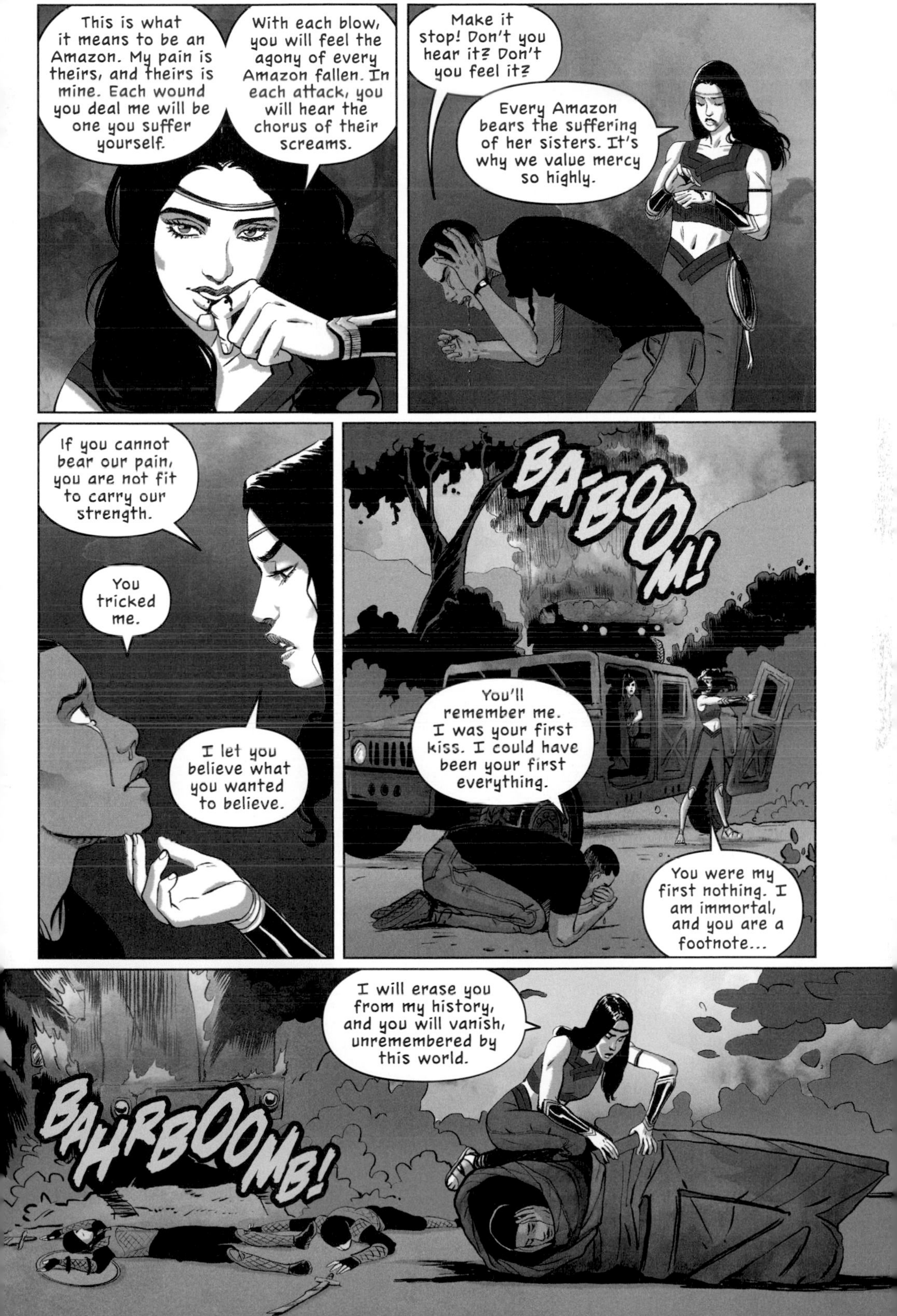
This is what it means to be an Amazon. My pain is theirs, and theirs is mine. Each wound you deal me will be one you suffer yourself.
With each blow, you will feel the agony of every Amazon fallen. In each attack, you will hear the chorus of their screams.
Make it stop! Don't you hear it? Don't you feel it?
Every Amazon bears the suffering of her sisters. It's why we value mercy so highly.
If you cannot bear our pain, you are not fit to carry our strength.
You tricked me.
I let you believe what you wanted to believe.
BA-BOOM!
You'll remember me. I was your first kiss. I could have been your first everything.
You were my first nothing. I am immortal, and you are a footnote...
I will erase you from my history, and you will vanish, unremembered by this world.
BAHRBOOMB!

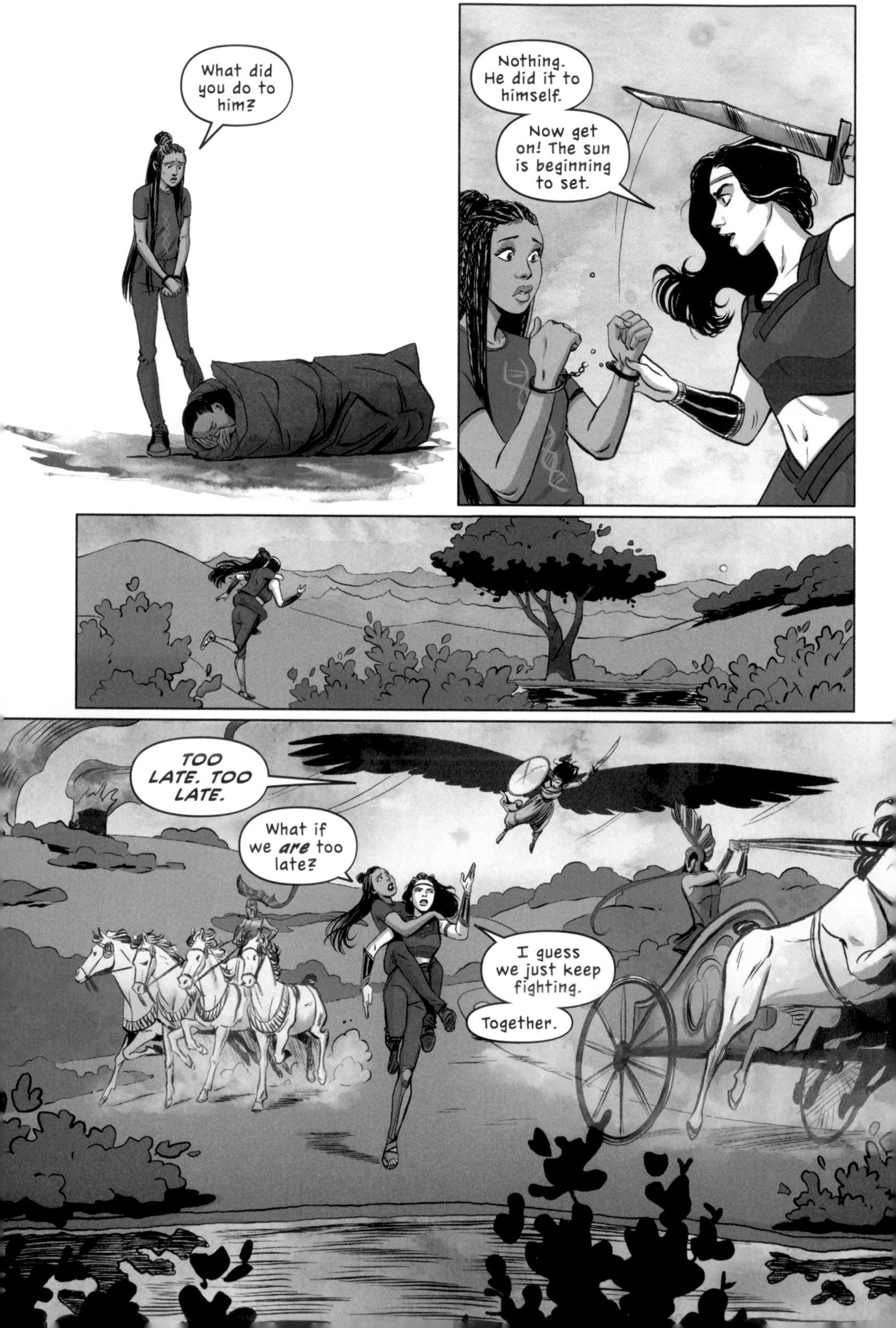
What did you do to him?
Nothing. He did it to himself.
Now get on! The sun is beginning to set.
TOO LATE. TOO LATE.
What if we *are* too late?
I guess we just keep fighting.
Together.

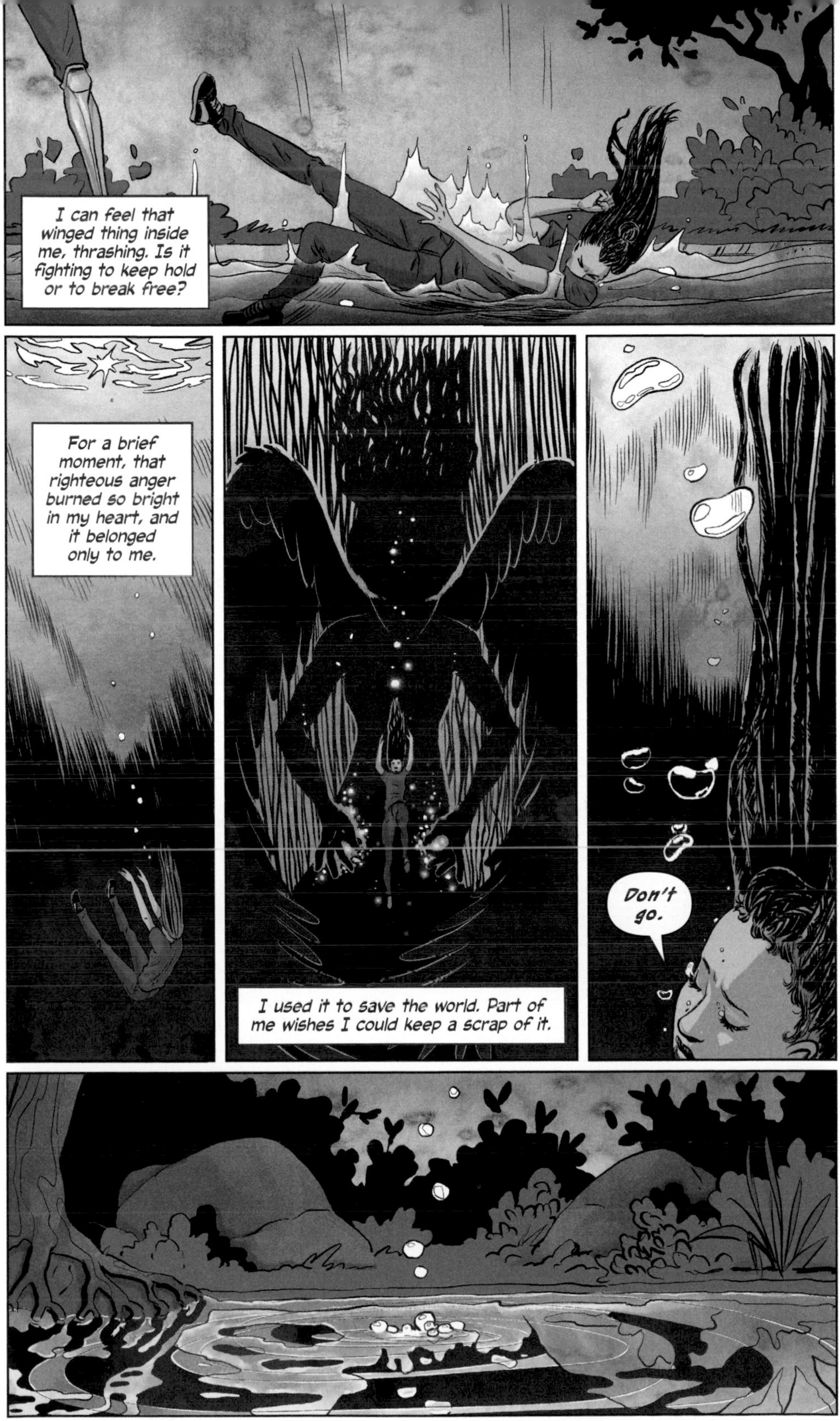
I can feel that winged thing inside me, thrashing. Is it fighting to keep hold or to break free?
For a brief moment, that righteous anger burned so bright in my heart, and it belonged only to me.
I used it to save the world. Part of me wishes I could keep a scrap of it.
Don't go.

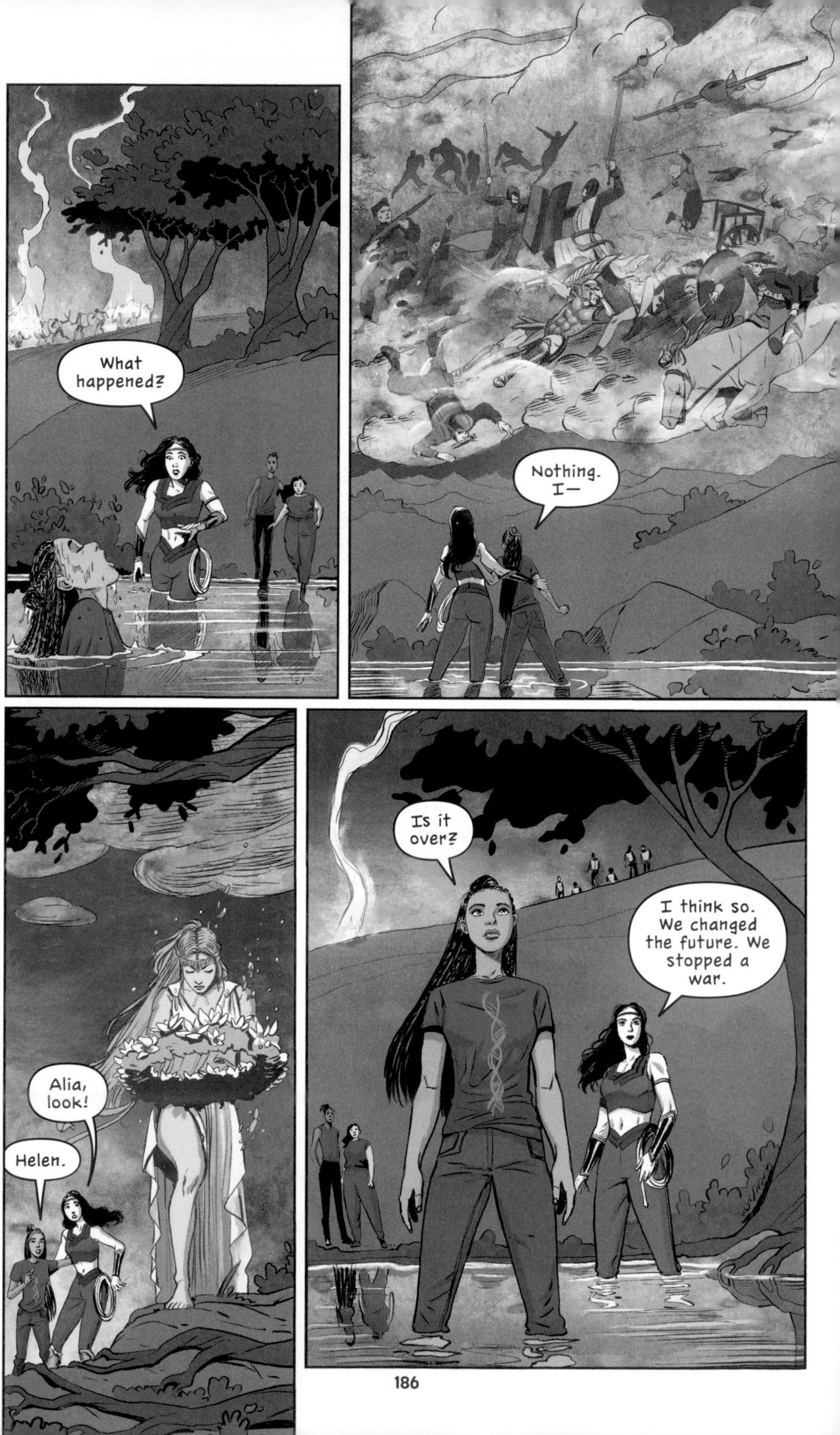
What happened?
Nothing. I—
Alia, look!
Helen.
Is it over?
I think so. We changed the future. We stopped a war.

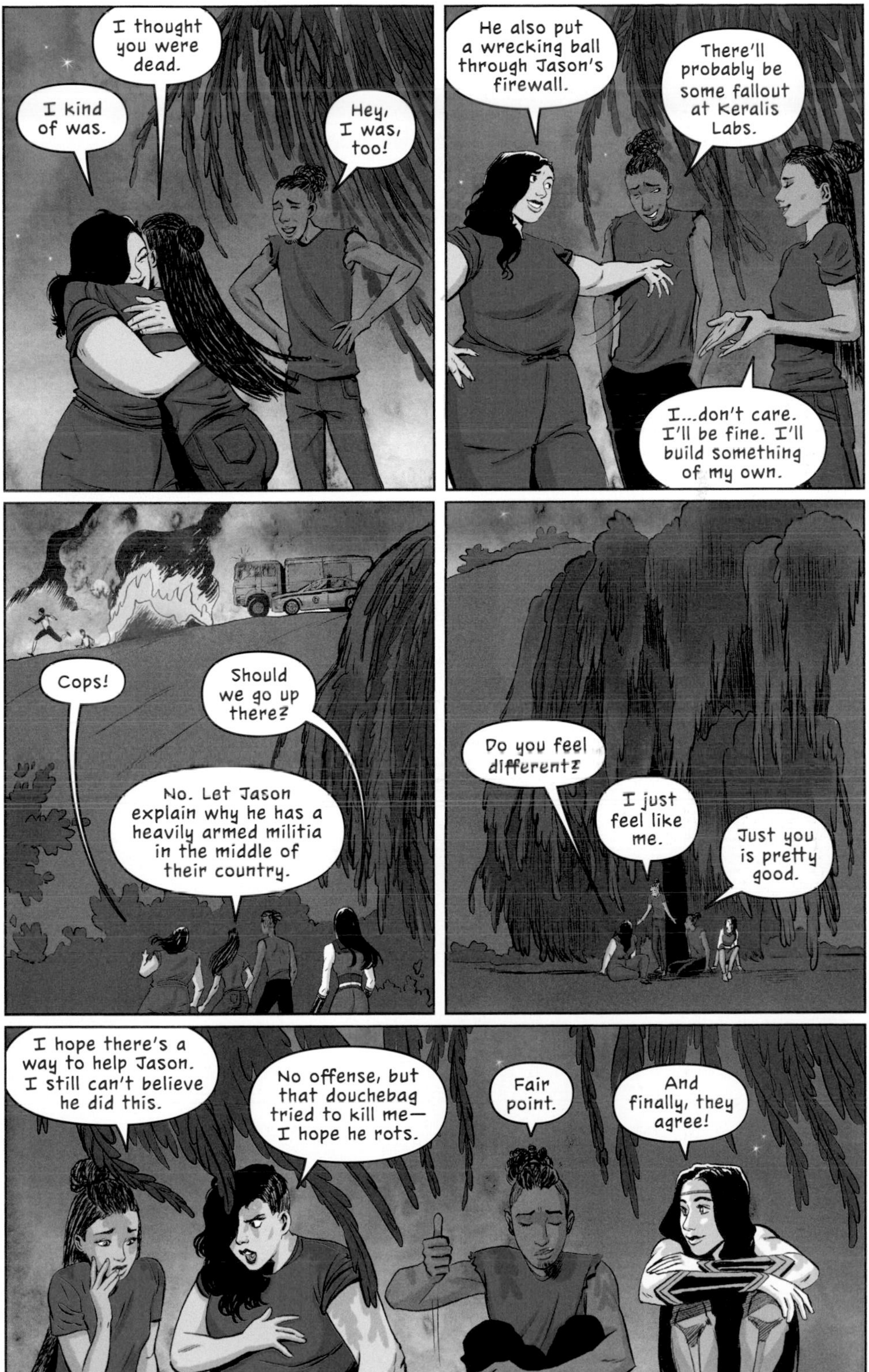

I thought you were dead.
I kind of was.
Hey, I was, too!
He also put a wrecking ball through Jason's firewall.
There'll probably be some fallout at Keralis Labs.
I...don't care. I'll be fine. I'll build something of my own.
Cops!
Should we go up there?
No. Let Jason explain why he has a heavily armed militia in the middle of their country.
Do you feel different?
I just feel like me.
Just you is pretty good.
I hope there's a way to help Jason. I still can't believe he did this.
No offense, but that douchebag tried to kill me— I hope he rots.
Fair point.
And finally, they agree!

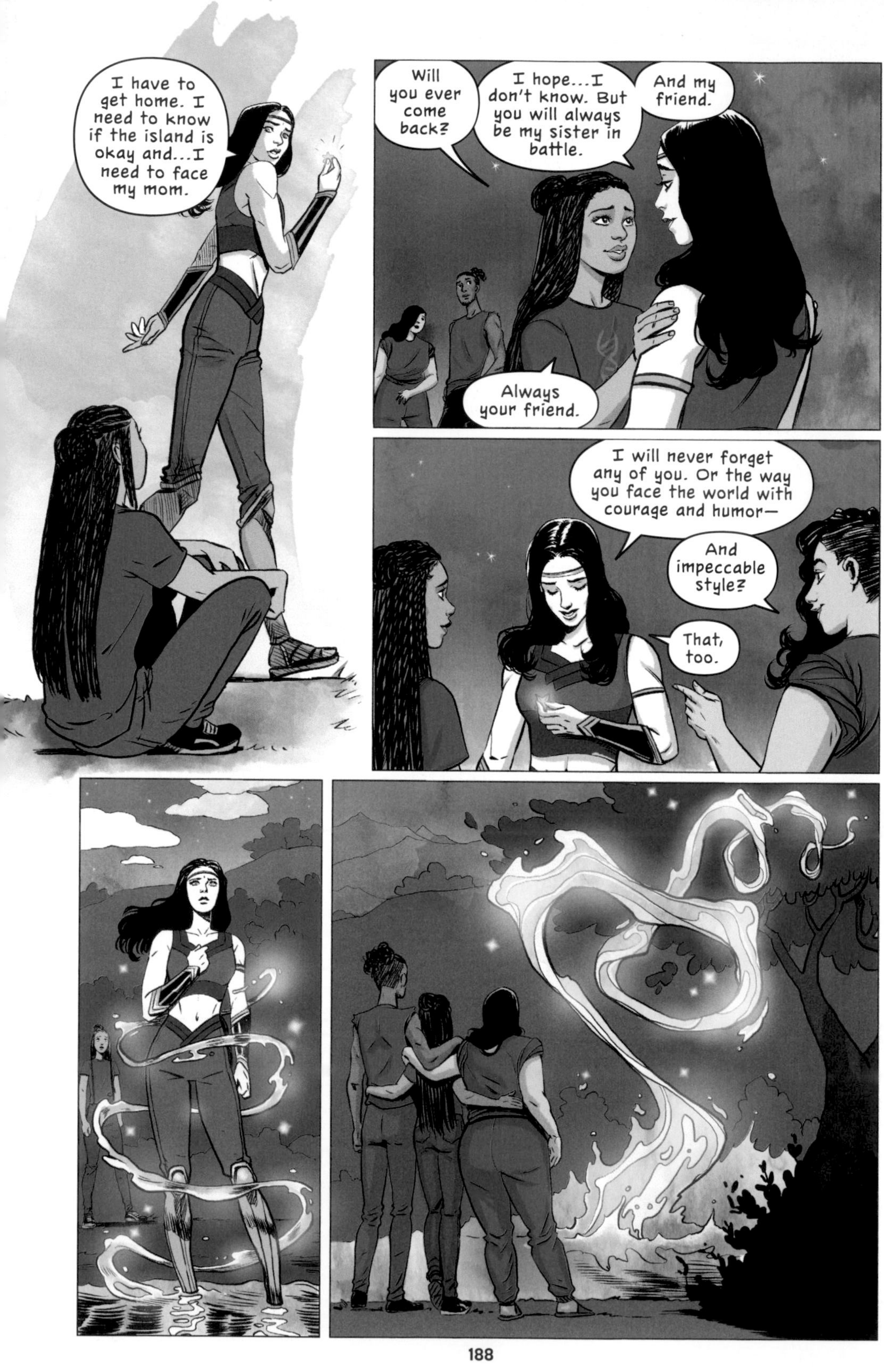
I have to get home. I need to know if the island is okay and...I need to face my mom.
Will you ever come back?
I hope...I don't know. But you will always be my sister in battle.
And my friend.
Always your friend.
I will never forget any of you. Or the way you face the world with courage and humor—
And impeccable style?
That, too.

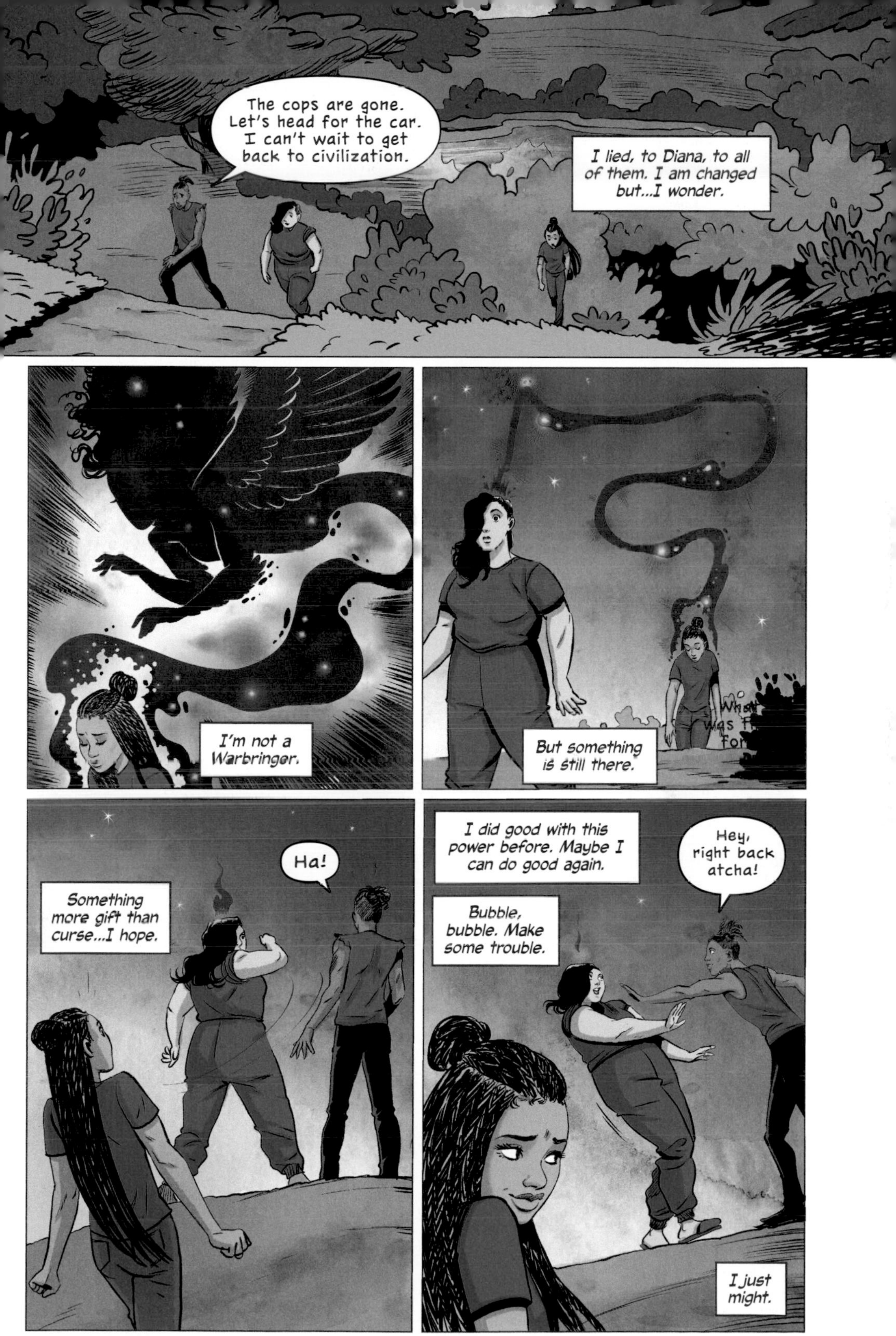
The cops are gone. Let's head for the car. I can't wait to get back to civilization.
I lied, to Diana, to all of them. I am changed but...I wonder.
I'm not a Warbringer.
But something is still there.
Something more gift than curse...I hope.
Ha!
I did good with this power before. Maybe I can do good again.
Hey, right back atcha!
Bubble, bubble. Make some trouble.
I just might.

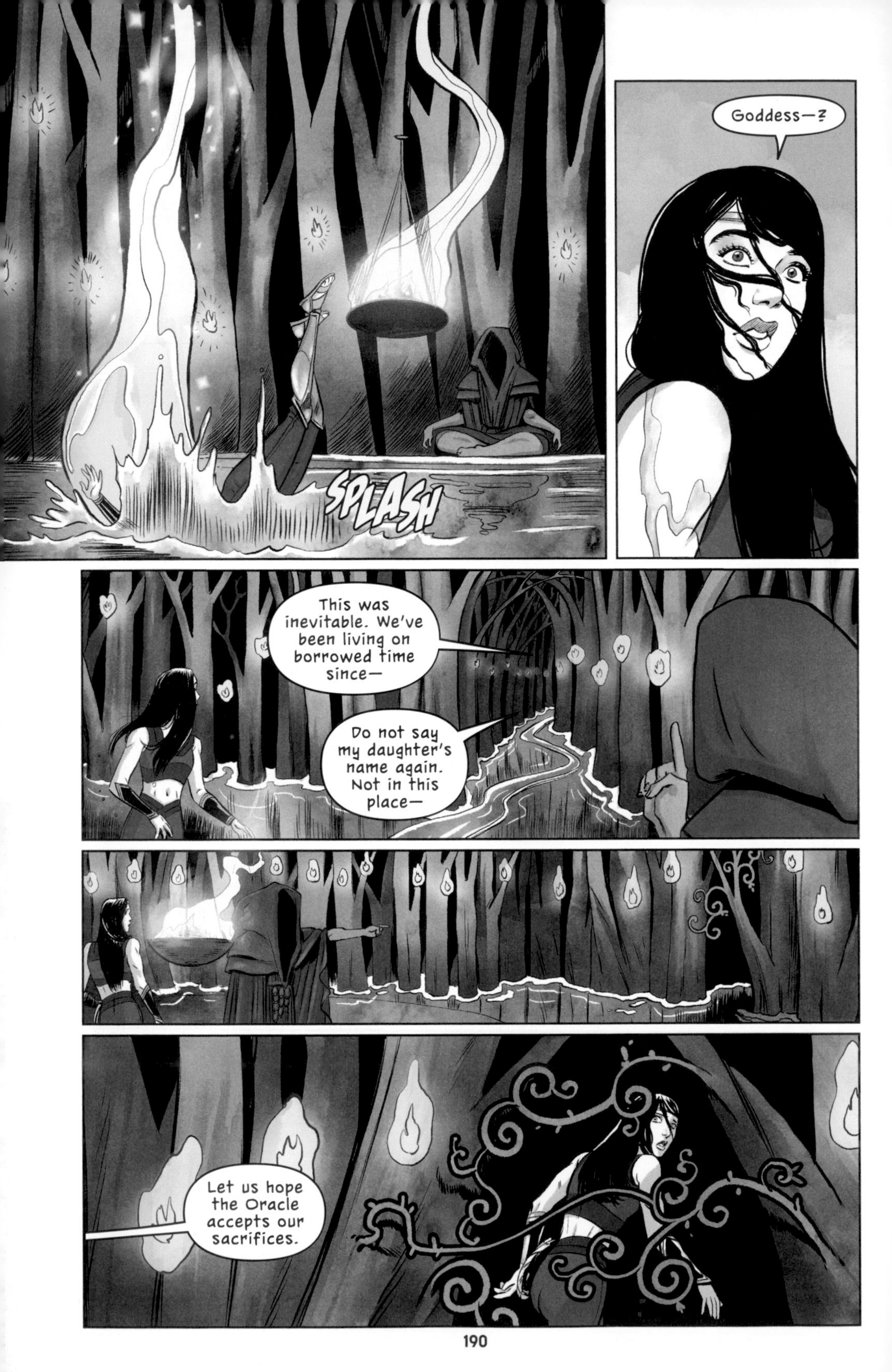
SPLASH
Goddess—?
This was inevitable. We've been living on borrowed time since—
Do not say my daughter's name again. Not in this place—
Let us hope the Oracle accepts our sacrifices.

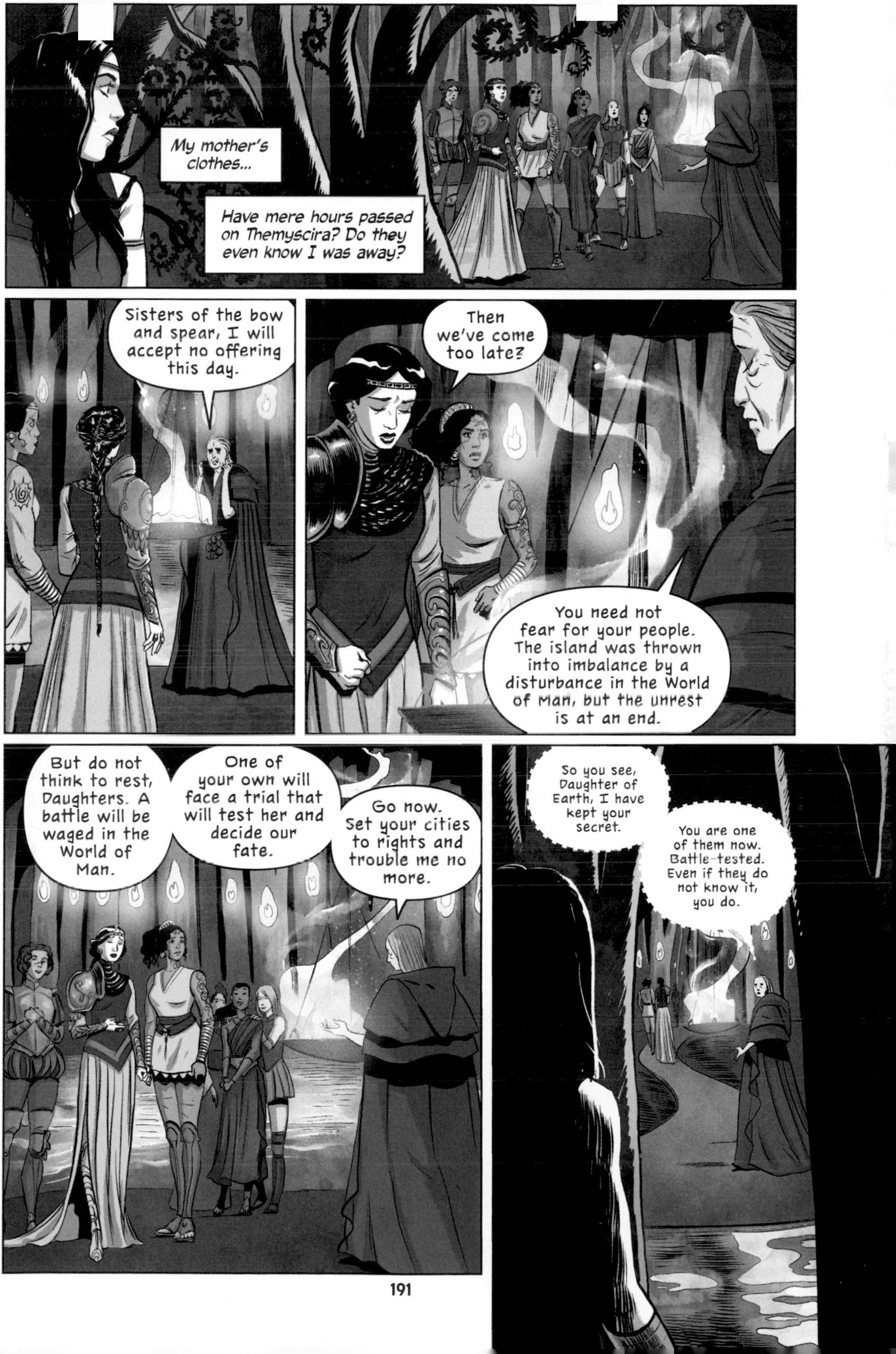
My mother's clothes...
Have mere hours passed on Themyscira? Do they even know I was away?
Sisters of the bow and spear, I will accept no offering this day.
Then we've come too late?
You need not fear for your people. The island was thrown into imbalance by a disturbance in the World of Man, but the unrest is at an end.
But do not think to rest, Daughters. A battle will be waged in the World of Man.
One of your own will face a trial that will test her and decide our fate.
Go now. Set your cities to rights and trouble me no more.
So you see, Daughter of Earth, I have kept your secret.
You are one of them now. Battle-tested. Even if they do not know it, you do.

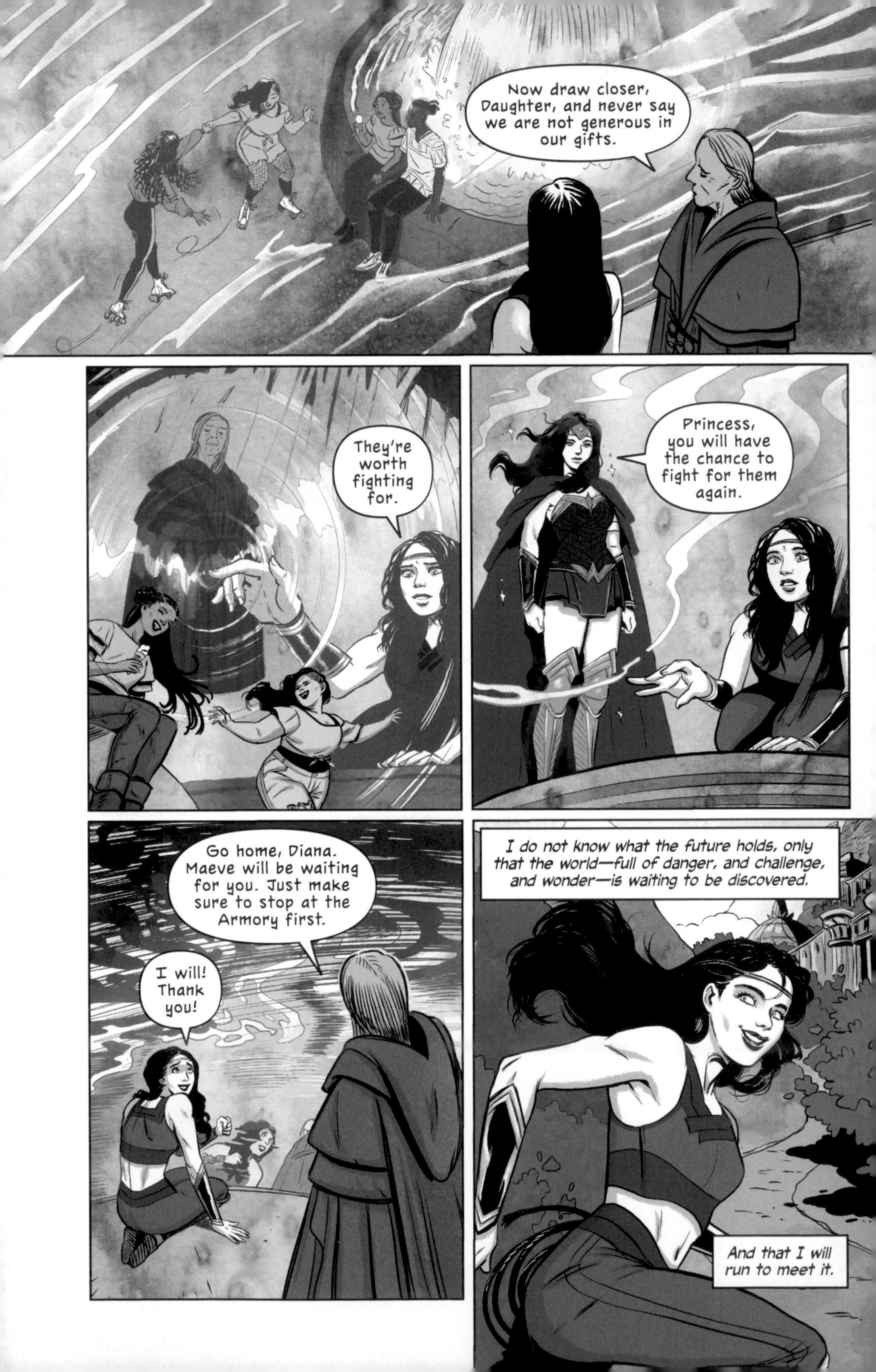
Now draw closer, Daughter, and never say we are not generous in our gifts.
They're worth fighting for.
Princess, you will have the chance to fight for them again.
Go home, Diana. Maeve will be waiting for you. Just make sure to stop at the Armory first.
I will! Thank you!
I do not know what the future holds, only that the world—full of danger, and challenge, and wonder—is waiting to be discovered.
And that I will run to meet it.

Leigh Bardugo is a #1 *New York Times* bestselling author of fantasy novels and short stories, including *Shadow and Bone*, *Six of Crows*, and the forthcoming *Ninth House*. She was born in Jerusalem, grew up in Southern California, and graduated from Yale University. These days she lives and writes in Los Angeles.

Louise Simonson writes comics about monsters, science fiction, superheroes, and fantasy characters. She wrote the award-winning *Power Pack* series, several bestselling X-Men titles, and *Web of Spider-Man* for Marvel Comics and *Superman: The Man of Steel* and *Steel* for DC Comics. She has also written many books for kids. She is married to comics writer/artist Walter Simonson and lives in the suburbs of New York City.

Kit Seaton grew up on a steady diet of comic strips, '80s cartoons, and volumes of illustrated fairy tale books. She's bused tables, sold computers, slung coffee, directed plays, and designed costumes before finally finding her home illustrating comic books. Kit earned her master's in illustration from the Hartford Art School and has taught comics and illustration at Rocky Mountain College of Art and Design, Savannah College of Art and Design, and California State University Fullerton. She makes her home with an old snuggle-grump housecat named Gus and a puppy named Panya in the Inland Northwest.

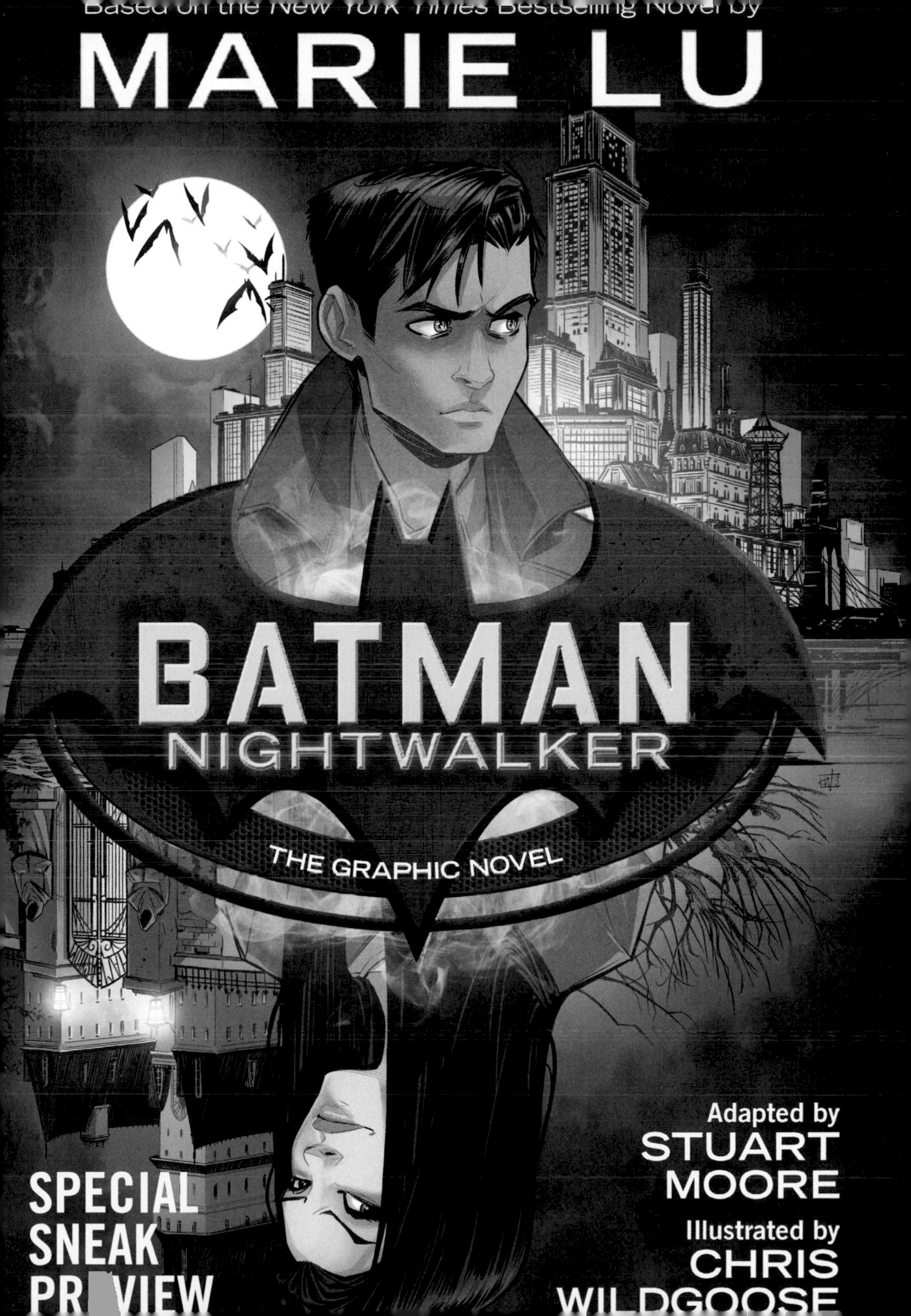
Based on the *New York Times* Bestselling Novel by
MARIE LU
BATMAN
NIGHTWALKER
THE GRAPHIC NOVEL
Adapted by
STUART MOORE
Illustrated by
CHRIS WILDGOOSE
SPECIAL
SNEAK
PR VIEW

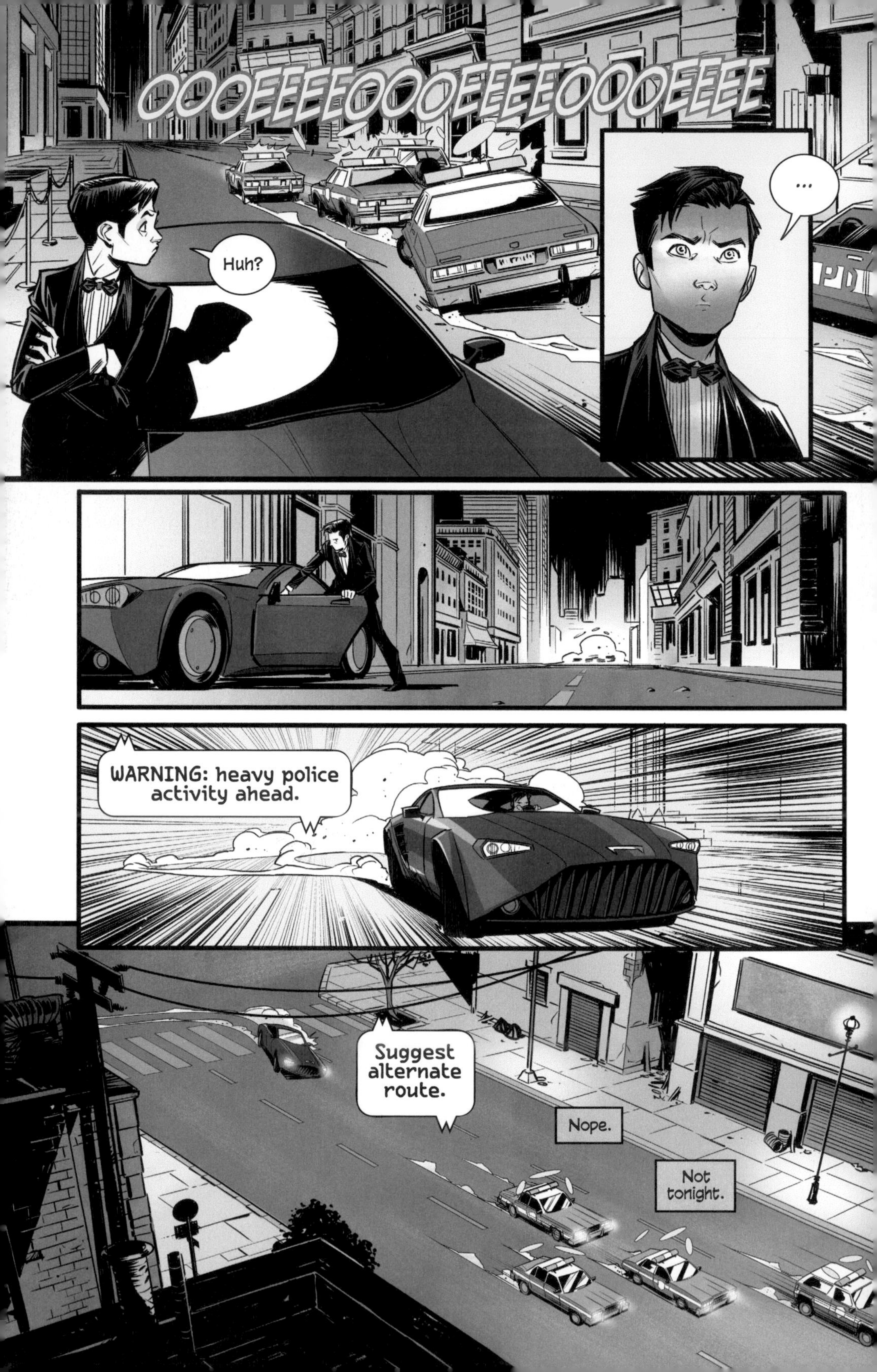
OOOEEEEOOOOEEEEOOOOEEEE
Huh?
...
WARNING: heavy police activity ahead.
Suggest alternate route.
Nope.
Not tonight.

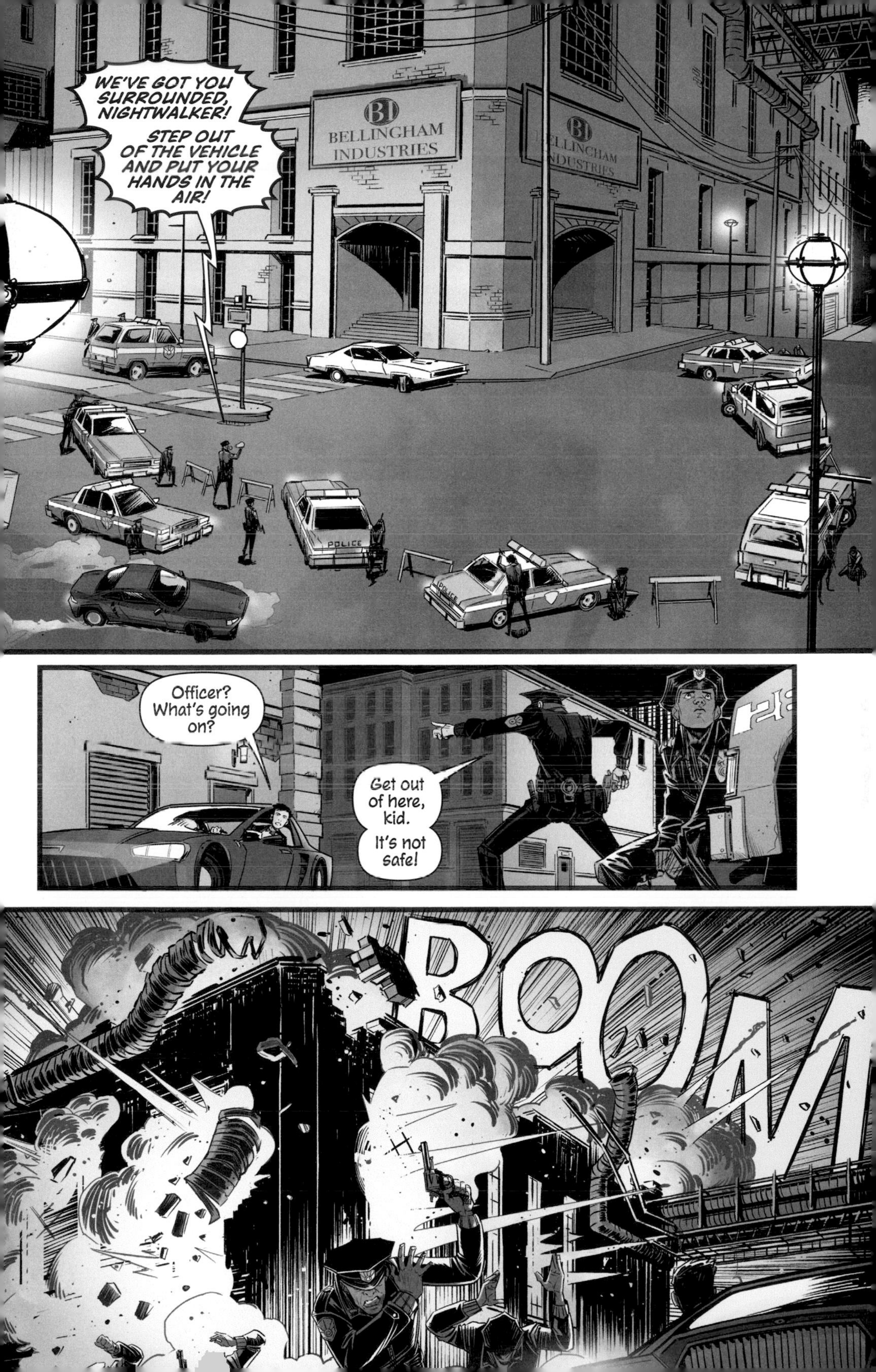
WE'VE GOT YOU SURROUNDED, NIGHTWALKER!
STEP OUT OF THE VEHICLE AND PUT YOUR HANDS IN THE AIR!
BI BELLINGHAM INDUSTRIES
BI BELLINGHAM INDUSTRIES
POLICE
POLICE
Officer? What's going on?
Get out of here, kid.
It's not safe!
BOOM

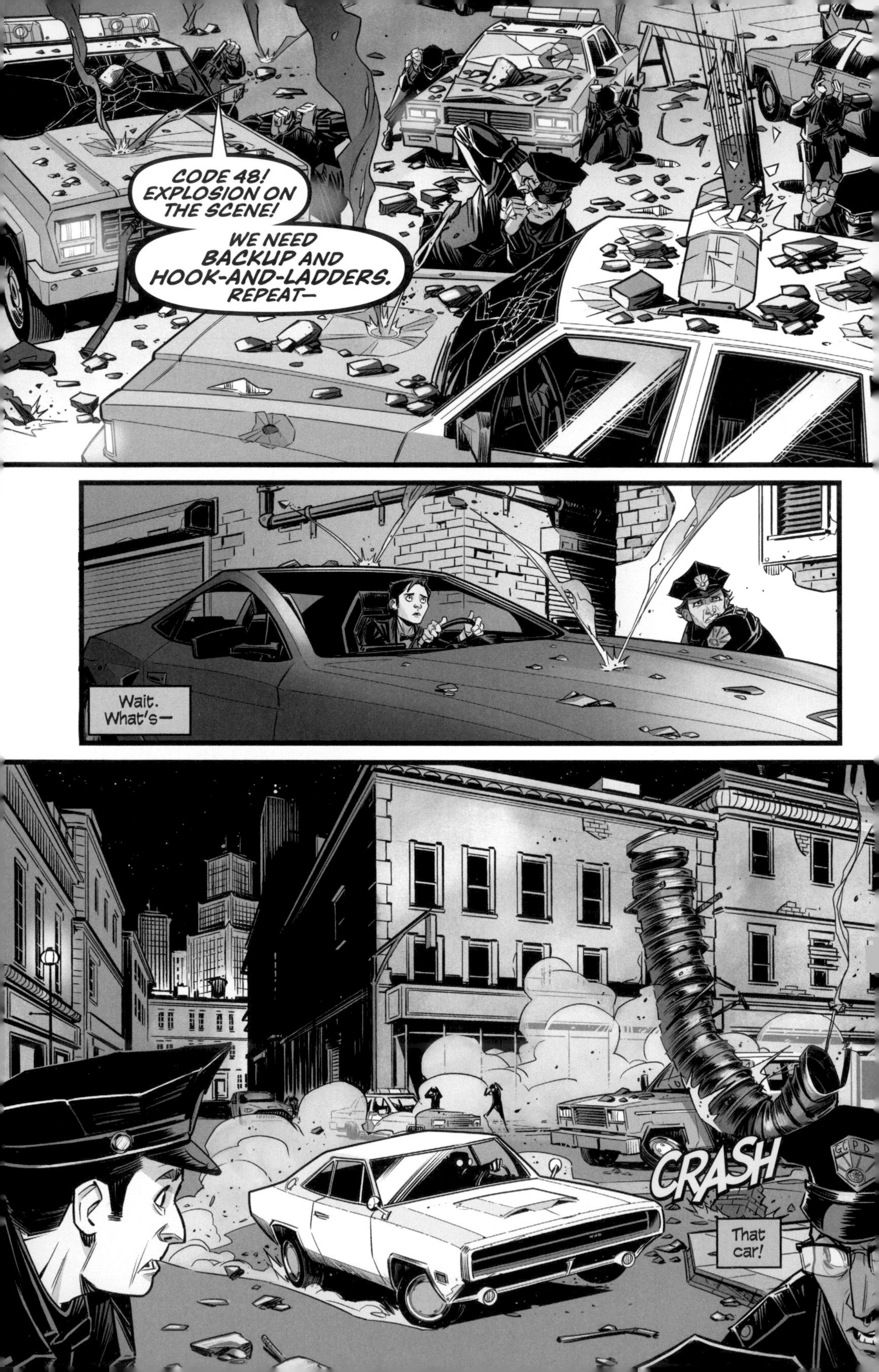
CODE 48! EXPLOSION ON THE SCENE!
WE NEED BACKUP AND HOOK-AND-LADDERS. REPEAT—
Wait. What's—
CRASH
That car!

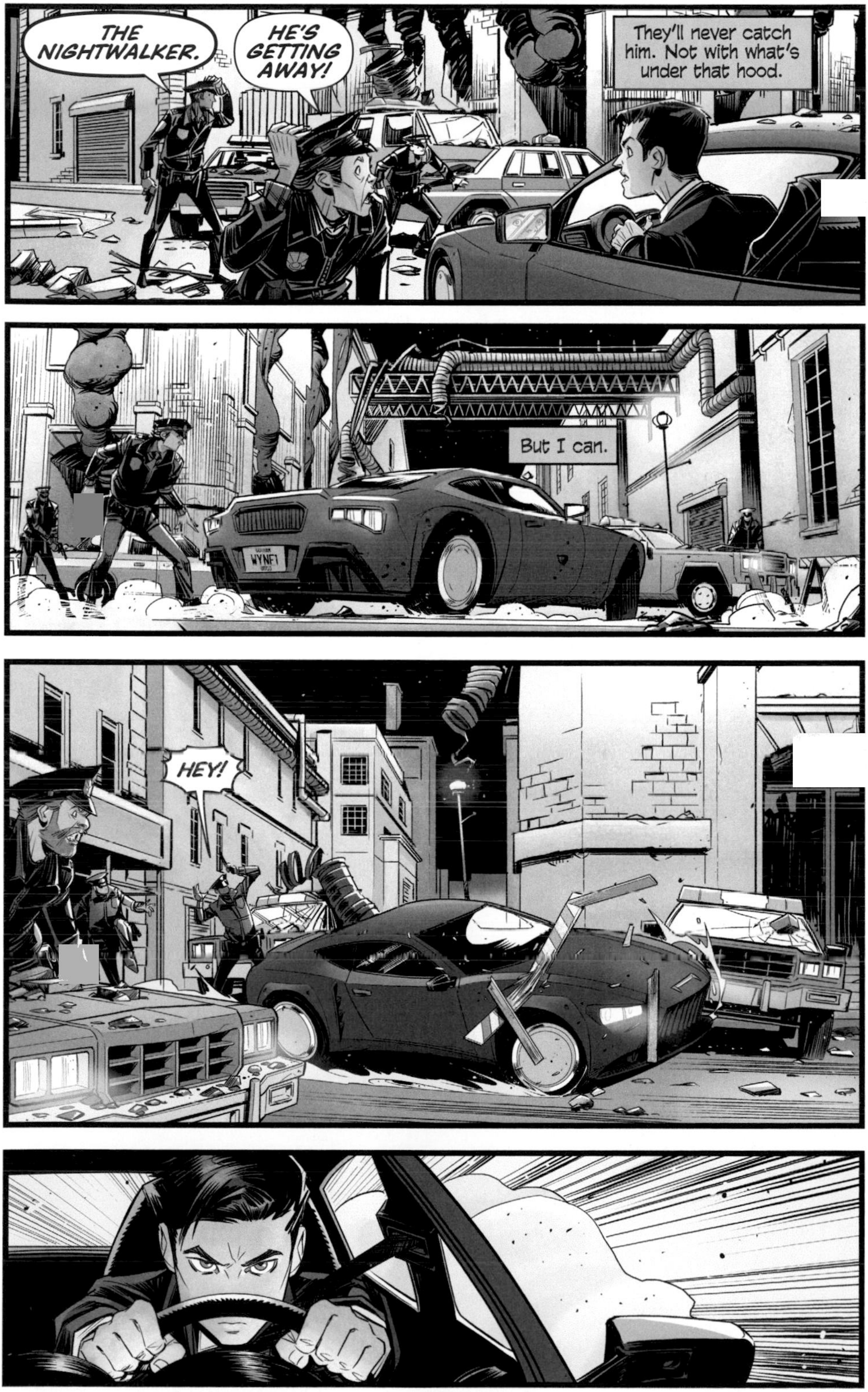
THE NIGHTWALKER.
HE'S GETTING AWAY!
They'll never catch him. Not with what's under that hood.
WYNF1
But I can.
HEY!

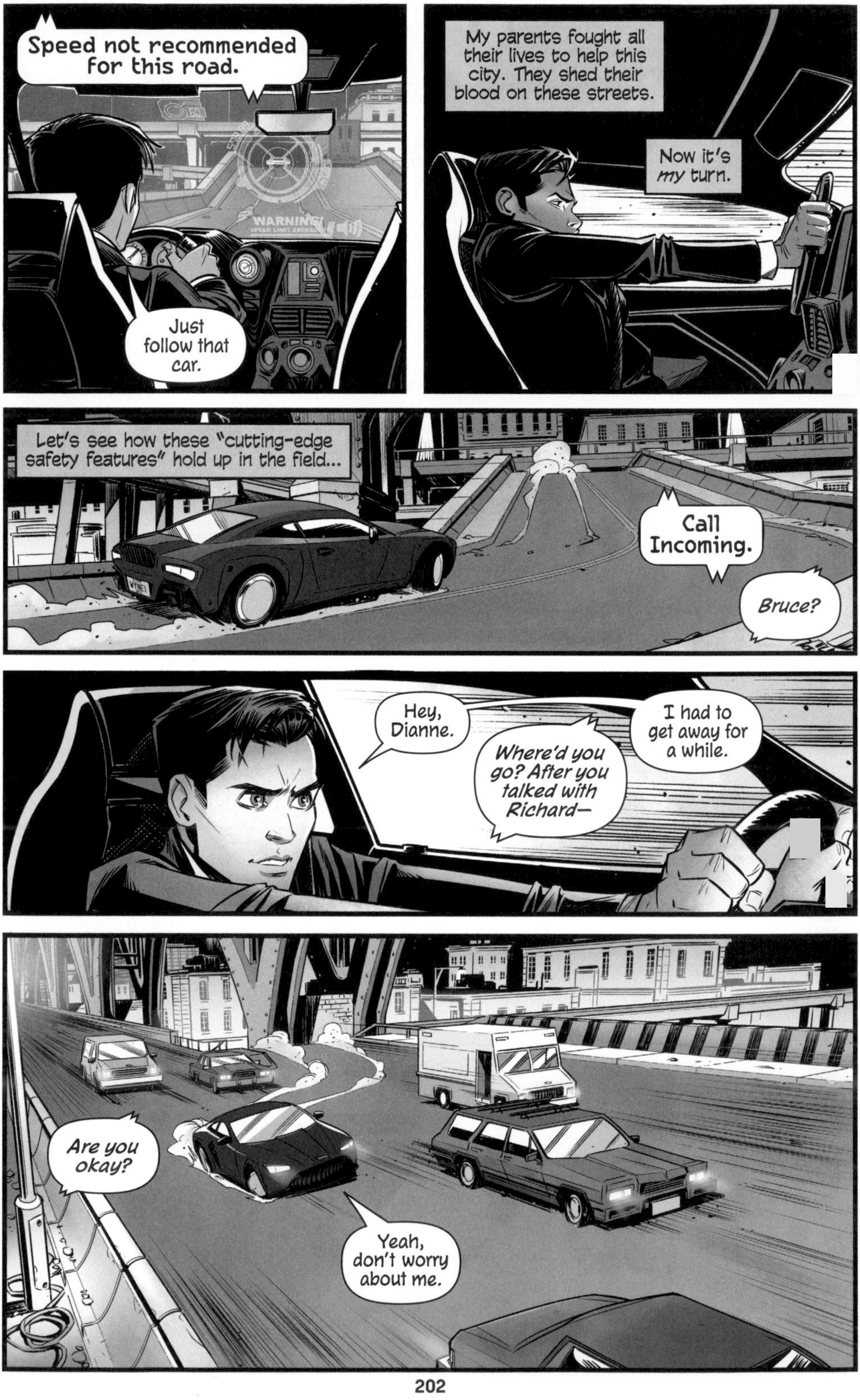
Speed not recommended for this road.
WARNING! SPEED LIMIT EXCEEDED
Just follow that car.
My parents fought all their lives to help this city. They shed their blood on these streets.
Now it's *my* turn.
Let's see how these "cutting-edge safety features" hold up in the field...
WYNE1
Call Incoming.
Bruce?
Hey, Dianne.
Where'd you go? After you talked with Richard—
I had to get away for a while.
Are you okay?
Yeah, don't worry about me.

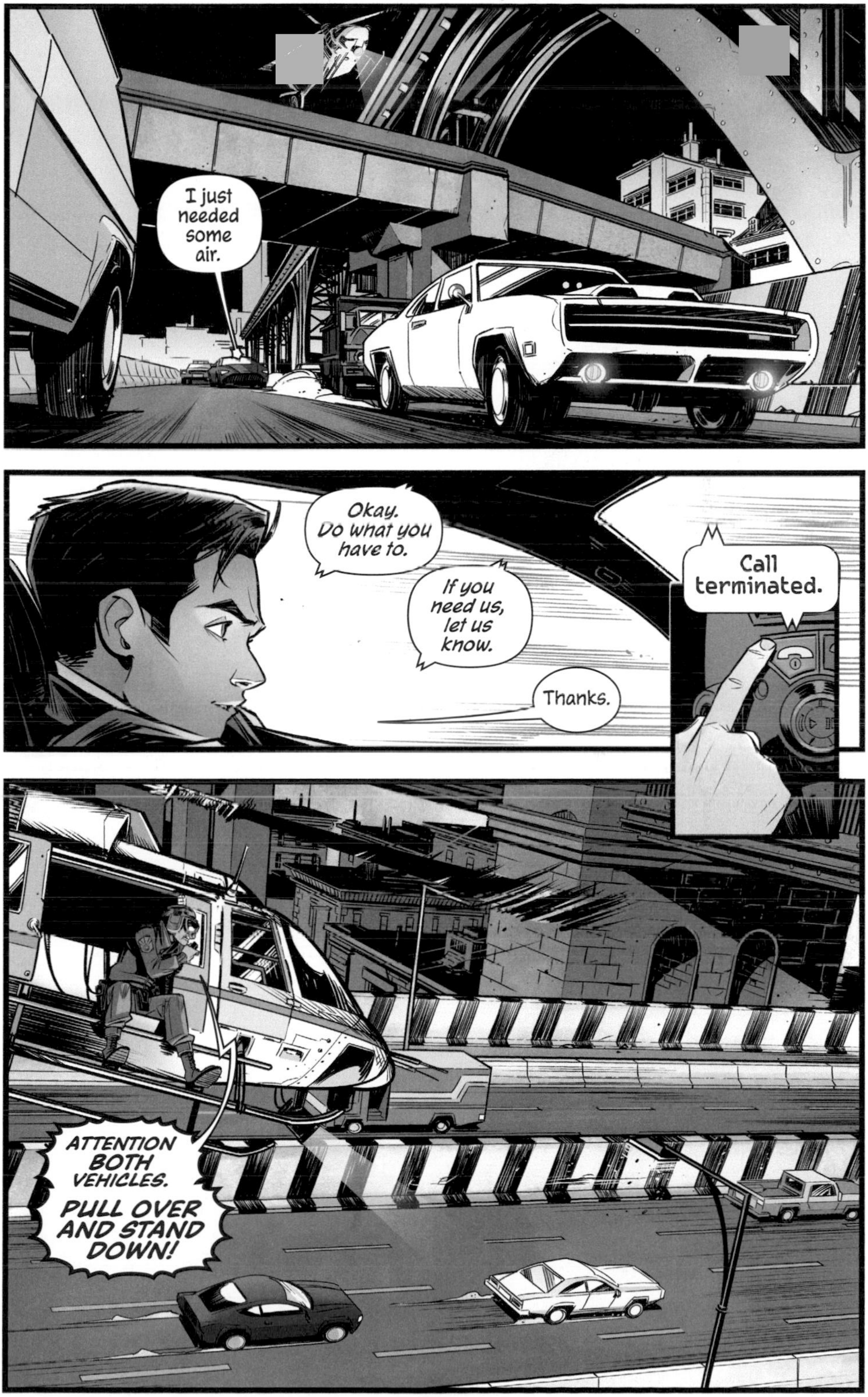
I just needed some air.
Okay. Do what you have to.
If you need us, let us know.
Thanks.
Call terminated.
ATTENTION BOTH VEHICLES.
PULL OVER AND STAND DOWN!

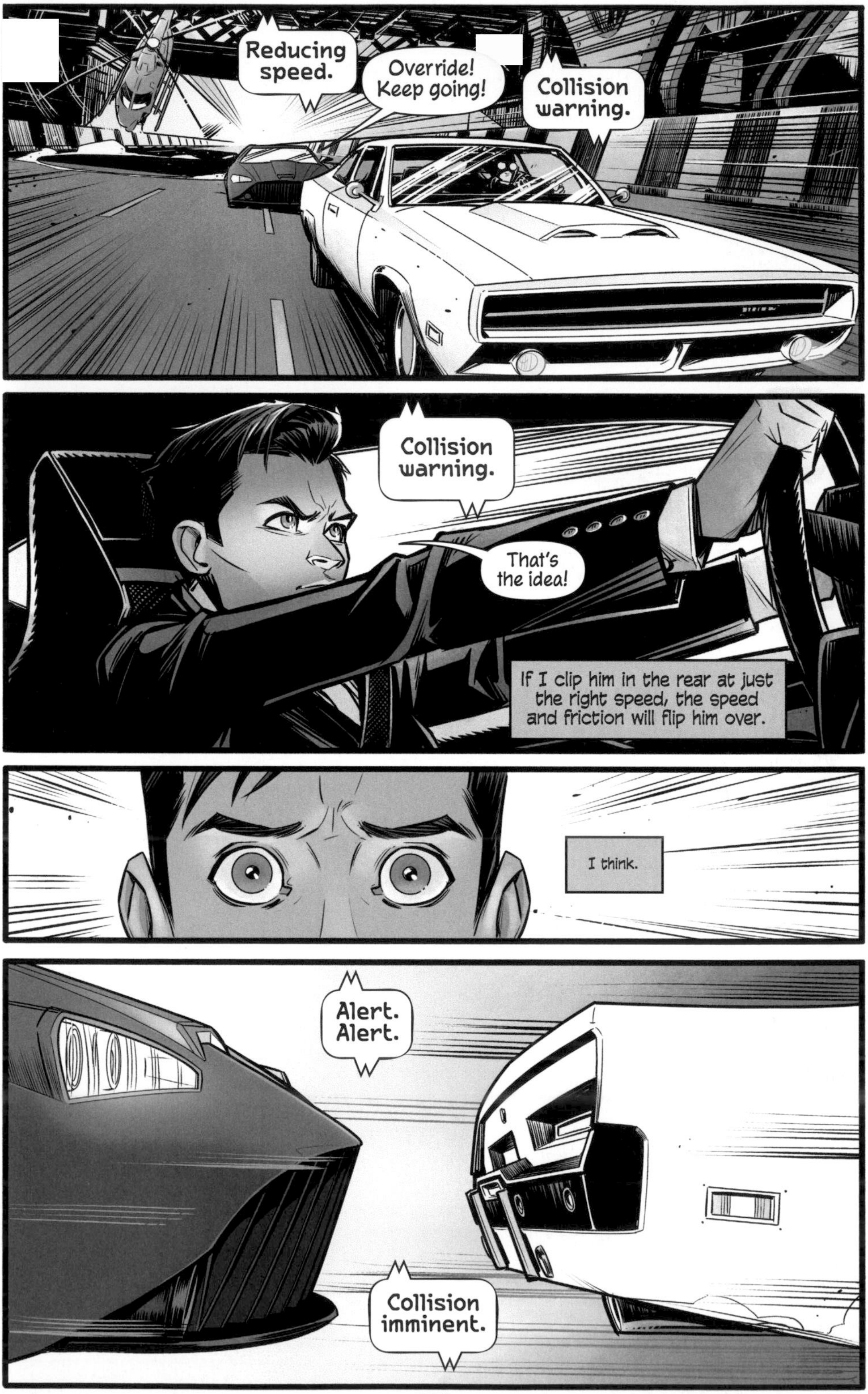

Reducing speed.
Override! Keep going!
Collision warning.
Collision warning.
That's the idea!
If I clip him in the rear at just the right speed, the speed and friction will flip him over.
I think.
Alert. Alert.
Collision imminent.

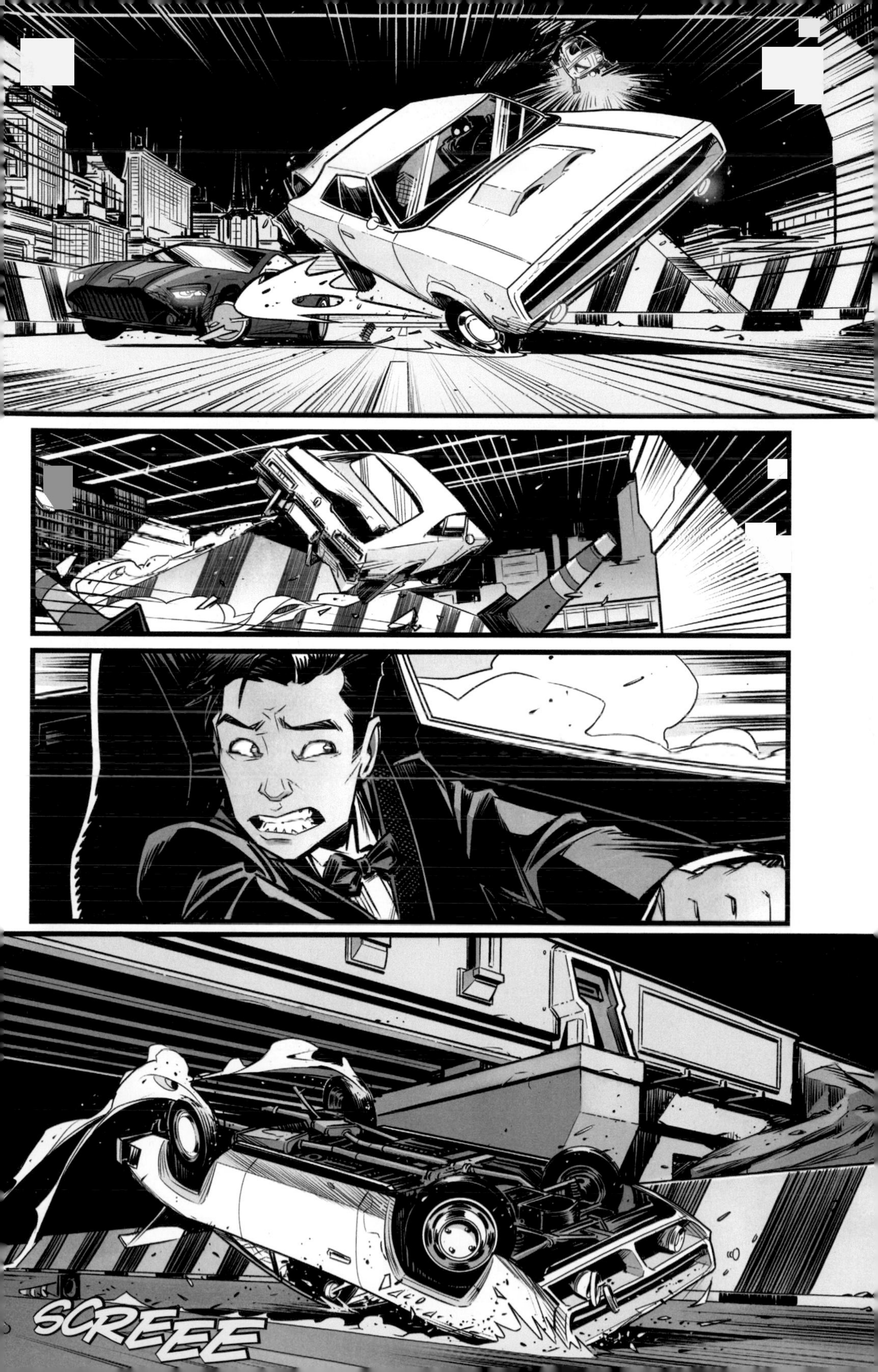
SCREEEE

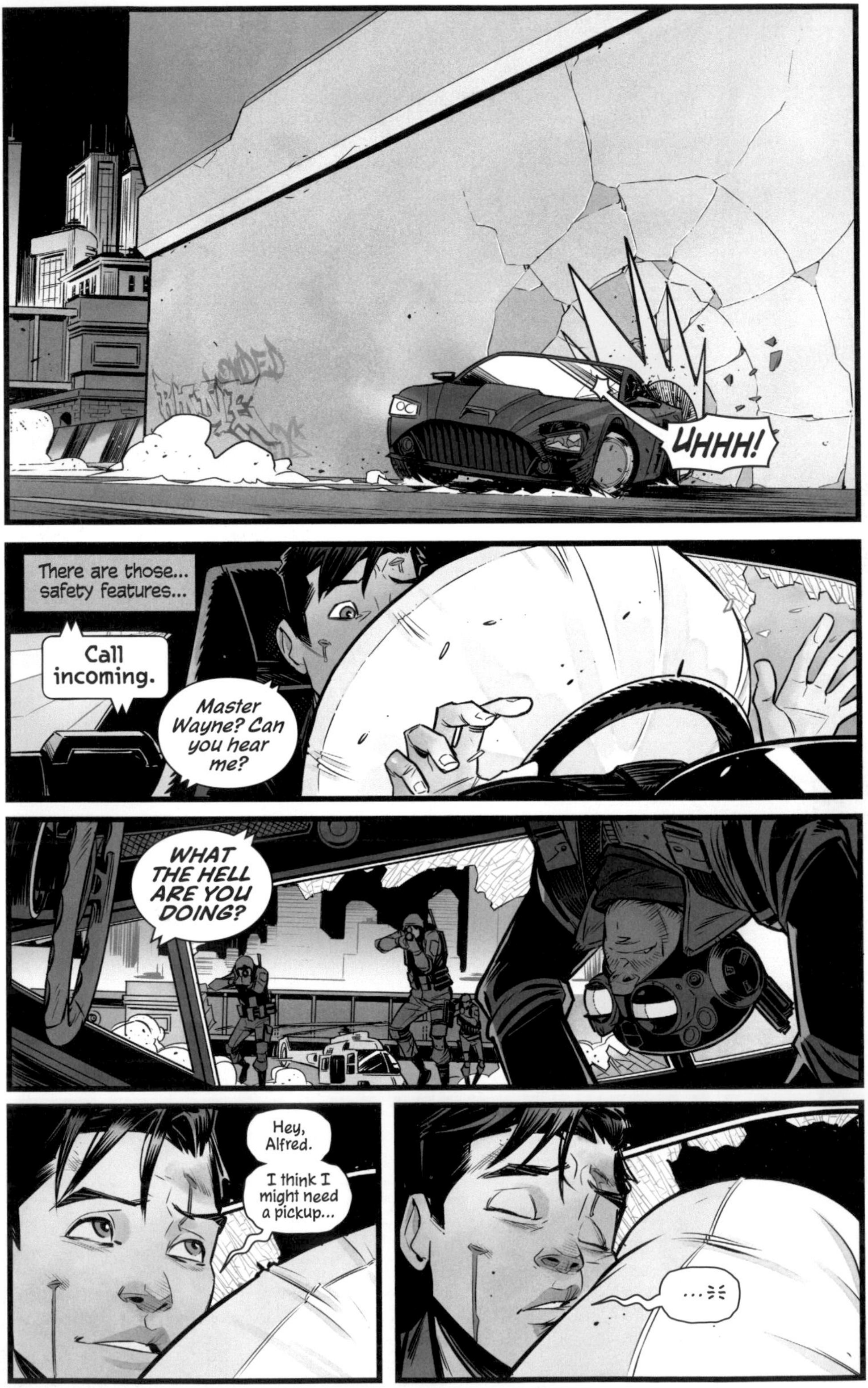
UHHH!
There are those... safety features...
Call incoming.
Master Wayne? Can you hear me?
WHAT THE HELL ARE YOU DOING?
Hey, Alfred.
I think I might need a pickup...
...

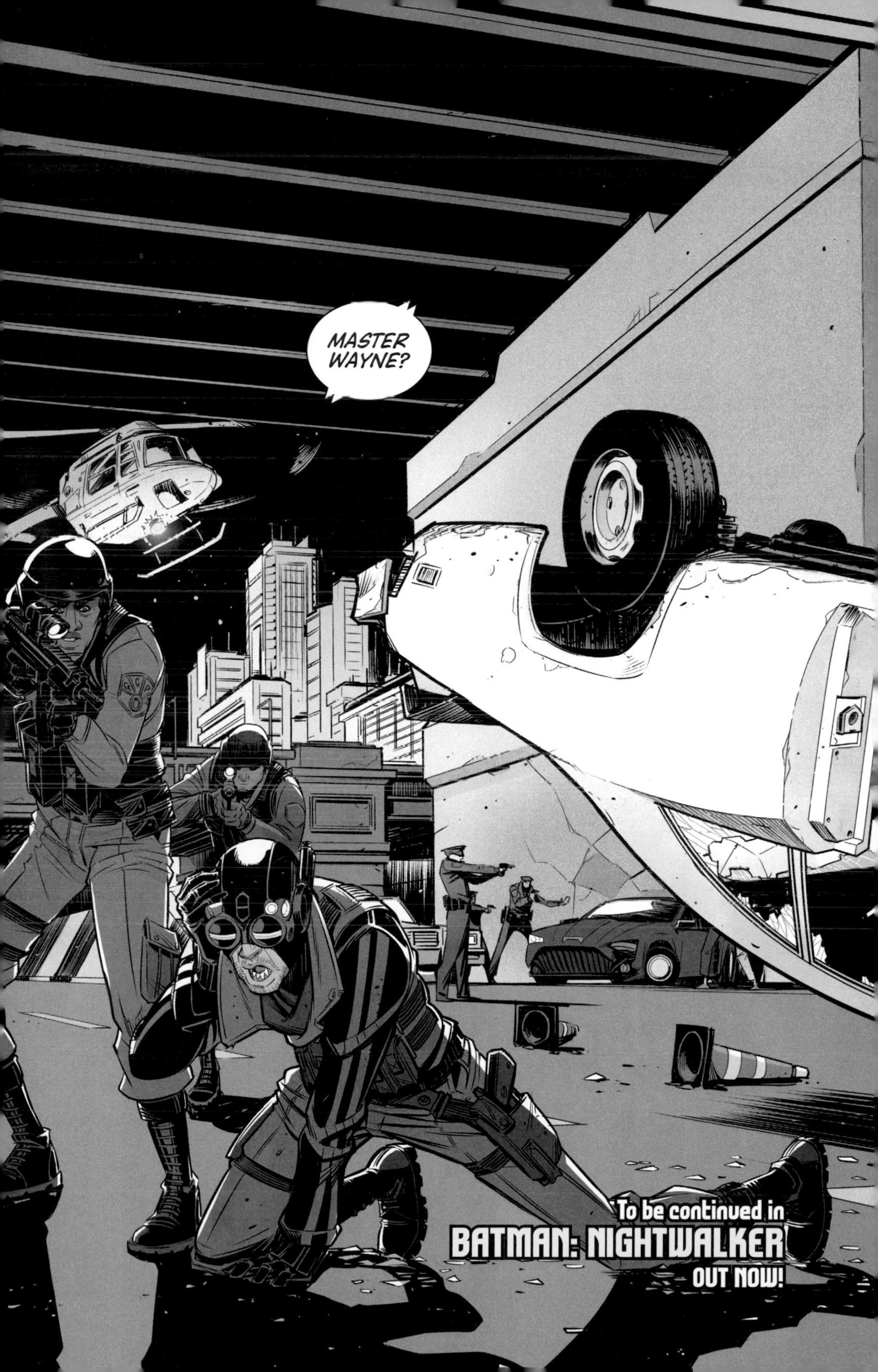
MASTER WAYNE?
To be continued in
BATMAN: NIGHTWALKER
OUT NOW!

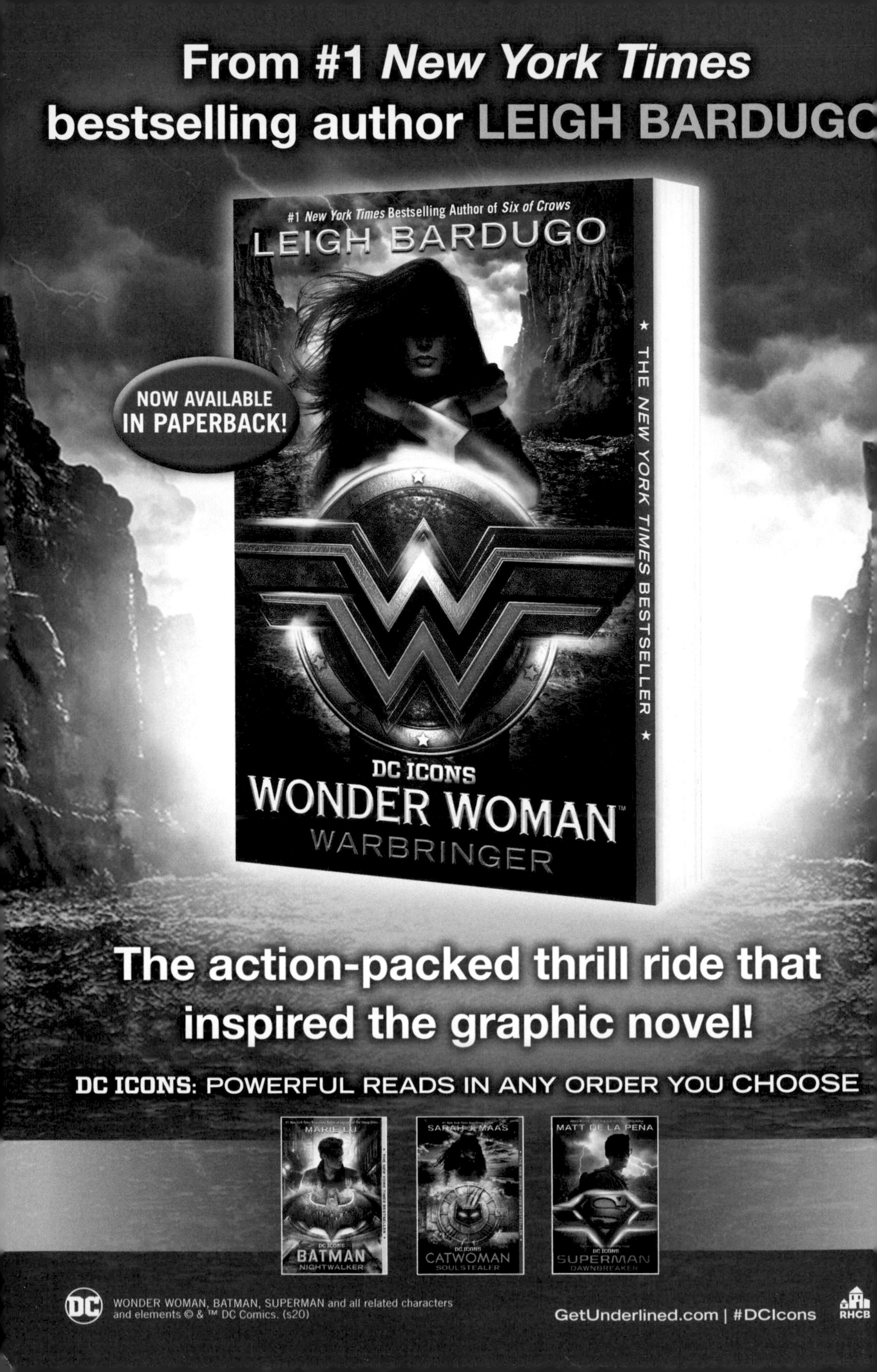
From #1 New York Times
bestselling author LEIGH BARDUGO
#1 New York Times Bestselling Author of Six of Crows
LEIGH BARDUGO
NOW AVAILABLE IN PAPERBACK!
★ THE NEW YORK TIMES BESTSELLER ★
DC ICONS
WONDER WOMAN™
WARBRINGER
The action-packed thrill ride that inspired the graphic novel!
DC ICONS: POWERFUL READS IN ANY ORDER YOU CHOOSE
MARIE LU
DC ICONS
BATMAN
NIGHTWALKER
SARAH J. MAAS
DC ICONS
CATWOMAN
SOULSTEALER
MATT DE LA PEÑA
DC ICONS
SUPERMAN
DAWNBREAKER
DC
WONDER WOMAN, BATMAN, SUPERMAN and all related characters and elements © & ™ DC Comics. (s20)
GetUnderlined.com | #DCIcons
RHCB